Rafferty

A.S. ROBERTS

DEFAULT
DISTRACTION

Jeanette

. It will never
be too late
for us :

xx

A.S. Roberts

Version 1F
ISBN: 978 1796960471
ASIN: B07NQQT2NW

Image copyright©2018
Edited by Karen J.
Proofreading by The Fireball Fillies.
Beta read by The Fireball Fillies.
Cover art by J M Walker @justwrite.creations
Formatting by Brenda Wright, Formatting Done Wright

All songs, song titles mentioned in this novel are the property of the respective song writers and copyright holders.

Playlist

Chapters

Dedication

As always, this book is dedicated to my husband. I would be nothing without your never-ending love and support.

It's also dedicated to my relentless alpha and beta team, Sarah, Debi, Kirsty, Crystal, Cassandra, Amo, Sheri, Tammi, Debbie and Jen. Without them, this story wouldn't be here. Thank you for helping me put the strange world that lives in my head onto paper.

A huge shout out to my editor Karen, how she puts up with me I'll never know.

Also, to my readers' group, The Anomalies and my lovely admin Jo (I couldn't run it without you). Thanks ladies for making me laugh daily and waiting patiently for my words.

It will never be too late for us. For us there will always be a way back to who we once were.

Rafferty Davenport.

Other books by this author

The Fated series

Fated
Inevitable
Irrevocable
Undeniable

Default Distraction series

Brody
Rafferty

Coming soon

Cade
Luke

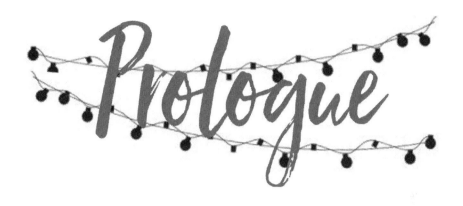

Prologue

Lauren

Seventeen years ago

I heard my breath escape my body on a shaky exhale.

My head was pounding so badly that the need to lift my hand up to hold my forehead was all-consuming. Concentrating hard and ignoring the rising pain under my scalp, I slowly lifted my fingers one by one and then eventually my hand. All the time, I was encouraging my arm to follow, but from the wrist up it felt like a lead weight and reluctantly I let my hand fall back down.

What is going on? Why do I feel so weak?

My eyelids refused to open, no matter how hard I tried.

So, enclosed in the blackness, with fear beginning to take over and with my head pulsing out pain with every beat of my heart, I reluctantly fell back into the softness underneath me.

I picked out the unmistakeable sound of a pillowcase crumpling as my head settled back down.

I'm in a bed?

I tested out my theory by rubbing my fingertips over the material underneath them and quickly concluded I was right.

I haven't slept in a bed in weeks.

Aware that my hearing seemed to be one of the only senses that hadn't deserted me, I scrunched up my face as I tried to concentrate on any sound I could find. I focussed my attention on the quiet beep that seemed to be coming from the side of me. I quickly realised that as each beep sounded another pulse of pain hit the inside of my head.

I'm in hospital?

I didn't understand.

How could I be in hospital?

A sudden need to wet my dry and very sore lips took over me and with immense effort, the tip of my tongue pushed its way through the almost sealed together fissure and slowly ran over the cracked, dry skin it found.

'Get the nurse, Adrian, quickly. She's awake.'

My mum's voice hit my ears and caused a wave of pain to crash over me. I held my breath, willing it to leave as quickly as it had come. Then I heard my dad's footsteps and a door opening.

'Mum?' I tried to force out, but it didn't come out as I intended and instead I heard an unidentifiable sound leave my lips.

I felt her hand move over my left one for the first time and realised she had been holding it all along.

'It's okay, Lozzie. You're safe now. You're in hospital, but you're going to be okay, we're here.' I could hear her voice trembling with emotion as she squeezed my hand as much as she dared, trying to convey the words she had spoken.

Suddenly, the room was transformed from what felt like an empty void to a bustling hub of activity as the door opened again with a whoosh. I felt myself flinch in response to the abrupt invasion.

'Hi, Lauren. I'm Anna.' Came from the person who had just entered.

'Can you open your eyes for me?' Anna questioned, using a soft a gentle tone.

I managed to gingerly turn my head side to side.

'It's okay if you can't, you'll be able to soon. You've been ill, but you're going to be fine. I promise,' she whispered as her voice got closer to me. 'Are you in any pain?'

I finally managed to separate my eyelashes, and squinting at the sudden flood of light from the room, I choked back a sound that answered her question.

'Not to worry. I've brought you something for that, now relax.'

I felt a gentle tug on the inside of my left elbow and then a small sting as the drug entered my blood stream. With every breath I inhaled, the pain in my head that had been coinciding with every beat of my heart lessened. As it did, so my head began to fill with unanswered questions.

'Now take a few sips of this,' she persuaded.

I felt a small straw being placed in between my lips, and I did as she instructed. The heavenly nectar touched the parched skin in my mouth and all too soon the straw was removed.

'There you go, Lauren. You'll be back to normal soon. Just relax. Your family are here with you. You're safe.'

Turning my head slightly, I found my mum's tired and worried face to the side of me and then I looked beyond her to see my dad. At first my eyes struggled to focus on him standing by the window of the hospital room, but eventually they corrected themselves enough for me to be able to see him wiping away the tears that fell in quick succession down his face.

'I'm sorry.' Finally, my throat complied, allowing me to whisper the words.

My mum nodded quickly at me. I watched her face crumple as a loud gut-wrenching sob left her mouth and she finally allowed herself to succumb to the agony in her heart. Her hand came up and she cupped her mouth as her emotions got the better of her.

A feeling of overwhelming guilt washed over me. I tore my eyes away from her and searched the room.

At last, I found what I was looking for and my heart leapt as I recognised him. He was a complete mess. His T-shirt and jeans were crumpled, his pallor was grey and several days' worth of patchy stubble had grown across his jaw line. His almost black hair that was normally perfectly placed, looked dirty and untidy. It fell over his face, effectively blocking his eyes from mine, but I knew he was watching me. I couldn't be sure, but I guessed he had probably been sat in the same position for days, looking at me through his curtain of dark hair.

He was here and the awareness that I now felt complete was overwhelming. Every part of my body that had been on alert before, now felt peaceful.

I watched as he flicked his hair up and away. As his silvery grey eyes found mine, I managed to convince my almost non-compliant body to offer him a small smile and sighed at him in relief.

However, his response wasn't what I had been expecting. He began to fidget where he sat, his feet moved up and down on the spot and his hands rubbed up and down his denim-covered thighs. I heard him sniff and then, instead of reciprocating my smile, his eyes closed briefly in resignation.

Pain ripped through my heart as I watched him. I turned my head as fast as I could to look at my mum and dad. They refused to meet my gaze and it answered every unspoken question I had.

In those few seconds, I understood that I had witnessed him turn off the switch inside his heart, effectively shutting me out. As my brain interpreted what it all meant, I audibly heard my heart rip into pieces inside my body. I couldn't save myself. I willed myself to close the eyes that just a few minutes ago I had struggled to open, but I couldn't. So, with my eyes now wide open with fear, I continued to watch my whole future disintegrate in front of me.

When Raff opened his lids again, his soulful eyes had gone. They'd been replaced with dark, closed-off pools. Silently, he stood up to make his way over to me. An extremely unwelcome premonition ran through me and unable to control anything, I started to shake in reaction. I felt like a voyeur or someone watching a film, because this… *this* couldn't be happening to me. After all we'd been to each other. All the promises we'd made. After all the hours he had spent making love to me and whispering his inner most thoughts and desires. After me following him across the ocean just to be with him, he was going to let it all go. He was going to leave me and effectively destroy us both.

Raff took the few steps required to arrive at the side of my bed. I felt the lump in my throat expand, until the constriction was so tight I thought I would never be able to speak again. He fell to his knees, placed his forehead on my bare arm and inhaled deeply to compose himself. Within a split second he moved again, lifting his head up and away he picked up my hand and pressed something cold into my palm, closing my fingers tightly around it.

Tears sprung to my eyes and I tried to voice a simple "no," but my body hadn't the capacity to help me achieve the sound. Instead, all I could do was turn my head from side to side.

I watched as his head bent down and he placed his lips lovingly over my closed fingers and for a few frozen minutes that's where he remained.

'I'm so sorry, Loz,' he whispered as he stood up and then bent over me to gently kiss the tip of my nose. Without ever making eye contact with me, he turned and left the room.

An agonising scream left my body, forcing itself painfully out of my narrowed throat. Mum gripped onto my arm, as if she was trying to stop me leaving my hospital bed to follow him.

I lifted my still closed fist away from the bed and up high enough to see what it was he had placed there.

I needn't have bothered. I knew exactly what it was without looking.

Through my watery, blurred vision I saw the silver chain hanging there. The half heart pendant Raff had given me a few months earlier was dangling from it, and it had never seemed more significant than it did now. It would never be whole again and neither would I.

My whole world was spinning on its axis with his departure, as the pendant turned slowly to reveal its one word.

"Always."

Chapter 1

Lauren

Present Day

The phone ringing incessantly dragged my focus away from the lists I'd been poring over to ensure I'd got all the food I required for the next couple of weeks. Thankfully the ringing stopped and I assumed that one of the waitressing staff had finally managed to pick it up. I smiled to myself, it looked like someone had actually taken in what I'd said at the ten minute meeting we always had before the day started. I'd explained that I was locking myself away to do a double check and would be unavailable, as I needed to be sure we were prepared for what were historically two of the busiest weeks of the year for The Fairy Garden.

I'd already had to stop what I was doing once. Our family doctor, Dr. Carpenter, had called with my latest test results. My diabetes was starting to put my kidneys under pressure and this was a concern to him. He'd advised that I now required monthly monitoring. I had sighed out loud at his request, but I'd agreed all the same. Once he'd got my agreement, he'd wished me a Happy Christmas and rung off.

Finally, I'd been able to get on.

Removing my reading glasses from my nose, I pinched the bridge and sighed at the release of pressure. The orders were complete and I'd triple checked them. I now needed to phone to check the suppliers had everything in hand. Only then would I relax, but knowing the phone was probably still busy, I decided to have a quick break.

Standing, I pushed my chair away from my desk, just as a sharp rap on my closed door echoed around the small, confined space of my office.

'Yes,' I answered as the door swung open.

The glorious smells of the tearoom entered the small space as Kirsty poked her head around the door.

I inhaled deeply and briefly listened to the happy voices of our customers with a sense of pride. It was moments like this that I gave myself an imaginary pat on the back. It hadn't been easy setting up my own business, even with all my friends and family behind me. With all the support in the world you still needed to believe in yourself, and until The Fairy Garden took off, my self-esteem had always floundered.

'Sorry, Lauren. I know you're busy, but the phone call was from Winter and she sounds in a right state about something. I told her to phone back in ten, because as you know it wouldn't allow me to put the call through to you... Is that okay?' She was referring to the antiquated phone system that had been installed many years before, when the out buildings we occupied would have been garaging for the estates' cars and before that the housing for the carriages.

'Oh, yeah that's fine. I'd finished anyway,' I replied, as I pushed a pod into the coffee machine and pressed the start button.

'I bet the orders were spot on. I bet you didn't need to check them at all?' she teased, narrowing her eyes at me.

I answered by offering her a small grimace and shrugging my shoulders. Kirsty had worked at The Fairy Garden with me since the doors had opened just over five years ago and she knew me so well. I was meticulous down to the last detail with my work life, but my personal life… well not so much.

I lost my train of thought as the phone rang again and Kirsty disappeared, closing the door behind her. Hastily I checked my watch before I spoke, wanting to answer the phone correctly.

'Good morning, The Fairy Garden, how can I help you?' I smiled into the heavy, black Bakelite phone that I had also inherited from the estate, and sat back down.

'Oh, Lauren. Thank God it's you,' came a flustered voice at the other end.

'Winter? Are you okay?' I replied.

I knew it was her, but the way Winter sounded was so completely alien to me, I had to check. I was sure she had never been harassed in her life. It was her upbringing. I loved the bones of her, she was one of my best friends, but our upbringings had been completely different. I came from a 'normal' working-class family who worried about everything, and she had been born into something much grander. Although times had now changed for her family's fortunes, Winter had come out fighting and grabbed hold of the opportunity that had been presented to her and now she also owned her own business. She had become a caterer and event planner, using her wide range of contacts from her large social circle, and her new business was going from strength to strength. I'd known her for over twenty years, from when we had joined the local Guides at age eleven. In all that time, I had never known her to be agitated. At the slightest sign of a problem she poured a large glass of wine and told whatever it was to fuck right off.

'NO... I'm not. It's all going tits up.'

I knew immediately what 'it' was. I let out a quiet sigh and closed my eyes. I dreaded hearing exactly what she was going to say, but equally as one of her best friends I wanted to hear what was going on, in case I could help her in any way. I picked up the heavy phone base and placed it nearer to me on the old oak desk, so it would be close enough for the plaited cord to stretch and I could lean back into my chair.

'What's happened, Winter?'

'Everything was perfect. I mean I have lists to check my fucking lists. It was all going according to plan, and now THIS!' I could hear her heels hitting the floor and I visualised her pacing up and down.

'Winter! Calm down and tell me what's happened?' I'd raised my voice in the hope that I could somehow be assertive enough to talk her down off the ledge she had placed herself on.

'They're ill. Would you believe it?' In my mind's eye, I could picture her spare arm waving around as she signalled her distress. She didn't wait for me to answer her question. 'Two of my hand-picked chefs have caught a sickness bug. The same chefs I vetted especially for the opening day and night for my biggest contract yet, are bloody ill. What the hell am I going to do now?'

'Oh no! I'm so sorry, Winter.' I pinched the bridge of my nose again and exhaled before I asked the next question. 'Is there anyone else you know who could help you do the job at the last minute.'

'What do you think?' she replied in a slightly sarcastic tone. I didn't bite, I knew she was worried out of her mind. For a few seconds, the line between us was empty of sound, but the thoughts that surrounded the two of us were so loud they were almost audible.

'I mean I can pitch in to help, but after that there's only you,' she whispered. 'But I can't ask. As your friend I won't ask you to help me... It's asking too much.'

My fingertips had started to turn white as I gripped hold of the receiver so tightly my blood couldn't pump to the ends.

'I...' I tried to answer her, but my throat had begun to feel dry and tight, my heart rate had increased and I could feel a sheen of sweat already covering my body. A wave of anxiety was flooding through my system. My stomach turned over as the ball of worry unfurled itself inside me and a surge of nausea hit. I knew what I needed to do. To calm myself, I looked down at one of the orders in front of me and when I could focus, I started adding the figures again and again.

Breathe in, breathe out.

These were tricks I'd taught myself over the years. I just needed to focus on something else and my body would start to return to my control.

'Lauren? Are you still there? You know under any other circumstances I wouldn't ask you. But, I don't know what else I'm going to do,' Winter carried on.

I knew she needed me, but I still couldn't answer her. My heart rate was slowing down slightly and I knew I was coming through the other side, but I couldn't trust my voice to reply. She would hear I was in a mess and her guilt would make the whole situation worse.

I could still hear Winter talking, but I was no longer focussing on her words as I continued to focus on the maths and the slow calming breaths I was willing my lungs to take. I was thirty-two years old and I needed to let this go, I needed to move on.

I grabbed at the glass of water to the side of me and sipped a little.

'I need more in the kitchen, I need at least one more capable chef, because...'

'Winter?' She stopped speaking as a voice interrupted her.

In the background, I had heard a strong male voice call out Winter's name. I let the deep voice wash over me and felt tears prick my eyes. It was a voice that I could sometimes make out on the radio, before I moved quickly to turn it off. It was the voice that on my lowest days I deliberately played on a DVD, just so I could cry. It was the voice of a boy I once knew, who had long since turned into a man.

No more, I'm not doing this anymore.

'Winter.' I interrupted their conversation, as he had ours.

'Yes,' she replied immediately.

'I'll do it.' The words came out of my mouth without any struggle at all.

For the past couple of years, I had been doing my best to completely ignore anything that was going on at The Manor. But now it appeared that my ignoring it, keeping myself busy and locked away when necessary, was to no avail.

I was going to face my heartache head on. I would get through it and then I would walk away with my head held high.

Chapter 2

Rafferty

'No, I'm telling you, Lawson, on behalf of us all. We're not doing any more gigs until the planned tour next year.' My empty hand was clenched into a fist, apart from my index finger. That was pointing at my reflection in the glass, as I tried to drive my point home.

I listened to his reasons, shaking my head as once more he tried to convince me otherwise.

'Speak to any of them, if they'll take your fucking call. They, unlike me, have no emotional tie to you. If they even pick up, the answer will be the same one you're refusing to listen to now… NO.'

The man was fucking relentless, but then the heartless bastard was more machine parts than flesh and bone.

'Yeah, you know damn well the new album will be recorded before then, this isn't our first rodeo, man.' I shook my head. My tone had taken on an air of sarcasm. I reined it back in and internalised what would have been an extremely loud, pissed off exhale. I placed my once pointed, but now bent index finger into my mouth and bit onto the knuckle, effectively stopping myself from swearing at his dogged refusal to listen to what I had been saying.

We couldn't have asked for a better fucking manager. Over the years, he had proved his worth many times. His business brain was phenomenal, as like a fucking tracker dog he sniffed out the next fifteen per cent he could make from us. We had made him into a millionaire. He, in return, had guided the four teenagers he had found playing their alternative rock music to anyone who'd listen in a seedy dive on the outskirts of Vegas, into fame and more money than we'd ever dreamt of. But as a person he was an A+ rated arsehole, whose family were just accessories he paraded out now and again. The fact he was my ex father-in-law and my son Flint's grandfather didn't help matters. Lawson looked after our PR, contracts and staff, but he didn't give a flying fuck what sort of lives we had or if we had any at all. As long as we turned out an album a year and were on stage at the required place and time, the fact we'd turned into addicts and lost people along the way didn't even deserve a second thought from him. His only concern was earning more and more money.

With the four of us now singing from the same hymn sheet, he had for the past few years, struggled to deal with the fact that although he was still our manager, we were now in charge of our lives. While we had been happy to hand them over to him for the previous fifteen years while we lived in a catatonic stupor, since Luke's wife Cerise had died, we'd taken a step back to see what we'd become. What we had found had shocked us to the core. We had two children between the four of us and there was no fucking way the drug and alcohol dependant fuck ups we had morphed into as we got high on fame, were going to be able to give them the life they deserved.

Hell, we were in our mid-thirties and we had no fucking life either. Apart from when we were on the stage in front of thousands of our fans playing our music, we were the empty, numb vessels we had created. We had money, sure, but inside and for all different reasons we were effectively fucking dead.

Three years ago, after Cerise died from a heroin overdose, we'd finally come to our senses, thank Christ. It was then that I knew right where we all needed to be. So slowly, as we helped Luke grieve for his beautiful wife and care for his eighteen-month-old daughter, we'd come up with a plan.

Now we were all here, back in the place I'd been born, and here I was staring out of my newly renovated, stone-columned bedroom window, looking out onto the snow-covered grounds of The Manor House I had as a kid regularly wandered into. This place had been my sanctuary as a young boy, as I scrumped from the fruit trees and kept away from my demanding father.

My refuge later, as a teenager, had been her and our young love. Her touch, trusting smile and amber eyes had fed my soul, and kept the pressure in my life contained. We had shared our hopes, dreams and passion. Lauren and I knew each other inside out and the further I pulled away from the demands of my family, the closer we'd become, until eventually I pushed her away too.

I blinked away my memories, but almost on instinct I placed an open palm onto the pane of glass in front of me, as I tried to touch the beauty of the countryside around our hotel. I knew what I was doing, through the glass I was trying to absorb what Lauren and I once were. I shook my head and heard myself exhale loudly as I tried hard to dislodge the thoughts in my head. My open palm curled up instantly into a tight fist as I mentally tried to shut down. Anger fuelled my system, but I wasn't exactly sure what the driving force was. Coming back to live here was one hundred per cent my idea, it wasn't as if I'd been out voted and made to come. But feelings that I'd long ago successfully pushed to one side were consuming me. I knew inside that this new venture was fucking paramount to our survival, not as a band but as actual functional human beings. But I'd made so many poor fucking decisions before, perhaps I was walking into another one?

How is she?

Does she still think of me?

What the fuck am I going to do if she doesn't even want to look at me?

Those questions and others had been going around my head on fucking repeat since we'd all arrived four days ago. The confusion inside my head was submerging me, taking me under and making my heart pound out of my chest with all the what ifs. I lifted my hand and pushed the longer strands of my black hair off my face and back to where they were supposed to go.

And still Lawson went fucking on, chewing my ear off with his selfish reasoning. His voice in my ear and the turmoil inside me as my heart and head demanded to be heard, were stoking the embers of my foul temper. I couldn't shout and scream at myself, God knows I'd tried it many fucking times before.

I was going to vent my spleen and his endless talk was killing the buzz I had from being home.

'THAT. IS. FUCKING. ENOUGH!' I shouted into the phone.

Stunned silence answered the words I'd shouted with force into his ear.

'Do you, or do you not, Lawson, want to carry on managing us?' I carried on speaking through my gritted teeth, while he was too shocked to voice his retort.

'Yes.' His answer came back on the very next beat.

'Then do it, carry on sorting out what needs to be done. Then we can carry on here knowing you've got it all in hand. Brody is halfway through writing the album already, it's a done deal. Now, answer the question I phoned to ask you in the first place. Did Flint make the plane an hour ago at McCarran?'

'Yes, I put him on myself.' I closed my eyes and pictured my stroppy, fourteen-year-old mirror image sitting in his first-class seat, pissed off with the world at leaving his friends and having to come to the UK to be with the father he hated.

I smiled at the thought and my anger fell away.

'Great, well nice to speak to you, Lawson. We'll speak soon, yeah?'

He said his goodbyes, but I'd already switched off. There were only two people in the world who could do that to me, our manager and his spoilt daughter, my ex, Ashley.

As the room fell into silence, I chucked my phone onto the large bed that dominated my room. I watched the phone bounce on the charcoal coloured covers and I threaded my fingers together and flexed them forward, listening to the click each knuckle made. I continued to release pressure by rolling my shoulders back and clicking my neck, alleviating some of the compulsory pressure that talking to him had forced into my muscles.

'Uncle Riff,' came a high-pitched voice from behind me. I smiled to myself as her baby name for me hit my ears. It had become a standing joke that while she could now pronounce everyone else's name correctly, she still clung on to the name she had labelled me with.

I immediately stopped what I was doing and turned to grin at the red-haired ball of energy, as she burst through my open doorway. Bending down I positioned myself to receive her up into my arms as she did her trademark leap of faith. It seemed that having a dad and three very protective uncles made her feel like she would never fall or struggle in any way and that was how we wanted it to fucking stay. I held her close to me, inhaled the coconut conditioner that she insisted was used on her hair, to "always smell like Mummy," and twirled her around a couple of times as I breathed in the joy of life she always carried with her.

'Hi, Bri, sweetheart,' I replied as I placed a kiss on her forehead. 'Whatcha up to?'

'Daddy asked Biscuit and me to come and find you.'

I glanced at the open door, there was no sign of her much-loved puppy.

'Okay, you've found me.' I placed her back down to the floor. 'Where's Biscuit gone?'

'He's in Uncle Cade's room across the hall, he's found his toothpaste.'

'Oh, shi...' I reined it in before the expletive fell out of my mouth. God knows we were trying to improve our language in front of her, but years of cursing were making it hard. I wasn't sure why we bothered, she already knew most swear words in existence, but she was intelligent enough not to use them.

So, high five to our parenting skills with that one.

'Uncle RIFF, you nearly said SHIT!' I closed my eyes and sighed.

Nice one, arsehole.

'Come on, let's go and rescue the toothpaste and then you can take me to Daddy, okay?' I tried to change the subject quickly and smiled at her as she turned and with her long red hair trailing behind her, she tore out of my room.

'Raff?' I heard behind me.

'I'm in Cade's bathroom,' I shouted out.

The wriggling puppy squirmed around even more under my arm as he heard Luke's voice and I struggled to hold him, as I continued to try to rinse out the pieces of chewed plastic and the constantly foaming, white bubbles from his mouth. All the while his jaws remained clamped shut on his prize.

'Honestly, I'm not sure that Biscuit is a dog, he's more like a fucking goat.' I grinned at Luke as he took the bedraggled, struggling puppy from my arms.

'Leave him to me and Bri, we'll deal with it. You need to go and see Winter.'

'Yeah?' I questioned, feeling my eyebrows raise as I answered.

'She's on the phone trying to sort out a... quote "problem" with the catering. I couldn't make out what the problem was, but it didn't sound too good. I thought you'd wanna know before the meeting.'

'Right?' I shrugged at him and looked down at the watch on the inside of my wrist. We had an hour. Without bothering to change my soaking wet, toothpaste covered T-shirt, I jogged along the corridor that held all our rooms and down the stairs. Eventually, a few corridors later, I came to the hotel's purpose-built kitchen.

I pushed open the door, then stopped dead as the aluminium swing door shut silently behind me and watched Winter as she paced from one side of the room to the other. Her heels clicked on the slate tiles as she spoke into her mobile.

'I need more in the kitchen, I need at least one more capable chef, because...'

'Winter?' I interrupted her and crossed my arms over my chest as I leant my arse onto the shiny worktop behind me. I didn't need to say any more, I knew my body language was asking all the right questions.

She spun around to face me and then I started to worry.

My always immaculately turned out sister had mascara running down her face. The fact she was so upset knocked me for six. I'd only ever seen her like it once before and that was many years ago. She never let anything get to her. Maybe letting her have this job was going to prove to be a mistake after all.

Three years ago, as we struggled to set our new life plan in motion, Falham Manor had been placed up for sale and even though I hadn't been home in seventeen years, I knew it was exactly the place I wanted to be. I bought it without thinking twice and for the first time in years, I offered the others an idea that had absolutely nothing to do with the music world.

In two days, our flagship, and the first of many luxury hotels, would be opened to the world and we'd happily given Winter the contract for the opening. Family meant everything to us and after everything we'd been through family would now always come first.

Fuck.

I looked at her again and she raised her palm at me asking me to be silent. I gauged my reaction inside and realised that it was true, I was very nearly human again. Years ago, I'd have been worried about what the press would say if something went wrong with a venture like this. Now, all I was concerned about was the fact this job might have been too much for her and it was going to break her.

'Yes,' I heard her reply into the phone.

Her face changed instantly as she listened to the voice on the other end.

'Thank you. I'll see you later at yours?'

She disconnected the call and stood in front of me. She dabbed at her eyes and lifted her blonde hair away from her face as she calmed herself down and tried to regain the control she always wore.

'Are you okay?' I asked.

'I'm fine, everything is under control.'

'Do you want to tell me about it?'

'No, I'm being paid to do a job here, not to whine at my big brother when the going gets tough.'

I shifted my arse away from the worktop behind me and walked nearer to her, until I could gently take hold of the tops of her arms. I rubbed my hands up and down them offering her my comfort.

'Are you sure?'

'Yes,' she emphatically replied. 'There was a problem, but it's dealt with. I'll tell you more in just under an hour. In the meeting, I'll update all the shareholders, not just you.'

I lifted my arms off her and held my open palms up to her in defence.

'Right, well let me know if I can assist you at all as your brother, not *just* a shareholder, won't you?' I sarcastically added, offering her a smile and moved back towards the swing door.

'You know I love you, don't you, Rafferty?' she called out from behind me and I could hear the hesitation in her voice as she thought about continuing. 'But there's a couple of us living here who have done alright without you being around to look after us.'

I stopped dead in my tracks at her words. I knew she didn't mean to hurt, but her words cut me to the fucking core. Without turning back to her I ran my hands through my hair, momentarily closed my eyes and expelled a huge sigh of resignation.

'I know. But I'm here now and I'd like to try to sort out some of the damage I left behind, if I can.'

'She's moved on, you know?'

I turned on the balls of my feet to face her as I concentrated on exactly what it was she wanted to say. I found her with her arms wrapped around her body as if to offer herself comfort.

'Once she thought the sun rose and set in you. If she could have chosen any boy in the whole wide world, you know damn well she would have chosen you. I love that you're back, Raff, but the reasons you gave me for being here, well they worry me. You nearly broke her in two, but somehow she survived. She's more than just my friend, I love her like a sister. I love her like I love you. I... I don't honestly believe she'd survive you leaving her again.' I watched as Winter wiped her fingers across her cheeks to remove a few tears that had fallen. 'I think after all these years you need to accept that it's all in the past, and leave it as a distant memory that can then hopefully fade.'

I looked down at the floor and stubbed the toe of my Dr. Martens onto the slate. 'I appreciate your love and concern for her, Winter. But the life I've had over the last few years has opened my eyes to what I really need from life.'

'Are you telling me you still love Lauren?' she questioned me with a hardness to her voice.

'No, I'm not saying that at all. All I want is to...' I struggled to provide a definitive answer. 'All I want is to mend a few bridges, so we can all move forward. Okay? Happy now?'

For a few seconds she stared at me, as if she was trying to read between the lines. I raised an eyebrow at her in question.

'Mend a few bridges?' she quietly questioned. 'I can understand that needs doing with Mum and Dad, but with Lauren?'

'Yes, with Lauren.' I crossed my arms over my chest. 'She's not married, is she?' She confirmed what I already knew by shaking her head.

'So, what if we need to sort out all the crap that happened between us? And I didn't even try to put things right.'

I watched her offer me a sad, resigned sort of grimace. 'What if you should have thought about that years ago?'

'I have thought of it, more than once a day, every single day, every fucking month and every lonely year, since the day I left her.'

I walked towards her and gathered her up into my arms, the way a big brother should always be able to do for his little sister. I had so fucking much to make up for and I knew it. I had promised myself that I would spend the rest of my life trying to make things right, as long as those I loved were willing to let me.

After a few seconds, I leant back, kissed the top of her blonde hair and released her from my hold. Stepping away from her I turned around once again to face the door. 'See ya in the meeting.'

'Yes, see you there,' she replied. 'Oh, Raff.' Her voice rose in volume. 'Before you go. Did Flint get on the plane?'

'I'll tell you later when you morph back into my sister and not some holier than thou events planner.' I gave her amused but indignant looking face a quick wink and a smile, before I retreated to the safety of the other side of the aluminium door, as once again it swung shut behind me.

Lauren

I drove down the lane, looking from left to right and taking in all the Christmas lights twinkling through the snow bespattered windows of the houses. Slowly, I pulled up across the road from my nan's shop and switched off the engine. Opening the car door was difficult as the winter winds were so strong. I pulled my hood up over my head and ran across the narrow lane. With relief, I pushed open the door and heard the welcoming ring of the antiquated bell.

'Bloody hell… It's cold enough to freeze the balls off a brass monkey,' I exclaimed as I walked through my nan's shop doorway with my eyes searching for my cousin Amy.

Unfortunately, I then heard the glass panes rattle in their rotten, wooden frames. The door had slammed behind me, as it caught on the cold gust of wind that was blowing up a storm in the lane outside. I closed my eyes and clenched my fists, waiting for the glass to fall out and shatter onto the floor behind me. It was the last thing my cousin needed, coping with our nan and trying to run a shop that had been my nan's life's work was more than enough for one person and I didn't want to add to her ever-growing list of woes. Luckily, the smash of glass never came and I let out the breath I was holding.

'Whoops! Sorry, Amy! That was close, wasn't it?' I offered her a grimace.

She sighed and hurriedly finished tidying away the pieces of scrapbooking papers she had in her hand. I watched her close the well-worn wooden drawer, by lifting the brass cup handle and sliding the wood back into place at the right angle. Then she jumped down backwards off the steps, holding tightly to the long pole that served as a handle. As her feet found the ground, I watched as she became lost in thought for a few moments. She was a beauty, my cousin. With her thick chestnut brown hair and her dark eyes, I couldn't believe some man hadn't found her, fallen for the amazing person she was and refused to let her go.

I looked away, not wanting her to see me appraising her, and allowed my eyes to wander around my second home. My nan's shop would be somewhere I would always find comfort and solace. "A Stitch in Time" had diversified several times over in the last ten years and it no longer just sold haberdashery items. If you had a need for it in your life, then one of the sectioned glass counters, or one of the many different sized wooden drawers that were built floor to ceiling along the walls of the shop, probably contained it. The only problem was people didn't seem to need places like this anymore. Let's face it, all you had to do was search online and with one click you could have almost anything delivered to your door. I knew what Amy was trying to do and I loved her so much for it, but trying to save our nan's shop was, I was saddened to admit, futile.

I jumped up to sit in my favourite place in the shop. It was the same spot I had been sitting since I had been tall enough to push myself onto the counter that ran down one of the side walls. It had been my favourite spot, because it had made me tall enough to see everything that was going on in the small but perfectly laid out space. I used to love to watch my nan with her customers, it all came so naturally to her. She would listen intently at the things they said they needed and when she didn't have quite what they were looking for she would find them something else. Then, in clever conversation, she would convince them it was better than what they had originally wanted. She would look up at me, sat here watching her and taking it all in, and offer me a small smile. Her customer service was something I had been adamant would be offered in my tearoom, The Fairy Garden. Whatever generation, we all yearn to be looked after properly and I was sure that was why my business went from strength to strength while others crashed and burnt.

Nan was an amazing lady and here in this tired and, it had to be said, somewhat tatty space, I would always feel close to her. Even now, when she was away for respite care at our local care home, I could feel her in the shop with us. Her blood, sweat and tears had been poured into the place. In doing so, she had left some of her soul and compassion rubbed deep into the wood grains that made up her home.

Lots of important events in our lives had happened here. My dad had proposed to my mum in here. Amy had been dropped off here with our nan as her mum left for a new life in America. My brother Mark had been benched during a football match and had punched through one of the glass counters in temper as a teenager – Nan had torn him off a strip or two, then calmed him down and patched him up. When my world had fallen apart when Raff had left me, she had offered me her crisp, white hanky from the pocket of her apron and spent many hours talking me through my pain. I often went over the words she had said to me then.

"Sometimes I think we meet the right person at the wrong time. In my experience, some people need to be with the wrong person to realise what they once had. Only after fighting, failing and with

their heart bleeding in pain, can they look back and appreciate what they had, but let go. If two people are meant to be together, call me old-fashioned, but I believe that love will always find a way."

I looked down at my hands holding the thick, wooden edging and smiled at the memories. Our nan had long since given up asking me to not sit on the ancient counter. I let go of my reminiscences and looked up at Amy again, who also seemed to be in a world of her own.

'Earth to Amy, I have news!' I spoke loudly attempting to get her attention.

I watched her sigh and then shake her head as she came out of her daydreaming. As her eyes found mine she offered me a huge grin.

'Where did you go to?' I teased her and smiled at her reaction.

She shook her head at me. 'It doesn't matter. Come on then, spill it,' she said and returned my smile.

'I need your full attention before I do,' I stated and I pointed towards the opposite counter, wanting her to jump up onto it and sit down.

First, she walked towards the door, shot the bolt across and turned the sign to closed. Her hand hovered for a few seconds over the fairy lights that decorated the main window. I knew she was looking for a reason to leave them on. The pretty coloured lights gave the run-down shop an extra Christmas sparkle and showed all the handmade items our nan had made. She walked back, having decided to leave them on.

'Well?' she questioned as she crossed her arms over her chest.

'Ok, you're going to be shocked at what I'm about to say, but before you go off on one, please understand that I. Have. Thought. About. It.' I looked down at my hands and realised I was trying to placate her with them as I spoke.

'Go on then,' she probed and I watched her brow furrow.

'Okay, you know that group, band, whatever they are… that have been doing up Falham Manor for the last couple of years?'

Her eyes opened as wide as I had ever seen them, almost perfect circles were staring back at me in wonderment. At last, her mouth opened to reply, 'Of course, I do live here too, you know… and it's Raff's band. They're called Default Distraction,' she answered, shaking her head at me.

'Well… Winter called me a few hours ago and she needs my help with their opening day.' She didn't say anything, I could feel her staring at me as she tried to work out what the hell was going on. I started to tap the wooden surface underneath me with my fingernails in agitation. It felt like minutes before she spoke again.

'She needs your help with what?' Her tone was understandably one of concern. I had known she would react like this, knowing the history between me and Winter's older brother, Rafferty.

'Half of her chefs have come down with some sort of lurgy. You know the shit and vomit sort of lurgy. They can't go near the kitchen, let alone the food. She needs help preparing the food for the big open event they're having on Sunday.'

I watched her taking in what I had just imparted to her.

I could almost read the thoughts in her head.

A few years ago, I had opened a beautiful tearoom in the old coach houses of Falham Manor. They had been sold with most of the other out buildings of The Manor itself. The Fairy Garden was doing astonishingly well. The risk of opening my own business had been daunting, but the hard work and the success of the place had somehow helped to heal some of the pain I had been carrying around for years.

We should have known then, with the sale of the outbuildings, that The Manor was also in trouble and would eventually have to be sold, too. It was happening throughout the country when upper-class families no longer had the money to sustain their substantial properties. It had been a shock however when we had learnt, via Winter, that The Manor had been bought by Default Distraction.

Slowly, I had mulled it over and realised that although they may have bought the building, there was no way in hell they were likely to ever see the inside of the place. They probably owned real estate all over the world. The reasoning in my head had helped to calm the panic attacks that had been reawakened by the news.

Then, all of a sudden, I was receiving information from other villagers. They'd seen Rafferty, he was back for a week to oversee the renovations and imparted just how good he looked. Then the questions started.

"Have you seen him?"

"Do you know why he's back?"

"What are they going to do with the old place?"

When I'd replied, "No, I haven't seen him and I didn't know," to most of their questions, they would then look at me in sympathy or sometimes, even worse, in pity. Often, they replied how it was such a shame we had lost touch with each other, and what an ideal couple we'd made when we were younger, then they'd add at the end "Never mind, that was years ago, you've both moved on since then." The conversation was often over after that and they'd say their goodbyes and leave me with my thoughts. He had most definitely moved on, but I was devastated to admit that I wasn't so sure about me.

Winter began to subtly warn me when he would next be back and I often managed to take myself away for a few days.

Amy shook her head at me. 'I can't believe Winter would ask you. I mean, I know you're a superb cook and are probably the very best person to help her. But, let's face facts, you've been steering clear of the actual Manor house for the whole of the time they've been doing it up... I'm sorry, Lauren, but we both know why, don't we?' I could feel my eyes filling with tears at her words. The pain he had left in my heart came pounding back. I refused to let the tears spill and I swallowed down the tight constriction that was building in my throat.

'I know, but she's our friend and she needs help. I've decided I need to do this and I need to show…'

'What?' she interrupted. 'You need to show Raff that you no longer care, is that it? And if it is…Why? Why would you put yourself through that?' I could hear the concern in her voice as she pleaded with me to rethink my decision.

I shook my head at my words. 'No, you're wrong. I really need to show myself, once and for all, that *I've* moved on.' I crossed my arms over the top of my thick cream jumper.

I was doing this with or without her emotional backing.

'What does Toby say?' I felt my face react at the mention of my boyfriend's name. Our relationship was only a few months old, but I already knew how he would react to my news and that concerned me.

'I haven't told him yet… It's my business, not his.' I heard Amy sigh as she realised she'd made me feel uncomfortable.

'Forget I said anything,' she added as she pushed herself away from the counter she had been leaning on. She walked the few steps across to where I sat. As she arrived next to me she took hold of my left hand in both of hers and gripped it tightly.

'Look, take no notice of me. What do I know? I may have been married once, albeit for a short time, but I know that I've never really been in love, ever. As you know, I'm not sure it even really exists… well not for the likes of people like me.' She shrugged her shoulders attempting to drive her point home. 'As well as poor romantic decisions, I am also the queen of making appalling business decisions… instead of taking the opportunity of a lifetime when you wanted me to go into business with you, I stayed here to run Nan's shop, thinking my business degree would turn a failing business into a thriving one. So, what the heck do I know?' She turned her head to the side to look at me. I knew she was attempting to convince me of what she was saying and I appreciated her trying.

I snapped myself out of my thoughts and managed a small grin at her.

'Oh, come on! You never thought that Nan's shop would get any better, even you're not that stupid,' I laughed, relieved that the fraught few minutes between us seemed to have passed.

'Oi! You cheeky bugger. I could go off you, you know,' she retorted.

'No, you're stuck with me. We both know the reason you stayed here at the shop. It was for love, not for any business reason.'

'Yeah, you're right, that's the sort of love I do believe in.' She smiled in acceptance at my words.

'And what do you mean, people like you? Love can be just around the corner for us all, just waiting for our right moment to meet *the* right person.'

She shrugged her shoulders at me. It was a long-standing argument between us. I still believed in love, even after losing Raff. Even though I was the only one between us to have had my heart shattered into a million pieces, I wanted to experience that love again, it was addictive. I wanted to believe in the happy ever after.

'So, let me ask you... Are you helping Winter for business reasons, or for love?'

'Definitely business,' I answered adamantly.

'Then if you need my help, I'm all yours. I know it may surprise you, but I could do with the extra money.' She knocked her shoulder against mine.

'Pack a bag then, you're moving up to The Manor,' I added.

'God, they won't know what's hit them. With the two Harper girls and Winter Davenport in the same place at the same time,' she laughed.

Still holding hands, we separately contemplated what the next few days were going to mean for us. I knew how many hours the three of us were going to have to put in to achieve everything that needed to be done. However, it wasn't the hard work that scared me, but the thought that after all the hurt and pain I'd suffered and the grieving I'd gone through when he pushed me away and left me behind, despite my many avoidance tactics over the last few years, sometime this weekend I would with absolute certainty be seeing Raff.

Lauren

I heard Amy's footsteps as she came down the wrought iron staircase, situated on the outside of the building. The stairs were the only entrance to my spare bedroom. I glanced around the kitchen and knew she was going to be able to see right through me as soon as she walked in. Ignoring the heavily laden surfaces, I put my head down and carried on creating the pastries and cakes that would be required today for The Fairy Garden.

We'd had a fantastic girlie evening last night and probably let our hair down a little too much. I had realised quite early on into our evening, that it didn't matter how much alcohol I was consuming, my body was churning around too much adrenalin for me to get drunk. My blood sugar wasn't good when I'd tested it after they had left to go to their beds. I knew that having had no sleep at all last night, wasn't going to help matters either. I hadn't tested again so far this morning and wasn't going to until I had time to sit down and eat properly.

After years of controlling my diabetes, I knew I should be stricter with myself, but sometimes I had too much else going on. Truth be told, I had always resented it. I always made sure I tested my blood the bare minimum of four times a day, but I wasn't always as careful with my diet. After my reading last night, I knew that I needed to do better, but today like often, it wasn't at the forefront of my mind.

How I was going to get through this weekend was.

Before Amy and Winter had arrived in my flat above the tearooms last night, I had thrown myself into creating the spreadsheets I knew would make our weekend more organised. I had watched them whisper their worries to each other over how I was going to handle this weekend. I'd ignored their whispers and the growing ball of anxiety in my gut and as I lounged on the carpeted floor of my flat, I'd focussed on the times and hours we would all need to work and tried to ward off yet another panic attack.

'Morning!' I heard Amy shout as she pushed open the front door. She banged her feet on the doormat trying to rid them of their snow covering. I looked up at the translucent window to the side of me. The snow seemed to have stopped falling now, which was a godsend. The little flurries we had been getting for the past few days were enough to make The Fairy Garden even more magical, but much more this weekend and I knew it would cause problems for my customers getting to me and the reopening of The Manor.

'In the kitchen,' I shouted out to her, trying to make my voice sound as normal as possible. I turned my head to offer a welcoming smile.

'Bloody hell, how long have you been here?' I watched as she lifted up her arm to check her watch. Then her eyes swept over the almost fully-laden worktops and cooling racks. A few seconds was all it took for realisation to hit her features.

'A while,' I replied.

'You haven't slept at all, have you?' she questioned, crossing her arms over the top of her cardigan.

I shook my head in response. 'Once you and Winter left, I sobered up quickly and my brain wouldn't shut up. The tearooms are completely booked out today from ten a.m. right through until we close. I knew just how much needed to be baked.' I paused for a moment trying to read her expression. 'So, I came down and got on with it.' I couldn't look at her anymore, I knew exactly what she was thinking. I turned back around to face the worktop in front of me and once again squeezed the icing bag with the right amount of pressure.

'How do you expect to last the next few days on no sleep at all?'

'Don't be so dramatic, Amy... I'll be fine, we're in our thirties not our seventies,' I answered, throwing a smile at her over my shoulder.

'Point taken.' She shrugged at me. 'Have you had breakfast?' she asked as she walked further into the furnace-like room.

'No, not yet. I've just got this and one more batch to decorate. Then all the cakes, pastries and desserts will be finished. So, when I leave here in... What's the time?' I shook my head in confusion as I couldn't read the hands on the clock face. It took me a few seconds before I realised that the clock face had just steamed up due to the heat in the kitchen.

'About twenty to six,' she replied.

I knew she was trying to work out what was going on with me, but I couldn't yet put everything into words, so for the moment I kept my feelings to myself.

'Ah, okay. So, when I leave here in about three hours, everything should be ready for the day ahead.'

'You can finish decorating the cupcakes, you're much better at that than me. I'll cook us breakfast and we can sit down and eat together. Then, you are off upstairs for a rest and a shower before you join Winter over at The Manor.'

'Well, I...'

She held up her hand to me. 'Not taking no for an answer.' I watched her pull out the schedule I had made for her from her cardigan pocket and she pinned it onto my neat corkboard which displayed our health and safety posters. 'Anyway, we're still waiting on deliveries to complete the sandwiches...and you know as well as I do that freshly made sandwiches are always better than those made earlier.' She grimaced at me. 'Nothing worse than an immaculately cut finger sandwich with curled up, dry edges.' Her eyebrows raised in question and she smiled at me.

'What would I do without you?' I asked.

We both knew that it wasn't her kitchen skills I was referring to, but her ability to see exactly what I needed to help me out of the emotional crisis that was threatening to engulf me whole.

'Anytime,' she replied, putting her hand to her mouth and blowing me a kiss. 'Now, go and sort yourself out. I bet you haven't tested this morning, have you?'

'No.'

'Do you know, for a person that's organised almost to the point of having OCD, you completely astound me. Please tell me you tested last night?'

'Of course, and I had my insulin. Now, I know you mean well, but get off my bloody back and get on with my breakfast.'

Happy in each other's company, but somewhat lost in thought, we both ploughed on with our jobs in hand.

Chapter 5

Raff

'Yesss.' I growled into the phone.

At fucking last I'd been able to reach my mobile after it had vibrated all over the bedside table next to me. I'd smacked my hand around the top of the cabinet for ages and finally relented in opening one tired eye so I could find it. My relief that the persistent ringing had finally stopped was overriding. I was exhausted, having fallen asleep around five in the morning.

'You have thirty minutes, okay?' Cade replied.

'What's the time?' My dry mouth made my voice sound hoarse as I spoke.

'Eight thirty.'

With my eyes still screwed up tight, I managed to laugh.

'Fucking hell, Cade. I can't remember the last time you even saw this hour of the day, unless you were just arriving home. You're fucking eager.'

'And you can suck my cock, dude. You remember that we agreed after the meeting yesterday that we'd help Winter with whatever we could…'

'Yeah, I know, thanks for…' His voice interrupted mine.

'And when I watched her giving us that report yesterday, in that tight-fitting skirt, Louboutin heels and pretty little top, I sure saw a lot that I could help her with.'

The change in his tone made my eyes open wide and then in turn squint tightly in pain, as the bright light of the winter's morning hit them.

'She's my fucking sister, man. Whatever it is that's going on in your depraved, cess-pit of a fucking head, lose it and fast.'

The sound of his laughter hit my ears as I put him on speaker and back down onto the cabinet. I swung my legs out of bed and stood up to stretch out my naked frame.

'So, how's Flint?' I heard him ask as I picked up the clothes I'd dropped on the floor last night.

'I think you can imagine how happy he was to see his old man?' I answered, throwing my black jeans onto the bed to wear again. 'I think the only whole sentence he uttered was as we pulled off the lane and came down the driveway, "Why the hell have you dragged me outta Vegas to go and live in bum fuck nowhere?"'

I'd picked up a sullen looking Flint from Heathrow airport and after pulling him reluctantly into my arms for a man hug, we'd driven straight back to the hotel. I'd looked over at him several times during the journey, but with his headphones in their normal place and with his eyes shut as he pretended to sleep, he effectively blocked out my attempts at any communication. He didn't even want to know about the brand new Bugatti Chiron I was driving and seeing as cars were his passion, I knew it wasn't a good sign. But it wasn't just him that had been lost in thought on the car ride home.

'You can sorta see why he'd feel that way? You were young once, old man. Tell you what, I'll go and see him later,' he added.

'Less of the old man and thanks… I think, now fuck off and I'll meet you downstairs in ten.'

'I'm showered, dressed and my hard on has been taken care of.' I shook my head at him as I walked into the bathroom and turned on the walk-in shower. The water immediately started to steam up the room and I pulled the door shut on it and jogged back over to my mobile, just in time to hear, 'I'll go down now and see if she needs a hand, my expert fingers, masterful tongue or even my rock-hard dick.'

I heard him roar with laughter at himself, then the line went dead as he rung off.

I pushed my hair off my face as I stared at the disconnected phone. That was all I fucking needed, Cade sniffing around Winter. Cade was an ex addict, tattooed male slut, as well as being one of the best fucking drummers I had ever heard or worked with. He had been born into a life where family was everything and he'd had all the privileges that money could buy. But being in his family came at a price, so as soon as he could he'd turned his back on it and walked away. He had embraced the life of being a rock star with every sinew of his body and was like a brother to me, as were Brody and Luke.

Winter was laughingly more upper-class with every year that passed. She wouldn't take any of his crap, but fuck, I didn't need any additional worries on top of what had been piled on me in the past twenty-four hours.

But him and Winter, together? As far as I was concerned it was no fucking way a match made in heaven. I loved him, but fuck, touching my sister when I knew where his fucking hands had been, I didn't know whether to laugh out fucking loud or to throw up with the thought.

Mind you, it could be fucking entertaining… and shit, I needed some diversion from my seriously fucked up life.

I quickly moved into the shower and for a few minutes I let the water pound onto my face and then rush over me, hoping it would erase the confused feelings coursing around my body. As the water run over my naked body, I placed both of my palms onto the cold silver tiles in front of me and leant forward. I watched as the water gathered into thick heavy rivulets before it disappeared down the drain. But it didn't work, the feeling stayed and the memories took over my head.

I closed my eyes and allowed the thoughts of Lauren to consume me and as I did so my semi-hard dick, not long ago woken from slumber, engorged itself with blood and began to throb.

Removing one hand from the tiles, I encompassed it and wrapped my fingers around it tightly. I interspaced my fingers in between the piercings of the Jacob's ladder and squeezed firmly. I felt a momentary spasm of relief fill my system and dropped my head forward in resignation. I hardly ever touched myself, I had endless streams of women that would do it for me and like the shameless fucker I was, I willingly let them. The squeeze I'd given myself only gave me a few seconds of relief and it wasn't nearly enough.

Being back here, memories and visions of her were driving me to the brink.

I rolled my hand up the full extent of my shaft and over the bulging crown.

'Fuck.' The word forced itself out of my mouth and my body began to shake with the feeling of absolute fucking pleasure coursing around my veins.

So, I gave in.

I moved my hand up and down my shaft, taking turns to touch each one of the four barbells on its length and rubbed over the crest of my dick with my calloused thumb. The piercings only added to the fucking pleasure as the pressure on my dick sent me quickly higher.

The memories of Lauren going around in my head were of a time gone by, so I'd reinvented them with an older her in place. She was now the fucking gorgeous woman I'd only seen in pictures. The moment I imagined her creating a small fissure between her lips to invite me in, I blew my load all over the tiles.

'Lauren... FUCK, Lauren.'

I sunk down to my haunches as wave after wave of pleasure rolled over me and then finally as it ebbed away, the unmistakeable stench of guilt followed in its wake.

After helping ourselves to what would easily have provided at least two cooked breakfasts each, Cade and I, along with several members of staff, had begun to shift everything that had been delivered in the last couple of hours. Fuck knows where Brody was when we needed him? I had to hand it to Winter, she had dotted all the I's and crossed all the T's. She was colour coding every box and package as it arrived at the back of The Manor, then Cade and I delivered it to one of the various rooms we were using for the opening tomorrow. This meant she could concentrate on the food preparation in the kitchen.

I'd been so fucking proud of her yesterday, as standing in front of us all she had explained that despite a couple of the chefs being ill, she had already dealt with the situation and had come up with a contingency plan. I'd sat in the large conference room, with my tall frame hunched over the table in front of me, smiling at the way she handled everyone. I'd doodled on the piece of paper in front of me and listened to her confidently address the band, the shareholders, and the skeletal management team we had headhunted a year ago, and answer every question that they, Brody and Cade had come up with.

My drawing had grown and so had the smile on my face the longer she skilfully kept charge of the meeting.

'So, what you're saying is, if we help you out with some of the distribution of the deliveries tomorrow, you'll have enough hands in the kitchen?' Luke had asked.

I'd turned my head to look at him. He had hold of his thick, red beard in his right hand as he asked the question. Like me he had kept quiet for the entirety of the meeting until now, but that was nothing unusual. Since Cerise had died he'd changed from giving Cade a run for his money as one of the most extrovert of our group, to being the quietest and most serious member.

'Yes... I have enough help in the kitchen,' Winter answered him. Luke nodded his head and said no more. But the slight hesitation in her voice had made me shift my gaze from him to her.

'Who did you manage to get to help, with such short notice?' I'd questioned.

'Ermmm... I asked a friend who I knew had the skills to assist me,' she'd answered, managing a small smile. With a sudden flourish, she'd closed the leather folder in front of her, effectively trying to shut me and the meeting down, which had intrigued me even more.

'Who's helping you, Winter?' I could feel my eyes narrowing at her as I pinned her down with my question.

The room and everyone else in it had disappeared from my view as I'd looked at her and waited for her to answer me. For the first time, she had started to look uncomfortable. I could feel all the eyes in the room looking between the two of us.

'Lauren Harper.'

At the sound of her name, I'd dropped the brand new pencil I'd been drawing with onto the highly polished mahogany desk and sank back into the chair. I'd slow blinked at my sister. Every cell and sinew in my body had swiftly become aware of my grandfather's wallet which was closeted safely in the back pocket of my jeans.

Because I knew that inside the treasured wallet, in its own fastened section, was a dog-eared piece of Kodak paper. The long strip was folded into four, which separated the four pictures we'd crammed ourselves into the booth to have taken, during our last summer together. The colours had faded, the film was peeling off and separating in places. But it didn't matter, I knew the pictures off by heart and inside out. Lozzie had sat on my lap for them all. The first one had captured us with our heads leaning together as we both smiled into the camera lens. The second, I had turned her head to face mine as I cupped her face to kiss her. The third, we were lost in that same kiss and the last, we were laughing at having had our passion for each other caught on camera. Four small snippets of what should have been our life, were captured there for eternity. They were seventeen years old, but the love and happiness still shone through.

The four small, indiscriminate, two by one inch pictures showed me on my darkest days what my life could have been. Before I made the biggest fucking mistake of my life and left her.

Now I was back, with a sulky teenager in tow and a depth of hurt between us that could easily fill an ocean with all the tears that we'd shed. I'd sat down in the early hours of the morning after Cerise had died and come up with this idea in desperation, to make sure we all survived, and had fucking sprinted with it.

The meeting had been drawn to a close and with me still sitting in the same fucking prone position her answer had forced me into, the staff had filed out followed by the rest of the band.

'Is it a problem, Raff?'

I had stood suddenly, causing the chair I'd been sitting on to slide back abruptly over the wooden floor and as she walked out of the door in front of me I'd replied, 'Of course not.'

But it was a problem, maybe coming back here to put things right had been a mistake.

I brought myself back to the here and now. I pushed my hands deep into the back pockets of my jeans and let the peace in the empty room I was stood in surround me. For a few minutes, I stared out of the window looking at The Manor's snow covered terrace.

We'd finally done everything that Winter had instructed needed doing. It had taken a couple of hours and I'd lost my hoodie on the way, throwing it onto a dark green Chesterfield as I'd walked past it for the hundredth time. My white T-shirt was sweat stained and I needed water. I knew I could no longer put off the inevitable.

'Oh, Riff Raff.' I heard Cade's piss taking voice and brought myself out of my fucking pity fest and back to reality.

'Yeah, I'll be there in a few minutes.' I stayed for as long as I could without it being obvious that I was scared to see her. Then I turned around and walked out of the small sitting room and back to the corridor that would lead me to where I needed to be.

I placed my hand on the aluminium door that led to the kitchen and prepared to face up to my biggest mistake, and the love of my life.

Lauren

Mentally I'd been preparing myself for my first encounter with Raff, since the moment I'd agreed to help Winter. But it was now eleven a.m. and it still hadn't happened.

I knew I was still running on the porridge Amy had made for me earlier and the nervous energy flowing through me. What I couldn't fathom out for the life of me was why every time the thought of bumping into Raff entered my head, a burst of panic erupted inside me, followed quickly by my heart rate accelerating and butterflies flying around my stomach like a summer's afternoon in a meadow.

I had been dashing around all morning, helping the "real" chefs create the extensive menu Winter had devised and had tried in vain to push him far from my mind. That had been made more difficult as Cade seemed to have made it his number one priority to get Winter to sleep with him. I'd forgotten just how full on he could be, until he'd swaggered into the kitchen for the first time, hugged me so tightly he'd lifted my feet off the ground and declared that I was a very welcome sight. It was as if no one else was in the room, even me, as his eyes and actions thereon had all been for Winter. Some of his antics had made me laugh as I watched my normally well put together friend blush under his administrations, then she'd snap back to normality and tear him a new one.

We had come to the end of what needed to be prepared first and were now waiting on some more deliveries. Now with my stomach once again moaning, and knowing I needed to take better care of myself, I decided to set up brunch for us all to one end of the L-shaped kitchen.

I had fetched everything we needed and placed it on the centre island, when from behind me I heard the familiar sound the large swing door made as it opened into the kitchen.

I inhaled a deep breath, steadied myself and forced my head to turn around, prepared to face my demons head on. I looked over my shoulder and recognition washed over me at the sight of the young man who strolled through the open gap. Instinctively my fingers clutched at the metal work surface to steady myself. His gait was familiar and my stomach turned over in equal amounts of excitement and apprehension. He looked up from under his baseball cap and his silver coloured eyes found mine. He offered me a small smile and continued walking towards me. I swept my eyes up and down him. He was the correct build and on first glance his eyes were an exact match to Raff's.

Surely my eyes were playing tricks on me?

I slowly blinked, trying to focus to get better clarity and started to shake my head with realisation as he came closer. It wasn't Raff. The adolescent boy that was now stood in front of me looked like Raff, walked like Raff, but he was his own person. In those few seconds, I could see his mannerisms were completely different.

I let out the breath I'd been holding and attempted a smile when I saw a look of concern come over his face.

His hand thrust out in front of him as he offered to shake my hand. I released my fingers from the work surface and held it out to receive his.

'Hi, I'm Flint,' he smiled. 'Are you okay? You look like you've seen a ghost.'

I nodded my answer, too stunned to reply, and he carried on.

'Is there any breakfast going? I know I'm late, but I thought I'd give it a try.'

'Flint,' came an almost scream from the other side of the kitchen.

Of course, it had to be. The last time I'd seen him was as a baby on the cover of Hello magazine, when the celebrity mag had done a feature on Raff and his family. I'd looked at it more than once as I dreamt of what might have been, and then I'd marched down to the end of our garden and thrown it on the bonfire my dad was having.

I watched as Winter came running towards him and pulled him into her for a hug. Embarrassed, Flint wriggled away from her hold, but she persevered and clutched him by the forearms as she gave him the once over.

'Just look at you!' she exclaimed as she looked him up and down. 'You grow like a weed.' Then she looked at me and smiled. 'Sorry where are my manners?' she grinned. 'Lauren this is my nephew Flint, Raff's son. Flint this is Lauren, one of my best friends.'

I went for a broader smile now as he turned away from Winter and looked at me again. 'Hello, nice to meet you. You can join us for breakfast, we're just about to eat.' I waved my open arm towards the island.

He took in the area I had gesticulated at and moved quickly towards it. 'Thanks.'

Without any guidance from me he immediately began to look around for nearby stools we could use and began to position them around the island.

I sat down on one and watched as Winter took the stool next to her nephew, so she could interrogate him as they ate. Although I smiled and listened to their conversation, inside my head I was lost to the memories that seeing an almost exact replica of a teenage Raff had brought to the forefront of my mind. My head took me back seventeen years ago, to the day I had found Raff waiting at the end of the long school driveway.

As my eyes first sought him out leaning against the old wire fencing, my heart had skipped a little. He was simply the coolest thing I had ever seen. I had offered Winter's big brother a smile and tried awkwardly with only one hand to sort out my vile burgundy and grey school uniform as I prepared to walk past him. Then I'd looked around me as I clutched my school books to my chest, expecting to find some other lucky girl running down the drive to meet him. When he peeled his sunglasses off, his eyes had found mine. A blush hit my face as he said my name and then didn't look away. In shock, I'd stood in front of him as he told me that he wanted to go out with me and he was going to walk me home to ask my dad's permission. I never answered him as we walked, but just occasionally I'd nodded my head at him as he spoke. I remember looking at the frozen puddles on the lane as we walked home and seeing the almost magical shimmering in them for the first time.

He had entered my world and suddenly everything about it fell into place.

With my hands on my lap under our kitchen table, I had pinched my flesh on the back of my hand as I watched him chat effortlessly to my mum as she plied him with her fresh baked biscuits and warm milk, at the same time as she banged on the kitchen window at my brother Mark to stop kicking his football against the wall or she would box his ears. Finally, my dad had arrived and taken him into our lounge and closed the door behind them. All the while they had been talking I had stood outside the glass panelled door with my fingers crossed, occasionally daring to peak through one of the glass panes. I had watched as Raff had thoughtfully nodded at my dad's words, with his hands pushed down into his jeans pockets.

The glass panelled door had eventually opened and he'd strode back into the hall, grabbing me by the hand on the way past. He had pulled me with him while shouting out his goodbyes and thanks to my family, then led me into the porch and closed the door behind us. Before he even spoke to me again, he pulled me tight into his arms and pressed a chaste kiss to my lips.

"Your dad said yes, Lauren." He had still held me close in the cramped porch, filled with coats, shoes and family life. "Now you're my girl."

'Hey, Flinty boy, how are you, dude?' came the booming voice of Cade as he re-entered the large kitchen.

Flint jumped off the stool he had been sitting on and with a broad grin on his face he made his way towards Cade to receive his welcome. With elbows bent they clasped their hands together and slapped each other on the back, finally pulling each other into a hug. Cade stole the cap off Flint's head and turned it backwards on his own, making his dirty blond hair lift away from his face, exposing his dark, Mediterranean eyes. Without another thought he promptly sat down on Flint's vacated stool next to Winter.

'Hey, that's so not cool,' shouted out a smiling Flint as he searched around for somewhere else to sit. Finally, he pulled up a small step ladder, turned it around and put it in the only space available, next to me. He perched his backside on the handle at the top before he grabbed at some more food.

The distraction of watching Cade interact with Winter was exactly what the doctor ordered.

Cade had sat down and had not removed his eyes from her once. I watched as he took her knife out of her hand, placed her plate in front of him and began to butter her waiting croissant.

'What the hell are you doing now?' she exclaimed in anger but with a half-smile on her face.

'Feeding you,' he retorted as if she had asked the most stupid question in the world. 'You're going to need all your energy, Winnterrrr,' he overly pronounced her name and I looked on in amusement, her eyes watching his exposed tongue in his open mouth, as he deliberately rolled the R in her name.

Oh, my God. Cade most certainly has her number.

I rolled my lips over my teeth and inside my mouth, biting down on them slightly as I tried to contain my amusement at his antics. Winter shot me a look across the island to let me know I hadn't fooled her and I stared her out while pulling my small croissant into small pieces, placing them into my mouth and chewing slowly.

I looked at Flint next to me and smiled at him again as his eyes caught mine. Thank heaven he was either so used to the way the guys in the band acted or he hadn't caught on to the game Cade was playing. But taking him in again I could see he knew exactly what was going on, he was much older than his years. I was about to look away when a small movement behind Flint took my breath away and all the air in the large kitchen was suddenly vacuumed out. I couldn't see his face but knew without any doubt it was him.

The moment that I had played out in my head for more years than I wanted to think about had arrived.

I tried desperately to pull my gaze away, but I knew it was hopeless. My eyes were literally magnetised into watching him approach. Slowly, he came near enough for me to see him around his son. I swallowed a large gulp and hurriedly wiped off the few crumbs of croissant from my lips with the napkin I had previously held in my lap. I knew I had seen him over the years on TV, in magazines and newspapers, but nothing compared to seeing the man I used to love, in the flesh.

He was wearing his dark hair shorter at the sides than he used to wear it, and longer on top and due to his exertions, I could see that it still flopped forward over his eyes. His face was the same shape as I remembered, although now it was covered in a thicker dark stubble and his bottom lip had been sucked into his mouth in thought. At last he stopped walking and I cast my gaze over his body, the body of the slim boy I had once known and loved had filled out. Raff was broader, taller and beneath his dirty, sweat stained T-shirt I could see he was harder and more muscular.

Bloody hell.

In my head, this wasn't how this part of our story went. I was going to be calm, polite and resolute at our first meeting. He would then be able to see that I had moved on, that I'd grown up and first loves that had gone on to become hot rock Gods were unquestionably no longer on my radar. We would pass the time of day and move on with our lives.

To conclude my ridiculously long perusal of a man I shouldn't even want to look at, I forced my eyes to travel up to his. They progressed slowly up the T-shirt that was stretched so magnificently over his torso, and they stopped to watch as he crossed his arms over his chest. Then they skipped over his large Adam's apple, skirted over his still sucked in bottom lip, and at last my eyes found his. I tried so very hard to put a look of friendly welcome on my face, but knew I'd failed magnificently when I heard a gasp leave my mouth.

My whole body awakened. It was as if I had been hibernating for years. My heart accelerated and opened up like a flower in bloom.

My skin began to tingle, with the hair on my exposed forearms standing to attention.

This can't be happening, it's fucking crazy.

My heart was banging in my chest and I felt punch drunk, but still I couldn't remove my eyes from his. I had to fight to keep my hands still, my whole body was screaming at me to stretch out my hand to touch him. In response, my hand lifted to my chest and covered over my heart, trying to add another layer of protection.

The world around us had disappeared and although I'd spent years climbing out of the deep, painful place he had left me in, I was instantaneously catapulted back. Seventeen years had come and gone. In that time, I had grown, discovered the real me, I had laughed, cried and even managed to somehow love again, of sorts. But in the exact instant my eyes found his, those experiences were erased. They became rapid eye movement dreams, dreams that I could barely remember having after I'd woken up.

Yet he'd awoken me just by walking into the bloody room.

This isn't good.

I just about managed to talk myself out of physically shaking my head.

I watched as small creases appeared at the corner of his eyes and he offered me a warm smile.

'Loz, it's *really* good to see you.' He emphasised every word. Listening to him say my name like he used to, was too much. Seven simple little words that oscillated themselves through the many layers I'd taken years to fabricate. He had exposed me and opened me up raw, in one minute flat.

'Please don't call me that, no one calls me that anymore.' I felt flustered at my reaction and got down suddenly off my stool. I was aware that all the conversation around the island had stopped and they were now watching the two of us. 'Nice to see you, Raff. I can't stop to chat, I've got far too much to do. Excuse me.'

I moved away as far as I was able, refusing to allow myself a second glance.

Chapter 7

Raff

I made myself stand still as she walked away. The urge to follow her and to try to make her listen to everything I wanted to say was overpowering.

It was a relief when I could no longer hear her feet on the slate flooring and I knew she was no longer in the same room.

'FUCK!' I roared as I kicked the small step ladder Flint had recently vacated as he stood up to watch Lauren go.

As it skidded across the slate tiles the noise was deafening. It was only when it finally crashed into an aluminium bank of cupboards and fell silent that I remembered that our whole couple of minutes meeting had witnesses. I lifted my eyes up from the overturned step ladder, pushed my hands into my back pockets and turned my head to stare at them all.

Shaking his head, Cade immediately shifted to go and right the steps.

The kitchen staff stood and made their excuses about having to get on and that left Winter and Flint.

'Well that went well.' I heard Winter's sarcasm trip off her tongue smoothly.

'Don't say another fucking word.' I growled over at her and stomped away.

Lauren

My feet moved automatically until I found myself once again in the large space at the back of The Manor. What would have once been the ballroom stretched across almost the whole of the ground floor at the back of the property. All the windows were floor to ceiling to capture the light, with arches that matched those in all the different buildings on the estate. The room was traditionally decorated in duck egg blue with golden tones and dated back to a more opulent time. I'd fallen in love with it as soon as Winter had shown it to me this morning.

I had no reason to be in here again, but walked around running my fingers over the tablecloths as I tried to connect with the beautiful room and control my overflowing emotions. I looked at the layouts and centrepieces on the tables, pretending to check on things and smiled at the decorators as I did so. I even straightened things that didn't need correcting in the first place. Luckily, they in turn got on with everything they needed to do and didn't question my reasons for being there. Eventually, I found my way to the end of the room and moved quickly behind a small makeshift stage that I knew at some point tomorrow Default Distraction would be playing on.

Behind the stage was a square bay window with a window seat. I knew I couldn't be away for too long, but I needed a few minutes for me. I sat down on the overly-stuffed cushioned seat and leant my back against the purposefully placed back cushions, which were hung by tabs from the white gloss wood panelling.

I heard myself sigh as I sunk further into the downy comfort and closed my eyes, sighing loudly at the embarrassing predicament I now found myself in.

I need to get over this.

I had moved on, my life was complete without him in it. Wasn't it? My eyes opened widely as I heard the question go around my head.

YES. YES. YES! Inside my head, I screamed at myself in reply.

I tried to clear my thoughts of Raff and closed my eyes once again, to think of Toby. We hadn't been together long but he had a good job, treated me well and had even hinted that he wanted to settle down with me. I could have the life I'd always wanted and maybe even a child if I looked after my diabetes well enough. But as I envisioned a picture of Toby in my head, like a slide show my brain replaced it with a picture of Raff.

As he smiled at me in my mind, I quickly opened my eyes, 'Oh, for God's sake!' I punched my tightly closed fist into the plump cushion by the side of my thigh.

Refusing to give in to his smile, I looked out of the window to watch the sun's reflection glistening on the thick ice of the large lake to one side of The Manor. I slipped off my Converse by treading on the back of them and put my bare feet up on the cushion. With my knees bent in front of me, I hugged them with one arm and trailing one finger from my other hand through the condensation at the base of the window I semi-reluctantly gave in to my memories. Closing my eyes again I leant my head to the side and onto the welcoming strip of cushioning.

'Mum, I'm off, Raff's here,' I shouted behind me, expecting my voice to travel down to the kitchen. Then turning back to the window, I lifted a hand to wave at him. As the car came to a complete stop his head turned towards our house and I watched him smile as he saw me there waiting for him. The four weeks we had been apart had been torture, but at last his A-levels were finished and he was home.

My heart completely stopped as his eyes found mine and then it restarted, accelerating into a full, very excited gallop. The butterflies in my stomach joined in instantaneously, reacting to the corners of his mouth lifting in greeting. My flesh prickled in anticipation of being with him, being near enough to have our skin touching each other's and him holding me tight in his arms like I might break if left to my own devices. I let the pristine white net curtain fall back into place and behind its camouflage I took in a deep breath, placing a hand over my heart before I propelled myself forward. I grabbed at my Kipling rucksack, flew out of my bedroom door and down the stairs as quickly as possible.

'Let's have a look at you then.' I heard my mum's voice as my jewelled flip-flops found our carpeted hallway. I turned my head to see her sitting at the kitchen table sipping at the coffee she was holding and smiling at me. 'You look really nice, Lozzie.'

'Thanks. Do you think Raff will like it?' I touched my long, loose pony tail making sure it was still in place and looked down at my short denim ruffle skirt and the pink, crop vest T-shirt I was wearing. I'd bought my new clothes with my wages from my Saturday

job and the two babysitting jobs I'd done this week. Even after buying my new clothes I'd still had some left to save.

'He'll love it. But then he'd love anything you wore. Where are you two off to?'

'I'm not sure, for a drive maybe.' I knew we would be going anywhere we could be alone. I tried to make my voice sound as nonchalant as possible and offered her a small smile to appease her questioning.

Finally, she answered me with a knowing nod of her head. 'Okay, well make sure you're back by nine.'

'Oh, Mum, really? I'm sixteen in ten days' time, surely I can stay out until ten now?' I heard myself tut, but somehow I managed to do it quietly.

'You know the rules, young lady.' Her eyebrows raised and I knew I was pushing my luck. 'And so does Raff, your dad explained our rules to him. While we are happy for him to take you out, he has to remember that you're three years younger than him.'

Even now, when we had been seeing each other for six months, I had to pinch myself to believe we were together. I'd had the biggest crush on him for... well, since forever. I'd read in magazines that it often happens when one of your best friends has an older brother, but this was different. It wasn't just a passing crush, an infatuation or even teenage hormones. I knew, even though I was only fifteen, that I would never love anyone the way I loved Raff. He was my first love, and would be my only true love.

'But...' I countered with.

'No "buts."' She stopped my attempt at swaying the conversation dead in its tracks. My dad might think he was in charge in our house, but my brother and I knew it was our mum, and any argument or resistance we put up was often futile.

'Okay, I know.' I sighed in acceptance at what she had said, gripping the bag I was holding tighter with both hands. I needed this conversation to end. I was desperate to get outside and into the car that was waiting for me.

'Two more weeks, Lauren, and you'll be sixteen. Dad and I will up your curfew time then, as long as you treat our rules with respect now.'

'Okay.' I sighed in resignation, turned and fled down the hall to the front door, before she held me back any longer.

'Have fun and be safe,' was her parting call as I turned the handle and pulled open the front door.

I found Raff on the other side. I gulped a breath of air and swallowed as I looked up at him. He didn't seem to have stopped growing in the last few years and he was now well over six feet. I watched him smile at my reaction. His black hair was flopped down over one eye, but then it always was in at least one place, and it usually covered one of his deep silver grey eyes. His face was clean shaven, showing more of his inherited olive skin that was already tanned by the early summer we'd had this year. My eyes unashamedly took all of him in, his teeth biting his full bottom lip and finally, the Adam's apple that seemed to be growing more prominent with every week that passed.

His hand that had been lifted with his finger poised at my doorbell came down quickly to grab onto mine and he pulled me quickly towards him. I landed against his firm body, made hard with all the competitive rowing he did at the private school his father insisted he attended. My whole body relaxed against his and my eyes closed as his fresh smelling soap filtered through his thin black T-shirt. One of his strong arms came around me so he could hold me close.

'I've missed you,' I spoke into his chest.

His spare hand weaved its way into my long hair and he gently guided my head tighter into him. I willingly placed it against his heart and listened to the steady rhythm it offered. He leant down to me and whispered into my hair as he kissed the top of my head. My pulse beat in giddy excitement at his words. 'Exams are over, now you're all mine for the summer and forever. I promise, no more time apart, Loz.'

Listening to his words and the sentiment behind them, made my skin tingle. I pulled one of my hands free to steady myself by placing it on his torso. The act didn't steady me at all. As soon as my palm found his well-defined muscles, my pulse beat so strongly all I could hear was the sound of the blood whooshing past my eardrums and all I could feel, see and taste from the air around me, was him. The way I reacted to him was at first something I didn't understand, but I was learning fast and now craved the heady way us being together made me feel.

The memory was so powerful I could remember exactly the way he smelt, even now. I inhaled deeply and let the smell wash over me, but it was almost too strong.

'I'm sorry if I upset you, Lauren.' Raff's deep voice interrupted me.

My whole body jumped out of the semi-relaxed state it had been in and my eyes flew open. I looked down at the small heart I'd unwittingly drawn on the window beside me and immediately rubbed it away.

'When?' I answered defensively and I turned my head a little to look at him.

'Just now.' I watched his posture change as he prepared to stand his ground. He widened his stance and crossed his bare arms over his chest. It made his forearms bulge against the many leather cuffs and bracelets.

'Oh, I wondered *exactly* which time you were talking about,' I retorted sarcastically and shot him a quick look to see him raise an eyebrow at me.

I swung my legs back down to the floor and slipped my loose Converse back on. I was going to stand up, but he was too close and effectively blocking my way. So, instead of standing and looking at his face, I was forced to remain seated and my eyes were made to focus on his well-fitting black jeans and black leather, studded belt. My hands gripped the cushion beneath me as I watched, unable to tear my eyes away, when he pushed his hands down into his back pockets, making his low-slung jeans pull tighter across his hips and then ride a little further down. His dirty T-shirt lifted from the top of his jeans, exposing the bottom of his abs and giving me a small glimpse of his dark happy trail. All of this was not helping me initiate the conversation I needed to have.

I swallowed and hoped he couldn't hear it.

He rocked back slightly onto the heels of his boots and cleared his throat.

'I'm so sorry for causing you so much pain.' I knew the moment his words left his mouth that he wasn't talking about a few minutes ago. He was thrusting both hands into the barely healed scars of our past. His fingers were tearing apart the delicate scar tissue left behind and hoping that by doing so, it would knit back together stronger and better able to bear the rigors of life's demands. He didn't know how wrong he was with his assumptions.

I made myself look up at his face and our eyes met. There was so much emotion between them and feelings that had long ago been stored away as no longer needed. It would have been heart breaking to stand by and watch our silent connection, but to endure that moment was more than I could bear.

I managed to clear the unyielding constriction in my throat to speak. 'Is this the bit where you want me to smile and say, it's all okay, Raff?' I looked at him in question. 'Because if it is, hell will freeze over first… because I can't. You walked away from me when I needed you the most and for that I can never forgive you.'

The first of many tears began to spill down my face. I wasn't ashamed to show him the pain he'd left inside my heart and I did nothing to wipe away the evidence of the grief he had left me with. But I swore in my head it would be the first and last time that I would allow him to see the heartache I lived with daily.

I saw his stance change and his hands appeared from his back pockets, they were now either side of my body about to touch me.

'Don't *you* dare.' I didn't recognise my voice, as I threatened him with more strength than I could have ever imagined I even had. 'Don't even *think* about trying to touch me, *you* don't get to offer me consolation. I'm not yours and I haven't been for more years than I can even remember. I'm with someone else now.'

'So, I've been told.' His eyebrow raised and his voice deepened.

I wasn't sure but I think I saw him momentarily flinch at my words, but I carried on regardless. 'I have lived without you now for over half my life.'

I summoned every ounce of strength I had and stood up, making our bodies collide in the small space. The connection caused my breathing to immediately ramp up and the stupid bloody butterflies in my stomach to once again take flight.

I made myself look up into his eyes and I could see my words had penetrated, pain and remorse were shining right back at me.

Hell yeah, take some of that.

'I deserve all of that and a lot fucking more.'

I nodded at him and made to walk past him. 'You're not worth it. Excuse me,' I muttered politely. Our conversation was over.

I'd made it all of three steps when I heard him speak again.

'This new bloke of yours, does he treat you well, Loz?'

My feet stopped moving and the squeak my shoes had been creating on the recently polished Parquetry flooring faded away.

'Does he make you feel, like you know I can?'

'Leave me alone... I'm not interested in you!' I shouted out into the now thankfully empty room.

'I don't for one fucking minute believe that and neither the fuck do you,' he replied.

I had to force my motionless feet to move one small step at a time, as it appeared they wanted to stay and listen to him. But I couldn't, I wasn't prepared to answer his questions, because he had always been able to tell when I was lying and I couldn't give him that open door into my present life.

I patted my cheeks dry as I walked the length of the ballroom and when I reached the main doors I convinced myself to smile broadly.

Lauren

Raff grabbed my rucksack and held on to one of my hands, threading his fingers through mine in the way he always did. I moved quickly trying to keep up with his long, powerful legs as he strode down our path and out to the old Ford Zephyr he had found in one of his family's garages and subsequently over the last year, had painstakingly done up. As we reached his car that was double parked in our street, he pulled open the heavy looking, two tone door and as it let out an indignant creak, he threw my rucksack onto the seat at the back.

I jumped in through the open door and sat down, adjusting my short skirt as he walked around the front of the car twirling the car keys around his finger. He jumped in, lowering his frame by gripping his fingers onto the roof of the car. He turned the key in the ignition, the engine revved to life and we pulled away. I let out a sigh of relief as the curtain twitching neighbours were left behind.

'Come here. You're too far away.' His silver grey eyes looked me up and down fleetingly before his eyes went back to the road ahead.

I slid over the bench seat as carefully as I could, which wasn't easy in a short skirt with my bare skin sticking to the cream leather. The moment my right thigh touched his jean clad one, my heart rate leapt in response and goose bumps rose on my bare leg. One of his hands left the steering wheel and came to find mine. I watched as his fingers threaded through mine and he squeezed his reassurance to me.

It wasn't necessary, with him was the only place I felt fully comfortable in my own skin. The curse of being a teenager my mum called it. Apparently, everyone questioned who they were, how they looked, what their future held, and if they would ever find someone to see through the teenage pretence and love them for the truth behind it. But when I was with him I asked myself none of those questions. He gave me confidence in the fact that he loved me, when sometimes all I could see was an awkward, sporty, gangly looking girl with tits and hips that were too small to be an attraction to anybody.

Thirty minutes later, Raff parked the large car in a very nearly empty carpark high up on the cliffs of Dover, overlooking the English Channel with France on the distant horizon.

'Just look at that view. Apart from you, it's the thing I miss the most when I'm away at school.' His hand left mine and his arm came around my shoulders to pull me in tighter against his body. 'Is here okay, Loz?'

'It's the perfect place, I didn't care where we went this evening. All I wanted was you to myself. I've missed you so much. The last four weeks have dragged by.' I turned my head to look up at him as looked down to me and I got lost in the depth of his grey eyes. The feeling coursing between us was still a wonder to me.

Was it always like this between a boy and a girl?

Or was it just us?

I'd spoken to my cousin Amy, and Raff's sister Winter, about the way he made me feel, and although they had crushes on boys neither were in a relationship and they couldn't answer me. Only my nan seemed to understand as she too had fallen in love with my grandad when she was young.

I knew he was going to bring his head down to kiss me and my body reacted instantaneously. I licked my bottom lip in readiness as his head came closer and a long strand of his thick, dark hair fell forward and touched my cheek. As his lips finally came to mine I heard myself sigh with the feeling of completion he gave me whenever we were connected in some way.

His tongue caressed mine and I teased his tongue in the way that being kissed by him had taught me. Every part of the sensitive flesh around my lips was teased and flirted with. I felt my tiny nipples bud inside my bra and my stomach muscles as they clamped tightly. As our kiss continued I was silently asking him to touch me, desperate to feel his rough fingertips gently slide over my bare skin. Almost as if he had heard my plea his fingers, calloused from doing up his car and from his other great love, guitar playing, touched the bare skin below my new T-shirt and I gasped at the contact. I felt them brush over my side and slide behind my back as he pulled me closer into him and I opened my mouth wider to subconsciously allow him greater access. His tongue became more insistent, more demanding and I found it difficult to keep up with him.

All I knew was I didn't want him to stop. I never wanted him to stop.

At last his fingertips returned and skirted underneath the bottom of my bra and then further upwards. My back arched further towards him as I lost control of everything and my body instinctively implored him to touch me. As his thumb rubbed over my bra-clad nipple, my body quivered in response and I groaned into his mouth.

We had been here a few times and we both knew what was coming next.

But tonight he broke away from me. 'Raff?' I breathlessly questioned as his lips left mine.

'I can't, Loz. God knows I fucking want to. But we can't keep doing this, we've come to that precipice where I can't fool around with you anymore without going the whole way.'

'I want to go the whole way with you, Raff,' I whispered. 'I love you and I'm ready.'

'I love you too.' His lips came back to mine and he kissed me with love and tenderness, effectively pushing the passion to one side. As his lips left mine he spoke into the small fissure between us. 'I love you so much, but you won't move me on this. You're under age for one and I'm NOT taking your virginity in a fucking car park.'

My brain kicked into gear on hearing his words and I pulled away from his arms, sitting up straight and folding my arms over my chest I stared out to what I hoped would be the calming sea. Slowly, tears began to roll down my cheeks at his refusal to give in to what I had thought we both wanted.

'Oh no, you don't.' His arm pulled me once again into his side, holding me tightly to him. The fingers from his other hand found my chin to tip my face up towards him and he kissed the tip of my nose. 'Don't pull away from me, Loz.'

'What's wrong with me? Why don't you want me?' I childishly blurted out.

His head shook from side to side as he wiped the tears off my cheeks and then ran his thumb along my jawline as he kissed me chastely.

'There's absolutely nothing wrong with you. You are fucking perfect in my eyes and because of that, this between us is going to be

done right. When we look back in fifty years' time, everything we ever did together will have been done properly.'

'You've had others, so why do I get the special treatment?' The child in me was turning into a brat, but I couldn't stop myself.

His hold on me tightened as he stared down at me, narrowing his eyes and stopping me from seeing into his soul. Then he shook his head from side to side. 'Because you, Lauren, are the only one I've ever loved. Because I will always look after you, Lauren, and I will always put your needs before my own. Because you are mine and will always be mine.'

His hold changed on me and he lifted me up onto his lap and groaned in my ear as my body came into contact with his. He wrapped his arms around me tightly and lowered his head onto my shoulder as he fought to control himself. I could feel his denim covered erection underneath the bare skin of my leg.

He lifted his head again and stared at the side of my face. 'Can you feel how much I want you?'

I nodded in answer, not daring to move a muscle. I wanted to, but my inexperience got the better of me and I sat still. But feeling him and hearing the strain in his voice helped to dampen down my fears.

'I just know that I will always put what is right for you before anything else, Lauren... and that's the way it's going to be. Tell me you understand that?'

Reluctantly, I nodded my head.

'Tell me with words that you understand what I'm saying?'

'I think so...' I answered.

'Then kiss me like you understand,' he demanded.

I turned my head to look at him properly. My eyes found his and I was lost. I placed my lips to his and tried hard to convey how much he meant to me and how much I wanted to be with him. His hand came up to cup the side of my face as he always did when we *kissed and his thumb brushed along my jawbone in tender affection. Finally, our lips broke apart and I leant my forehead to his as I circled my arms around his shoulders, holding him to me.*

'Why does being young have to be so difficult?' I smiled at him as we took long, deep breaths to recover.

He laughed and somehow that sound made me feel warmer inside. 'Yep, I agree it's difficult... But it's a couple more weeks until your sixteen, that's all... Anyway, cheer up, I've got something for you.'

I lifted my forehead from his and looked at him. My face, which had been sad before, broke into a wide smile.

'Why?' I questioned.

'Because one day I'm gonna give you the world. But this will have to do for now. Hold on while I get it.' He stretched behind me and down to the side of his door to reach my gift. 'Now, it's nothing expensive, I don't want you to get your hopes up.'

'That's fine, I don't need expensive,' I answered, trying to reassure him.

'Okay, then close your eyes.' He shifted again so he was once again comfortable underneath me. I felt his hands touch my skin as he placed a chain around my neck and then I heard the clasp flick shut. 'You can open them now.'

I did as he instructed, then my hand shot up to my neck and I picked up the chain I found there. Lifting it up in front of my eyes, I could see it was a silver coloured fine chain that held half a heart. I twisted the pendant around so I could read the one word written on there.

'Always...' I whispered.

'Yep, and mine says...' He pushed his hand into the already stretched neck of his old T-shirt and pulled out a more masculine looking chain, with the other part of the heart swinging on it. 'And

mine says, forever. It's only a whole heart when they're placed together, like you and me.'

'Always and forever. I love it, thank you, Raff.'

'It's how I feel about you, Loz. We're always going to be forever.' Then he pushed the pieces together, showing me how perfectly they fitted against each other.

I pulled him closer to me and we held on to each other tightly as we watched the sunset to the west of us, lost in the emotion of our love for each other and the fragility of our years.

Little did I know then, that this was one of the last sunsets we would see together, before life got in the way and broke our hearts into two, like the pieces of the necklace we were wearing.

Four months later he would be gone.

Forever and always holding half of my heart captive.

I heard myself cry out with grief and sat bolt upright as I tried to work out exactly where I was.

I clutched the duvet to me and searched around the room, lit by the white, snow-filled landscape outside. I was at home. I saw the dull red, luminous figures beside me, it was three in the morning.

It was a dream. Seeing him today had stirred up my memories.

I clutched the back of my neck and began to massage it as I rolled my neck around, trying to relieve myself of the tension that had built up in the five hours I'd slept.

I flung myself back down on my bed and tried to once again empty my mind.

I looked up at the stars through the skylights above me. This was getting crazy. I hadn't slept at all last night because of him and tonight I'd managed five hours before a dream of him had woken me up.

'No more!' I yelled out to myself.

I flung myself over onto my side and snuggled back down into my comfortable bed and thought of my cousin Amy instead. I hoped her night with the tall stranger called Daniel was still going well. I felt a smile push up my cheeks as once again I visualised him carrying her over his shoulder up the wrought iron staircase to my spare room. I was happy for her. Just with the fleeting glimpse Winter and I'd had of him, I could see he was a seriously good-looking guy and she deserved to have a tall, handsome man paying her a huge amount of hopefully very obscene attention.

After working bloody hard at The Manor all day, Winter and I had finally managed to escape, and it had been a relief to leave the place behind. As the three of us had finally sat down together in the closed tearooms, Amy had been teased and cajoled by the both of us into telling us about the handsome stranger who had rescued her and nearly ended up fucking her in the kitchen of The Fairy Garden. I had never seen her so irradiated. She told us about meeting him and how he made her feel, but to be honest all her words meant nothing, her body language and the bright light of hope in her eyes said everything we needed to know. Her second thoughts about meeting him had been fleeting, as Winter and I urged her into spending some time with him, and the last we'd seen of her was him carrying her off up the stairs.

My mind left them behind and went back to my own day. Raff and Cade had continued to "help" us and after our last conversation, I hadn't been able to look him in the eye. He had done whatever he could to make sure he was as close to me as possible for every excruciating minute. Every opportunity that had presented itself to him, he had made sure he could brush past me or touch my fingers with his. I knew exactly what he was trying to achieve. He was trying to remind me without words, how he could make me feel and it had worked every fucking time.

I couldn't lie here going over and over our fraught conversation. Then it came to me, I knew what I had to do.

I flung back my thick duvet and jumped out of my antique framed bed, hearing the familiar squeak as my weight left the springs. Then I moved around my bedroom, using only the light from outside. At the bottom of my bed was my grandfather's chest, which I used predominantly as a blanket box.

I crouched down onto the fluffy, dark red rug that was beside it and lifted the lid. Luckily, I knew the old chest and all the important things it contained so well that searching through it was something I could easily do with my eyes closed. My fingers rummaged in the far right corner until finally they rested on the tissue paper I was searching for. I snatched up the small offending package, walked quickly out of my bedroom and into my living area, then made my way over to the corner where my kitchen was located.

I stamped my foot hard on the pedal of the bin and the lid lifted with such force it clanged on the kitchen cupboard behind it. The sound echoed around the space, like a bell chiming in a clock tower. Extending my arm, I offered up the tissue paper covered package to its dark oblivion, but couldn't release my fingers to let go.

'Just do it, Lauren. Let it go. Let him go.' I talked out loud trying to offer myself the reinforcement and encouragement I obviously needed.

It was no good, my fingers were holding on tightly no matter how hard I tried to talk myself into doing it. Disgusted with myself, I pulled my arm sharply back into my body. Resigned, I slunk down the opposite kitchen cabinet and sat down onto the cold floor. Closing my eyes, my head fell backwards to the support of the wooden cabinets behind me. I clutched the tissue paper to my chest with both hands, hearing the small chink of the pendant touching the chain inside the paper. The small almost insignificant sound made my stomach knot against itself with panic at the many thoughts that were going around my head.

I was never going to be free of him, of us. The pendant had one word on it that I didn't have to look at as I had seen it so many times before. I knew every flourish and swirl of the font that had been used to engrave it onto the metal.

It seemed that "Always" meant exactly that, he was branded onto my very soul.

Chapter 9

Raff

I pulled down on the bar until I felt the cold of the metal touch across the bare flesh of my shoulders and exhaled through gritted teeth. 'Shhhhhhhh.' I held it there momentarily and then permitted the contracted muscles in my back to release and my arms to once again raise high above me. I concentrated on holding the tension in the bar before I drew the bar down again, completing my repetitions.

I let the bar go, and the plates came together as they fell on top of one another in quick succession with a resounding clank. I leant down beside the bench, grabbing at my towel. I wiped the sweat away from my face and had a quick swig of water, before I pulled the pin out and added another two plates.

I was just starting the repetitive exercise again, when I became conscious that it didn't matter what weight I was pulling, I couldn't feel the exercise at all. My mind wasn't on what I was doing. I immediately let go of the bar and the plates crashed together so violently the pin flew back out of the hole.

'FUCKING HELL!' I picked up the metal pin and feeling the anger inside me being released down every vein, I threw it at my reflection staring back at me from the mirror. The glass cracked, spread and then the offending mirror shattered, falling into a million pieces all over the new sprung rubber flooring.

'For fucks sake,' I muttered under my breath.

'Mr. Davenport, are you alright, sir?' I heard Paul the gym manager asking me as he rushed over.

I stood up from my position sitting astride the bench and ran my hands through my hair as I blew out the rest of my anger before I gave the poor bastard a mouthful that he didn't deserve. After running the towel over my face, I turned to face him.

'Yeah, I'm good, sorry about the mess.' I lifted my arm, with the towel wrapped around my hand like a boxing glove, towards the shattered mirror. 'What's the chance you can get the designers back in here to replace the mirror before we open?'

'I'm not sure,' he answered, still not removing his eyes from the silvery shards.

'Well, do what you can, I'll pay whatever they ask,' I replied, moving away to one of the running machines. I felt his eyes following me. The poor bastard was probably trying to work out which one of his new machines I was going to break next.

I could almost hear him thinking in his head how he could ask me to leave while still keeping his job. I didn't want to antagonise him, but my need to annihilate what was going around my head was greater than his need to protect the brand new gym. Add that to the fact I was one of the owners and he didn't stand a fucking chance.

I dumped my towel, pressed the start button and jumped onto the treadmill. I started ramping up the incline almost immediately.

My mind was stuck on her and the way she had reacted to me yesterday. I hadn't meant to corner her behind the stage we'd had set up, but I'd known the second she'd left the kitchen that I needed to follow her and try to let how know how much I desperately fucking regretted what had happened between us. When I saw her sitting in the alcove with her eyes closed, I'd stopped dead in my tracks and taken the chance to take a good fucking look at her. In nearly seventeen years, I had only seen her one other time. About five years ago, she'd attended the wedding of a mutual friend and Winter had sent me over some pictures. I could see what a beautiful woman she had grown into, but it didn't do her any justice at all. Seeing her yesterday, she'd literally taken my breath away. It's strange how many years can go by without you being in the presence of someone, but the very moment you meet again, you're back surrounded by memories that consume you. The way she used to twiddle her hair when she was thinking, the amber in her eyes that caught alight when she was angry. The sweet noises she would make when I was deep inside her. Everything flooded back in those few minutes.

She was absolutely fucking beautiful, just as I had always known she would be.

I'd run my eyes over and over her, trying to take in everything about her. Her chestnut brown hair was longer and now had lighter shades running through it, and although I couldn't see them I knew it matched her amber coloured eyes. The young body of a sporty girl had blossomed into full womanhood. She was curvaceous and completely different to the fucking stick thin, Barbie-doll women that had been keeping my bed lukewarm over the years. The moment she turned to me and opened her eyes I was back. I wanted her with a passion I hadn't felt in a long fucking time.

I'd had a sleepless night going over all the memories I had of us. All the times I'd loved her, all the times I'd made her laugh and the moment I'd personally ripped her heart out of her by walking away. I'd loved her all those years ago, in a way that I was damn sure only the young ever get to experience. I'd always thought it was a rose-tinted love, it had to be, because I remembered it as being too damn good. In the years that had followed, during days spent in drunken stupors, when I'd often drunk myself fucking sober, I could still remember how that love felt. On my lowest days, when getting so far off my fucking head to blank out the conniving, money-hungry bitch I'd married, it was memories of her that pulled me through. Winter had nearly got me to admit yesterday that I was still in love with her, which I had thought couldn't be true. I mean, how can you spend so many years away from that person and still say you were in love with them?

But now I knew, after seeing her, that I'd never stopped loving her. I looked up from my feet pounding the rubber matting and pressed the stop button. Holding on to the bars either side of me, I leant forward onto my forearms and inhaled deeply. I inhaled in through my nose and exhaled out through my mouth, as I tried to slow down my breathing in order to concentrate. For a few minutes I observed my reflection, sweat was running down my face and my hair was plastered to my head, but I looked past my façade, stared into my eyes and looked deep into my own soul.

It was true, I still loved her.

I didn't need to spend time trying to work it out. The brutal truth was, I loved someone who would probably never give me another chance and why the fuck should she? I knew I didn't deserve her. I had to face facts, I was in love with a woman who'd sworn she was with someone else and had moved on.

I watched my own eyebrow lift in defiance.

I wasn't willing to accept it, because I didn't believe her, not for one solitary, fucking minute. After all these years, her body still spoke to mine. She couldn't hide the way she reacted to me, I'd seen her inhale suddenly and could almost hear her heartbeat accelerate when she'd tried so incredibly hard to remain detached. I didn't give a fuck who he was, she was mine. She had always been mine and I was back to claim her.

For the first time in many years, I was being honest with myself and it felt fucking good. Now all I had to do was to get her to do the same thing. I was back in the place of my birth to mend some bridges, but with Loz, I was going to have to build the thing from the fucking ground up.

'Rafferty,' I heard

I tore my eyes away from the truths I could see reflected in the mirror and turned to see my son staring at me. I couldn't imagine how Lauren had reacted when she'd first seen him. He was every bit me and thank fucking God nothing of Ashley. His build, his colouring and most of all his attitude, God help him, were all me. Even the way he crossed his arms over his chest, twisted his head to the side and looked through the dark fringe of his long hair. He took people in, like I did. I could see him wordlessly asking me so many fucking questions that I didn't have the answers to, and the assumptions he came up with.

The truth captured in his eyes was a sucker punch straight to the gut, exposing exactly what he thought of me. It showed me wanting as a dad, and I wasn't fucking proud to see it there.

'Hey,' I replied as I started to move over towards him, offering him a smile that wasn't reciprocated.

As I drew closer he began to shake his head at me, unconsciously letting me know he didn't want my company. 'I came to tell you that Grandma and Pops are here.'

'Thanks, Flint... Hey, wait up, I'll walk back with you.' He shrugged his shoulders at me, like he couldn't give a shit one way or the other and turned towards the doorway.

I moved quickly to keep up with my son.

I was thirty-five years old and had made mistakes in my past that I didn't want to think about.

But it all seemed so clear to me now.

Flint and Lauren.

They were my future and I'd do whatever it took to make it up to them and to get them back into my life on a permanent basis.

Lauren

The whoosh of the kitchen door closing sounded again, as the staff left with yet more delicious samples of what The Manor was going to be offering to its paying guests. It snapped me out of the thoughts on constant bloody play in my head. The closing of the heavy metal door signified to me, the difference between my life and Raff's.

I audibly sighed and then looked down to concentrate as I washed my hands. I shook off the excess water, ripped the blue paper from its holder and turned around quickly as I began to pat them dry them. Everywhere was clean, shiny and in order. I glanced over at the last few trays of food left on racks in the large, aluminium space. Everything was going to Winter's very detailed plan and I couldn't be happier for her.

I looked over at the closed door and shook my head to dislodge my thoughts, as I prepared to busy myself checking and redoing what had already been done. Anything to keep myself occupied. I dropped the scrunched blue paper into the bin and reached over to turn the radio up a little so I could hear **Duffy** singing **Please stay**. It seemed that almost everything they played on the radio today was aimed at me, but I was probably being over sensitive and dramatic. It seemed that Raff still had that effect on me and I wasn't at all comfortable with the realisation.

I had peeped outside the kitchen a few times since the doors had been opened to the invited reviewers and national papers. The multitude of people in and around the building appeared to be very happy, comfortable and well fed. Winter had done a first-class job. The Manor was already breathtaking, but she had surpassed herself with the finer details of the day's events. She had chosen decorations and centrepieces that picked up on the opulence of the Victorian era, which was when The Manor had been built for an Earl and his growing family. I knew my friend was brilliant, but after floundering for a few years she seemed to have finally found her calling. She and Amy deserved every success and so much more. All this "leaving school and knowing exactly what you wanted to do with your life" rubbish, had never happened to any of us. I would honestly say that we were only just about mature enough now to know what we wanted to do with our lives. Perhaps the three of us were late starters? Maybe until we hit our thirties we hadn't felt the deep passion you needed to be certain about what you wanted from life. Or maybe we had all had that deep passion for something when we were younger and it had moved out of our reach? I knew both things had happened to me. I heard myself sigh again and shaking my head I tried to pull myself out of my melancholy thoughts.

Picking up my glass of water, I sipped at the cool contents and leant my Capri pants encased bum against the sink behind me and tried hard to stifle a yawn.

Even from the side of the vast property where the kitchen was situated, I could hear the low hum of the chatter going on all over the building. The noise sounded encouraging and I knew, without reading the reviews that would be written in tomorrow's papers and this month's magazines, the guests had been won over. I wanted to take a good look around and had tried to summon up the courage several times during the day to do so. But, I'd wandered earlier today and had seen Raff, and that one look was enough to send this supposedly brave thirty-two-year-old, independent businesswoman scampering back into her hidey hole.

I had entered the ballroom four hours previously, as per Winter's instructions to check everything was going according to schedule, and found him standing there with his parents and an uncomfortable looking Flint. Never had I seen Raff in a suit, not even at those award things they often televised live from the U.S. The awards that I only watched to remind myself that I felt nothing for him, then punished myself by turning them off while he was still on the stage, when my throat tightened, tears painfully pricked the back of my eyes and my heart began to ache with a deep sense of longing.

The man that had stood in front of my eyes earlier was spectacular. I wasn't sure if I'd ever hated or loved him more.

Loved? I heard a low groan leave my mouth, as it had the countless other times I had gone over seeing him today, and listened to that word reverberating in my head. Hate and love were very close bedfellows, weren't they?

I must be tired and confused.

As I had looked at him and his family, I had slowly become aware that my feet had frozen to the spot and the head waitress who had been chewing my ear off asking constant questions fell silent to me, as every sense I had, honed onto him and him alone. The charcoal grey of his expensive three-piece fitted him to perfection, showing off his broad shoulders, muscular toned torso and long defined legs, all the way down to his tan coloured, leather brogues. To top it all, it made the silver grey of his eyes appear like mercury filled pools.

He was simply mesmerising. For the first time I'd ever witnessed, he looked every bit part of the upper-class family he belonged to.

At least that's what the untrained eye would see, but I had once been so much more than that. I had swallowed deeply and stood mute, watching him flicking his index finger with his thumb on his right hand as it supposedly hung relaxed against his side, and swirling the small amount of amber coloured liquid in an expensive crystal-cut tumbler, which he was holding with the fingertips of his left hand. A smile might have been on his face, but he was agitated. We had been apart for years, but those two mannerisms showed me in a matter of seconds exactly how he felt.

I had stood frozen, unable to hear a word that was being spoken, until I heard his mum's voice call over to me.

'Good morning, Lauren.'

Those three words made the room once again come to life. Colour once again bled into my peripheral view, which had turned black and white as I had concentrated hard on scrutinising him. The small party had opened up their circle and turned around to face me. Two wide smiles had appeared immediately in greeting, followed by a stern nod from Colonel Davenport.

Raff however, had taken his time. I had watched as he slowly tilted his head towards where I stood. He'd then pulled his eyes away from watching the swirling whiskey in his glass and found me, immediately penetrating my pretence of working. Small laughter lines had appeared beside his eyes as he smiled knowingly. His gaze in turn darted all over me, silently acknowledging that he knew I'd been admiring him. Heat swept over my skin where his eyes travelled and then milliseconds later when they came to rest on the skin of my shoulders, left bare in a cream Bardot top, my body ignited. His eyes on my bare flesh might as well have been the calloused skin on his fingers caressing me. My body was instantly set alight, even from twenty feet away. My breathing changed and a blush hit my face that I knew even his father with his poor eyesight would be able to see. Somehow, my body had sensed the panic building inside me and miraculously began to move as I offered them a small wave in greeting. I steered the head waitress by the elbow along with me as we left the ballroom. As we departed the room, finally the breath I had been holding in released and I focussed everything I had on the waitress walking beside me, until she had at last had all her questions answered.

One of the chefs still working in the kitchen laughed at something on the radio and brought me once again out of my recollection.

I need a diversion.

I knew what I could do.

The old kitchen in The Manor had a fantastic L-shaped walk-in pantry. The architect who had refurbished the building had done so sympathetically and anything that could be of any use had been left and integrated into the new design. This had left many feature fireplaces, three secret passages, ceiling roses and my favourite, because cooking was my true love, a north-facing pantry.

I walked in, making sure the old panelled door didn't close fully behind me. Closing my eyes, I let the cool room embrace me and chill the feverish skin I had been carrying around since our moment in the ballroom. Walking around the corner away from the door, I took my phone from my trouser pocket and scrolled down to find Toby's number. A few minutes talking with him was exactly what I needed. As his phone rang, I pushed myself up on my toes and edged myself backwards to sit onto the marble surface that ran around the entirety of the large room.

'Hello, Lauren,' he answered. 'Are you okay?'

I held in a sigh of exasperation. I knew it wasn't his way, but truthfully, I was desperate to hear a change in his tone when he knew it was me on the other end of the phone. I wanted to hear his voice deepen with lust and longing. I needed to hear his footsteps on the floor and the voices of those around him begin to drift further into the background as he walked away from them. I wanted him to want to be with me in some small space of our own, even if we were only on the phone.

You're in your thirties for Christ's sake, grow-up.

'I'm fine, a bit tired, but good.' I could hear other voices talking around him and tried desperately to remember his itinerary that he had printed out for me.

'I bet the tearooms have been busy today. It should be a very profitable week for you.'

Please don't talk business.

I rolled my lips over my teeth and wordlessly looked around the empty space I was in. I hadn't lied to him, but I'd also not been truthful either. He didn't need to know I wasn't where he thought I was, he was working away until just before Christmas and I'd gone with "what he didn't know wouldn't hurt him."

'It should... How's the business trip?' I decided as much as I didn't want to, to change the subject.

'It's going well, we may be able to fold it up early and Lucy is keeping up with my demands.' He carried on talking about his media marketing business and the meetings they were attending. I zoned out and offered the occasional listening noise in return.

I bet. I felt my eyes roll up towards my forehead.

I could see Toby's PA in my mind's eye right now. I bet she was enjoying her upgraded role as his plus one for the trip. She was an attractive twenty-seven-year-old, with no other ties on her time other than to be at my boyfriend's beck and call. I'm sure a lot of women would have been jealous of their time together, but I had decided a while ago that I was obviously too mature for those feelings as it didn't bother me at all. Business was business after all.

Winter and Amy had opened their eyes wide when I'd told them how he was going away without me and taking her. Them probing as to whether I was happy with that and telling me exactly how pissed off they'd be if it was their partner, had me asking myself questions that I didn't want to know the answers to. What they didn't understand was I'd done the young love, the first love, the intense love thing before and I'd been crushed when Raff had left me. I was looking for a companionable sort of love now, one that included a mature respect for each other, even if it meant compromising on a lack of passion. Winter had told me I was in my thirties and not my seventies and I needed to snap out of it, she had only climbed down off her soap box once Amy had shot her a look. I knew they meant well, but they needed to understand that this was right for me.

I glanced around the empty pantry as he carried on talking and tried in vain to relax into his voice. Toby knew that I'd once been involved with Raff, our previous relationships were one of the things we had shared with each other a few months ago. I could see it had been hard news for him to take in. I mean, what normal working guy wouldn't feel threatened when they found out that their newish girlfriend had lost her virginity to a guy who had twice been voted World's Sexiest Man? I'd lost other boyfriends before, to the same male insecurities. Toby had been unhappy when he had realised that Raff was once again turning up in the village when he visited The Manor to check on the renovations. It seemed that Raff also made Toby feel insecure, when there was no need. But I knew it affected him, I'd watched his whole demeanour change any time Raff's name was mentioned. Only a couple of inches taller than me, any talk of Raff made Toby try to stand a little taller and to hold in a breath to try to flatten his stomach. He was a decent looking man in his late thirties, but corporate life had already taken its toll. Rich food and too much alcohol meant he carried a little extra weight around his middle and with his sandy coloured hair beginning to thin on top, I could see he felt inadequate.

I had weighed everything up and decided he didn't need to know exactly where I was working this weekend.

'So, what's been the best seller then this week, Lauren?'

Oh God, really? Couldn't he for once ask what colour underwear I was wearing? Or tell me how much he wanted me and describe all the wonderfully delicious things he was going to do to me, and would do, once he got home?

I sat up a little straighter at his question as I jumped to attention. A sudden noise from the kitchen had me peering around the metal racking to see if anyone had come to find me.

'Oh well you know, the usual,' I replied, feeling suddenly flustered at the fact I hadn't a clue.

'I bet those individual samples of different countries' Christmas cakes are doing well?'

'Yes!' I answered almost a little too enthusiastically, grasping hold of his idea and running with it. 'Almost every afternoon tea has requested at least a couple of them today, they were a fantastic idea of yours, Toby.'

And there it was, now I was blatantly lying to him.

'I knew they'd sell. I have so many more ideas for your little business, Lauren. I just wish you'd allow me to contribute more.'

I felt the hackles rise on my back and started to slow breathe as my anxieties of never being quite good enough began to rise up inside me.

'You know how much I appreciate that, but I've explained before. I welcome your input, but it's my baby and I want The Fairy

Garden's achievements and failures to be down to me.' Absentmindedly, I started to flick irritating specks of nothing off my black trousers. This conversation was one we'd had many times before, and it exasperated me beyond belief that he wanted to have it again. When he added in "little business" I was ready to bite his balls off with annoyance.

I'd rung him wanting to feel close to him. I'd wanted the conversation with him to erase whatever the sensations were that my body was feeling being here and around Raff. I wanted him to fill in the vast chasm that had opened itself inside me. Instead it was pissing me off and making me annoyed with him. I turned my head to the side when I heard another clicking sound coming from the kitchen end of the pantry.

'Sorry, Toby. I'm being called by Debbie. The tearoom is swamped and she needs my help.'

And that's how one lie became two.

'That's fine, Lauren. Speak soon.'

Another click sounded, but this one was in my ear as Toby cut off our call.

A shiver came over me as I realised he hadn't even waited to hear me say goodbye. There had been no expressions of love or sentiment, no "I'll call you tomorrow" or "I miss you." Sadness washed over me as I contemplated that our relationship seemed to be more of a meeting of minds, rather than the all-consuming passion I knew deep down I wanted.

Lauren

I jumped down off the marble ledge and pushed my phone into my back pocket. I sighed with the knowledge that I hadn't achieved what I'd set out to at all. I wandered around the corner of the L-shaped pantry, walking on the black grouting and following the pattern of the black slate flooring.

The sound of movement in the empty space made me look up suddenly.

My eyes found Raff sitting on another part of the marble work top. I stopped moving and crossed my arms over my chest as I looked at him in question. All at once I realised that he had probably heard most of my conversation with Toby. A flush of embarrassment and anger lit up my cheeks.

For a few seconds, we looked at each other. He looked dishevelled. The hair that had been nearly immaculate when I had seen him this morning was messy, where he'd been running his hands through the longer top strands, and the dark stubble on his face was already thicker. His once smart charcoal three-piece suit had lost its jacket and his waistcoat was unbuttoned and hanging loosely. His white shirtsleeves had been rolled up until they were tight around his forearms and the shirt had been pulled out of the waistband of his trousers.

I considered his eyes briefly and finding a flicker of amusement held deep within them, I narrowed my own at him and then looked down. I followed his movement as he leant forward, placing his bare forearms to rest on the top of the suit fabric that stretched magnificently over his thighs. I watched mesmerised as his hands clasped together in front of him and the veins on his arms became visible as his muscles flexed. I was aware that my heart rate had quickened at finding us on our own in the same room and inside my head I was already screaming at myself for my ridiculous response.

I almost visibly nodded as I decided there and then that I had nothing at all to say to him and turned towards the door shaking my head.

'You can't keep running away from me, Lauren.'

I ignored the voice behind me, filling the cavernous space with his deep bass tones and reached out for the brass door handle in front of me. My fingertips contacted with the freezing cold metal and I turned it quickly to release the catch that was holding me confined with the person that was both my worst nightmare and constantly reoccurring favourite dream. The handle turned, but the catch remained solid. So, I tried again, making sure I turned the handle to the left, as far as it would go. Still nothing. I resorted to rattling the thing to see if that would free it. I was confused for a few seconds and I could almost feel him smirking behind me.

I don't believe it. He wouldn't have, would he?

'The door's stuck.' I said the words out loud, but knew he was already aware of our situation.

My anxiety began to unfurl inside me at the unexpected situation. I leant my forehead against the cool wood of the door, licked my suddenly dry lips, closed my eyes tight and drew in a deep, calming breath as I fought to keep a lid on my panic.

Not here, not now, not in front of him.

'Yeah, the catch is old and sometimes needs releasing with a screwdriver. The builders were supposed to sort it out. But... well they haven't and I wanted to talk to you.'

I spun around, as anger flooded my system. In my rage, my anxiety surprisingly faded away. I focussed straight on him, something that up to now I'd avoided like the plague. He was still leaning forward on his forearms

'What the actual fuck? You've deliberately shut us in here?' My hands found either side of my hips and I glared at the arrogant bastard. 'I can't believe you would do something so stupid! It's your hotel's opening day, there are things I need to get on with. There are people you need to mix with and speak to. And all because YOU WANT TO TALK TO ME?' I knew I was grasping at straws, anything not to have the conversation he seemed so desperate to have. I'd had the conversation many times in my head. I'd even shouted it out loud a few times when I'd been drunk, but in real life? No bloody way was I having it.

Witnessing my anger or possibly the fact I was shouting at him, seemed to create a spark inside Raff. His brogues hit the floor with an unexpected click as he jumped down in one fast movement and strode the few steps towards me. Stopping himself a few inches short of our whole bodies being in contact with each other's, he swept his hair away from his eyes and twisted his head to look down at me.

'Do you not know me at all? I don't give a fuck what I'm supposed to be doing, this here is what needs to be done.' He moved one finger backwards and forwards between us both. 'You and me, this whole sorry fucking situation needs to end.' Irritation bristled off him as I stared into the angry, mercurial swirl of his grey eyes.

'I couldn't have put it better myself.' I thrust my arms straight down by my sides and reached behind me to find the closed door, needing to feel the steadying effect of the solid wooden object beneath my fingers. Then I lifted my chin and stared defiantly at him. 'So, is this what spoilt, rich brats do when they're not getting their own way?'

I watched him twist his head further to the side and look through the few errant strands of his dark hair as he absorbed my question.

'No, this is what they fucking do.'

With the words barely out of his mouth, his lips came crashing down to mine. My body was forced backwards against the door under his sudden onslaught. My mouth, which had been open ready to retaliate with more words of anger, reacted immediately and was suddenly trying to consume his. I'd forgotten just how good Raff could kiss, he paid loving attention to every single sensitive nerve ending and I was lost to all the sensations, to the want and need he conjured up inside me. The kiss felt like more than just spur of the moment passion, I could feel his fury, his impatience and his need to control. I needed to push him away, but as soon as that thought occurred to me, it was as if he read my mind. His large hands came up to cup either side of my face and he held me there, at his mercy. At the touch of his lips on mine, my body had started to ignite, a hot pit of long forgotten fire uncurled deep inside my stomach and it spread quickly until I was a molten mess in his hands. The more his tongue caressed mine, the more any notion I had of pushing him away dissipated.

I was gone, so far gone I stood no chance of removing him from me. The battle was over.

Damn him to hell.

He'd demanded.

And I'd let him take.

I was trapped between the want, need and desperation for the man I had been in love with for seventeen years, and all the hurt he had caused me. I brought my hands up to the bare skin above his waistband and felt a shiver devour me as our flesh connected. I held on for dear life as I silently gave him permission to carry on. Holding me captive with his mouth on mine, he pushed his hard, muscular body against mine, pinning me against the door with his hips and steel like erection. Happy that I was secure in his hold, his hands travelled down my neck, trailing his thumbs slowly over my throat. Finally, they stilled over the already sensitive bare skin of my shoulders.

'You are so fucking beautiful, Lauren,' he whispered into the small fissure he had created between our mouths.

As his lips found my bare neck, I waved the white flag of surrender. I was ready to take everything he was offering and to give him back anything he demanded.

A heavy knocking sounded behind us and Raff broke away. Lifting his head, his eyes remained fixed on mine, but he couldn't hide the regret trapped within them. His hands left my shoulders and simultaneously he smacked his open palms onto the door either side of my head as he showed his anger.

'Lauren, are you okay in there?' I could hear the concern in Winter's voice as she spoke from the other side of the door.

I touched my swollen lips with my fingertips as Raff moved further away and turned his back to me as he straightened himself out. Then he whispered the words I didn't want to hear.

'I'm sorry, Loz. I shouldn't have done that.'

Seventeen years had come and gone, but with one simple sentence he had taken us right back. He regretted what he had done and I was once again left rejected and confused. I leant my head back onto the door behind me and closed my eyes, blinking away the tears that threatened to fall.

Winter hammering on the door again brought me out of my pit of despair.

'YES…YES. I'm fine, Winter. The door's stuck. You need to get a screwdriver to the catch… apparently,' I shouted back to answer her banging.

'Thank God! I was getting worried you'd been taken ill. Just relax, I'll find one somewhere.'

'Taken ill?' he questioned as he turned back around.

I glared back at him and shook my head, refusing to answer his question. He broke our eye contact first and turned back to where he was sitting a few minutes previously.

I heard Winter's heels clopping off into the distance as she left the other side of the pantry door. I crossed my arms over my chest, suddenly feeling extremely cold at the loss of his body on mine. I watched Raff's back as he grabbed up his creased suit jacket from the marble he'd been sitting on, forced his arms back into it and straightened himself up.

'I need to know. Why exactly are you here, Raff?' My voice was small and shaky, but I was determined to stand strong and to get some of the answers I felt he owed me.

He turned around to look at me and with his arms hanging down by his sides he began to crack the knuckles on his fingers. 'I'm back for lots of reasons.'

'Uh, huh,' I agreed with him. 'So, are you using me as some sort of ego boost? Or a bet? Poor old Rafferty, doesn't have enough women throwing themselves down at his feet, let's see if he can fuck Lauren, for old time's sake?'

'You're so far off the fucking mark, its laughable.' He smirked at my growing anger.

'Really? I've been trying hard to work it all out, but I don't see it. I'm sure you've more money than most people can dream of. You could live anywhere in the world you wanted. But you've chosen to come back to a small village in England, deep in the Kent countryside. A village, that at eighteen you couldn't wait to leave behind along with all the rest of us in it,' I accused.

He pushed his hands deep into his trouser pockets and stared at me as he shook his head. 'Money doesn't buy you everything.' He sighed. 'I always wanted to live in our village and you fucking know it, Loz.' His voice grew in strength as he answered me. 'And I never wanted to leave here, because you, Mum and Winter meant too much to me, but you knew I had to go.' I could hear the pain in his voice as I opened up the Pandora's box of history between us, but I was on a bloody roll and couldn't even begin to think about stopping.

'Mmmm… You say I meant too much to you? You were my whole world, I ran away from home and followed you to the U.S. But I didn't even mean enough to you for you stay by my bedside in Vegas, did I?' I pushed myself away from the door, feeling a sudden surge of strength as I pressed him with my words.

I wasn't proud of myself for hurting him, but some things you can go your whole life carrying around, I'd done it for years and I knew it wasn't healthy. I needed to voice the sentence I had only ever said before inside my head. 'So, you need to listen to me. If you're back here for me, Raff, then know this, that ship sailed a long time ago.'

Raff stepped back into my space and grabbed hold of my forearms, sending another annoying zing around my body, then he pulled me towards him until every inch of me was touching some part of him. He buried his fingertips into the back of my arms and held on tightly. I could feel the beat of his heart against my chest. His warm breath hit the shell of my ear as he bent his head down and spoke into it, causing the skin around it to tingle. The undeniable fresh smell of Raff rose up with the heat of his body and into my nostrils. It was an automatic response when I inhaled deeply.

'You're right, you are one of the reasons I'm back here... Brody has been taking the piss out of me about you for the last few years. But truthfully, I didn't believe it myself until I saw you again. I thought I was coming home so I could find the peace I've been searching for. Fuck knows I needed to make a proper home for Flint and I wanted this new business venture to help to ground all of us in the band...'

I went to interrupt him but he seemed to sense it and acted faster, moving his head suddenly and grabbing my face with one hand he placed his lips quickly down onto mine in a chaste, but rough kiss. I was stunned, and when he pulled away just as rapidly, I couldn't talk. Then he carried on as if nothing had happened.

'... cause Christ knows we've been spinning so far off the fucking rails in the last ten years we need it, we need this place to simply survive.' He stopped talking momentarily and sucked in his bottom lip as he thought. 'You know, I'd hoped I could see you, that we could talk and clear the air, because I had reasons for the decision I made all those years ago and someday you *are* going to hear me out on them. But seeing you now and holding you, all those other reasons for being here feel like complete fucking bullshit... YOU are the reason I'm back here. It's still there between us isn't it, Lauren?

No! It can't be.

I felt my eyes open wider in fear, like a rabbit caught in the headlights. I stepped back, wrenched my one arm from his hold and moved back to the door, unconsciously bringing my fingers up to my lips to touch where he'd kissed me yet again.

'What?' I managed to force out in disbelief. 'What's there?'

'The love, the passion, the pain...' His tone dropped as he went on. 'I've never had this emotional connection with anyone else. You're it and I'm ashamed to say, without a doubt I knew that all those fucking years ago and I let you go. You've gotta believe me when I say, I've never felt this way about anyone else in my life. Leaving you *is,* and always will be, the biggest regret of my life.'

I was enraged.

No, I was fucking furious.

How bloody dare he?

'Little old me? Surely not? Perhaps that should be saved for the breakdown of your marriage to a woman you loved enough to stay with. Shouldn't that be your biggest regret?'

God, I'm a sarcastic bitch.

I saw pain flicker through his eyes once again and I shook my head at him. 'It's too bloody late, Rafferty, and STOP kissing me.' My heart was pounding, but I wasn't sure if it was in anger or from the fact that I wanted him to take me back into his arms and to kiss me properly. Then my voice quietened as the hurt came flooding back like a tsunami. 'You left me,' I whispered into the emotionally charged air.

The anguish was there in between us both, stripped bare and hurting like hell. The pain in my chest was threatening to open wide and swallow me whole.

I needed to get out of here. My emotions were rolling back and forth and upside down. Once again anger took over as my eyes filled with pain induced tears.

'Just who the hell do you think you are? You don't get to bounce in and out of my life, like a bloody yo-yo just because I happen to cross your mind occasionally. What we had between us *was* years ago, you *were* my whole world. But you need to listen to all the past tenses I'm using here, Raff. It's over... YOU. LEFT. ME!'

'I know what the fuck I did! And you don't fucking cross my mind, you live in my mind every fucking second of the day.' He lifted his left hand and tapped his index finger against his temple. 'You're imprinted deep down inside me, the way you smell, the way you smile, the way you move, and the way your skin reacts to my touch. I dream about the way your lips move and part just a little as I bend to kiss you, like they're giving me an open invitation. And just so *you* know, you still do that just for me.'

'I'm *with* Toby,' I forced out between gritted teeth, using him as my last-ditch attempt at keeping Raff at arm's length.

My words obviously hit home, his fists clenched making his forearms strain against his leather cuffs and bracelets. He looked down to the floor, pushing his arms straight down to his sides and let out a loud exhale.

When he lifted his head, and composed himself, amusement had spread across his face.

'Winter said you had someone and *then* you also told me.' A small laugh left his mouth. 'But, I heard most of your conversation in here today... You're not in a relationship with that stupid wanker on the end of the phone, it's more like a fucking business arrangement.'

I shook my head at his words, but I knew they were true. 'I am, and we're going to get married.'

Watching him shake his head and tut at me was maddening.

'You've gotta be fucking joking,' he stated.

'No, I'm not. I love him.'

The sound of his sudden laughter filled the air around us as his head tipped back. Then all at once his eyes were back on mine and penetrating my crumbling resilience with an angry swirl of grey.

'You might think you love him, but you're not *in* love with him. There's a huge fucking difference.'

'How the hell would you know how I feel?' I spat out in anger at his assumptions.

I watched the cocky bastard nod his head. 'Oh, believe me I fucking know… Because there is no way in hell a woman like you would let me touch her if she did. He's a fool, he had an opportunity to claim you as his and he did a fucking poor job, and that will be his downfall. He doesn't make you smile or laugh enough. He doesn't love you as much as he should and he certainly doesn't kiss you as much as a passionate woman like you needs kissing.'

The tension between us ramped up several degrees as once again he stepped nearer. He bent his knees and crouched down slightly in front of me, making our eyes level. 'You should be kissed all the time, you were made for it. Hell, *I* tutored you for it. *You* need to be kissed every hour, every minute and every second of every day, by me and only me. I'm going to make sure that happens from now on.'

'Oh no, you bloody won't!' I almost screeched out.

He nodded and raised a questioning eyebrow at me. 'Loz, believe me when I say, I *know* that this between us isn't over and it never will be. Very soon you'll be begging me to fucking kiss you. You're mine… forever and always.'

The words he uttered were like being slapped around the face and I woke up from the dream I had allowed myself to almost stupidly follow him into.

I heard the connection of metal on metal and then the air was suddenly sucked out of the pantry as the door was forcibly pulled open.

I turned and fled quickly through the gap and past Winter's questioning expression.

Raff

'What the hell is going on?' My little sister asked as Lauren rushed past her. I tried to keep my eyes on her to see where she was going, but I could feel Winter's violet-blue eyes boring into the side of my head and looked over at her instead.

I knew Winter's question had been directed straight at me.

'The door closed behind us.' I shrugged at her as I made my way out of the cold pantry and back into the heat of the kitchen. I looked around, Lauren was gone.

'The door closed behind you? I don't believe that for a minute. Lauren knew the door was iffy. And even if it had, how did you both end up in there together?' I watched her cross her arms over her chest and she stared at me with the same penetrating gaze she had been using on me since she was a toddler.

'Okay, I needed to talk to her… we need to talk to each other.'

'I agree. But, let me get this right. You *shut* her in a room with you? Even for you, that sounds a little… what's the word? Oh yes, unhinged.' I looked down following a sudden noise, to see the toe of her Louboutins beginning to gently tap on the slate flooring and held back a grin I knew would wind her up even more.

'I came to find her in a rare few minutes of downtime and saw her going into the pantry, it's not as if I dragged her in there kicking and screaming.'

'But, you made sure she couldn't get out?' Her voice was quieter now, but her anger was still just below the surface waiting to cut off my dick.

I ran my hand through my hair with exasperation, knowing she was right.

'Yes.'

'Seriously, Rafferty? You need to think before you act in future.' I watched as she shook her head from side to side. 'She has anxiety attacks.' Her voice dropped to a low whisper.

'She does? Fuck.' I felt every bit the complete fucking bastard I already knew I was.

Winter grabbed hold of my arm, and suddenly we were moving. Her tight fist screwed up the fabric of my expensive Armani suit, as she dragged me back inside the pantry. The kitchen had begun to fill with the waiting staff, looking for more trays of food. I followed her lead and as soon as we were both inside the door she pulled it to. I found a ledge behind me and placing the back of my thighs against it, I leant back to listen to what she wanted to say to me in private.

I owed her that much at least.

'You need to understand a few things. You, leaving Lauren, left her with more than heartbreak...' She walked over, crossed her arms over her chest and leant next to me. 'I'm a shit friend, I shouldn't be telling you any of this, she's one of my best friends.'

'No, you probably shouldn't, but as your brother I appreciate it.'

Winter's hand came up and touched my arm making me look at her. 'She's suffered really badly with anxiety issues for years, and they only started once her parents brought her back from Vegas, when you were no longer on the scene. Although, they have been less frequent since she opened The Fairy Garden.'

'The Fairy Garden?'' I felt my forehead crease as I pondered her words.

'Yes, her tearoom. What of it?' She glared at me and my stupid question.

'Nothing.' I shook my head at her.

'Shutting her in a room, Raff, that was a shit move!' Her voice raised and then, remembering where we were, she whispered to me. 'You wouldn't know this, but she has never spoken to Amy or me about what exactly happened between you two. Amy and I have often talked about whether Lauren knew the reason you left her? I'm your sister and you've never confided in me either... although, I have to say we've got our thoughts on what happened.'

'Yeah, I bet.' I couldn't help the anger that came out as I answered her. 'Go on then, let's think.' I paused for a split second in sarcasm. 'Couldn't keep his fucking dick to himself is probably in the No.1 spot.'

'I'm sorry to say, it's one of the possibilities we've thought of, yes. Lauren told us a few weeks before she came home about Ashley hanging around you all the time and you did end up marrying her.'

'There was nothing going on then, not for me anyway.' I sighed as I spoke, I'd known all along how it looked.

'Then maybe you should have confided in me and I wouldn't have had to think so badly of you?' I saw her shoulders shrug as she questioned me.

I blew out a long exhale, feeling my nostrils widen. 'The only person who needs to know why, is Lauren. I appreciate your concern but it's our business and no one else's.'

'That's true, but... Oh, sod it. I might as well say it, as it seems to be obvious to everyone else apart from you two. You still *love* her, Raff. She still loves you... Look, if you want my opinion?'

'Since when did you, Winter, give a fuck about asking anyone before you gave them *your* opinion?'

'Right okay, that's true. *You* should never have walked away. But by God, I'm hoping you had a bloody good reason for doing so. If you did, then *tell* her.'

'I'm not sure if you've noticed, she's not too keen on talking to me.'

'Then grow a fucking pair!' Her voice raised again. 'And think of a better way to communicate with her. Don't corner her so she feels the need to run away from you.'

'Do you think it could be that easy?' Inside me a bud of hope was growing larger the longer we talked.

'No, it's not going to be easy, but then you don't fucking deserve easy. She is way out of your fucking league. But for some stupid bloody reason my best friend loves you. Sort this bloody mess out, Raff.'

I nodded in agreement, and for a few minutes we sat side by side as I let her words sink in and, recognising the possibility that I had not only broken Lauren's heart but also caused her other problems, filter around my system. Life was fucking cruel that was for sure. My mind however was focussed more on the other words she had just spoken.

She still loves you.

I bent my arm up and placed it around her shoulders and by holding the side of her face, I gently pulled her to me and placed a kiss on top of her head. 'Thanks, Winter. Sometimes you're not a crap sister.'

I felt her shoulder knock into my side. 'You, on the other hand, are *always* a crap brother.' I heard the laughter in her voice and smiled.

'A different way to communicate, huh? Yeah, I think I can do that, thanks for the advice.'

'Just don't mess this up. Don't hurt her... I shouldn't have told you anything at all. Don't make my telling you her secrets count for nothing. She deserves love and passion, she deserves a man who worships at her feet. I believe that after watching the two of you over the last couple of days and seeing the chemistry between you, not trying to blow your trumpet, only you can give her those things. And I want them so badly for her.'

Winter's honesty meant everything. 'So, I take it you're not a fan of that Toby bloke, then?'

'Oh, my God, NO! Don't get me started on him. He puts in no time and effort, he doesn't deserve her. Amy and I don't like him at all.'

'Noted. Now, I know you're busy, but go and make sure she's okay for me, please.' I kissed her head again and left her. I wanted to search the place for Lauren but had to get back to the paparazzi and reviewers I knew were either going to make or break our new venture.

As I strode out of the kitchen, making sure I was once again tidy enough to face them, I contemplated how much this new business meant to me. Having started this whole idea to, I thought, keep us all alive and to offer our children stability, I now knew it represented even more.

I was back, because in truth my heart had never left here. As I walked back into the busy hotel, I smiled, posed for pictures and answered questions when necessary. But in my head I was lost to memories of her and us.

'Hello, Rafferty,' I heard Lauren's nan's voice call out from the kitchen. I hadn't even realised she was there.

Immediately, we sprung apart a few inches and looked at each other, smiling. I saw a blush consume Lauren's face. I placed a kiss on the end of her nose and grinned.

I'd been brought up to be a gentleman, so I turned my attention from her and down the hallway, to the ladies in her family, who seemed to be catching up on gossip in the kitchen.

'Hi, Mrs. Harper, and Mrs. Harper.' A smile spread over Lauren's face as she turned in my arms and looked towards her nan and mum, who were now standing watching us. 'Nice to see you both,' I offered.

'Take care of our girl, Rafferty,' her knowing nan added. 'She's looking forward to her birthday evening with you.'

'I promise I'll look after her, and that's good because I've had it all planned out for weeks.' Lauren hugged me to her so tightly, I felt the smile she offered them pull up her cheeks.

'And, Raff, you make us feel old. How many times must we tell you? Please, it's Vera and Lisa,' her mum reminded me. I nodded at her words.

'Would you like a drink?' came from Lauren's nan.

'NO! NO! NO!' burst out of Lauren's mouth. 'Knowing Raff, he'll politely say yes and we'll never get out of here. Enough, you two, *you are not sharing our date. He does not want a drink and he certainly doesn't want to come in and answer twenty questions, which is what you'll have him doing the moment you get him into your lair.' I smiled at them both as they laughed and waved us off.*

We moved backwards and Lauren pulled on the lion shaped front door knocker to close the door behind us, effectively trying to shut us away from their interference.

'Bye, Vera. Bye, Lisa,' I shouted out before the front door closed completely and I heard them both laughing. 'Come on.' Suddenly I was as desperate as her to be away from her front doorstep.

I opened the door to my car and watched as she slid over the bench seat in her short skirt and then I ran around to jump in myself.

Pushing the keys into the ignition, I fired up my old Humber and pulled away from her house. With one arm on the steering wheel, I lifted my left arm up high signifying that she was too far away. I exhaled as I relaxed the moment she moved over and into my hold.

'Happy sixteenth birthday, Loz. I love you,' I whispered into the top of her hair and breathed in everything about her. She calmed and centred me in ways that she didn't understand. I'd had another shit day. The constant demands of my dad were beginning to make me feel cornered like a wild animal. He phoned again, we'd shouted and screamed at each other until my mum had wrestled the phone away from me and with tears in her eyes she'd replaced it back in its cradle. I couldn't do what he wanted, it wasn't in me, and it wasn't what I wanted for my life. The disagreements at home were affecting all of us. Every time the phone rang Winter was now sprinting to get it first, she was hoping she could help me out by lying and saying I wasn't there. The pain this was causing Mum and her, was breaking my heart. No way was I getting Lauren any more involved than she needed to be.

The sound of her voice broke up the dark thoughts in my head.
'I love you, too,' she replied.

I took my eyes off the quiet road for a few seconds and looked down at her beaming up at me, and bending my head forward I kissed the tip of her nose then I looked back up.

'Stop looking at me like that, Loz. You're distracting me.' For a while now a growing sense of urgency to be more to each other had been growing between us. When we'd first got together, she'd not even been kissed before. But, as we spent as much time together as we could, I'd taken the lead and she'd followed wholeheartedly.

Her happy giggle made me smile. 'I'm allowed, I'm sixteen today.' I felt her arm tighten around my body. My dick twitched in response to her words and confidence. I glanced down to see her tongue flick out quickly to wet her lips and I exhaled loudly. She didn't understand just how much she'd learnt in a few months.

We drove on in silence, happy to be in each other's company and I ran over the latest argument with my dad.

'What's wrong, Raff. Holding you, I can feel you've just tensed up.' Her voice penetrated my sadness.

'The normal, I've had another row with the Colonel, I'm not sure how much longer I can put him off.'

Lauren shifted in my arms to look up at me. 'Tell me what he said, please.'

'Another day.' I shifted in my seat and pulled her tight to me once again. 'This is your birthday night and he, no matter how hard he tries, is not going to fucking spoil it.'

I felt her strengthen her hold on me and focussed my eyes back on the road.

'Okay, but promise you'll tell me tomorrow?'

I nodded in answer as I swung the car into my family's crumbling wreck of an ancestral home. The familiar crunching gravel under the tyres of my car was like music to my ears, yet at the same time the sound of my impending doom, but my dad wasn't going to ruin tonight. Tonight, was going to be just me and Lauren.

'*We're at yours?*' *she questioned.*

'*Yeah. Wait there for me.*'

I switched off the engine and climbed out of the Humber by holding onto the roof to support my tall frame. Twirling the keys around my index finger on my right hand, I shoved my other hand into my back pocket and I strode around the front of the car. I could feel her eyes watching my every movement and offered her a grin and a wink. I knew it was enough to make her blush and I loved the way she responded to me.

I pulled open the heavy door and offered her my hand. She took it immediately and I pulled her up and into my body. As soon as she was where I wanted her to be, my hands found the bare skin of her neck and my thumbs caressed her throat with my long fingers supporting the back of her head. Her head tilted back on instinct and I smiled down at her, watching her amber eyes darken, the longer I held her.

'*Kiss me,*' *she whispered.*

No fucking way. *I wasn't sharing the way she looked in my arms with any other fucker that was for sure.*

I felt her thumbs thread themselves into my belt loops to pull me into her and hold me closer.

'*Not here. We're probably being watched. Later, when we're all by ourselves, I'll kiss you,*' *I whispered down to her.*

'*You're such a tease, Rafferty Davenport.*' *She smiled at me.*

'*I aim to please.*'

'*Do I have to beg?*' Fuck, she was learning fast.

'*You can try.*' *I grinned at her.*

I felt her hand leave my belt abruptly and then a smack on my arse as she reprimanded me for not giving her exactly what she wanted. I moved quickly and caught her small wrist in my hand before she hit me again. My other hand snaked around her waist and I pulled her against me with force. She gasped as my erection pushed into her.

'Are you ready for your birthday surprise, Lauren?'

'Yes.'

I pulled myself away from her and pushing my hands into my jeans pockets, I walked backwards towards the side of my overly large family home.

'Come on then.' I crooked my index finger and narrowed my eyes at her as I beckoned her forward. Quickening my step, I managed to keep her at arms' length and it was just far enough away for me to take a good look at her.

I'd never been in love before. But the vision in front of me, dancing and skipping along as she messed around ahead of me, had captured me and I knew then and there that I would never not be in love with her. It didn't matter what crap life threw at us, she was it for me and the way her eyes sparkled under my observation, they told me that I was it for her. I couldn't give a fuck what he said about us being too young, what the hell did he know anyway?

She made a grab for my hand and I snatched it away.

'Oh, no… I haven't finished looking at you yet.' A laugh left my mouth as I took in her momentarily cross expression.

Still moving backwards, I made my legs move faster. I crooked my finger at her again.

My girl was fucking beautiful. Her chestnut coloured hair was loose, it tumbled down over her shoulders and half way down her back. Her smile was wide and her amber eyes danced with amusement at my antics. She was breathtaking, her eyes set my insides alight, and every time she focussed them on me, the rest of the world faded away.

Studying her more closely, I could see she was wearing a little make-up, but thankfully not enough to cover the freckles on the bridge of her nose.

One day I was going to count every single one of them.

I smiled at her again and blew her kiss. Then I stopped dead and waited for her to throw herself into my arms. With our eyes closed and her arms securely around my neck, I picked her up off the floor. Carrying her small frame, our mouths pressed together like they were magnetised. As we consumed each other, I turned around and began to walk towards the side entrance of the house. I pressed my very needy mouth further into hers, taking everything I needed from the connection. I knew we'd reached the heavy oak gate when my boots found the cobbled paving in front of it and I booted it open. As the gate banged against the stone wall of the house her eyes flew open and she looked at me, silently giving me her permission.

I broke my mouth from hers and kissed the tip of her nose, smiling again at the freckles staring back at me.

One day I was definitely going to count them all.

But, not tonight. Tonight, I had other plans for us.

Lauren

'There you are.' A few hours had passed since my altercation with Raff in the pantry and I hadn't seen him since, which meant I'd been on edge all day. I walked into the kitchen, barely glancing at the offending storage area, just in time to see Amy press a button on one of the huge dishwashers in the kitchen. Although she hadn't a clue, just by being here she made me feel more comfortable and at peace with myself. Amy had finished her shift at The Fairy Garden and was now helping Winter and I for the less formal open evening of The Manor. At the sound of my voice she turned around to face me and standing up straight she smoothed the fitted black dress she was wearing back down over her hips.

It wasn't often I got to see my cousin looking like she did right now, her normal attire was jeans and worn out hoodies. But tonight, she looked stunning. She was done up to the nines, wearing what looked like one of my dresses, and black high heels.

'Look at you… nice dress.' I smiled over to her as I teased her. She really did look beautiful.

119

'Oh, this old thing.' She smiled back at me. 'Sorry, I borrowed it. I *thought* I had nothing suitable with me to wear. Who knew I could have come in comfy jeans and a pair of Converse?' She stared at me, raising one questioning eyebrow and looked me up and down.

Oh shit.

I'd showered and changed about an hour and a half ago into some boyfriend style jeans, Converse and a white, Bardot styled T-shirt that read, "My heart belongs to you..." Not a good choice I'd thought as I had checked my reflection in the mirror, but it was the only one I'd put into the small holdall this morning after hearing the change of direction on suitable attire for this evening.

What I hadn't done was inform Amy about the change.

I grimaced back at her and silently mouthed my apology. 'It looks better on you than it ever did on me,' I offered, trying to appease her.

I watched her take another look at herself. There was something different about her this evening. She looked as tired as Winter and I did, but there was another addition to her normal look. Her eyes were alive, her skin looked almost iridescent and I truly hoped as she looked herself up and down, she could see what I could.

She lifted her eyes from the beautiful black lace and asked, 'So, what brings you to my lowly domain?' She opened her arms up wide and turned around in a circle, gesticulating the kitchen.

'Well, Cinderella, Winter and I want you out of here. All the guests have gone into the ballroom to watch the band and we thought we could share a couple of glasses of bubbly together and then hopefully go to find our beds.'

'I'm a little overdressed.' She shot a quick look down at her tits. I knew what she was thinking, but seriously, she looked hot. Held in a decent bra they were almost spilling out of the space in between the plunging V neckline of the dress.

'You look beautiful, even stunning.' I smiled at her and she raised her eyebrows at me in question. 'I know. Not to worry, we'll hide you away in the drawing room, because God forbid anyone should get an eyeful of your tits.' My laughter filled the kitchen. 'Come on, we deserve the celebration and we're dying to know how last night went?' I tried winking at her, but I wasn't good at it and often stupidly found both of my eyes closing at the same time, and shot her a knowing smile.

'I bet you do, but that will have to wait for another day. I'm too exhausted to talk tonight, just take me to the alcohol.' Her eyes left mine as she answered.

Okay, that wasn't quite what I'd been expecting. I'd hoped she'd had a good night, I wanted it for her and selfishly for me as well. I needed her joy to counteract my confusing day. I took a step towards her and grabbed hold of her hand. As we left the back of the house and began to move forward down the empty passageway, the sounds of the band tuning up reached my ears. My stomach turned over in excitement and my heart began to pulse in time to the beat Cade was producing. I rolled my eyes at my reaction and bit both of my lips between my teeth, to hold in a sigh.

I seriously need a distraction.

As we arrived through one door, Winter was closing the grander double doors to the ballroom behind her. She'd brought a small silver drinks trolley with her. On it, I could see two bottles of Champagne and three glasses. I smiled broadly at her as she began to push it towards the two overly large settees, placed either side of a roaring log fire.

Amy walked to one and flopped down.

'I'm knackered, completely cream crackered,' she declared as she kicked off her shoes and proceeded to make herself comfortable on the overstuffed settee. I smiled at her almost being engulfed by the leather that surrounded her and then looked at Winter as she fought to release the cork from the first bottle. I took a seat opposite Amy and sank down, my back and legs screamed out in relief.

POP!

Finally, the cork wiggled free and shot off towards the ceiling. The three of us smiled at each other. Hurriedly, I pushed the glasses under the stream of the escaping Champagne.

'To us!' Winter shouted into the warm room.

'To us!' we called back, clinking the expensive glasses together.

I wasn't a great lover of Champagne, I was more of a beer girl, but this was Winter's celebration and I was happy enough to drink a little with her. My last reading for my blood sugar had been surprisingly okay and with my shot of insulin, I felt my body could withstand a couple of drinks.

'I don't know what to say to you both, other than thank you. But that doesn't seem nearly enough.' Winter drunk the rest of her Champagne down quickly and sat down next to me.

'It went brilliantly, Winter. You should be so proud of yourself,' I offered into the quiet room. 'I saw you handing out your business cards left, right and bloody centre today.'

'Well, I couldn't have done it without you both, thank you from the heart of my bottom.' She smiled at us again and topped up all our glasses. I managed to get my fingers over the top of mine, before she overenthusiastically filled it to the point of it slopping over the rim.

'The Fairy Garden had one of its best days ever today, Lauren... I'm so proud of you both and your achievements.' Amy lifted up her equally overfilled glass to us and took another sip.

I looked at her, trying to read between the lines and then looked sideways at Winter who caught my eyes with her own.

Wordlessly, we jumped up in unison and made our way around the large, low table in front of us and plonked ourselves down either side of her. We both pulled her into our arms and for a few minutes we sat together, offering each other our solidarity and strength.

'We're proud of you too, you know,' Winter whispered to her.

Looking at the side of her face, I saw the ghost of a smile grace her lips. She held onto us both firmly, squeezed a little tighter and then we broke. Winter and I went back to our original places on the settee opposite. I knew why. We both wanted to hear about her evening last night with Daniel, the guy who had carried her up to my spare room after hoisting her over his shoulder. Each of us in our own way needed the diversion from our day. Personally, I needed something to clear Raff out of my head. He'd occupied the space for far too long in the last few days, I needed it back for my own sanity and I knew Cade had also gotten under Winter's normally cast iron veneer.

'So?' I questioned Amy and interrogated her with a stare.

She shrugged at us in reply.

Okay, so she was going to play it like that. I smiled, she really should know Winter and I better than this by now. Ever since we were young we could coerce Amy into telling us almost anything and it was a game we loved to play. Without looking at Winter, knowing she would follow my lead, I made the first attempt.

'Okay, let us recap. When we last saw you last night, the very lovely Daniel was climbing the wrought iron staircase to your bedroom, doing the stairs two at a time. Let us remind you, *he* was carrying you over his shoulder as if you were as light as a feather.' I placed an open palm over my heart.

She shook her head slowly from side to side.

'Oh, come on, Amy, spill it. We need to hear it all.'

'My night was amazing. Having never had a one-night stand before, I don't know what I was expecting. He was attentive and gave me exactly what I needed.' Her words sounded wooden, almost as though she'd practised them over, and over again.

I looked at Winter and she raised her eyebrows at me.

'Oh dear!' I pushed into the silent room.

'Indeed,' added Winter. 'So, it was either bloody awful or the best sex you've ever had. He was that good, huh?'

'Yes, he was good. I had a really good night,' she answered as nonchalantly as she could manage.

'So, let's get this right. He's tall and good looking?' Winter asked, turning her body away from Amy towards me. I in turn took her lead and copied her.

'Yes,' Amy answered.

'He was *so* strong, we saw that by the way he picked her up,' I added.

'We did,' Winter answered, as she feigned fainting like a southern belle. I suppressed a laugh, feeling lighter the more Champagne entered my body and the longer the conversation went on.

From my peripheral view, I saw Amy nod in response. Playing our game, neither Winter or I looked over at her.

'With that sort of strength, he probably has the most fantastic body?'

'Yes, he had a really good body.' Amy almost sighed as she answered.

'We witnessed he had a sense of humour.' I was adding up Daniel's list of plusses on my fingers as Winter and I carried on having the discussion between ourselves.

'A man like that is sure to know exactly how to use all those qualities to best effect,' added Winter, nodding her head.

'I bet he knew just how to use all of those skills.' I sighed, finding it hard to keep in the laughter that wanted to burst out of me. I leant back into the comfy cushions behind me and fanned at my face with my hand.

'He did,' Amy added.

'He exuded confidence, I could sense a bit of a bad boy about him,' Winter continued.

'His body was covered in the most beautiful, brightly coloured tattoos and his fingers were covered in rings. Sex with him was amazing… the way he controlled my pleasure and then held me close afterwards was more than I could have ever imagined.'

I watched her as those words left her body. A wide grin attached itself to my face. I was so pleased for her, she was locked away too much in a life that belonged to our nan. I wanted her to feel, to experience, I wanted her to love and be loved in return. I knew the feeling, I understood how it worked, and when it lasted, it was *the* very best thing in the world. Even when there was a chance it would shatter you into a million pieces and leave you destitute in its wake.

'So, when are you seeing him again?' I questioned.

She looked at us in disbelief, as if she was trying to gauge our responses to her admission. Winter seemed a bit lost in her own thoughts even though our conversation carried on.

'It was a one-night stand, we made no other plans. I told him to make sure the door closed behind him on his way out.'

I felt my face change into one of complete shock. I knew she pushed people away, but seriously after the words she had used to describe her evening with him, I couldn't believe it.

'So, you're telling us that you effectively kicked him out of bed and slammed the door shut on his face?' Winter asked in a tone of voice that told me was as shocked as me.

'Stop it!' Amy was shaking her head at us both. 'It was a one-night stand. He's here for Jack's wedding, after that I'm sure he'll be on his way back home. By the looks of his clothes and the car he was driving, he has money. So, what on earth would tempt him to stay here in our sleepy little village?'

'Did he tell you all of that?' questioned Winter.

She shook her head a little. 'It's just what I got from our few conversations.'

'What sort of car did he have? Just as a matter of interest. Was it a sports car?' I looked over at Winter and her new line of questioning, making note to question her later.

'No, it was a Land Rover. A Defender I think.' She smiled, seeming lost in thought.

'Oh.' Winter nodded. 'Well, I for one think you'll be seeing him again…'

Amy looked at her in question, furrowing her forehead.

'I mean, we're going to the wedding, aren't we?' Winter smiled.

That was it, Winter knew something and I needed to know what it was.

Just then a loud cheer went up next door. Instinctively, my gaze left Winter and travelled towards the closed double doors. A beat was being tapped out on what appeared to be one drum and then the guitars joined in. I realised it was a tune I recognised.

It was exactly what we needed. It was what I needed at least, with Raff only separated from me by the double doors, I wanted something to try to take my mind off the fact he was next door. Every strum of his guitar reverberated around my heart. So, I tipped my Champagne flute up and I swallowed deeply until it was once again empty and it had dulled my feelings down.

'Oh, I love this one.' I jumped up and began to dance around the room, holding my empty glass tightly. Winter jumped up to join me.

'Come on, Amy!' I shouted at her hesitant figure still on the settee.

She finally jumped up to her feet and danced towards us, picking up the Champagne bottle on the way.

The more Default Distraction played, the more we danced, the more we drank and luckily for me, the more I could pretend I wasn't thinking about him.

I managed to pretend for nearly two hours. We had long since tucked Amy up on the settee, as tiredness and too much alcohol had overtaken her and then we had carried on dancing, until Raff came to the mic and announced he was singing the next one. I'd spent years feigning the fact that I knew nothing much about Default Distraction, but what I did know was that although Raff had a good voice, Brody always sang, as his voice was the instantly recognisable sound of the band. My body froze and I looked at Winter in question. As she shook her head at me, I made my way to the double doors and listened closely as he spoke to the crowd in the room.

Intrigued and unable to stop myself, I opened one of the doors and slipped through the small gap followed closely by Winter. Once I was inside the ballroom, I pressed my back against the cool wall and confident in the cover the semi darkness offered, I stood and watched.

Under the one spotlight that had been set up to shine down on the lead singer, I saw Raff. He looked more comfortable this evening, now he was out of the suit he'd been wearing earlier. Or did his comfort stem from the fact he was where he had always been destined to be? I wasn't sure, but then I no longer knew the man, so why should I know the answer?

He was dressed in solid black jeans and a white shirt that was completely unbuttoned, exposing his bare torso. His dark hair flopped down over his eyes in various places and as I watched him push it back to the top of his head, I managed to stifle a gasp and I knew I hadn't moved on at all.

I watched him in the place he was meant to be, the place he was born to be and I was transported back seventeen years ago. The two of us could have been in one of the seedy bars he used to play in Vegas. Time had gone by, we'd both had other relationships and led lives separated by an ocean. But somehow nothing seemed to have changed at all. I watched him pull his jeans up his legs, so he could sit down on the stool. As his position changed, his white, button down collar shirt fell open, fully exposing his chest. I inhaled and then quietly, so Winter couldn't hear my reaction, tried to blow the air slowly back out over my lips as my eyes fell to his tattoo free, bare skin.

With a silver plectrum held in his full lips, he once again pushed his always errant strands of hair away from his face and then altered the mic stand in front of him. Tapping it, he raised his eyebrows and smiled at the audience and my heart broke all over again.

Rein it in, Lauren, you're stronger than this. Thinking myself immune was one thing, believing it was quite another.

'Yeah, I know, this is a bit of a surprise to me, too. So, here's hoping I don't damage your eardrums too much. I know my dulcet tones aren't what you're used to, when you normally listen to the golden boy behind me.' He looked back at Brody who was picking up a bottle of water, having been made redundant by Raff's move to the mic.

'Get the fuck on with it,' yelled Brody, as he laughed in response. The crowd reacted to the two of them and an amused murmur went around the audience.

Raff swung around again, bringing his acoustic to his lap and grabbing the mic with his free hand. 'Yeah, okay. It's a long story, which not to worry, I'm going to make short. A long time ago I made the biggest mistake of my life and I need to say sorry, but she won't listen.' The crowd in unison produced an "Ahhhhh" and Raff acknowledged them by nodding slowly. 'Yeah... Well I was told this morning, by someone who knows me well, that I need to start communicating differently.' Winter who was standing to the side of me grabbed my hand as he carried on speaking, but I couldn't tear my eyes away from watching him to ask her why. 'I agreed... so, here goes. This song is one that we've never covered before, but the crew behind me have always had my back, and they're talented enough to keep up with me. It's a song that takes me back to when my life was simple. When all that mattered was that she loved me and I loved her. This song is for my girl, the one that after all these years still makes my heart beat faster. One of these days I'm going to count all her freckles again.' He stopped speaking momentarily and cast his eyes downwards, then he cleared his throat and spoke again. 'She knows who she is.' A murmur went around the crowd as they started to look around. I quickly removed my hand from touching the bridge of my nose, not wanting others to see that I had raised it up instinctively as he mentioned the freckles.

I knew before he strummed the first chord on his acoustic guitar that the words of **Ronan Keating's – If Tomorrow Never Comes,** would leave his lips. Tears chased each other silently down my face as I watched him sing into the crowded room. The words washed over me, catapulting me back to a time when all we had was each other and it had been more than enough.

Lauren

'*Where are you taking me?*' *Instinctively, I touched the wool concealing my eyes. Raff had tied a scarf around my head, making sure I couldn't see.*

'*You'll find out when we get there. I'm going to stand in front of you and guide you, okay?*'

'*I think so.*'

'*So, put your fingers into the top of my belt and follow me. Okay?*' *he lightly demanded as he placed my hands exactly where he wanted them.*

'*Yes, okay.*' *I smiled in the direction his voice was coming from and we started to slowly move forward.*

I knew we were inside his house as I'd been blindfolded in the kitchen, much to the amusement of the cook, Mrs. Clark, who Raff had clearly roped in to help him. I heard my feet fall on the flagstones of the back rooms of the ground floor and then we started climbing. The smooth, worn oak of the banister slid through my fingers as we climbed higher and the fact I was walking on bare wooden stairs told me we were taking the back stairs, the servants' stairs. After going up twenty-two steps my feet finally hit carpet. We walked a few steps along a corridor and stopped. I listened to the whirring sound the lift made as it climbed its way slowly to us and while we waited he pressed a quick kiss to my lips.

'You still okay?' I'd felt his lips smile as he pulled away from me ever so slightly to ask the question.

'I think so.'

'Good, got any ideas yet?' I could hear the amusement in his voice.

'You're smuggling me up to your room, so your parents can't see you've been captivated by a poor village girl, whose dad is their gardener and who isn't quite up to their standards?' I spoke in a jokey voice, but it wasn't far from the truth.

'Nope.' I heard a deep laugh leave his chest.

'Then, no, I've got no idea.' I shrugged my shoulders at him.

'Good, because it's a surprise.'

The lift arrived and I heard Raff pull open the cage doors, then he guided me in. The doors closed and the lift started to move. As the lift ascended, so did my excitement as I wondered what exactly he'd come up with for my birthday evening.

'Right, once we get out, we've got another two flights to go, its narrow and you're going to need to trust me.'

'I do, with all my heart.'

'I know, and that's what makes you my girl.'

From behind, he guided me up the tight, confined space until we came to an abrupt halt. His arm left my waist and I heard a door open in front of me as he pushed it. A light breeze touched my skin and I realised we were once again outside.

'A few more steps and then you can take off the blindfold.' We moved forward slowly, I reached out with my hands instinctively *looking for something to hold on to, but found nothing. 'Okay, Lauren... You can stop right here.'*

His hands left my waist and I felt him move around and in front of me. Then he was back. I felt his arms as they snaked around my waist, pulling me into him and kissing the end of my nose. My breath hitched and I froze so I could concentrate on the feel of his skin on mine. His fresh body wash was all I could smell on the soft summer night's breeze and it was all I needed to remind me that we were here together.

'You can take it off now.' His voice was quiet and low. I could feel him watching me as he spoke.

'Just give me a minute, I'm taking all of this in.'

A laugh came from deep inside him. 'All of what? You can't see anything yet.'

I gripped tightly to the sides of his jean jacket and pulled him further into me. 'All of this, you and me together. I want it to be like this always.'

'Always and forever,' he whispered back at me. 'Now take off the blindfold and let me see you.'

I let go of one side of his jacket and pulled at the knot to the back of my head. My makeshift blindfold fell away and to the floor. I ran my hand through my hair and shook my head relishing the sudden freedom. It was a relief to feel the air on all my face. I breathed in the fresh air and slowly opened my eyes to look up at him.

A small smile spread across his mouth as he watched me. That simple gesture took my breath away. His hands came up to cup my face and his thumbs ran over each of my cheek bones. Then his lips came down to mine, the touch of his flesh on my skin sent waves of want and need coursing throughout my body. My body sprang immediately to life as we kissed. His tongue tentatively swept over my glossed lips and I reacted instantaneously by opening my mouth to feel more of him. I needed to feel as close as we could get, I wanted all of him. His more experienced mouth brought our kiss to a close and I felt a tear fall from my eye as he slowly pulled away from me. I could see the concern on his face as he watched it descend.

'Hey... what's that for?' His silver eyes clouded with worry, but his hands never left the sides of my face as he gently held me.

I blinked the collected moisture away. 'It's nothing.' I tried to shake my head to convince him of the what I had said.

'You haven't even looked around yet, but I want you to know, this is a birthday evening picnic. It's you and me spending time together by ourselves, it's not me trying to get in your knickers. If you're not ready or have changed your mind, I can wait.'

I tried to move my face from his tightening grip, to shake my head at him, but his grip tightened.

'Do you understand?' he asked, as I tried to remove my eyes from his deepening gaze.

My hands came up to hold his. 'You've got it wrong, Raff.'

'Yeah?' His eyebrows raised in question and concern and his knees bent as he looked at me again with our eyes at the same level.

'I love you so much, Raff Davenport. So much it scares me.' The previously blinked away moisture once again poured into the bottom of my eyes. 'I want us to always be this way. I know we're young, but I can't see myself in the future without you. I'm only sixteen but I know I'll never love anyone the way I love you... I love you so much it terrifies me. I want you to always look at me the way you do now. So, you see, it's not the thought of being with you that scares me, it's the thought of us not being together that frightens me.'

I watched his eyes fill with tears at my words as his lips came down to kiss the tip of my nose. For a few seconds, we stayed in that position as we held each other close and tried to convey our feelings wordlessly to each other, until his lips left me again.

'Don't be scared, Loz... There's no need. Without you there is no me. I already know that I'll hold you in my heart forever. Music is my life, but you? You're more... you're the very reason my heart beats. Everything I write and play is because your love inspires me. You make me see and feel things that I'm sure any other bloke my age wouldn't even imagine existed.' He stopped speaking for a moment to refocus his thoughts and stood back up to his full height. His mouth came down to the top of my head and he rested his lips against my hair. 'You make me whole, and without you my existence would be pointless. Wherever I go, you're coming too, because I told you, Loz, me and you are always and forever.'

Suddenly, he was back in front of me. A smile ghosted his lips and I smiled back. The dull ache that had momentarily filled my heart lifted away with my confession and his confirmation that he felt just as strongly about us.

He sniffed suddenly, blinked his eyes and cleared his throat. 'Now, serious shit over with, can we get on with me romancing you?'

'Romancing me?' I smiled back.

He moved quickly, revealing what he had organised.

I lifted my hand and placed it over my heart as I took in the scene. We were on the roof of his family's stately home and the view was striking. But, it was what he had prepared that took my breath away. To one side of the huge roof, in a small secluded area, he had thrown down various blankets and pillows. He had hung fairy lights between the tall, narrow chimneys that jutted out from various obscure places. A small picnic basket was sat to one side of the blankets, along with a small digital radio and his acoustic guitar, which was leant against the base of a chimney stack.

'It's magical, just look at all the fairy lights,' I whispered.

I felt his hand grab mine as he stood to the side of me. His fingers threaded in between my fingers and then he lifted up my hand in his to press his mouth to it.

'Good, I'm glad you like it.' I looked over at him to see him twist his head a little to the side as he shrugged. 'I have to be honest though, I had a bit of help.' His spare hand came up to show me his thumb and index finger showing a small gap between them.

I grinned at his response. 'Let me think,' I began playfully. 'Music by you? Food by Mrs. Clark? Design by Winter?'

Letting go of my hand suddenly he clutched at his heart and pretended to fall backwards. 'You wound me.'

'STOP IT!' I shrieked at him, remembering we were up high on the roof. Laughing loudly, he righted himself and grabbing at my hand again, he pulled me into his body. With his arms wrapped around me tightly he pressed his mouth quickly to mine.

'Come on, sweet sixteen, let's get this party started.'

Having eaten all the things Mrs. Clark had made for us, we had turned on the radio and to whatever they played we managed to find the slowest beat to dance to. With our arms entangled around each other we danced, talked and made out under the stars.

One song blended easily into another as we kissed and explored each other without fear of being interrupted.

'You're so fucking beautiful.' One of his hands left my back and casually his thumb brushed over the ridiculously sensitive skin of my lips as he stared at me in what seemed like amazement. 'I think

this is the first time I've ever seen you look so alive. Your eyes are huge and your lips are full of colour, it looks like kissing me is better for you than any fucking make-up.'

'Being with you, makes me feel alive,' I answered, and feeling brave I ground one hip against his erection causing him to widen his nostrils as he drew a quick intake of breath. He answered me in kind as he smiled, narrowed his eyes and his hands moved their hold on my body. They went down behind me, flicked up the back of my short skirt and he grabbed on to the bare skin of my bum cheeks, lifting me off the ground. All at once we were moving as he begun to walk me backwards towards the pile of blankets and pillows on the floor.

Ronan Keating's – If Tomorrow Never Comes, came on the radio.

'Stop for a minute, please... I love this one,' I whispered into his neck and he met my request by instantly stopping his advance. He lifted me further up into his arms and I gave in to what felt like the most natural thing in the world. I lifted myself further up his torso with his help, wrapped my bare legs around his waist and looped my arms over his shoulders. Our mouths found each other's with more passion than I had ever felt between us before and he began to move us slowly around to the song. I heard every word **Ronan** *sang and pictured us in my mind's eye as the couple he sang about. By the time the song had finished and he'd pulled himself away from me, I was so turned on I could barely think straight. Once again, he was walking, the radio played on but no other song penetrated my thoughts, my head was full of Raff and us. He found the blankets and cushions and slowly lowered us both down.*

What happened between us happened naturally, almost organically. It was like it was written that we would find each other and consummate our love under the stars. Wordlessly, he began to worship me with his heart, his honesty and his touch. He undressed me slowly, every piece of my skin that he bared to his eyes was kissed and savoured. After the few pieces of clothing I had been wearing had been removed, he draped a corner of a blanket over me and stood up. I watched, unable to tear my eyes away as he kicked off his boots, removed his jacket, T-shirt and finally almost on a go slow he flicked open his belt and unbuttoned his jeans, pushing them and his boxers down his hips. It was the first time I'd ever seen a man naked and Raff was beautiful, more beautiful than I could ever have imagined. For a few seconds, he stood in front of me completely unabashed at his lack of clothes. As he questioned me with his eyes, unknowingly he tilted his head to the side. Silently, he asked for the answer to an unspoken question, his silver-grey eyes finding mine as he looked through the longer strands of his hair. I replied by offering my hand up to him, he accepted it willingly and fell back down into my arms.

Slowly and gently we explored each other until finally he penetrated me, easing my fears with his words and actions as he did so. Once he was convinced I was comfortable and he was satisfied I was enjoying it as much as him he quickened his pace, answering my pleas to him to help me quell the ache that had built up inside me. We came apart in each other's arms, declaring how much we loved each other. I watched as my beautiful man called out my name before he collapsed onto my shoulder. Suddenly, I felt like the older of the two of us. I wrapped my arms tightly around the seemingly vulnerable man in my arms and tears once again fell down my cheeks.

Sensing my tears, his head lifted from my shoulder and he looked down at me with concern.

'Awwww, Loz, don't cry, please don't cry. Did I hurt you?' He seemed so young as he questioned me.

I shook my head at him, unable to voice all the feelings that were coursing rapidly around my system.

'Lauren, you're gonna give me a complex if you cry every time I make love to you.' He gently placed his lips to mine and then lifted his head away. He moved in my hold until he had removed his weight from me. He propped himself up on his elbows either side of my face and looked down at me. I gazed up into his face, realising that in that minute I'd never loved him more. His hair was a sweaty mess and his eyes showed just how exhausted he felt. Releasing an arm, I pushed his hair away for him and offered him a smile.

In one swift movement, which made me squeal out loud, he rolled onto his back taking me with him. Comfortable in his hold, I laid my head down onto his chest

'I'll never forget this evening.' The evening sky had darkened and the stars were out and twinkling down on us. He kissed my forehead as he tightened his hold on me. 'Thank you, Raff. I can't believe you did all of this for me.'

'I'd do anything for you, Lauren... even create a fucking "Fairy Garden."' His deep laugh vibrated from his bare chest, underneath my ear.

'Just to get into my knickers?' I trailed one finger over his bare chest, teasing his erect nipple with my fingers. His hand moved quickly and slapping down on top of mine he stopped my teasing finger instantly.

'Fuck me.' He spoke and half exhaled in reaction to my touch. 'You learn quick.'

'I had a good teacher and he's SO romantic.'

'The romance was just to get in your knickers.' I lifted my head and then pulled my hand out from under his and playfully grabbed his face, turning his handsome face towards mine. The moment his silver eyes swirled in front of me and he blew his errant hair away from his face, I knew I would happily walk barefoot to the ends of the earth to be with him.

'Happy Birthday, Lauren. I'll love you, forever and always. You're my girl and don't you ever forget it.'

I watched his lips speak the words and I placed my mouth down onto his.

Chapter 15

Raff

I leant down and into the mic, feeling the cold metal brush against my lips as I began to sing. I was completely out of my fucking comfort zone. I was used to backing Brody, but being the lead vocal was something I hadn't done for what seemed like a fucking lifetime.

In fact, she'd been in the audience the last time I'd sung lead, back in Vegas.

I was hoping Lauren was somewhere nearby as I poured my heart into every word that left my mouth. The song wasn't one that I'd ever liked, but I remembered that night on the roof of my old family home, like it was fucking yesterday. Listening to the words being sung, moving around, holding her in my arms and kissing her like she was all I needed to survive, was imprinted into my soul.

I'd watched earlier as Winter slipped into the drawing room off to the side of the ballroom as we began to set up. I could have bet everything I owned that Lauren and her cousin Amy were in the room with her, celebrating Winter's success with the Champagne she'd wheeled in on a trolley.

As I went into the first chorus Cade and Luke joined in with my acoustic and I hoped the increased volume was enough for Lauren to hear.

I sang with all my heart how "If tomorrow never comes" for us, I'd want her to know how I felt and then lifted my eyes to search the doorway I was sure she was still behind.

When I found her there, leaning against the wall with her eyes focussed on me and my singing, my heart leapt. She had barely entered the room, obviously having crept in hoping no one would see her standing there. My voice became stronger as I twisted my head to the side and stared at her, trying to convey the way I felt behind every word I sang.

I took her in, holding one hand over her heart, like she was trying to stop it from hurting, or trying to protect it from me. Or maybe she was trying to stop it beating as our eyes fell into each other's. I couldn't be sure, but I loved the fact her mannerisms were everything I remembered from our past. She looked every bit the girl I'd left behind, stood there in her jeans and T-shirt, and my throat began to swell with the emotion I was struggling to keep deep down inside. I cleared it, swallowing down the lump that had formed and missed my next line. My eyes darted back to the audience, made of mainly friends, family and acquaintances. I watched the audience smile back at me, as they thought I'd made a mistake. I offered them a grin and carried on singing, allowing my eyes to dart back and forth between the audience, her and the other side of the room.

All at once one of the few lights we'd had erected for this evening swept past her, reflecting off her wet face. I could see she was crying and I was convinced that her tears were for us. Jealousy released itself inside me and I realised I didn't want anyone else to witness them but me. I didn't want her to have to explain to anyone other than me why she was crying, and how she was feeling. I wanted to be the one to comfort her and hold her. I watched as Winter squeezed her hand in solidarity, and offered her a quick nod of thanks.

She deserved much more than a nod of fucking gratitude. Thanks to Winter it seemed we had cleared the overgrown path of communication between us. I hoped that we could just as easily seal over the large cracks of hurt I'd created.

The moment the song ended and Cade's drumstick came down signalling the final beat, I wanted to jump down off the small stage, run over and take her into my arms. But there were two problems with that want.

One, she still hadn't heard me out.

Two, I had a set to finish.

The crowd cheered as I stood up and the lighting increased for a couple of minutes while we retook our correct places and I dared to properly look at her for the first time.

I watched as she smiled over to me and whispered a "Thank you."

That single acknowledgement and the small smile she bestowed on me, to me they meant everything. For the first time since Flint had been born, my heart filled up. It was all I was looking for, that one simple gesture that gave me the confidence to think that she would listen to what I had to say. And the hope that this was always how it was meant to be between us. That this was our story, and finally we had a chance of making our way back to each other.

Luke fist bumped me as he passed me to take his normal place onstage. That one act acknowledged he knew exactly who I was singing for.

Brody grabbed me to him for a man hug and I heard him speak into my ear.

'At long fucking last, man. She heard ya. I watched her take in every fucking word. We've got two more songs to do and then you make sure that this time she doesn't get away.'

Cade offered me a shit eating grin as I made my way to the guitar rack beside him and I offered him my middle finger in response. I wasn't convinced he had any idea how I felt, I knew that a long time ago, way back when, he'd lost his heart. That was the only time he'd ever allowed a woman to come close to him, but once he realised, he pushed her away. He didn't do family, well not anymore, and he never connected with anyone, because he never stayed long enough for anybody to affect him. He went through life like a hot knife cuts through butter, sending the people who dared to try to get close to him spinning away in his wake.

Apart from us in the double D's, we were his safe place.

I placed my acoustic gently down into the rack and then crouched down. Sitting low and resting back on my haunches made sure that my eyes couldn't wander into the crowd. I was afraid they would be magnetised straight to her. I wanted to make sure the crowd, who were no doubt by now searching the room for "my girl," couldn't watch me and follow my gaze. I waited, lifting the strap of my Gibson up and over my neck and then plugged it into the amp. As Brody ditched our second to last song for one of our biggest hits and the finale to this set, "Regret," I appreciated that he was ending our set early for me. I knew how much it affected him when he sang it and knew then that I wasn't the only one feeling fucking emotional tonight. I flicked the amp on, stood and spun back around to face the crowd, only to find her and Winter gone.

Disappointment flooded my system as I looked around as much of the room as I could see with the stage lighting in our eyes and comprehended that I couldn't find her.

We were four blokes on a small stage in a county of England and between us we had more regrets than the captain of the Titanic.

This was our time, I was convinced of it.

This IS our time. I closed my eyes losing myself to the sound of us and as I played the familiar chords, I prayed. For the first time in Christ knows how long, I fucking prayed.

I prayed she'd be back.

I prayed for forgiveness.

I prayed for acceptance.

I prayed for the chance at a future.

But most of all, I prayed for the chance to hold her in my arms and to once again tell her how much I loved her.

I lovingly held my old Gibson Sunburst and relaxed into the familiar feeling of holding the depth of its body under my forearm. I'd chosen to play this exact guitar tonight, because she'd been with me since the beginning, and holding her in my arm was the second-best thing to holding the woman I loved. As I plucked at the strings with my longer thumb nail on my right hand, I tapped out the rhythm with my fingers on the pick board and then finally, at the right moment, I took my silver plectrum from my mouth and went into the riff. The unmistakable sound of the metal connecting with the strings of my guitar was now my only drug of choice. To be allowed to fashion this sort of magic was the reason I'd left home all those years ago. I touched the strings and I was lost to the sound she created. Most of my life, music and my guitars had been my solace. I'd never let them down and vice versa.

But then that might be because my life had always been about choices. I'd always had to choose one or the other, not once had I been able to have everything that I wanted or needed. Well not anymore, because it was no longer a pattern I was willing to follow. This time I was going to do the right thing by everyone and that included me.

I lost myself into the sounds we were producing and effectively gave Lauren the space she needed away from prying eyes in the room. All the time the song went on I prayed she would be waiting for me when it finished.

I found my mum in the crowd and offered her a smile, which she returned and I nodded at my step-father.

I knew then, as I stood on the stage, that this was how it was always meant to be. Lauren and I were meant to lose each other, so we could reconnect and find each other again at some later stage. Lauren would never have been able to stand the lifestyle we had to lead all those years ago, and that I'm sure would have eventually come between us. It was almost better this way, we had found each other at a time in our lives when we could truly appreciate exactly what we'd been denied and what we'd been missing.

Raff

I knocked hard on the door using my whole hand. I wasn't happy I'd been summoned to his office, why we couldn't have a conversation over the dinner table was beyond me. But I knew why, we weren't a "normal" family.

'Come in and close the door behind you.' I heard my father use the same tone of voice he would use when he was at work. He didn't seem to be able to differentiate between the two places and that fucked me off even more.

The ultimate professional, the colonel and my father were the same man. It was a shame that he couldn't seem to separate the two.

I walked into the mahogany wood-panelled room and breathed in the stale air that I knew I'd find there, ever since I could remember the room had smelt of cherry and vanilla tobacco from his pipe. I looked over to where he was sitting and found the said pipe in its normal position, clasped in between his thumb and index finger. He always smoked when he was thinking and that, I was sure, meant bad news for me. I'd already noted that Mum had been busying herself all morning, so he'd probably warned her he was about to have another 'talk' with me.

'Sir, you wanted to see me?' I offered as I pushed the door closed behind me.

I walked nearer to where he was sitting, in the worn, old wingchair beside the fire and took the seat he had offered using his free hand, opposite him. The chair beneath my backside wasn't as comfortable as his and knowing the man like I did, I knew it was to make me feel as uncomfortable as possible under his examination.

Once an intelligence officer, always an intelligence officer, even in parenting.

'So, Rafferty, my boy. Your exams are over, and I've given you the few months break your mother insisted you needed... Now, I need a date to give to Sandhurst.' He spoke from the side of his mouth and then drew in another puff from his pipe. As he did so he turned over a thick, expensive piece of paper in his hand and waved it around to attract my attention. I could see the crest of the officer academy on the top of it.

'I thought we were waiting for my results?' I questioned hopefully. Although that fleeting hope was pushed away as he removed his pipe from his mouth and tidied his thick, greying moustache between his thumb and forefinger. His eyebrows then dipped in the middle at me as he frowned and he slowly shook his head.

'They're not necessary,' he answered, before the mouthpiece of his favourite pipe was once again sucked into his awaiting mouth and clinked against his teeth.

And there it was.

God forbid if something I'd achieved or not, counted for anything. I belonged to the Davenport family, where for years, one boy from each generation went to Sandhurst to become a member of *the next cohort of young officers, and I was it. I was the only male in the family, bloodline or not.*

I looked at him through the longer strands of hair over my face and chewed the inside of my cheeks as I narrowed my eyes at what he was asking. I knew I had to choose my words carefully. Winter and Mum didn't need the shit that would ultimately hit the fan after I'd given him my answer.

Truth be told, neither did I.

I'd known that what he was asking of me, had been expected of me since I'd gone into sixth-form, but those two fucking years had gone quicker than I'd expected. In that time, Lauren had come into my life and become more than I had ever thought possible. I never thought that I'd fall in love in with her and as much as she gave me, bringing her into the equation added even more possible heartache and someone else I had to protect from the fucking fall out.

I sat myself up as straight as I could and swept my hair off my face. Taking in a deep breath I steadied my breathing and prepared to give him my answer.

'I have no date for you, sir.' I lifted my gaze to meet his.

'Then I'll give one to you, Rafferty. You have two weeks.' Silence consumed the room as we stared at each other.

I began to shake my head, slowly at first and faster as I grew in confidence. 'It's not happening, I won't do it... because I can't do it.'

The speed in which he stood took me by surprise and I fell back further into the firm seat back behind me. He dropped his beloved pipe into the large glass ashtray beside his favourite chair and it landed with a loud clatter, shattering the silence in between our fraught conversation. He leant forward swiftly, until his large, paw-like hands gripped the arms of the chair I was sitting on and he moved further forwards into my space, trying to intimidate me.

I heard the ticks of the mantelpiece clock as we stared each other out, noting that his face was becoming redder as his anger intensified.

'It is what is expected of you, my boy, and no one has never not done what is expected of them in this family. We pride ourselves on doing what is required of us.' He stood up and away from me as quickly as he'd arrived and moving himself into the very centre of his office he turned around, gesticulating at all the portraits of previous generations of the family in uniform, on the panelled walls.

'I'm sorry if it upsets you, sir. But it's not for me. I want something else from my life.'

'WANT?' he almost screamed back at me. 'Do you think I give a damn about what you want? Playing music and acting like a degenerate are not acceptable for the life of a Davenport. We're men and we act accordingly.'

His words hurt, they cut so deeply that I struggled to keep a lid on my emotions. Unable to sit any longer, I stood up to my full height, knowing I already had a couple of inches on him and stood unmoving. I crossed my arms over my chest and looked at him.

'I know you don't and I know what you think, but this is my life, mine. And this is what I want from it.'

He stepped closer to me until our faces were a couple of inches away from each other's.

'When I took your mother in and married her, she swore her and your allegiance to my family.' Anger was bristling off him and with every word he spoke bits of spittle left his mouth in his fury.

I knew he loved my mum, but Christ, the man had a shitty way with words. He made it sound like they hadn't fallen in love and that he'd instead found her destitute on the streets.

'You may not be my son by blood, but I've given you every opportunity being a member of this family brings. This, my boy, is

what the men in my family do, we train, we go to war and we fight for our country. This is what you've been brought up to do and you will go to Sandhurst, or I'm telling you, that you will no longer belong to this family. Your mother will no longer be your mother, Winter not your sister, and I will no longer be your father.'

For the first time in my life I understood what a red mist of anger was. I blinked and blinked, trying to clear my vision as it closed in on me and wrapped me in its cloak. But it was no fucking use, I could no longer see him and the home I'd grown up in. All I could feel was rage thundering throughout my body at his threats.

I took a deep breath in through my mouth, tasting the pipe smoke left in the air and spoke back at him.

'That's where you're wrong, Rupert.' No fucking way was I calling him sir like he had demanded of me ever since I could talk. I took a step towards him, until we were nose to nose. I wanted to show him I was every bit as adamant in my choices and words as he was. 'My mum will always be my mum and Winter my sister. But you're right, Rupert, you'll no longer be my father, because you never were in the first fucking place.'

'GET OUT!' he blustered. 'Not just out of this room, but out of my house. You, my boy, are no longer welcome.'

'I'm not your boy, and I never was, was I? From the very moment you realised you couldn't mould me into your exact image.'

He didn't reply and I watched as he stepped around me, turned his back on me and picked up his beloved pipe, the one that he'd carved lovingly by hand, and thought how ironic that was. As he struck a new match and started to draw through the mouthpiece I spoke again.

'Don't worry I'm going, not on your say so, but on mine.'

I walked out of the room and slammed his door shut, knowing how much he hated it.

Lauren

'Come on, otherwise you're going to make it pretty obvious who he was singing to if people catch a look at your face,' Winter yelled in my ear, and grabbing my arm she guided me around the edge of the large room. Without, I hoped, catching anybody's eyes, we exited through the main doors and went across the hallway to the ladies' restroom nearest to us.

'HELLO!' Winter shouted out as she pushed open the door. Luckily no one answered her call and I realised I might get the chance to sort myself out before I had to face anyone but her.

'Well, thank fuck for that, they're all in there watching the boys,' she gesticulated by throwing her arm behind her at the ballroom. She moved quickly into a cubicle and I heard the toilet roll unravel as she pulled on it hard. I relaxed a little and moved to the vanity unit to take a good look at my undoubtedly red and blotchy face. I saw her to the side of me running the paper under the cold tap and then she turned to catch my eyes in the mirror. Her eyebrows raised at me in question.

I took in a deep breath as finally her focus landed squarely on me.

'I know, I look a mess,' I offered, as her enquiring eyes swept over my face.

'That's the least of our problems, that I can patch up… here.' She offered me two pads of toilet paper. 'Sit down and hold those over your eyes for a few minutes. While you do that, I want you to listen to me.' She pushed a chair up behind me until it hit my knees, forcing me to sit as she'd requested.

I put the cold paper over my eyes and sighed in relief as it immediately began to relieve the burning sting that my tears had left in their wake.

'I love you, you know that, don't you?'

I began to move the cold heaven away from my eyes, to look at her. 'Stop, put them back!' she shrieked at me.

'Sorry… of course I know you love me.' I sank back further into the chair and prepared myself for whatever she was going to hit me with. She knocked into me as she clambered up to sit on the vanity unit in front of me.

'Then I'm going to ask this only once. Are you ready?... No that's wrong. Are you strong enough to open up all these old wounds with Raff?'

I peeled the by now warm paper away and blinked at her as my sore eyes refocussed. 'I love him, Winter. I've been ready to sort this out since the moment he left me. In fact, for years I longed for the chance. I used to daydream that he'd come back into my life, you know… that we'd bump into each other somewhere and he'd still want me the same way I wanted him. But, you know the story and all the years that have passed, his marriage…'

'And divorce,' she added.

'Yes, and his divorce and their son... I never dreamt he'd still feel the same way.' I was stunned by my own honesty.

She looked away and answered as she began to rummage through the complimentary cosmetics in the wicker basket to the side of her. 'I know you love him. You've always, for as long as I can bloody well remember, loved him. But you've not answered me. Are *you* strong enough?'

I took the mascara she was holding out to me as she turned back around, unscrewed the lid and looked back to the mirror. 'I know this sounds crazy.' I stopped speaking for a minute as I contorted every muscle in my face into the exact position I needed to sweep the first lick of black over my top lashes. 'The only way I can answer that is, the few times I've been with him in the last couple of days, I've felt everything.' I stopped again as I stretched out my face to apply the liquid to my other lashes.

'I don't understand what you mean.'

I looked over at her. 'When you have anxiety, Winter, it quickly becomes the first, the second and sometimes the only thing you feel. Everything else becomes secondary to coping with it, until the worry of it becomes all consuming. Being with Raff, I've felt anger, I've felt rage, exasperation and passion. But most of all, I've felt the love that I long ago locked inside my heart come spilling out. Never once did I feel my anxiety was out of my control, not once. Being with him, and around him, he seems to make me stronger. I seriously think I need to hear him out.'

I watched her nod at my words and then, lifting her head higher and tipping it back, she fanned at her face to dry the tears that had started to collect in her eyes. Winter Davenport hadn't cried in years, she loved to give off the air of a hard bitch and only those of us close to her got the occasional look at her fragility underneath the make-up and expensive clothes.

I loved her, but seriously? And she thought I had problems.

When she brought her face back to mine she fell forwards into my arms. After a fleeting hug, she pulled away from me and jumped down off the light grey vanity unit. I watched as she systematically shut all the doors on her emotions one by one.

'Right, let's do this. I can hear "Regret" winding up. Let's get you back to the boyband.' I smiled at her choice of words. She grabbed at my hand and pulled me along with her.

Boyband, Default Distraction were certainly not. They were four extremely attractive men in their thirties who'd lived through more than their fair share of life's extreme highs and lows. As a package, I'd been stunned at how well they still fitted together both as a team and friends, on the small stage in the ballroom. Two of the boys I'd met and put up with in Vegas almost a lifetime ago, had been egotistical jerks in their own way. But life had smoothed down their rough edges, as only life could. They were all even better looking now, even with their faces showing wear and tear. But that always seemed to be the way with good looking men, they seemed to get even better looking as time passed. They exuded tolerance and experience, and after everything the four of them had lived through and come up against, could I dare say it? Maturity.

'They're certainly no boyband, Winter.' She flashed a smile over her shoulder at me as she pulled open the door to the ladies'.

'Oh, I know, it winds Raff up, so I use it from time to time. In fact, I knew a boyband once.'

'Oh my God, I bet you did! And how many of them did you do?' I stopped dead in the small ante-room of the ladies' and pulled her shoulder so she would look at me again. I was wondering if this was yet another little snippet she'd forgotten to share with Amy and me.

Her beautiful smile lit up my insides as she turned around to bestow it on me.

'Just the two.'

'Just two? Surely not?' I answered with laughter in my voice.

'Yep,' she replied as we made it out into the empty hallway. 'But, both together of course.'

I froze, looking at her in question as she pulled open the door in front of us. As the music got louder, I smiled and shook my head at her. She walked in with her head held high and I followed behind her.

One of these days she would have to stop keeping all males at arms' length. I knew how she saw life, having two men at once meant she didn't have to worry about any meaningful connections, she got what she wanted and so did they. But, she worried Amy and I, the way she would no longer let anyone penetrate her smokescreen. The optical illusion she had created was stunning, but no one was allowed to see around the edges, to the reality of her beautiful soul, in case she got hurt again. I understood, but hoped she might one day be able to find another way.

The door closed behind us and as Default Distraction finished the end of "Regret," I watched as Brody sang his heart out to the speechless crowd and I was swept along with the emotion in his voice. Raff and Luke strummed the final chord, Cade hit the snare and Brody fell forward as the last of his breath left his body. The room erupted around us and as the lights came back on there I stood clutching Winter's hand, the same hand that I hadn't even realised I'd made a grab for.

As the band accepted the cheers, handshakes and congratulations, my eyes were fixed on only one man, Raff. He jumped off the stage and the sound of his boots hitting the floor travelled over to me, stirring up feelings of impatience inside me as I awaited his arrival. He turned his head around the room. I watched as he nodded at his family and kissed his mum as he walked past them and then as he stood in place in the centre of the room looking through and around the vast amount of bodies. I knew he was searching for me and I stood patiently waiting for our eyes to connect.

The moment he found me, relief swept over his face and his strides became more purposeful as he made his way over. He had to stop several times to be polite to people who wanted to say a few words to him and he did so, but not once did his eyes stray from mine. With pleasure, he accepted their congratulations and handshakes, he offered them his words and a smile in return, but his eyes were all for me. It seemed he was reluctant now he had found me, to remove them.

He was stood with his arms crossed over his chest as he listened to a male unknown to me. He nodded, bent his ear in closer to offer his undivided attention and then uncrossing his arms, he clasped the man's upper arm as he made to move himself away.

Once the way was clear and there was no longer anyone in between us, he mouthed "Thank you" at me and I answered him with a smile as I was transported back in time.

Tearing my captive eyes away from his, I ran them over his longer stubble, noting the salt and pepper effect of it. I watched him take the few strides towards me, almost now wishing it was a longer walk.

God, could the man swagger and with so much fucking attitude, too.

His white shirt opened as he came nearer, revealing a body that I hadn't ever in my wildest dreams been able to visualise. In his teens, Raff was tall, lean and had hard muscles from all the rowing he did. But as a man, he stole my breath away. He was much broader across the shoulders and working my eyes down the gap created by his shirt moving to the sides of his body, I could see every worked-hard-for contour and muscle. Well defined pecs met my approving gaze, I saw that his chest was still hairless and then a tiny shard of silver caught my eye and although the shirt closed over again, I was sure his nipple was pierced. At that thought a flood of arousal hit the top of my thighs. Involuntarily, I responded by licking my lips and after a fleeting look at the rock-hard abs he seemed to be packing, my eyes flew back up to his just in time to see a smirk leaving the corner of his mouth.

I'd been caught admiring him, but I no longer cared. Butterflies danced around my stomach, my core clenched tight and a dull ache of want that I hadn't felt in many years hit my lower body. My heartbeat was quickening as I anticipated his touch. He came up in front of me and grabbing both of my hands he pulled me into his warm body. The smell of his sweat from the gig floated up on the heat of his body and I melted into him.

'You and me, we're outta here,' he spoke into my ear and I immediately complied, holding on to him as we vacated the room.

Chapter 18

Raff

Holding her hand and feeling her almost running along to keep up with my lengthening stride was one of the biggest fucking rushes I'd ever felt. All I knew was that I needed to leave everyone else far behind us. I wanted her all to myself and it seemed that surprisingly she wanted the exact same thing.

I was moving fast, with the disbelief that what had happened back there was true. The song I'd sung to her had penetrated through the many barriers she'd set up between us, and I could hardly believe my fucking luck.

She wanted to be with me and she was happy to let me lead us away.

My heart filled with hope that the connection between us was strong enough to fight off everything that had come between us. The voices behind us got quieter the further we walked and by the time we got to the bottom of the back stairs, knowing we no longer had any spectators, I couldn't wait any longer.

I turned around quickly and pulled on the one hand I was holding until she collided against my bare chest. The gasp of shock and then the quick intake of breath that she took as our bodies connected, was better than shooting up any drug I'd ever been in fucking contact with. Adrenalin flooded my system as I twisted her arm and put the one hand of hers that I was holding behind her back. My other hand weaved its way into her thick, chestnut hair at the back of her head. I leant my back onto the large newel post behind me and held her securely. My fingers cupped the back of her head gently but firmly and I made her look up at my face.

I watched through the strands of hair that had fallen in front of my vision as her eyes found mine and in slow motion I saw the fiery amber flecks in them begin to disappear as her dark pupils enlarged. At the very edge of my view I saw her tongue come out to wet her lip and then the tiny gap she opened between her full lips. My eyes left hers and all I could focus on was the plump, pink flesh of her mouth. Slowly, I tipped my head to the side and started to lower my mouth to hers. Her small hand left the side of my waist where she'd been gripping my loose shirt and then reconnected with the bare skin above my jeans. I sucked in a breath at her touch.

No woman apart from her had ever turned me on so fucking much just by placing their hands on my skin.

Our mouths were so close together. Every breath she took travelled over the needy flesh of my open mouth. I brushed our lips together feeling the electrical surge come between us, as I whispered to her.

'We need to talk.' It was the last fucking thing I wanted to do with her compliant in my arms.

'Later... Just kiss me.'

I couldn't help but smile at the desperation in her voice.

'Yeah, but I need to tell you how it all went down.'

'Yes, you do, but for now... just bloody kiss me.' The pleading tone in her voice heightened.

'I told you, you'd beg,' I answered, smiling at her impatience

I crashed my mouth to hers quickly, knowing I was pushing my fucking luck. The moment our needy flesh touched, my need to physically consume her took over. I wanted her in every way possible. I wanted her smiles, her laughter and her fury. I wanted her to need me in her life, I wanted everything about her and I didn't want to share anything about her with any other person. Not anyone.

My hands started to move of their own accord, one wound up her hair tightly to maintain our union and the other released her hand and started to travel over any part of her body that I could reach.

The groan she emitted as I grazed my knuckles slowly down her spine was like music to my ears. She hadn't removed her hand from behind her back, so I grabbed it again and pushed it tighter into the middle of her back. I made sure she was as close to me as possible. With our mouths still fused together, I pushed off and away from the post at my back and started to walk her backwards, fast. The need to feel her body trapped under mine was becoming impossible to ignore. Finally, we came to a stop as my knuckles touched the recently painted, cold wall of the hallway. Releasing my hold on her hair and hand, I pressed my body firmly against hers. Moving to the side I pushed one of my thighs in between hers, making her part her denim-clad legs. I began to grind my hip into her, giving her purchase and effectively holding her in place.

Our mouths became more demanding the longer we kissed, our teeth clashed together as we changed position time and time again and the silent thoroughfare around us began to fill with the noise of our breathing and desperation. I used my now empty hands to explore the woman I loved.

I took them symmetrically down the sides of her face, over her bare shoulders. They travelled further down her arms. Unable to refuse myself a moment longer I lifted my chest away from hers and pushing my hips further against her, I cupped both of her heavy breasts. As a teenager she'd been gorgeous, but now her body had blossomed into full womanhood she was indescribable. I wanted to see every single part of her, I wanted to explore her with my mouth, my fingers and watch her come undone with my caress. I rubbed my thumbs over her already rock-hard nipples and then pulled my mouth away from hers slightly, to hear the moan I knew she would release.

'Ohhhhhh,' she moaned. Her eyes were closed and her head tipped back just a little, exposing more of her throat. The bare, flushed skin called to me. I fought the need to sink my teeth into it, wanting to mark her as mine.

'You're beautiful, Lauren,' I whispered into the small fracture between us.

I lifted my thigh in between the apex of hers and watched as she closed her eyes at the motion.

'We need to fucking move, because if we don't soon, I'm gonna be taking you in this corridor and I won't give a fuck who sees us.' I spoke the lie into her ear, before I gave in and let my mouth bite its way softly down her neck. In reality I knew I would kill anyone who dared to see her like this in my arms. When I reached where her neck joined her shoulder, my hands hurriedly pulled her slash-necked top down. It gave way all too slowly, further revealing all her clavicle and I softly licked the whole length of it. Her hands grasped my head and her fingers buried themselves into the longer lengths of my hair as she held me to her.

'Fuck, the taste of your skin, Loz. I thought I could remember how exquisite it was, but it's far better than I memorised.'

I ran the tip of my tongue with perfect precision along the prominent bone once again. I stared, unable to pull my eyes away as goose bumps began to rise in my tongue's wake and as Lauren started to shiver slightly in my arms.

'I don't care about moving, I... just...'

'Just what? Tell me what you want,' I almost hissed at her in desperation to hear the words spill out of her mouth.

'I want... I want you, Rafferty.' No one ever used my full name anymore, and nobody had ever said it the way she said it now. I couldn't fucking wait to hear it fall from her mouth as she came with my dick inside her.

'And I want you, but you don't know what you're asking.'

'I know exactly what...' Her words faltered momentarily as I softly bit into the exposed skin at the nape of her neck. 'I... I want you.'

Looking quickly upwards, I could see she was too far fucking gone to care. I placed my mouth back to hers and found her willing tongue with mine as I caressed and then forcibly consumed her, demanding with pressure that she open up wide and let me in.

I should have been man enough to take her somewhere private, but fuck me I was so fucking lost in the woman. She was my first drug, my rediscovered drug and now my forever drug of choice. I would never get enough.

My hands quickly forced her top down further, feeling the material resist as it got tighter and then as her bare tits revealed themselves by almost bursting out of the slash neck. The soft fabric cleared her arms and she lifted them out suddenly. It then fell away from my hold and pooled at her waist. I braced myself with my mouth still on hers, answering her demands and lifted my arms up to cover her tits with my hands. I had large hands and it took the entirety of each of them to fully cup them both. My dick twitched uncontrollably in my jeans and it took every molecule of self-restraint that I had to stop from exploding behind my button fly.

'No fucking bra, Loz?' I whispered to her as I pulled my needy mouth away from hers.

'This top doesn't need one,' she answered back.

I could see the corners of her mouth lifting in a shy smile. Sucking in my bottom lip I chewed down on it for a split second and raised an eyebrow at her. Then, once again, her mouth pulled mine back in and our needy lips crashed together.

She'll be the fucking death of me.

I brushed both thumbs over her needy nipples and gave her exactly what she was sub-consciously asking for. The skin of each of her areolas was tight and puckered as she exposed herself to me and the chill of the hallway. We kissed until almost all the air had gone from my lungs. I wasn't sure what I needed more, her or oxygen. Finally, I broke my mouth away from hers to look at her face. Her lips were engorged with blood, her cheeks were flushed and her head was turned slightly to one side as it rested on the wall.

I could feel the heat from her body and almost feel the quickening beat of her heart. But, I still couldn't fucking believe I was holding her in my arms.

I could tell she felt safe with me, we were out in the open and any bastard would be able to see us if he dared to take the wrong fucking turn. But with her eyes closed and caught up in the moment, she had relinquished her faith and trust to me.

I'd had women out in the open before and couldn't have given a fuck if anyone had seen us. Like the egotistical bastard I'd been, when high on drugs or consuming my almost hourly amounts of Bourbon, I couldn't have given a shit about them. They didn't care if people saw my fingers in their arse as long as those people also thought my dick had been inside them. Quite often, that wasn't the fucking case. I'd let them suck me off or give me a hand job. My dick, I'd been a bit more choosey about.

But seeing her here relinquishing her faith and trust to me, I'd never been so fucking turned on in the whole of my life.

I rolled both of her nipples in between my thumb and forefinger and watched her mouth open as she gasped her appreciation to the sensation travelling through her. She began to grind herself into the top of my thigh and I knew that every single strand of my dwindling restraint had fucking snapped.

I quickly pinched her nipples and watched her eyes open up to stare intently back at me.

'Jeans off.'

With no hesitation whatsoever, her hands left me and without looking down I could feel from the movement in between us that she was doing exactly what I'd demanded of her. As she shimmied around between me and the cold of the wall behind her, I bent my knees to lower my mouth to her tits. Even as she continued to push her jeans and knickers down her legs, she unconsciously pushed her tits further towards me. Just before I sucked her needy flesh into my mouth I looked down at her almost fully exposed body.

'You are so fucking beautiful, Lauren.'

Her eyes came to find mine and she watched as I let my eyes wander quickly all over her exposed body. I licked one nipple fleetingly, hearing her gasp her appreciation and effectively slowing up our movements, which up to now had been frantic and hurried. I bent down further to help her out of her shoes and clothes. Propelling myself forward I fell onto my knees in between her bare legs and inhaled deeply. She was so fucking aroused it killed me to pause in front of her, but I had an ultimatum and before I thrusted my dick deep inside her she needed to know exactly how it was going be from now on.

'You have one chance, Loz.'

I grabbed hold of both of her knees, making her bend her legs a little, and licked my tongue a couple of inches up them one at a time.

'Oh... God, Raff.' Her voice was husky with need and it took all I had to continue.

In front of my eyes she began to shake and I looked up in time to see moisture begin to appear at the top of her legs.

'You have one fucking chance to say no, because once you let me deep inside you, Lauren, that's it. I'm not leaving, not ever.'

Her head that had been thrown back in the ecstasy of feeling my tongue on her skin, teasing and caressing her, fell forward. Feeling her eyes on the top of my head I looked up at her. I lifted my arse from sitting on my haunches and coming up onto my knees, I gently ran my hands up the back of her legs. I let my tongue run further up her left thigh and tried to not taste the woman I loved for fear of losing all fucking control. Her hands threaded into the hair at the back of my head.

'I don't want you to leave, I never wanted you to leave.' She slowly pushed the words out as she absorbed the feelings I was creating inside her.

'Good, but here's the deal.' I let my warm breath caress the wet of my saliva on her thigh and then turned my attention to her right leg and slowly ran my tongue over that too.

'You don't get to push me away, either. Once I take you, Lauren, you need to remember that you're mine... What are you?'

'I'm yours, Rafferty. I've always been yours,' she whispered.

The instant the words left her mouth, I was moving. I knew she was wet enough for what we both wanted and I wasn't prepared to make either of us wait any longer.

I stood suddenly, and crashed my mouth back to hers. Her arms instinctively came around my shoulders and she held on tight. In the space of a few seconds I'd released enough buttons on my jeans to allow me to pull my throbbing dick from its tight confines. I fisted myself a couple of times trying to get some relief. Then placing my hands underneath her bum cheeks, I lifted her up and positioned the almost purple looking head of my dick at her entrance and rubbed it once the full length of her wet slit.

'FUCK.' Realisation hit me like a fucking freight train and I pulled my mouth away from hers. I had no condoms on me.

'Loz, are you still on the pill?'

'Yes, and I'm clean. Are you?'

I rested my forehead to hers. I hated that she had to ask me, but I understood why. The lifestyle that had come between us was once again rearing its very ugly fucking head.

'I'm clean, can you take my word?' My eyes implored hers.

She didn't answer with her words but using her arms she lifted herself and shifted herself slightly. I was holding her too tightly for her to see in between us, so on instinct she moved onto the crown of my dick. As she slowly impaled herself she cried out her answer and it echoed around the hallway.

'YES!' she cried out.

Unable to contain myself any longer, I moved my hands behind her and placed them onto the cold wall, not wanting her bare flesh to be rubbed against the unforgiving, textured paint at her back. I inhaled a deep breath and pushed myself all the way inside her. For a few seconds, we held on tightly to each other and wondered at the feeling of the two of us being connected. Her warm, wet walls gripped tight and I groaned in response.

She was my fucking home and I would never leave her again.

'It's too much, Raff.' Her voice brought me back. 'Oh, my God... you feel, it feels different. It's too much... I can feel too much.'

'It's never too much, Lauren. This right here is what should be, always and forever, because you're my girl.'

Our mouths crashed back together and I finally allowed myself to move.

The pace I wanted to set was frantic and explosive, but I held myself back, not wanting to hurt her. Until I knew she was ready I moved firmly but controlled. Then, holding her weight on the top of my thighs and with her shoulders pushing onto my perfectly placed hands, I fucked her deep, like a man possessed. There would be a time later tonight when I would worship every fucking inch of her, but it wasn't here and it wasn't now. Instinctively, her legs opened wider and I drove my dick into her, time and time again. Her cries of pleasure met my ears and my pace quickened. The need to be inside her, to fuck her and to cum inside her was almost primeval. The feelings of need between us were made of pure passion. Our gasps and moans filled up the open space, all I could hear was our mutual pleasure-filled noises and the bracelets around both of her wrists as they clinked together with the force of our conjoined movement.

I felt the first pulsing of her walls around my dick and I was gone.

'RAFFERTY.' And there it was, the one fucking word I'd been hanging on by a thread for.

The heat of my orgasm was chasing down my spine as Lauren sank her teeth into my shirt covered shoulder, and my body froze as my dick convulsed inside her. My neck arched and I looked skyward as I discharged hot bursts of semen into her, repeatedly.

I came roaring her name and then dipped my head to rest on her shoulder.

As soon as I could, I focussed my eyes back on hers and to see a small smile of satisfaction on her lips was a relief. I'd been too rough with her, but by the look of the sated woman in my arms, she'd enjoyed all I had to give her.

I pressed my lips back to hers. Gently and with as much love and tenderness as I could find, I kissed at her smile.

My eyes snapped open as my mobile began to vibrate in the back pocket of my jeans. I ignored it and closed them again. I knew she'd heard the noise the moment her body began to tense up and she broke her mouth from mine.

'Your phone?'

'Mmmm hmmm,' I mumbled onto her skin as I began to nip at her jaw bone.

'Perhaps you should answer it?'

'Nah.'

'What if it's Flint?'

With those words, I came out of the thick air of lust around us and lifting my head I refocussed on the almost naked woman in my arms. Given a few more minutes, my semi-erect dick would have completely awakened and I'd have happily been pounding into her again. Her eyes sparkled as she questioned me and I knew she was thinking the exact same thoughts.

'Okay.' I reached into my back pocket and pulled the phone out.

Taking a quick look, I saw Winter's name flash over the screen as it pulsed in my hand. I used my thumb to swipe to answer and almost growled with anger into the phone.

'You've gotta be fucking joking me, Winter.' I spoke with annoyance in my tone. 'This better be important.'

'We can't find Amy. Lauren and I left her asleep on the settee when we came to watch you play and now she's missing.'

I was about to answer that she'd probably gone home without them when she spoke again.

'She's really drunk, I'm worried about her.'

Lauren heard every word Winter said and her eyes gradually opened wider in concern as she pushed me away from her.

'We're coming, give us five.'

I stepped back and lowered her to the ground. I quickly put my dick back into my jeans and buttoned up the fly. Then placing my open palms on the now empty wall in front of me, I inhaled deeply to bring myself back. All at once she was picking her hastily dropped jeans and knickers off the floor and forcing her legs hastily into them.

'Thank you, I need to go,' she whispered. From the corner of my eye I watched as she zipped up her jeans, wiggled her feet into her Converse and pulled her top back up.

'I know,' I offered. 'Fuck it.' Resigned to the interruption, I pushed myself off the wall and stood in front of her, watching as she tried to tidy herself up, getting more amused the longer it went on for.

I smiled and offered her my hand. 'You look sensational. You know you can brush yourself down and realign your creased clothing as much as you want. But nothing will remove the flush in your cheeks, your nipples pushing through your top as they cry out for more of my attention and the fact you look like I've fucked you... nothing.' I smiled at her as she took hold of my offered hand. I brought it up to my mouth and brushed my lips over her knuckles to hear her gasp once again. Then the boy inside me took over, breathing in sharply I plunged her hand inside my jeans and used it to straighten my dick out. My eyebrows lifted and waggled at her in amusement.

Automatically, her hand instinctively held me, moving as I directed her. Her eyes grew wider the more she touched. It took all I had not to change my mind about helping to look for her cousin. I inhaled deeply and closed my eyes as I exhaled. Once I was sorted, I could feel her touching the metal work that although wasn't new to me, certainly was to her. Her eyes began to question mine and I breathed in again to pull her inquisitive fingertips out from my jeans.

'Oh, my God.' She looked at me in shock and amusement. 'What was that?'

'Later,' I answered, winking at her and her thoughtful expression. It took all I had not to laugh at her furrowed brow.

'I can't believe you did that. Tell me, you didn't just do that?'

Not releasing her hand, I lifted it up in mine, turned her around in my hold and with my arm loose over her shoulder, I began to walk us back down the corridor to find my sister.

'Oh, yeah... I did.' I glanced down at her as we walked and as she looked up at me, I gave her a quick wink. I watched her roll her lips inside her teeth as she smiled and her eyes opened wider at me as she began to shake her head a little from side to side. She was no fucking innocent and I loved it.

'I've been waiting for years to feel your hands on me and I couldn't wait any longer. I'm annoyed at the interruption, but the anticipation of what's going to come tonight will keep me going.'

I turned and moved quickly in front of her, stopping her progression back to the others. With my spare hand, I placed my thumb and index finger under her chin and lifted her still dilated pupils to meet mine. Slowly, I twisted and lowered my mouth to hers, unable to go another moment without feeling her compliancy under my lips. Then I stood back up and looked at her as I gathered her into my arms.

'I can't fucking wait for them all to see that you are and have always been mine.'

She stood on tiptoe and brushed a quick kiss to my lips and then removing herself from my hold, she grabbed me by the hand and led me back down the corridor. 'Come on, I need to find Amy and then you need to take me to wherever the hell we were off to before we got waylaid.'

'Waylaid? Mmmm, it's my new favourite word. Be prepared to be waylaid often.' I nodded my head and laughed as I replied.

Lauren

My mind was still full of the fact that after us all searching high and low for a drunk and missing Amy, we'd realised that she wasn't actually missing at all. Cade remembered seeing Brody wander off into the room we'd left her in. When Luke had knocked on his door, and entered with permission into Brody's room, he had found Amy being lovingly cared for by the lead singer of Default Distraction.

Apparently, he'd found her drunk and decided she needed his help. He'd held her hair while she was sick and then tucked her up in his bed, while he sat and watched her.

I had wondered what Winter was on to earlier as us three girls had sipped on the Champagne together, and now it all made sense. She'd put two and two together and worked out who the mysterious Daniel was.

He was Brody Daniels, lead singer of Default Distraction.

A wave of worry washed over me. I wasn't proud of myself for leaving Amy by herself. Although in our defence she had been comfortable and asleep, and I knew we hadn't been gone long. But far worse, we had left her in the care of the man she thought was called Daniel, when he wasn't.

I knew the shit was sure to hit the fan on that one, but that was another story.

I touched the cold glass with my fingertips and looked out of the window at the white world and the starry, black night sky that surrounded us. The snow-covered land around us made me feel blanketed and protected. It was a welcome feeling, as my whole world had begun to feel like it's very semblance was cracking under the strain of all the unconscious and unrealistic demands I had placed on myself.

If someone had told me last week that I would be here with Raff, having let him kiss and touch me to the point of then having sex with him in a hallway, I'd have told them that they were delusional.

But here I was, sitting down low in one of his expensive sports cars, as he drove me home. In the warmth of the car I could smell sex on my skin and I could feel his semen soaking my already damp knickers. That was all the proof I needed that I hadn't been dreaming.

I looked down to the side where our hands were clasped together as Raff carefully drove us the short way up the drive, away from The Manor and back to my small flat above The Fairy Garden. His thumb rubbed over the back of my hand and shockwaves from that simple touch entered my system and travelled all the way to my core, where the dull ache of lust had spontaneously reignited again.

The car was quiet, the only thing I could hear was the whirring of both of our minds as we tried to unravel the years of hurt between us. I wasn't sure how he felt, but I was struggling. My heart jolted hearing the recognisable sound of a small patch of exposed gravel, it crunched under his wheels as we entered the area of the outbuildings.

'It's just over there, you have to drive through the narrow archway on the left.' I pointed as the shadowy outlines of the outbuildings appeared.

'Okay, I see it,' he replied.

As Raff leant further over his steering wheel, as he contemplated navigating his beloved car through the small opening in the light of the one orange lamp, and his hand left mine. I immediately felt a sense of grief at the loss of his touch. I pulled my now cold hand into my lap and pushed it down in between my legs.

Finally, we pulled up outside my tearooms.

Raff switched off the engine and adjusting his large frame as much as he could in the small interior of the car, he turned his body sideways to look at me.

'Can I come in?' he asked, as he tentatively reached out one hand. With his fingers, he pushed my long hair away from the side of my face and placed it behind my shoulder. I could now feel the strength of his eyes imploring me as he stared at the side of my face.

The words he asked, just about summed up the atmosphere that had wrapped its very unwelcome presence around the two of us. The passion we had felt earlier was still there in the background, but having to put it on hold to search for Amy had allowed the previous hurt to seep into our heads. It didn't matter how unwelcome it was, it had taken hold and I could tell we were both having difficulty shaking it off.

His warm knuckles grazed over my cheekbone and at his touch I summoned the courage to turn to look at him and face my fears head on.

I nodded at him and at last I found the nerve to bring my eyes up to meet his.

'Don't ever let me down again, Raff.' I watched him nod at me resolutely and I grabbed at the edges of the biker jacket he'd thrown on top of his now buttoned up, white shirt. I pulled his face to mine so I could press my lips to his. I wanted the connection between us to remind me why I needed to take a chance on him. His mouth found mine as he captured my lips with his, and between us we tried hard to erase the growing sense of unease.

'I won't,' he answered as he pulled away and leant his forehead momentarily against mine. I heard the creak of his jacket brushing against the leather interior, as he shifted the whole of his body awkwardly across the centre console to wrap me into his tight hold. He pushed the weight of his body into mine and pressed his mouth fleetingly back to my lips.

As he began to relax back into his seat and the fraught atmosphere returned, I wordlessly got out of the car and waited for him to catch up. Once he was out, I moved towards the stairs that led up to my flat and began to climb them slowly, hoping that he would follow my lead. I was taking him into my inner sanctum, no one apart from the girls ever got to stay here. My little flat was my everything. I'd designed it, so that it offered me everything I hadn't yet been able to find in another human being. When I needed solace, it wrapped its warmth around me in consolation. When I needed to escape, I came up here and closed its doors on the sometimes unrelenting world. When I was unwell, it offered me comfort and helped me to get better.

I was wordlessly inviting him up and knew I was opening up the whole of my heart by doing so. I wouldn't survive him leaving me again.

Of that, I was convinced.

The instant I heard his heavy boots clang behind me, my body relaxed and quietened. My pulse that had been beating a loud drum in my ear receded and the prickle of my anxiety fell away. Somehow our lives had been guided to this point, I didn't know how or why, but for the first time in as long as I could remember I felt at peace, knowing he was following my every step.

I placed my key to the door lock and tried hard to make it find its way home, but as my body began to shake with the cold and emotion I couldn't guide it to where it needed to be.

Raff's feet found the deeper top step behind me. I looked down and could see his black boots either side of my Converse as we stood there, my back to his front. His body moulded itself to mine and I felt the warmth of him begin to seep through my clothing. His left arm wrapped itself around my waist and his right grabbed hold of my shaking hand.

'Let me help, Lauren?'

I nodded in reply and swallowed at the trapped emotional knot in the back of my throat. His hand gripped mine and together we found the barrel of the lock. I knew the significance wasn't lost on him as I heard him sniff in my ear as the lock gave way and the door opened wide.

The warm air hit the bare skin of my face and shoulders as I stepped inside and slipped off the thick wrap I'd been wearing. I heard Raff close the door behind us and then I felt him stall on the door mat. I turned on the subdued lighting in the flat and watched as my place of comfort sprung to life.

'If you're staying with me, then drop the dead bolt.' My voice sounded far more confident than I felt.

Unknowingly I froze in place, awaiting the noise I desperately wanted to hear. As the metal dropped into place almost instantaneously after I'd spoken, I exhaled and closed my eyes as I prepared myself for what I needed to do next.

Lauren

I walked away from the doorway and Raff and into the small kitchen that was in one of the corners of my large, open-plan living space. Going to the sink, I washed my hands, then pulled open the fridge door and took out a small glass bottle, which I placed onto the side. Opening a drawer, I pulled out one of my glucose monitors, unzipped the case and turned it on. Still without turning to look at Raff, I picked up a lancet and clicked the hand-held device into my left index finger. I then squeezed a droplet of blood to the surface and placed it onto the waiting glucose monitor. I could feel him behind me taking in everything that was going on, but without saying anything I carried on. I opened another cupboard, dropped the lancet into the yellow sharps box and then looked at the reading on the screen in front of me.

I pulled my phone out of my pocket and opened the app I needed to check my daily readings. When it displayed my level I refused to show my concern, I simply took out a syringe and holding the glass bottle upside down I drew out the correct amount of insulin. Then I unceremoniously dropped my jeans, squeezed the top of my thigh and pushed the needle home into the layer of fat at the top of my leg. I knew I had to start doing better with managing my disease, but until now I hadn't felt the need to acknowledge let alone manage it.

Finally, I dropped the needle into the same yellow box, put away all the equipment I had used and washed my hands again.

I pulled my jeans back up and glanced over my shoulder at Raff.

I knew if I found any hesitancy whatsoever, then whatever had come to pass between us the last few hours would have to be forgotten.

'So, do you still want to stay, Raff?' I spun around to face him fully. He was leaning his backside on the back of my large settee.

His eyes came to find mine as he twisted his head in question at my words and I watched his arms cross over his chest. 'Yes, I want to stay, Lauren.'

'After what you've just seen?' I questioned him again and watched every expression on his face to get my answer. 'Diabetes controls my life, are you sure you understand that?'

'Your illness makes no difference to how I feel about you, Loz.'

I saw no hesitancy in his face at all and took a couple of steps towards him. 'You couldn't handle it all those years ago, are you sure you can now? Diabetes doesn't go away, not my type anyway. I have to test several times a day, I have to eat when I'm not hungry, and sometimes when I'm starving I can't eat at all because my blood sugar isn't at the right level.'

His left hand came up and swept his hair away from his eyes, it was as if he wanted me to see him more clearly as he spoke. 'I was scared, Loz. I'll admit it... When you first got ill, I was shit scared. I didn't know what to do for the best and I know I waited far too long before we took you to the emergency room. But, I didn't leave you with your parents because you were ill, it wasn't the diabetes that made me leave you in Vegas.' He was shaking his head slowly at me waiting for his words to reach me.

'It wasn't? So, was it because you wanted to be with Ashley?' I wasn't sure which was worse, to be left for another girl or left because you were ill. My heart was pounding in my chest and my hands began to sweat as I waited to be put out of my misery.

'Fuck no!' he spat out into the air and believing his response I exhaled a shaky breath. 'I knew what you'd started to think, I can still see the looks you used to give me when she hung around us and touched me when she was speaking to us all. And, I know... I know I was a horny teenager and wrongly lapped up the attention. But, I can categorically say, I had no intention of ever fucking her, no matter how hard she fucking tried to coerce me to.'

My head was a whirlwind. 'Then why did you leave me, Raff?'

He crossed the few steps in between us to reach me and crouched down so we were at the same eye level. His hands found the back of my arms and he held me gently but firmly in his grasp.

'Don't you see?'

I shook my head at him. 'No,' I implored.

'We were in the U.S. It wasn't good old Britain with its free health care. I didn't want to let you go, I wanted you where you belonged, with me. But, Lauren... I hadn't got the money to buy you the equipment and the insulin you needed to take care of your diabetes. You must remember how we lived?'

I knew that I had been looking back for a long time now only remembering the good times, but in the back of my mind I did remember.

We had rented a two-bed duplex apartment in one of the seediest areas of Vegas, far away from the pretty twinkling lights and the rich people spending lots of money. Each month I'd been there, I'd seen how hard it was for the boys to scrape together the money to cover the rent, we never answered the door when we were late paying as we were scared we'd be chucked out and end up sleeping in Luke's old car.

The place we lived in housed some of the hardest working people I'd ever met, it also housed the down trodden and unfortunately those who prayed on those weaker than them. We lived in the same place that the third-class citizens resided in, the cleaners of the twinkly lights, the street walkers, the drug addicts and those seeking to put their name up in lights. I could still see the dirty, old, single mattress that Raff and I slept on at night, covered with a sleeping bag. Some days we lived on Ramen noodles and on other occasions we didn't eat at all. It had been a shock to my system when I'd first seen where he was living. But when he'd taken me in his arms that first night, all my reservations had been swept away.

Raff's hands moved up my arms and over my bare shoulders, bringing my sleeping body alive once again at his touch. His hands didn't stop moving until they had travelled up my neck and had taken hold of my face. His large hands and calloused fingers gently cupped my head as he stared at me.

'Tell me you remember?' he pleaded.

'I do.'

'I didn't want to leave you, I wanted you to stay, but I had to let you go. Your parents made me understand that. It was only because your nan had bought travel insurance to cover you for six months that the hospital accepted you as an inpatient in the first place.'

'Travel insurance?' I could feel myself frown at him in question as I tried to take in what he was saying.

'Yeah.' I looked into his eyes and studied what I found deep within them.

'Oh, I didn't know.'

'You were too ill to know what was going on, it was terrifying watching you get ill over those two to three days... fucking terrifying.'

'I'm sorry,' I whispered as I saw the pain collected together in his eyes.

He shook his head. 'No, I'm sorry. I should have reacted faster. I should have got you the help you needed quicker. You nearly died and that would have been my fault.'

Why life had been such a bitch to us back then, I couldn't work out. But, it seemed it was making it up to us by bringing us back together. As Raff stood to his full height and pulled me into his arms, I happily leant my head on his chest and relaxed into his hold. I felt complete for the first time in many years. I had one more question and then I would let it all rest, back where it belonged in our past.

'Tell me you forgive me for hurting you?' he begged.

'Now I think I understand why... Of course, I do. I understand now that you had no other choice. But you should have spoken to me and *you* should have explained to me why. All these years, Raff... all these long, lonely years, I thought the very worst. I thought you no longer loved me and it was a way to get me to leave... All these wasted years.' My voice ended on a sob and he tightened his hold on me.

'I'm so fucking sorry, Loz. Your dad said he'd explain it all, he said it was better if I left, because it would cause you more heartbreak if I stayed and tried to explain. I sort of agreed with him, because I knew you wouldn't have accepted what I had to say.'

'My dad?'

'Yeah.'

'He never really explained anything, Raff. He just said it was better for everyone this way. He said you couldn't go home and I couldn't stay, so there was no choice. I suppose that sort of explained it.'

'That's it?'

'Yes, that's it. But, to be honest it's such a long time ago, it's hard to recall everything correctly.' Something didn't sit quite right, I just wasn't sure what it was.

'Mmmm,' he agreed, although I could see he didn't think it all added up either.

'I need to ask this.' I spoke quietly and gripping his clothes, I held him to me.

'Go on.' As he replied, the words reverberated inside his broad chest.

'Ashley?'

He sighed and let a breath out before he answered. 'I swear, I didn't have anything to do with her until months after you'd left, she played on my loneliness. I was often drunk and sometimes outta my head and she used it to her advantage.'

'So, you're saying it was all her fault?' My tone turned accusing.

'No, I'm not.' I felt him move and knew he had looked up towards the ceiling as he began to gather his thoughts. I heard a gulp as he swallowed down his exasperation. 'But I'd often wake up and find her where you should have been and I had no fucking clue how she got there. She wanted to be the wife of a rock star and I was her meal ticket. It's in her blood and to give her, her due, it's probably the one thing she's fucking perfect at.'

I was trying hard not to tense up as we discussed his ex-wife, but I would always hate everything she stood for. He may never be able to see it, but she had done everything she could to take him from me all those years ago. I bet she'd been so happy when I'd left for home. As far as I was concerned, women didn't go for other women's men, it was an unwritten rule, or at least it should be. Raff started rubbing his hands gently up and down my arms as he tried to get me to relax.

I pulled myself together, looked up and offered him a small smile.

'But, you had Flint together, so not everything in your relationship was bad, was it?' I tried and failed successfully to pull my face together as I mentioned the child they'd created while I'd been at home reading every snippet of information I could secretly find on the "A-list couple" they had fast become. I didn't resent Flint, really I didn't. But I should have been his mum, not her, and it had eaten away at me for years after he'd been born.

'I love Flint, with everything I have. He's everything to me, watching him grow up has been amazing and I'd have loved to have more children. But my relationship with Ash, for what it was, was on its way out, just as we got our first signing… You'll never know how hard that was.' I felt his feet shift as he increased the pressure of his hold on me as he unknowingly tried to convince me of the words he was saying. 'The times I picked up a pay phone and dialled your number to tell you. YOU were the one person I wanted to share the good news with, not her, not anyone but you. But I still didn't have the money to pay for your medical care, so I couldn't. So, I shared it with her. Then suddenly she was pregnant and you know all about my past. There was no fucking way I could turn my back on my child nor its mother.' His eyes looked lost for a few seconds and I was convinced he was going over his own birth and what his poor mum had gone through as a young parent with no support from his birth father.

So, that's how the bitch trapped him. What a conniving piece of trash she was.

'Our marriage started to die not long after Flint was born. She never wanted either of us, all she wanted was the lifestyle. So, finally I had the money and my marriage was heading for the divorce courts. I summoned up the backbone to contact you. Your mum was friendly when she answered the phone, but she quickly informed me that you'd moved on and were about to get engaged to a bloke called Bryan.' I pushed myself away from him so I could look up into his face. I knew that my expression would show him how confused I was.

'My mum?' I managed to ask. 'She never said you'd called and I have no idea why she would have thought that I was about to get engaged, especially to Bryan.' Shaking my head, I laughed a little at the irony.

I watched him nod as his eyes quickly locked onto mine.

'Your mum asked me if I wanted to upset your life again, when it had taken you until that point to move on.'

'I never got engaged to him and I can't imagine why she thought I would.'

Raff let out a huge sigh, 'Well fuck!'

His answers made my decision, he was all I'd ever wanted. So, when he followed it with the words that for years I'd only dreamt of hearing fall from his mouth, my heart burst out of my chest with happiness. 'So, here goes. I love you, Lauren. I've always loved you. Many, many times I tried to work out how to get you back. But, it wasn't meant to be then and I must accept that now. But this is our time, Loz, and it's like I said many years ago... We are always and forever.'

I grabbed hold of both sides of his leather jacket and pulled him to me. I buried my face into his chest and inhaled the smell of him that was teasing my nostrils.

'You've tried to get me back other times?' I spoke into his chest and could feel him nodding his head in answer. 'You'll have to tell me all about them.' Again, his head nodded and he exhaled a wavering, emotional breath and held me tighter to him. 'I can't believe you're here with me, I've dreamt about this for years.' I tipped my head backwards to look up at him gazing lovingly down at me.

'Believe it, I'm here and I'm not going anywhere. I've told you I love you, I'm not expecting anything in return, it can wait. I'll wait forever to hear those words leave your lips.'

'You don't have to,' I replied.

I saw a look of panic cross over his ridiculously handsome features and I smiled up at him. He released his hold around me to grasp the tops of my arms as he tried to work out what I was saying.

'I love you too, I never stopped loving you.'

Raff pulled me to him. Gathering me tightly, he picked me up and twirled me around. Eventually, my feet found the floor again as he placed me gently back down and pushed his errant hair out of his eyes, back to where it belonged on top of his head.

'I don't know what to say, Lauren.'

'Don't say anything at all.' I placed one finger to his lips and watched as he kissed it and grinned back at me. 'Will you dance with me?' I asked.

'I'm willing, but to what?' he countered with a low laugh leaving his mouth.

I shouted out to my smart system. 'Alexa play my "romancing" playlist, please.'

An amused smile broke out over his face and he mouthed "romancing" back at me and lifted his eyebrows in question.

Should I be embarrassed? I knew, and now he did too, how nearly everything in my life had something to do with him and the memories of our young love. But these little things had got me through and had made me feel closer to him, when in reality, he had been so very far away. Maybe I should have been embarrassed, but I wasn't, not with him.

Song after song came on as Raff held me tightly in his arms and we both wordlessly remembered another time when we'd danced under the starlight.

Chapter 21

Lauren

I couldn't recall the exact moment when our laughter and smooching around in each other's arms became something else, because it happened so naturally.

I'd been looking up into Raff's face as he sung the words of **"Sometimes when we touch" by Dan Hill.** Every single word had resonated deep down inside me. I couldn't wait any longer for him and he instantly recognised it.

He stopped singing and his eyes narrowed as they focussed on me and me alone. His longer strands of hair fell over his face and I smiled at him in response to the questioning look I found swirling around in his grey eyes. His tongue came out to wet his lips and then slowly he dipped his head to meet mine. Just as he said I always did, I anticipated his touch and my lips parted slightly to welcome him.

I heard him groan before he sealed his mouth over mine. I was shocked at how controlled he was, unlike earlier this evening when our mutual passion had burnt so fast and furious that we'd ended up having sex in a hallway where anyone could have seen us. His tongue teased, stroked and tasted, with long, far reaching caresses. He applied the right amount of pressure as his tongue and lips stirred up the whole of my body, until nothing mattered but the feel of him kissing me. I replied by threading my fingers into the back of his hair and directed his mouth over mine. Although, by the way he kissed me, I knew the man that had hold of me in his arms needed no such help. He knew exactly what I wanted and needed.

He gave without taking as he attempted to show me his love.

My palms which had been placed comfortably on his chest as we had danced together earlier, now left his hair and started to travel. I'd been occasionally rubbing over his nipples and connecting with the barbells that now pierced them and now I wanted to see them. Slowly, with shaking hands, I started to unbutton his shirt, until at last I could lift my hands to push the shirt off his broad shoulders and down his arms. The spark that ignited between us as I placed my hands on his exposed skin, temporarily slowed down my hands as I savoured the feeling. Then I continued leisurely, feeling every defined muscle under my fingertips, until finally the shirt became stuck around his wrists.

He broke his lips away from mine and gave a small laugh as he fought to pull the still buttoned up cuffs off his trapped hands.

Stepping a little away from him, I took in how beautiful he now was. The silver of his piercings glinted in the light. I remembered from years back how responsive his nipples were and needed to see if having them pierced made him even more sensitive. With one hand, I trailed a finger over his pec and then twisted one gently to the side. His nipple hardened and grew longer.

His eyes closed as he dragged in air over his teeth and he stopped struggling to free himself of his shirt. When he opened them again, the grin he gave me in return was magnetising.

'I think you like me trapped and at your mercy, Lauren.'

I felt a blush hit my cheeks as the realisation hit.

I certainly did.

'You've seen me almost naked today, Raff, and now it's my turn.'

He nodded at me and tilted his head to the side as he cocked up one eyebrow in question to me and tried to hold in his amusement. His feet moved as he widened his stance slightly against my possible onslaught. I stepped back further to admire the view. His chest widened as he instinctively stood to his full height, and with his arms relaxing into the position they were now trapped in, his chest expanded in front of my eyes as he took a deep breath in and slowly exhaled.

He was spectacular.

'So, what are you going to do with me, Loz?'

Every part of my body had sprung to life at his voice, he was no longer touching me and his arms were trapped behind his back, but his presence was enough to send me spiralling out of control. His eyes swept up and down my body, with intent. As they travelled over my clothing his breathing changed, he licked his lips and then on occasion sucked in his bottom lip as he pondered. I heard every hiss of air he dragged over his teeth and every exhale he carefully let go into the sexually charged atmosphere.

He took one step towards me.

'So, do you like what you see?' he questioned.

My eyes left his hard body and found their way back to his face. I nodded at him and returned his grin.

'Good, now undo my belt and unbutton my jeans… *carefully*.' He placed so much emphasis on the last word, it almost sounded like he was breaking it down into separate syllables.

I took one step towards him. It was all I needed to do, to be back under his control. Looking down I watched my fingers deftly and confidently flick open his belt. As it slackened, his jeans fell to hang loosely on his hips. I started at the top and undid the buttons on his jeans until finally I could see his sizable cock. My fingers froze and I looked up to meet his amused grin.

'You can touch it, it won't bite.' His tongue flicked out to touch his top lip and I watched mesmerised.

I narrowed my eyes at his teasing and shook my head at him.

'Oh, I'll do more than that, Raff. I'm not the naïve young girl you remember.' I did my best to wink at him and saw the moment my words hit home as his expression changed. I placed one hand on either side of his open jeans and pulled them further apart quickly as I sunk to my knees in front of him. With my eyes opening wide, I watched as his heavy, engorged cock sprung free of its confines and came into view. The glint of more silver caught my eyes.

I captured his wide crown into my mouth and tasted the pre-cum that had beaded onto his crest and by placing pressure onto it, I pushed his cock down with my mouth so I could see more. Swirling my tongue around and around the crown, I heard a groan leave his mouth as I counted four small, slightly curved barbells. Together, they created a ladder effect. I took hold of him with my right hand, placing my fingers in between the silver and slowly I began to pump up and down. He grew hot to touch and larger as blood flooded his cock. Satisfied I'd shown him what I was capable of, I freed him with a loud pop and looked up at him.

'I thought you felt different earlier.'

He smirked at me and then suddenly his arms flexed as he began to free himself. I heard material ripping. and I was vaguely aware of white fabric flying through the air. Then his hands came down to hang by his sides.

'But you liked it,' he stated. His freed hands found my shoulders and he pulled me to standing. 'Didn't you?' he questioned.

'Yes.'

'As much as I'd like to take you here and now, I made a promise to myself earlier that I was going to take my sweet fucking time with you. Is your bedroom behind that door?' He nodded in the correct direction.

'Yes,' I replied.

Moving quickly, he pulled his jeans up enough to walk. Then he turned me around and bent to place one arm underneath my shoulders and the other behind the back of my knees. Then he swung me up with ease into his arms and started walking towards the closed door. When we got to the doorway, he stopped suddenly.

'Tomorrow, you're going to phone that fucking excuse you call a boyfriend and tell him the two of you are finished, understood?'

'Yes.'

He smiled down at me. 'Yes? You're very agreeable tonight, Lauren.'

My arms that were looped around his shoulder and clasped together, released and ran up the back of his neck, until my fingers found his shorter lengths of hair at the back of his neck. His full attention was on me now as he waited for my answer.

'I've seen something I want, I'll agree to anything right now.' I rolled my lips over my teeth trying to control my smirk.

'Anything, huh?'

'Anything,' I whispered, before his mouth came crashing down to mine as he showed me how much he appreciated my answer. I took the time, as he stood in the open doorway holding me close to his chest, to explore every well-defined muscle and sinew on his back. Earlier it had been his hands on me and I longed to explore the man that the boy I'd loved had grown into. I ran my fingertips over his skin, trying to conserve every dip and rise to memory.

Our kiss that had started off with passion, was developing quickly. In that one kiss, I could now feel everything that was trapped between us, the years of loneliness, the pain of our enforced separation and the remorse. But most of all, I could feel our love. It was like we had been storing it away for each other for years and now it had been uncorked.

It was explosive.

The kiss wasn't gentle as our teeth clashed together and his teeth nipped my already overly sensitive lips. But it was us and we both knew we needed to feel everything. We needed to feel everything we had missed out on in the years we had been apart.

Suddenly, we were moving.

I was carried over the threshold of my bedroom. It was as if an imaginary line had been drawn in the sand and once we had taken the step over it, we were both giving in to the questions, doubts and obvious obstacles in the way of us being together. This wasn't about the earlier quickie we'd had in the hallway as we gave in to our lust for each other. This was us answering our hearts pleas to love each other.

Lifting his mouth away from mine, Raff slowly lowered me to the floor.

It was my turn. My hands started wandering of their own accord. I ran both palms up his chest, feeling the clarity of his defined muscles. In the light of the stars and moon flooding through my Velux windows, I could see him react to my every touch. His nipples hardened as my hands travelled over his bare skin. His breath hitched each and every time I withdrew my touch and then placed my fingertips back on his skin and his grey eyes darkened as his pupils dilated. I removed my hands from his chest and let them move smoothly around to his back, where I lightly scraped my short nails from his shoulder blades down to the waist of his jeans. It was intoxicating watching his reaction to my exploration, his eyes closed momentarily as if it was all too much having my hands on him.

Using the purchase of his loose waistband I stood up on tip toes and pressed my lips back to his. I licked the seam of his closed mouth and willed it to open slightly, the way I now knew I welcomed him. As his lips parted, I heard a drag of air being taken in and then when it seemed he could hold back no more his arms, which had been hanging loosely to his sides, came up to cup my face. Our kiss deepened as his thumbs caressed my cheekbones. The way he kissed me with such deep tenderness touched my heart.

As Raff kept his hands on my face, touching and caressing with such tender affection, the rest of my body began to feel neglected and needy. I could feel my body becoming fidgety and agitated. My feet started to move restlessly of their own accord and my fingers began to grasp his sides, where before they had only rested. I pulled his body closer to mine to seal the small gap between us and felt his hard erection pushing in between us both. Only then did I understand just how hard the man was fighting to control his need for me.

Still his hands cupped my face and his thumbs gently caressed my cheeks and cheek bones. But that simple tender action was now driving me wild with desire. I wanted and needed more. I wanted to feel that touch all over my body, I was on fire for him to lavish the same attention on the rest of my body, yet he continued making love to my mouth and caressing my face.

Finally, he broke away, leaving a fissure between our swollen lips. It was only when he dragged in air and his chest heaved, I knew he was probably even more affected than I was by his need to show me his love.

'I need you, Lauren,' Raff almost rasped out on his exhale of breath.

'Then take me,' I whispered back.

Then his mouth was back, no longer teasing and caressing, but demanding.

As one, we closed the couple of steps to my bed. Our hands were all over each other. It was ungraceful and we lost ourselves to our feelings of pent up want and need. His hands gradually stripped me of my clothing and his mouth only broke away from mine when it was necessary, in order that he could alleviate me of my confines.

At last, when I felt I could take no more, my naked body was lowered slowly backwards onto my bed.

There, with the light of the night sky to aid my eyes, I watched as he lowered his jeans, kicked off his boots and trod on the bottom of his jeans to free himself of them.

His hair had come down over his face, but I could still see his eyes behind it telling me wordlessly everything I wanted to hear. The man gave off dark and moody with his hair and eye colour and the title had never suited anyone more. The sparkling, silver piercings placed in strategic places on his body were in a complete contrast to his hair, eyes and skin colour.

He was truly magnificent.

Suddenly he moved, crawling up the bed. Eventually, his hands came down in place either side of my face and he slowly lowered his body, so it almost but not quite touched mine. In slow motion, his head twisted to meet my lips with his own. Before my arms had a chance to take a firm hold of him, he broke our kiss and directed his head downwards. His tongue, lips and teeth trailed a path down my body. They explored, savoured and teased every single inch of my sensitive and needy skin, until I was crying out with my need for him. Further and further down he went, until he was kneeling on the floor in between my open feet. His hands found their way under my bum cheeks and he pulled me to the edge of the bed, so that his tongue and mouth were exactly where I needed them to be.

His hands moved and his fingers opened me up wide to him. Then his tongue licked slowly up and down my lips, occasionally applying pressure onto the hood of my clitoris. I could hear my pleas and gasps as I took everything he was willing to give. He teased and toyed with me, taking me so far and then leaving me on the precipice of the cliff we had found our way up to. He read my signals so well and knew when I couldn't take it any longer. His warm, skilled tongue found its way back to my clit and he flicked and licked, until he drove me over the edge.

'Oh, God... Rafferty, Oh God... Yes, yes...please.'

My back arched of its own accord and pushed my pussy further into his face. My body was lost in its own dance and demanded he answered its request. His hands moved instantly, receiving me. He grabbed me forcibly by the hips and held me tighter as I rode out my orgasm on his face, until I was so depleted my body collapsed back into the soft duvet under my back.

For a few minutes, as the heady feelings of satisfaction coursed around me and took over my every sense, I reluctantly shut my eyes and relaxed into the powerless feeling of "petite mort."

The bed shifting as he lay down beside me brought me around, as did the feeling of Raff lightly trailing his fingers all over my sensitive skin. My whole body was on high alert as the aftershocks from the orgasm he had just given me sparked to life under the caress of his fingertips.

His lips pressed to my temple as he whispered in my ear.

'Are you back with me, Loz?'

My power of speech had been temporarily taken away, so I gently nodded my head and lifted my hand up to capture his muscular arm. I didn't want him to stop touching me, but I needed somehow to hold on to him as I rode through the feelings he had unleashed inside my body.

'I need to hold you, Loz. I need to be inside you when you come again.'

My eyes opened wide at his words. As my eyes found him, his face broke out into a huge grin. He was propped up, hand on the side of his face and elbow into the covers at the side of my head. His arm lifted and mine followed as my hand was still holding on tightly. He ran his index finger from my temple and down my jawline.

'There she is. Fucking hell, you're beautiful… I've never witnessed another woman come undone like that before, Lauren.' He dipped his head to chastely kiss my lips. 'When you're ready, I'd like it to happen again all over my dick.'

He winked at me as he teased.

I was lost, caught up in the here and now. I was lost to the feelings he produced inside of me and the overwhelming need to always feel this way. I was lost to him and knew I always had been. For the first time in many years, I felt intact and knew he was the missing piece of me that I had been waiting for.

I smiled back my answer.

As his body moved over mine, his mouth once again took mine captive. My body answered his demands and I was instantly ready for him. His cock entered me and for the second time that evening we became as one, conjoined by our love and need for each other. He rocked himself in and out of me gently at first as his eyes sought mine out. Our need for each other and the release we were galloping towards fed our motions until we were gripping hold of each other and crying out each other's names.

My orgasm hit quickly with no build up, as my body was still recovering from the aftershocks of the first. I could feel my vaginal walls squeezing him tightly, offering him the encouragement he needed to let go. As he came, he reared up, arching his back as his body reacted instantaneously to its sole purpose and forced his cock deeper inside me.

When he was spent, he came back down on top of me, guided by my hold on his shoulders. Our hot, sweat-soaked bodies came crashing back to earth, together. The need to sleep wrapped up together as we were, became all-consuming.

'This is us, Loz. We're always and forever. I love you, my girl,' was the last thing I heard as sleep captured me.

Lauren

The smell of bacon met my nostrils and coming to, I opened my eyes to meet the soft warm glow of the winter's sunrise filling one side of my bedroom from the Velux windows.

Slowly, I turned over onto my back and felt the delicious ache my body had been left with this morning. Smiling to myself I moved my arm from underneath my head and it glided across the empty space in the bed next to me. To my relief, the bed still felt warm to touch. Adding that to the delicious smells now making my mouth salivate and I knew without a doubt that everything had happened just as I remembered.

'Morning.' Raff walked back to the open bedroom doorway, wearing his barely buttoned up jeans and I could have sworn that I could see the unmistakable glint of silver at the top of the opening. I tore my eyes away. He leant on the doorframe and pushed both of his hands into his front pockets, pushing his jeans a little further down. Refusing to look, I stared at his gorgeous face with his bed mussed hair and noticed he was sporting longer, dark stubble.

And boy did it suit him.

I could tell by the grin on his face he could read my every movement and the thoughts in my head.

'How are you this morning?' he asked as he used one hand to remove his hair from in front of his eyes and back up on his head.

'I'm well and you?'

His eyebrows lifted at my question and then he crossed his arms over his chest.

'Yeah, I'm good... but I'm nervous.'

'Nervous?' I questioned.

'What happened between us last night, Loz...'

I tried so hard not to react, but I knew the smile I'd been unable to contain at his arrival in the doorway had just been wiped off my face with that one sentence.

'Don't look like that... It's not what you're thinking. I've realised that being with you in the same bed, making love to you and touching you all night long... Hell, fucking you when the mood came over us... and then holding you in my arms until you fell asleep, is what I want for the rest of my life. I know we haven't even been back together for twenty-four hours, but...'

His voice trailed off as he pushed himself off the doorframe. I grabbed the sheet to cover me as I sat up suddenly, wanting to know exactly where he was going with the conversation. A few steps later and he came to the side of my bed, where he fell to his knees as he grabbed at my loose hand. Stunned, I watched him look down to our conjoined hands as he rubbed his calloused thumb over my knuckles. Then almost at once his eyes were back on me.

'Lauren, I want to marry you. And honestly, I feel we've wasted too much time already.'

I slowly blinked at him, as I stared deep into the grey pools staring back at me as he waited for my response. My stunned mouth opened and closed a few times while I tried to let the words he had spoken sink in.

'I love you, Loz. I always have and always will. I didn't sleep much last night. I was too terrified to. Because I didn't want to miss anything about our first night together in far too long. I already knew how you slept and how you talk in your sleep. By the way, it's nice to know I'm "that good,"' he joked to cut through the tense emotional atmosphere and then carried on as a blush hit my face. 'But, the way you snuggled into me when I wrapped you up in my arms was new to me, when it fucking well shouldn't be.'

'You're asking me to marry you, Raff?' I questioned, making sure I wasn't dreaming. 'You don't have to.'

'Yes, I do. Because it's what I want, it's what I've always wanted.'

'Okay,' I offered back, still too stunned to add anything much to the conversation.

He let a small laugh go. 'Yeah, I know it's a surprise, but this is us. It's not too soon, hell we've loved each other for almost two decades. So, there's no fucking way it's too sudden. The way I see it is, we've wasted too much time already and it makes perfect sense to me, as I want to be with you forever. The question is, is it what you want?' His hand left mine and his index finger came up to my lips as they opened a little to reply.

'Don't answer me right now.' He nodded at me before he leant over to kiss me. 'I need to get the breakfast. Stay right there.'

He stood and jogged his way out into the living area. I grasped all my bedding to my chest, too stunned to know what to think and flung myself back down on my bed. So, I rested there, listening as he whistled a tune to himself and dished up our breakfast. I knew then that equally that was a sound I wanted to listen to every morning. He might not want it yet, but the answer I needed to give him was clear in my mind.

He walked back into the bedroom still whistling and although his eyes refused to quite catch mine, I knew he was analysing my every movement.

I sat up in bed once again and offered him a grin that must have matched the Cheshire cat's. He reached the side of the bed and positioning one knee onto the mattress, he placed the tray down onto my lap. I glanced down and looked at not only the food he'd prepared, but also at all the equipment I needed to test my blood this morning.

'I love that you cooked for me.' I looked up and admired the man who was now leaning over me to place a kiss to my forehead and couldn't resist running one finger over the barbell in his nipple and watching him inhale at the small touch. He quickly caught my wrist and stopped my teasing.

'Careful,' he warned. 'Otherwise you might not get breakfast. And yeah, I want to look after you and I *know* how much energy you expended last night.' I raised my eyebrows at the boyish grin that met my smiling face. 'Sorry it's so early, Loz. But, I have a meeting back at The Manor I need to get to.'

The feeling of disappointment ran through me, but looking at his contrite face I let it go. Monday was the only day my tearoom was closed before Christmas, and aside from having to take in a delivery that I knew was due, I'd hoped to spend every minute with him. Especially after the question he'd just asked.

'I promise I'll be back as soon as I can.' He placed a kiss to the top of my head and moved away.

'Okay,' I offered, barely managing to keep a lid on my disappointment.

I picked up my fork and began to play with the food on my plate. In the corner of my bedroom with his broad back turned towards me he thrust both his arms into his creased white shirt, with its ripped cuffs and began to do up the buttons.

'Do you really want to leave here and not know my answer?' I spoke and cut through the silence in the bedroom that had descended over us.

He spun around suddenly and fixed his mercurial eyes on me and for a second I was too stunned by his beauty to speak again.

'I don't want to force you into anything, Lauren. Just know that I'll wait forever for you, though I'd prefer it was sooner rather than later. You're mine, you've always been mine. I want to let everyone else know it. I want the world to know that at last I'm off the fucking market, because the girl I've loved since I was a boy, loves me enough to want to be my Mrs.'

I fell back onto my pillows and offered him a smile as I rubbed my open hand on the empty side of the bed next to me, consciously offering him the place.

'My answer is yes, a trillion times, YES!' I shouted out as happiness swept over me.

His fingers stopped their movement, leaving his shirt still half undone, and his face broke out into the widest grin I'd ever seen. His hand delved into his back pocket and he pulled out his mobile. With his eyes still focussed on me, he pressed a couple of buttons and then started speaking. As he spoke he took two steps nearer to me, prowling like a hunter does with its prey.

'Cade, I'm running late... Yeah, I know, I'd have your fucking balls for saying the same thing. But this once, I think you can all cut me some slack.'

He stopped speaking to listen.

'Yes.' His eyes narrowed as he looked deeper inside me, and then he spoke again. 'She is that important.'

With that he rang off and dropped his mobile to the floor as he prowled further towards me with a salacious look in his eyes. It was a while before he managed to leave for his meeting.

Lauren

I made it down to the tearoom with literally minutes to spare, unlocked the door, stepped inside, banged my snow covered boots on the matting and closed it behind me. Deliberately, I turned around just in time to see Raff pull out of the small courtyard. I raised up my hand and touched the necklace through the old sweatshirt I was wearing today. I'd purposefully dug it out of the blanket box to wear earlier. Raff hadn't seen it so far, but I was looking forward to later when he would hopefully undress me and find it.

Always and forever. I smiled to myself at that thought and felt my heart swell with happiness.

His tail lights disappeared through the narrow archway breaking me out of my daydreams and the headlights of the small delivery lorry I was expecting appeared.

Reluctantly, I pulled open the main door and undid the bolts at the top and bottom of its partner, making sure by opening both that the gap was wide enough to allow room for his trolley, without it removing chips of paint from the doorframes. I could feel the heat of the tearoom being sucked out into the cold of the morning and mouthed a couple of hot breath rings into the early morning. Offering the delivery driver a small wave, I stepped out further onto the crisp covering of snow and got on with the job in hand.

An hour later, I had put everything away and had done my weekly check of the tearooms. Normally, I would now make my way back upstairs to get back into bed for a while. But I already missed Raff and didn't need the smell of him on my sheets reminding me just how much. So, I walked around the tearoom instead, unnecessarily double checking everything and working up the courage to do what I knew I needed to. With relief, I heard a door close in my flat above me and knew Amy had found her way home. Hopefully we could catch up later, but for now I had other things to deal with.

I pulled out a chair from a small round table and sat down. My stomach churned and I forced myself to count in my head and control my breathing as I prepared to make the call I'd been dreading. I touched the correct buttons on my phone and closed my eyes as I heard it ring on the other end.

'Morning,' he answered.

At the sound of Toby's voice, I placed my phone onto the table and put it on to loud speaker. Doing so meant I could now use both hands to quietly tear up a Christmas napkin, which until one second ago had been carefully folded and placed there waiting for our next guests. As I tore long, straight pieces, I managed to keep a lid on the threatening anxiety that was beginning to bubble up inside me.

'Hi,' I answered. 'Hope you're okay.' I didn't wait for an answer as it wasn't really a question. It was more something I felt I should be saying to the guy I had cheated on several times yesterday. 'I was wondering when you thought you might be home?' I made my voice lift as I tried to keep the conversation light.

Please let it be soon. I had to get the conversation I needed to have with him over as soon as possible, but I refused to be that awful person who did it over the phone.

'Missing me, Lauren?' I could hear the smile in his voice and looking up I caught sight of the grimace on my face in the large French Baroque styled mirror that took up the whole of the chimney breast in the tearoom.

'Oh, you know,' I replied as I swallowed, panic took over and made my hands begin to shake a little. It resulted in one of my tears in the napkin going slightly wrong. My heart accelerated in response and my breathing grew shallow. I took a deep breath and held it, willing myself to calm down.

'Well, you'll be pleased to know that I'm on my way back now. I should be there in approximately two and a half hours.'

My hand screwed up the by now ruined napkin and I watched the knuckles of my hand go white in complete contrast to the red coloured napkin.

'That's great.' Anyone who knew me or paid me any attention at all would have been able to tell by my tone of voice that I didn't think it was great at all, but as usual it went straight over his head. 'Do you think you could come straight here to see me, please?'

I had never slept with anyone other than the person I was in a relationship with and I hated myself for doing it to Toby. He deserved more than that and I needed to tell him as soon as possible that our relationship was over.

'You are missing me… I'll be over as soon as I've popped in to see Mum.'

I shook my head slightly at his answer.

'Okay, see you then.' I touched the red phone icon and disconnected the call.

If being in love with another man wasn't enough of a reason to break off our relationship, there was another one. I had never come first in Toby's life and I knew that I never would, and now I understood that it wasn't enough for me. But, I couldn't lay the blame for the way I felt about Raff at Toby's door. I needed to tell him that although he had mentioned marriage to me a few weeks ago, we weren't meant to be together and that us getting married wasn't going to happen.

I stood up, tidied the mess I'd made at the table and pushed the chair back in. There was no way I could wait upstairs in my flat for Toby to arrive, so I walked over to the centralised log burner in the tearoom and throwing the used napkin inside I lit the already laid fire. A few minutes was all it took for the fire to take hold, then I closed the glass door and stood up. I rubbed my hands together and then held them open to the sudden invasion of warmth breaking the chill of the air around me.

Now, what can I do?

A knock sounding on the closed door of the tearoom brought me to and I turned my head to find a set of silver-grey eyes staring at me through the glass. I blinked and looked at them again quickly realising that it wasn't Raff, but his son Flint. On his back, he had a red-haired little girl and taking a look at her face as she peered up from the protection of his shoulder, I could see she was crying.

I weaved my way quickly around the furniture to open the locked door.

'Come in.' I opened the door wide and using one arm I waved them both inside to the warm. 'What's happened?' I questioned Flint as I reached behind him to rub her gently on the back.

'Hi, Lauren. Can I put Brie down over there?' He tilted his head towards a small two seater settee next to the log burner.

'Yes.' I nodded as I answered him and then I followed behind them.

I watched him twist his body slightly and then bend his knees so he could gently place her down on the settee. Without saying another word to me he rearranged the settee around her. I watched him work, wondering how a fourteen-year-old boy could manage to show so much control and empathy in a situation that involved a young child. Finally, making sure the pillows were comfortable under her head he brushed the hair off her face and then turned back to me.

'Thanks for letting us in. Brie has fallen over and she's cut both her knees through her leggings.'

I nodded at him and looked quickly at the bloodied dirt patches on her knees.

'What happened?'

He replied as I made my way to the counter behind me and grabbed the green first aid box from underneath it.

'We were out walking, when a gun fired in the woods behind The Manor and Biscuit, Brie's dog, took off. We ran after him, but we couldn't find him and then she fell over.'

'Oh, you poor thing, Brie. Well you've both come to the right place,' I empathised with Brie and nodded at Flint, mouthing to him that everything would be okay. I could see how worried he was for her. The concerned expression on his face was like Raff's. I could see how uncomfortable he felt as I watched him push his longer hair out of his face and behind both of his ears. I moved around him and crouched next to the settee. Brie was a pretty little girl and my heart broke for her as I listened to her sob for her dog.

'Hi, Brie. My name is Lauren. I saw you at The Manor yesterday.' I took one of her hands in mine, pulled off the dirty, holed mitten it was enclosed in and held it between my own as I tried to get some warmth into her. Then I did the same with her other hand.

Brie wiped her face on her other sleeve and looked up at me with the most beautiful green eyes I'd ever seen. Slowly, I put two and two together. She was Luke and Cerise's daughter. She had her mum's stunning bone structure and her dad's Irish colouring.

'My doggy, Biscuit. He can't die. He can't,' she sobbed.

'I'm sure he's just exploring. Your dad will find him and while he's looking we need to clean up your knees, don't we?

'My hands hurt too.'

She stopped sniffling and turned both of her open palms towards me to show me two pink looking hands that were scraped and full of pieces of grit.

'We'll start with those then, shall we?' I smiled at her and watched her nod her head and offer me a small smile.

'Have you phoned for help, Flint?' I could feel him behind me.

'I couldn't get a signal and there's nothing wrong with my phone, it must be this sketchy place.' I could almost hear the scowl that I knew without turning around, would most definitely be planted on his handsome face.

Like father, like son. I thought with a smile.

'You can use my phone. It's in the office, which is down that corridor behind me.'

'I'll be back soon, Brie. Lauren's kind, she'll look after you.' Looking at her face I saw her accept his words and got on with what needed doing.

Hearing his footsteps retreat behind me, I started to dab at Brie's hands with antibacterial wipes, doing it as carefully as possible. 'Oh, and, Flint,' I shouted.

'Yes,' he answered.

'The phone, it's on my desk. You have to pick up the receiver and dial the numbers.'

'Dial the numbers?' I heard the question in his voice and turned around to show him.

'Yes, you put your finger in the hole over the digit you need and make the dial go clockwise until your finger hits the bar and then release the dial. It will go back automatically, then you dial the next number you need. You can find the telephone number for The Manor on top of my desk, on a sort of emergency contact list I made for my cousin.'

I'd used my hands to show him in mid-air what was required and watched with amusement as his forehead creased in a "what the fuck" look. Then he was gone and I turned my attention back to the patient in front of me.

A few minutes later, I'd cleaned Brie up and Flint was back behind us.

'Lauren… Luke, Brie's dad, wants to know if we can stay here for a while, if that's okay?'

'Yes, that's fine.' I turned to him, just in time to see him disappear back down the corridor.

'So, what do you say to a nice hot chocolate with marshmallows?' I questioned Brie.

Her green eyes sparkled a little as she momentarily forgot her sadness and she nodded her answer to me.

'Lay there then for a little while and I'll start making it.'

She sat up quickly and flung her arms around my neck and squeezed.

'Thank you, Flinty said you were nice.'

Then her warm arms were gone and with her face only inches away from mine, I could see her fears creeping back into her head.

'I'm sure your daddy, Raff, Cade and Brody will find Biscuit. In fact, I know they will.' In my head, I was praying with everything I had that my words would come true.

'He has to. He can't die… My mom died. Please, Lauren, tell me he won't?'

I saw something flicker through her eyes as she sat there and realised that the beautiful young child that I pulled quickly into my chest to hug, was terrified of losing something else in her life. I'd known Cerise, albeit briefly, seventeen years ago. She was a dancer and had come into Luke's life a few weeks before I'd left Raff's. I had immediately been drawn to the vibrant girl and had cried when I'd read how she'd died, leaving her husband and daughter behind.

'I know they'll find him, Brie.' I said a quick prayer in my head. 'I knew your mummy and she would be so proud of how brave you're being.'

'You knew my mom?' Her green eyes were set alight as she questioned me.

'I did and she was lovely, you look like her you know?'

'Daddy says I'm pretty like her,' she whispered.

'Yes, she was very beautiful.' I stroked my finger along her jawline and then touched the end of her nose briefly with my index finger. 'And so are you.'

'She was a dancer and I dance too,' she offered.

'That's amazing, Brie. When you're all grown up and famous, I'll come and watch you sometime.'

For the first time her smile reached her eyes. 'I'd like that, Lauren. You can tell me if my mom would have liked my dancing.'

I was feeling emotionally fragile already and had to fight back tears at her words.

'All done.' I heard the shout from Flint and was grateful for the interruption, not only for myself but also for the beautiful little girl who was on the settee in front of me. I watched her peer around me and look for Flint.

The two of them may have been years apart in age, but they had a connection. She smiled her welcome to him as he drew closer to us and dropped to his knees to wipe away the semi dried tears that were forming salty tracks down her pale cheeks.

'That's better, shorty.' He smiled down at her. 'Now, you're not to worry, because your dad, Uncle Raff and Uncle Cade have walked out of the meeting they were in. They're out looking for Biscuit with the gamekeepers. I know they'll find him. You know what he's like, he probably ignored us earlier and got into trouble somewhere.'

Brie smiled gratefully up at him. At first I thought she looked up at him like a younger child looked at their older sibling, then I realised she looked at him more like her protector, her hero. The band only had the two children between them and I supposed that would make them close, whatever their ages.

Sniffing, I quickly swallowed down my emotions, got to my feet quickly and moved away, wiping my eyes with the back of my hand. 'Come on then, Flint,' I called over my shoulder. 'I'll need a hand with the hot chocolate making.'

Chapter 24

Lauren

The three of us had eaten our marshmallows without a spoon, after I'd declared a marshmallow bobbing war. Subsequently, Brie had stood up on her chair and the three of us had bobbed our heads down and plunged our faces several times into the oversized teacups. We were a mess at the end, all three of us had managed to cover our mouths and noses in freshly whipped cream and chocolate sprinkles, which we'd added to the top. Christmas music blared out from the radio I'd switched on earlier, as Flint and I had made the chocolate, and laughter filled the tearooms. I was more than happy to spend my time with them both, talking and laughing as we occupied each other, all the while waiting for our problems to hopefully resolve themselves. Snow continued to fall outside and although I had yet to have my conversation with Toby, it felt Christmassy and exciting.

Could I dare hope that this might be my life from here on?

Whenever I felt it was possible, I had looked intently at Flint, trying to work out from the few things he said and did, what made him tick. I was more than ready to be a mum to my own, with any luck. But, when I married Raff I was going to become his step-mum and I only hoped I would make a good job of it.

After finishing up our drinks and laughing at Flint mimicking Cade, we had gone to the kitchen to wash the large teacups. I wanted to keep the atmosphere happy and upbeat, not only for them both but for me too. I'd thought about what we could do while we all continued to wait. Suddenly, as I glanced around the clean, quiet space, an idea came over me.

'I need some helpers, so who's up for helping me bake some shortbread?' I placed my hands on my hips and spun around to face them both. I had asked the question with a smile on my face as I was convinced Flint wouldn't be up for it. I was certain a fourteen-year-old boy would think he had much better things to do with his time, but I also knew how concerned he was for Brie and knew he would do anything to keep her busy while we waited for news.

Imagine my surprise when I watched a broad grin grow until it covered the width of his face.

'What? Do you mean we could bake now?' he asked, as the grey in his eyes sparkled like silver glitter.

'Yes.' I smiled at him as I took down a few clean aprons from the linen shelf and piled them on the work top. 'Are you up for it?'

'Definitely, count me in. Shortbread, that's sort of cookies, isn't it?'

I wanted to answer that it was in fact a Scottish biscuit, but didn't want to catapult Brie into melancholy at me mentioning her dog's name, so I nodded instead.

'Great, then you both need to wash your hands, in the sink over there.' I put the dry teacups onto the china rack and followed them over to wash my own hands. Flint pulled the one and only stool in the kitchen away from the corner and placed it in front of the worktop. Then he lifted Brie up and onto it. Once he'd finished, I passed him a folded in half apron and he placed it on her lap, then looped his over his head with practised ease and tied it up at the back.

'My daddy loves cookies.' Brie clapped her hands together in glee at the thought of making something for Luke. He had lost Cerise, I thought sadly, but he was a lucky man and I hoped he realised it. The gorgeous little girl loved her dad with everything she had. *How lucky are people to have that kind of adoration and unconditional love?* I was happy for them both, but a little bit jealous.

I grabbed all the ingredients we needed and set them in front of the two children. The three of us set to work, chatting as we did so. It seemed easier to chat once we weren't all looking at each other over a table. Like a production line we set to work. I measured the ingredients and used the mixer, Flint rolled out the mixture and Brie cut out the shapes. Before I knew it, we were on our second batch with one already in the oven.

An immense happiness was taking over me as I watched Flint roll out the biscuit mix with ease and the look of absolute pleasure on his face as he did so. The kitchen was somewhere I'd always felt at home, courtesy of my lovely nan and her love of feeding her family.

'So, you like to bake then, Flint?'

I saw him nod in my peripheral vision.

'I like baking, but I love to cook. Whenever I'm allowed I make up my own recipes.'

'You do?' I answered, trying not to sound too surprised as I did so.

'Yes. But I don't get to do it very often,' he answered sadly.

'Oh, why's that?'

He was about to answer when the oven timer sounded for me to pull out the trays of shortbread. I moved quickly, wiping my hands down my apron as I stepped towards the aluminium beast that took up half of one wall in the kitchen. Stopping the timer and feeling fragile from a lack of sleep the night before, I sighed in relief as the noise left the small space. I opened the door to the oven and holding onto it, I rose up a little as the heat poured out into the room, I then grabbed at the oven gloves and placed my hands inside. Finally, I pulled out the first couple of trays and after tilting them slightly, so both the children could see their handiwork, I placed them on the cooling racks nearby. Brie had stopped cutting and squealed with excitement as she saw the many Christmas shapes she had cut, now come to life.

'They're great, guys, brilliant job.'

I offered Brie my palm on the way past them both and we high fived. Then I fist bumped with Flint as he grinned back at me.

Once again, I took my place in the biscuit production line. I poured more flour and I reengaged Flint in conversation.

'So, you were saying you don't get to cook much even though you enjoy it?' I hoped my tone of voice had disguised my nosiness and carried on. 'It's a shame to not be able to do what you enjoy.'

I watched him think over my question.

'What with schoolwork and travelling with the band, there's not that much time.'

'That's understandable,' I offered. 'Does your mum cook?'

The sudden laughter that left his mouth made me smile.

'Does Ashley make shortbread, Brie?' he questioned her. It didn't escape my notice that Brie called all the members of Default Distraction uncle, but Ashley wasn't called aunty.

'No, she's very busy being pretty,' Brie sassily answered from her end of the production line with a laugh. I rolled my lips over my teeth and held in my laughter.

Out of the mouth of babes.

'Well you can come and cook here anytime you like, Flint.'

'And me?' came a high pitched, excited squeal.

217

'Yes, Brie, and you. As long as your daddy says it's okay,' I added.

'Thank you,' she answered as she pushed another star shaped cutter into the rolled out shortbread mixture.

'I'd like that, thanks,' Flint finally answered.

'Can I hear a but?' I questioned and I turned towards him as I sealed the lid on the flour for the last time.

'I'm not sure how long I'll be here and I have to have my lessons with Cade while I'm here.'

'Cade gives you lessons?' I picked up a clean tea towel and wiped my dirty fingers on it as I leant my hip into the worktop.

'Yeah. Apparently, I'm talented on the drums and my family want me to go with it.'

'They do?' I could feel my eyebrows rising high in question as I looked at him.

'Uh huh,' he replied, still looking at me.

'Well that's fantastic... It's great to have a musical talent like that. Is that what you want to do?' I couldn't help myself and I pushed just that little bit more.

'I used to love playing the drums and I'd like to be in a band. So, sure it sounds cool... But, what I'd really like to do, is to be a chef.'

Silently, we looked at each other for a few seconds. I reached out and gently held on to his forearm.

What the hell was Raff playing at? If anyone knew what it was like to have the expectations of their family on them, it was him. I couldn't understand what he was doing, expecting his child to be something he didn't want to be. That certainly wasn't the Raff I used to know or thought I knew.

'You know where I am. You're always welcome to come and cook or bake with me, anytime you want. Okay?' I questioned to make sure he understood me and watched him smile and nod.

A bang on the tearoom door sounded, breaking our connection and my hand fell away.

'Okay, I'm going to answer that, no one touch the oven while I'm gone, please.'

Brie had left the tearooms, after a very intense and descriptive talk about how she would like the shortbread decorated, with a dirty looking Luke holding a filthy, shivering Biscuit in his arms. She'd left happily enough after she managed to get him to agree to bring her back soon.

The relief I'd felt as I'd answered the door to him standing on the doormat, was huge. The short time she'd been with me Brie had cut a little path to my heart and I wouldn't have been able to bear seeing the little girl lose something else. Luke had given me a hug when he'd arrived and told me how pleased he was to see me again after all these years. He looked different from our time in Vegas, worn down and most definitely sadder. I realised losing Cerise had taken its toll on him more than he probably cared to admit. He'd given his thanks to me for occupying Brie and for taking care of her.

All the time Luke had stayed talking, Flint had stood behind me and I could feel his reluctance to go. So, I'd agreed with Brie about the decorating and then swung around to tell Flint that I would need his help carrying out her wishes. Offering Flint the invitation had also given him an excuse to stay a little while longer.

Half an hour later, with our work done and boxed up for Brie to give to Luke, we were back out in the tearoom. With a cup of tea in my hands, I watched as he went through another large hot chocolate and a couple of what were supposed to be bauble shaped biscuits that hadn't quite come up to scratch. We'd felt after a cheerful discussion that he should eat them and get rid of the ugly evidence that they'd even existed.

'You're very good with Brie, Flint,' I offered as I blew a long wisp of steam away from the top of my Christmas decorated teacup.

He nodded at me and grinned.

'She's young, but I enjoy her company. She knows what it's like being us. With everyone else I have to explain it.' I knew he even meant me, when he smiled across the table. At the same time, he pushed a few odd crumbs that had decorated the edges of his lips into his awaiting mouth.

'I can see the two of you have a connection.' I smiled back and took a sip of the warm liquid I held in both hands.

'I would have liked to have been a big brother, but it's too late now.'

I tilted my head a little to the side and feeling my forehead furrow a little, I answered him. 'Well, never say never.' My heart jumped in response as happiness rushed around me. I was remembering Raff's proposal this morning and couldn't believe my luck at having had the chance to then spend some time alone with Flint to get to know him a little. He was amazing and I was desperate for the chance to maybe have another little boy who looked just like his dad.

He took another sip of chocolate and shook his head at me.

'No, it won't happen now.' I looked at the pain held inside him as it reflected in his eyes. I took a deep breath and tried to answer him as nonchalantly as possible.

'I know it must be hard for you, but your mum and dad might meet someone else, they could have more children and you could be the big brother you'd like to be. It's absolutely possible that you all could be happy again.' I gave him a small smile that I hoped he would take as reassurance.

'Mom is with already with someone else, Travis Somners from The Noise.' He stared at me a little harder to see if I understood what he was talking about. My eyes opened wider and I shook my head back at him. 'He's the lead singer with them, they used to go on tour with DD, but they're big in the U.S. in their own right now.' I continued shaking my head and opened my palms to him. 'Anyway, she can't have any more children.' He shrugged as he spoke to me.

'Oh, I'm sorry to hear that.' And as much as I hated her, I was a bit sorry for her under the circumstances. 'But she's got you and from what I've seen today, she must be so very proud of you. I know I would be if you were mine.'

'Thanks, I think she is… most of the time. And my dad probably won't have any more kids because he doesn't stay with anyone long enough.' I felt my eyes widen as I watched him sip at his hot chocolate, then his eyes were back on mine and I tried to blink the dryness away. 'It was sad when Mom lost the last baby early this year, especially as the doctors say she can't have any more.' He placed his mug down with a bang and took a deep breath. I could see by his body language that he was remembering something sad. 'That's why Dad finally left her, when the doctors said she couldn't have any more children. She's lost a few since they had me, he was alright after the first two, but the last couple…'

It took everything I had not to spit out the mouthful of tea that I was attempting to swallow. My head was spinning around. I was truly sorry for the boy who suddenly seemed younger than his fourteen years, sitting across the table from me. I could feel his sadness falling off him in waves and my heart physically hurt for him. I pushed my hand over the table and took his hand in mine to offer him some comfort. But, as I did so, I was trying desperately hard to run over every word Raff had spoken to me in the last twenty-four hours.

I knew they had only recently divorced, but I'd been under the illusion that they had gone their separate ways years ago. I was trying to work it all out, but truthfully, I was coming up with nothing.

'But, I'm sure that can't be quite right, Flint. Marriages are complicated things, especially to those watching from the outside.'

'It is…' I watched him shrug his shoulders. 'I heard him say so, back in Vegas. He told her in the hospital that he was sick of being by her bedside as she lost yet another baby and that he wasn't going to do it anymore. He left her room quickly, turned down the corridor and didn't turn to see me sitting waiting outside. Then they got divorced.'

'Oh, my God, Flint. I'm so sorry you heard that.' And I truly was, but I was also sorry for myself.

Alarm bells started ringing in my head. My heart started to bang in my chest in panic. I went over the conversation that we'd had yesterday. He'd assured me that he'd only walked out on me in Vegas because he couldn't afford my medical care.

But he had more than enough money now.

Had he left Ashley because she wasn't strong enough to carry another child, and he couldn't cope with it? What sort of man leaves their wife because she can't give him any more children? This wasn't the Tudor times. Then there was me, I was always going to have an illness, it would never go away. How long would it be before he possibly grew tired of dealing with my diabetes?

I felt sick to my stomach. I felt myself sag even further into the comfortable seat I was in. All the earlier euphoria that Raff had left me with was gone. I recognised the feeling, my body had started to crash. Having listened to Flint and taking in what he had to say, I now felt like I'd been dropped from a great height. I needed to test my blood, but right now, it was the last thing on my mind.

Lifting another Christmas napkin up off the table, I blew my nose to disguise what I needed the cloth for, and as I blew my nose I dabbed at the moisture gathering in my eyes.

Suddenly, all my new found confidence in Raff and our supposed everlasting love left me. Nagging doubt started to replace the earlier warm fuzzy feeling he had left me with. With one hand holding my teacup, my other went instinctively back to my throat and the necklace I could feel nestled under my clothes. I hoped it would give me the strength I needed to believe in Raff one hundred per cent, but it didn't. Doubt flooded my mind until I felt like I was drowning in it.

For a few minutes, Flint and I sipped at our hot drinks in silence. I had nothing else to offer the conversation and it appeared that neither did he. The scraping of his chair legs on the tiled floor brought me out of my thoughts. I watched as he stood up.

'Thanks for this morning, Lauren.' I looked up at the wall clock and realised I had about ten minutes left until Toby was due. I let out a quiet sigh at the thought. 'I'll go now as your friend is going to be here soon, isn't he?' My eyes found Flint again, he had obviously taken in what I'd said earlier about waiting for a friend to visit.

'Oh, Toby, yes… And it was nothing, Flint. I enjoyed your company, in fact you and Brie have brightened up my morning.' It was true, they had been a very welcome interruption, between the two men who both swore they loved me, but in different ways, I now knew they were equally wrong for me.

He smiled a small smile back at me as he made his way to the coat stand and lifted down his camouflage jacket from the hook. He pulled a black woollen hat down low on his head and moved the longer strands of hair from his view. He smiled as he grabbed the loop of Tartan ribbon we'd tied around the white box that contained the biscuits he was going to take back to Brie.

'Bye then.' He pulled open the tearoom door and offered me another small smile and a wave.

'Remember what I said, Flint. You're welcome here anytime.'

I watched as his face lost the pained expression reliving his memories had given him and once again he smiled broadly at me. 'I will, thanks.'

With that he was gone and so was the earlier feeling of immense happiness he and Brie had brought with them into my suddenly very lonely tearooms.

Chapter 25

Raff

I'd run my hand over my head and held it there for a moment, squeezing my fingers into my scalp as I tried to force my hair and my head back to where they should be. The meeting that had been postponed from earlier due to Biscuit doing a fucking runner, was finally happening. The business report was a long list of numbers that I'd long ago lost track of. I made up my mind then and there that I wouldn't be wasting my time on another meeting like this. We paid the lawyers and accountants a hefty sum of fucking money to keep track of our affairs and I, for one, wasn't prepared to pay them a few thousand more to read out the list of pluses and minuses ever again. Only Cade and I were there to listen. Brody hadn't turned up in the first fucking place. We'd made a guess as to where he still was, as he hadn't even got the decency to send one of us a quick text, and Luke had now gone to pick up his daughter Brielle from Lauren's. I wished I had a good enough excuse to leave Cade to it. Cade was after all our numbers man. As the brightest son of a Mafia family, and having been expected to take the bar exam in order that he could be their next consigliere, he was the most equipped one of us all when it came to understanding shit like this. I looked at my phone, to check the time. It had been the longest fucking morning ever and there was still about an hour and a half left. I was once again sitting at the large mahogany desk in the hotel's meeting room. I knew I was irritating the hell out of the accountant as I tapped my pencil up and down on the papers in front of me. I hoped it would in turn make him hurry the fuck up so we could get out of here.

As he flipped over to yet another fucking screen, I sighed out loud and leant back into my chair. I placed my hands behind my head, unable to focus on the whiteboard any longer, and looked down the length of my legs. I watched all the shit from running around the woods looking for Biscuit fall off my boots as I crossed my feet at the ankles and swore under my breath at the mess.

Everything was a distraction.

All I wanted to do was to race back to Lauren, take her in my arms and to lock us away from the world. Happiness that we had found each other once again was flying around my body and it was hard to concentrate on anything else.

As I rolled the heel of my boot over the clumps of dirt gathered around them, my mind wandered back to Vegas and the last time she'd been in my arms.

"What am I going to do?"

I pushed my hair out of my eyes before I looked back down at Lauren who was lying on the mattress we shared together. Then I lifted my head and looked around the room, every single face looked back at me with concern.

"She needs a doctor," Luke answered, saying the words that we all knew were true.

"I know what she fucking needs, but how the fuck do I pay for that?" I could hear the anger in my voice as I spoke. I knew I had to rein it in, but I was scared, more scared than I could ever remember.

I bent my knees and fell down on the floor next to her, taking her hand in mine and rubbing my thumb over her knuckles. She never even stirred.

"If I had the money, I'd give it to you, but I haven't, none of us have," Luke once again pitched in.

"I know."

"Raff you need to phone home and ask for help. She's really ill. And it's not a cold or a virus, like we first thought." I heard Cerise's soft voice as she too, raised her concerns.

"I'm not proud, if she needs help, I'll phone him and ask. I'll do anything to get what she needs."

"Right, let's get the car dude. I've checked, Federal law states that the ER have to treat and stabilise anyone who turns up on their doorstep, whether they have the ability to pay or not." I heard Cade's instructions to Luke and then Luke's sudden movement as he grabbed the car keys from the one hook we had by the door. The door slammed shut behind him as I put my lips down onto her forehead.

"You don't need to phone him, I'll contact my family once she's there and ask for help." Cade spoke again.

We hadn't been friends long, but in the few months we'd been playing together, some of our pasts had been shared over a beer. They knew how I'd walked away from my family and how Lauren had followed me. Equally, I knew what they'd left behind.

"Like fuck you will," I forced out. "I appreciate it, Cade, but you've only just got them to agree to butt out of your life. If you start owing them for something..." I let my words hang and twisted my head to look at him. He knew exactly what I meant. "No, she's mine, she's my responsibility. I'll phone home as soon as they take her in."

Wrapping the one decent looking blanket we had on our bed, around her, I swung her up into my arms and moved towards the door.

"Rafferty?" she whispered to me in question.

"We're going to the hospital, Lauren. You're not well. Don't worry, I've got you."

I walked through the open door and as carefully as I could with her in my arms I went down the wet metal stairs. My right foot slipped and the adrenalin released inside me made me hold on to her even tighter. I knew how fucking dangerous the steps were after it had rained. None of us that lived here in the depths of rental hell would dream of rocking the boat to demand basic health and safety was adhered to. That sort of thing got you thrown out by the locally employed heavies. The slippery metal under my boots felt like the rest of our existence here, fucking precarious. Things had started to change in the last couple of weeks, we'd had more call backs to local bars, all due to our new lead singer, Brody. Songs we'd been playing for a while got far more fucking attention when sung by him and I knew we were moving in the right direction. But it wasn't going to come quick enough for me to help her. I had to face the fact that we were still fighting to be heard and playing every gig we could lay our hands on, and I wouldn't subject our uncertain life on Lauren if she was ill.

Finally, I reached the ground. I passed Lauren to Cade and jumped into the back seat of the car. As soon as I was in, he passed her down to me.

She was as light as a feather and it made the whole manoeuvre easier than it should have been. She was slim normally, but over the last few days the weight had fallen off her. She was thirsty all the time and too physically tired to even get to the bathroom. I'd spent the last twenty-four hours giving her water and carrying her to the bathroom to pee.

For a couple of days, we'd thought she'd just caught a virus. But she hadn't gotten any better and even with a very limited medical knowledge between us, we knew it was far more serious. She was getting worse, not better.

Holding her tight in my arms, I looked down at the girl that had given up everything to be with me. The claws of fear had opened and attached themselves to my flesh. I couldn't lose her, I couldn't exist without her.

Please let her be okay. I'll give anything for you to make sure she's okay.

I didn't have a religion and I didn't believe in any God, but at that moment I let my silent prayer lift up to whoever might be listening and wiped away the one tear that had rolled down and off my face and onto the unusually pale skin of her cheek.

All these years later and I could still taste the overwhelming pungent smell of my own fear in the air around me. My stomach rolled around in protest at the sick feeling inside me and my arms ached to hold her encased within them. I needed to breathe her in and for some reason, even though I left her happy and sated only this morning, I needed to check she was okay.

A feeling of déjà vu washed over me and I knew that whatever it took I was leaving this waste of time meeting, as soon as fucking possible.

I lifted my focus from my boots and over the table to the overpaid suit who was still fucking rambling.

'Look I'm sorry… Mr…' I started to rudely click my thumb and index finger together, snapping them loudly to attract his attention as I was unable to remember the boring bastard's name. I knew it wasn't his fault that I wanted out of here, but I was prepared to cause all sorts of trouble to get my own way, even making him think I was a complete arsehole.

'It's Anthony McFarland.' I felt Cade kick my boots with one of his own as he shouted at me.

'Apologies, Anthony. Mr. McFarland.' My English upbringing got the better of me for a few seconds and then I was back to getting what I wanted. 'I know we had to run off earlier due to a family emergency, but how much fucking longer is this meeting going to take?'

I looked over at him as he tried to calculate what I'd asked.

'Just fucking go. I've got this,' Cade offered.

'You sure?' I asked the question, but was already standing up and getting ready to leave.

'Yeah, fuck off, you're useless here today anyway.' He grinned up at me. 'I'm pleased for you man, fucking pleased. Go get her, you've waited long enough.'

I grabbed at his head on the way past and placed a loud smacker on the top in thanks and then ruffled his hair.

'Just fuck off,' he shouted as my hand found the brass door knob and I pulled it open hastily in a bid to escape.

Closing the door behind me, for a split second I stood and contemplated. I needed a shower and a change of clothes, but what I knew I needed more was to get back to her. I checked my pocket and pulled out my car keys.

I came down the main stairs at The Manor in time to see Flint coming in the smaller door to the left carrying a small white box. He looked happy and that was rare these days. I slowed my pace down to almost standing, so I could watch him a bit longer as he walked further into the reception area.

Finally, he looked up and finding me on the first flight of stairs, his smile fell away.

I wasn't sure what I'd done, even though I'd asked him several fucking times in the last few months, but his reaction to my presence gutted me every time.

'Hey, Flint. What's in the box?' I could see it was tied up with Christmas themed ribbon and could have made a guess, as I knew he'd been with Lauren for most of the morning. But, it was getting hard to engage him in any conversation at all, so I asked the question anyway.

I watched as he lifted the box up higher and let it swing a little on his finger. 'We baked shortbread while we waited.'

'That was good of Lauren.'

'Yeah, I like her. She said I can go back anytime and help her in the kitchen.' He smiled as he remembered his time there.

'I like her too,' I answered, feeling pleased they'd spent some quality time together. 'And that's good, I know how much you enjoy cooking.' I cleared my throat and spoke again. 'She's an old friend of mine, she means a lot to me.'

He stared at me for a few seconds and his eyes narrowed. 'I need to go and find Brie, she made these for Luke.'

'I'm off out for a while. See you later.'

231

'Yeah?... Just to let you know, Lauren has a visitor. Someone named Toby.'

Lauren

As soon as the door banged shut behind Flint, I stood and began to tidy the table we'd been sitting at. I put the cups, plate and dirty napkins onto the tray I'd carried them out on, and with my hands I swept up the few crumbs from the table. The china chinked together as my hands shook with nerves as I walked back to the kitchen, looking once again at the weighted clock on the wall as I passed.

Five minutes and Toby would be here. Passionate he wasn't but punctual he most definitely was.

My phone vibrated in the back pocket of my jeans and I pulled it out to check the message. I felt sick as I read the incoming message from Raff, and realised he must have programmed his number in earlier today.

Fuck the meeting. I'm on my way back, because, Loz, I can't stay away from you.

'Oh no,' I whispered into the empty space around me. As much as I wanted him with me, I needed to speak to Toby by myself.

I replied quickly watching my fingers shake a little as I typed.

I'm expecting Toby.

The three dots started to pulse and I knew he was replying.

I know. Flint told me. I'll stay in the car until he drives away.

When I didn't reply, the dots started to jump again.

I know you're nervous. I can feel it. Do you want me in there with you?

No, I don't. Please no he can't!

My hand that was holding my phone began to shake too and I hurriedly replied.

No, I don't.

Okay. Just remember it's the only thing standing between us. Tell him. Otherwise I will, I don't want to spend any more time apart. And remember, I love you.

I flicked the switch on my phone to silent and placed it back in my pocket. An overwhelming sense to lock up the tearooms and to run upstairs to the flat came over me. I swallowed, took a deep breath and forced it back down.

I'd called Toby over earlier to break up with him and to tell him that I was now with another man. I didn't want to hurt him, but I'd sworn in my head that I was going to tell him the truth. I knew he'd be angry and he had every right to be, but he deserved the truth and then hopefully once he'd gone away to lick his wounds he would be able to move on. I was now convinced that however much affection we held for each other, we weren't in love. Two weeks ago, our strange relationship had been enough, almost a consolation prize for those like me, who had already loved and lost.

But the past twenty-four hours had shown me that it wasn't.

It wasn't even nearly enough.

I placed the tray down on the side in the kitchen and bent to place the dirty cups into the dishwasher. Dropping the required tablet into the machine, I turned the dial and listened to the whoosh of water as it switched on. Holding on to the side of the worktop with both hands I tried to compose myself. Earlier this morning, I had gone over the words in my head as I practised what I was going to say him.

Now, after Flint's revelation about Rafferty, nothing I was going to say to him seemed to make any sense at all.

'Lauren, I'm here.'

Toby's voice called out to me and I closed my eyes as I let out a long exhale. I gripped the side even tighter, wishing I could sink my nails deep into the solid surface. I braced myself as I let his voice wash over me and comprehended, not for the first time, that the tone of voice he'd used was the same one he always used to announce he was about to orgasm. A shudder rippled down my back as I was reminded of just how punctual the man really was.

Whatever decision I made about Rafferty, I knew that I didn't want to be with Toby either. Resolutely, I took off my apron and threw it onto the side. I turned, walked back out of the doorway and down the narrow corridor.

As soon as he heard the squeak of my Converse on the tiled floor he turned away from warming his hands over the log burner and offered me a smile. When I didn't reciprocate it, I saw his smile fade.

'Should I be worried, Lauren?' he immediately questioned.

Acting braver than I felt, I continued to walk nearer to him and offered him a small nod.

'I need to talk to you, Toby. Can you take a seat?' I pulled out the same seat I'd been sitting on earlier, when I'd spent time talking to Flint, and gesticulated to the one that was opposite mine for him to sit down on.

'No thanks,' he replied with a defensive tone already in his voice. 'I think I'd prefer to stand.'

Placing my forearms on the table I allowed my hands to clasp together and although they gripped each other tightly, I made them sit still on the table top. I knew Toby, if he saw any chink in my armour he would try everything to talk me around to his point of view.

Once I was convinced I was giving out the exact body language I needed to start the conversation, I looked up at him and began.

'Toby, something has happened while you've been away. It's… well it's sort of put things into perspective for me.'

I watched as his eyes narrowed and he crossed his arms over his chest. But he never uttered a sound, only nodded at me for me to carry on.

'I've realised that I can't ask you to continue in this relationship with me under false pretences.'

My eyes that had momentarily wandered, came back to his as he still didn't say anything. Although I'd been clasping my hands tightly together, my thumbs now began to move of their own accord and rubbed at each other in agitation. I watched his eyes take in the small movement and willed myself to stop.

'What false pretences, Lauren?'

'I'm sorry, I know we discussed the possibility of getting married only a few weeks ago.' I knew I was grasping at straws now as I continued speaking. 'Maybe that's what made me think, panicked me almost. But, I now know that I can't marry you.' A huge sigh followed the words out of my mouth on a rush.

'Why?' I had never known Toby to be a man of such few words.

I took another deep breath, I needed to find the words that would convince him of what I was saying, but also ones that would hurt him the least. But, right at this minute I was struggling to find ones that would do both.

'Because I don't love you like I should.'

'I don't understand. What's happened while I've been away to make you come to that conclusion?'

My eyes opened wider in exasperation, unclasping my hands I opened them up to him. 'I should love you with an all-consuming passion, but I don't. I like you... but it's not enough. You can't start a marriage on like.' His eyes opened in question at me and I knew he still wasn't taking in what I wanted him to. '*I* cannot start a marriage, knowing that I don't love you like I should. It's not *enough* for me and it really shouldn't be enough for you!'

I could see from his body language that my revelations had knocked his confidence. His shoulders had slumped further forward, making him seem slightly shorter than he really was.

'But it is. It's more than enough for me. You're an attractive woman. We have a meeting of minds. We run two small, but growing businesses in the same area. We're good together in and out of bed. I don't want or need anything more.'

I rolled both of my lips over my teeth and inhaled deeply. I couldn't help myself but I physically flinched as the last words came out of his mouth, and without even saying the words I knew that he knew.

'Do you have something else to tell me?'

I nodded and answered. 'I'm sorry, Toby... but while you've been away I've...'

'You've what, Lauren?' I knew he already knew by the way he questioned me.

'I slept with someone else.' I refused to use the phrase, cheated. Because in my heart I knew it wasn't true. I hadn't been cheating on anyone when I slept with Raff, because we were always meant to be.

I forced the words out and watched as they filtered through to him. Then I looked down as I waited for the shit to fly. I knew I had to let him have his say about what I had owned up to, it was only fair. We weren't young, stupid or even naive and I could use none of these things in my defence. So, I sat waiting for him to shout, accuse and hate me.

But nothing came.

I lifted my eyes back up to him, to watch his thin lips twist slightly.

'Say something,' I implored, waving my arms up in the air.

'What you've done is given in to lust. Lust is not a deal breaker for me.'

The scrape of the chair legs on the tiles screamed their protest as I stood up quickly and pushed myself away from the table. 'It's not a "deal breaker?"' I no longer recognised my own voice, it had gone up several notes and was now shrill, as I reflected my resentment in my tone. 'Well it is for me, Toby. And what you're saying is only proving to me, that we are not meant to be together. I mean what sort of man is happy and okay about sharing his woman with another man?'

I watched him laugh a little at all the questions I'd bombarded him with, and then he shrugged his shoulders. Then it dawned on me just what a stupid fool I was.

'You've already slept with someone else, haven't you?"

He didn't reply, but he didn't need to. It took everything I had not to move around to the other side of the table and to punch him.

Throwing my hands up into the air, I responded to his lack of response. 'I can't believe this. This is shit. Am I that stupid that you thought I'd never find out?'

'I thought you knew how our relationship was? You've never been bothered about me spending time away in the company of other women.'

'WHAT?... So, let me get this straight in my head. I'm confessing to you that I've slept with someone else and you thought we had an open relationship already?'

'That's right.'

I literally hated the bastard and the stupid smile that was now covering his entire face.

'I can't believe I didn't see this! This isn't the sort of relationship I want, or have ever wanted. So, how many women have you slept with while we've been "together?"' I air quoted the word either side of my head as I tried to understand just what a fool I'd been, once again. 'Have you always been careful with these sluts or do I now need to get myself tested for something?'

'No, I'm always safe and I can't believe you didn't realise before, we're in our thirties, we're not kids and we never discussed being monogamous, did we? Did you use a condom?'

I looked around the cosy, Christmas card setting of The Fairy Garden. I couldn't believe the ugly conversation I was having under the sprigs of mistletoe and twinkling fairy lights. My back pocket vibrated and I knew it was Raff, reminding me what I had to do, reminding me about him. For a brief moment, my head went back to yesterday, to when Raff was inside me and my heart remembered how good it had felt to be connected with him once again. 'That's not something I need to answer, as you'll never be anywhere near me again. I can't believe how far apart you and I actually are in our expectations of a relationship. Everything that is coming out of your mouth is only going to prove to me that we had no business even being together in the first place.'

I was shaking my head at him as he began to laugh at me.

Suddenly, my feet were moving, my hand raised and I slapped him as hard as I could around the face. His head turned with the weight of the blow and then came back to focus on me. The sound of my hand connecting with his cheek seemed to make the glass panes rattle in the door behind me. I grabbed my burning hand with my other one and squeezed as I willed away the pain.

'Okay, I deserved that,' he offered.

'You don't say!'

'So, what happens now then, Lauren. Do you expect the guy you had sex with to ride in here on his white charger and to sweep you off your feet? Are you breaking up with me to move on with him?'

I had been, but I couldn't tell him that. I also couldn't say that for a very short while I had been caught up in the wonderful future Raff and I were going to have now we were back together. Now the world had finally tilted on its axis and righted our situation. Flint's words had brought me back to reality with such an impact, I was surprised I wasn't locked upstairs struggling to breathe and crying my heart out.

'Not that it's got anything to do with you, but no, I'm not that bloody stupid. I may believe in happy endings. But, I no longer believe in them for me.' I could hardly believe how calm and resolute I was being as I spoke the words to him. Only this morning I had been so happy and idealistic. Hearing what Flint had to say about his dad, had then set me onto a different path. I would always love Raff, or maybe that was, I would always love what we could have been. But I now knew it was only an unrealistic dream. Perhaps if I'd never got sick in the first place, things would have been so different.

For a few seconds, we looked at each other. Toby was trying to take in what I wanted to say.

'We could make this work. A bit like a business arrangement.'

I crossed my arms over my chest and looked at him. 'A fucking business arrangement?' The exasperation in my voice made the words I spoke louder.

'Yes, you know,' he carried on.

'I don't and I'm not sure I even want to listen to what you have to say.' I was now shaking my head at him.

'A lot of marriages are arranged by families. We'd just arrange our own. I could be monogamous for you and I know you want children.'

'You have got to be joking?' I could still feel my head shaking a little from side to side as I looked at him. 'I know I'm not stunning like some women. But, never in all my wildest dreams did I ever think someone would propose a business arrangement to me, instead of marriage.' I was frowning at him. I was having the weirdest conversation of my life with a man I had only this morning set out to break up with. With a man, I now wasn't sure I even liked.

My insides felt like they were on fire. But, the feeling of anger inside me had its bonuses. All worries of keeping my anxiety in check were forgotten.

I was angry at Raff for showing me a tiny snippet of how we could have been together. He had spent one night in my bed and I knew I'd never be the same again. I now knew that the memories I had of him from when we were teenagers, when our love had been young, innocent and all-consuming, was nothing to what we could be together as adults. I knew my life would never be the same again. Truth be told, I'd had always compared every relationship I'd had since him, with him. But, in the back of my head I'd been able to argue that I was looking back with rose-tinted glasses. Now it was even worse, he had shown me what we could have been like for the rest of our lives. Hurt that it was all a lie that he had fed me, fuelled my anger to the point of combustion. Because he *had* served me up a lie and I couldn't accept what he wanted. I couldn't accept marriage to him, because I'd always be looking over my shoulder waiting for him to go. I knew that nothing was ever guaranteed, but with him I couldn't accept knowing when we started out, that it wouldn't stand a chance of lasting forever. I wouldn't survive him leaving me again.

So, I needed to leave him first.

Hearing a sudden noise outside in the otherwise empty courtyard made my head turn. I could hear the crunch of the snow under the wheels of a vehicle and as that vehicle slowly came closer to the doorway, I could now see what I already knew. It was Raff's car.

I knew my time had run out. I'd obviously taken too long and he had given up waiting for me.

'Fuck no.' I knew that Toby had followed my gaze out of the arched windows and into the courtyard. 'It was him. It had to be him, didn't it?' Toby spoke again. I didn't answer the question because I knew he already knew the answer.

In the couple of minutes it took for Raff to park, get out of the car and arrive on the doorstep of the tearoom, I thought over what a crazy, ridiculous mess my life had become. My future as I saw it, seemed to have three paths and I had this ridiculously tiny amount of time to choose one of them.

I could be by myself, which I knew Raff would never accept.

I could have an arrangement sort of marriage with Toby and hopefully children.

Or I could marry the only man I'd ever loved and have everything I'd ever dreamt about, until I became ill enough that he would walk away, like history had proven twice before.

I knew all three of my options would hurt me at some point, but I knew without a doubt which one would break me in two.

I had to avoid it all costs.

I had to avoid Raff at all costs.

To compose myself for what I needed to do next, I made myself look away from the man I would love forever.

The sound of the deep timbre of Raff's voice hit me as he swung open the door, along with a blast of freezing air.

'Lauren... and you must be Toby.' He spoke my name questioningly and I could already imagine the look on his face as he spoke.

I shivered slightly.

I turned to look at him and braced myself for my body's reaction to his presence. I tried hard to keep myself in check, but it wasn't easy. The man could fill a room with his quiet commanding authority.

Don't react to him. Just don't.

I heard Toby fidgeting behind me and could imagine him standing himself up to his full height and pulling in his slight paunch as he took in the same sight I was. Raff was making his way further into the tearoom only wearing dirty jeans, filthy boots and a thick, green cable jumper. His hair was damp from the once again lightly falling snow outside, and falling down messily in front of what I knew would be questioning, mercurial grey, swirling eyes. Against Toby's always immaculately put together appearance and his designer labelled clothes he should have come of worst, but I knew that we both knew he didn't.

'It had to be you.' I heard Toby's accusation and closed my eyes briefly to the situation that I knew was about to unfold itself.

'It's always been me,' Raff replied. 'Lauren is mine. She's always been mine. You had your chance and like a complete fucking prat, you didn't take it. Take it from me, it's always going to be me.'

'You're not welcome here, I think you should leave,' Toby vindictively spat out. Raff lifted one finger to his lips effectively signalling that Toby should shut up. My heartbeat accelerated at the intense atmosphere in the room. I could sense the testosterone and the subsequent pissing contest between them.

Rafferty lifted his arm up to me, as he continued to stare at Toby. I knew what he wanted, what he was expecting. Ninety-nine per cent of my body wanted to comply to his unspoken request. But, I made my feet stay still and I saw him raise one eyebrow at me and then twist his head in question. He lowered his arm when I still didn't move towards him. I wanted so much to feel his arm around me and to stand in solidarity against Toby, but after what Flint had told me this morning, I couldn't. It seemed that I would never understand men and as much as I dreamed of love and having a happy ever after, it wasn't written in the stars for me.

'What's going on, Loz?' Raff questioned me after taking in my reaction.

Movement came from behind me as Toby took in my response to Raff and he realised he now had his moment.

'She's about to agree to marry me aren't you, Lauren?'

Toby fell to one knee and offered me up a small square box. I didn't say another word but opened the box and without even looking at the ring inside, I placed it wordlessly onto my own finger, signalling the start of our arrangement.

Raff

Completely motionless I watched as Lauren slid his ring onto her finger. Confusion and anger seeped into every cell of my body and my eyes narrowed as I took in the sight of them both. He was on one fucking knee and they were both positioned in front of an open fire. I flicked my eyes up quickly and just as I knew it would be there, I saw the mistletoe hanging above them.

Had she played me?

Quickly, my brain thought back to the last few days and especially to yesterday and last night. There was no way she could fake how we'd been together. I'd spent enough years with Ashley to know exactly how fake felt.

My heart beat faster and adrenalin flooded my system. Several times I felt myself blink, obviously thinking I could clear the picture I was watching, from my sight. But nothing worked. Thankfully he wasn't touching any part of the woman that was mine, otherwise I knew I wouldn't be standing still.

So, like the man my step-father had always wanted me to grow up to be, I held in the cry of pain my body so desperately wanted to release and swallowed it down deep, to sink with all the other heartache I'd forced down inside me.

'What the fuck is going on, Lauren?' My throat sounded hoarse with the emotion trapped inside it.

When she didn't reply, I moved nearer to where they both stood, wanting her to remember I was still in the room. But I refused to look at his ring of ownership on her finger.

I was too fucking angry.

I was convinced it meant nothing.

So, what the fuck was she playing at?

When she still refused to look in my direction and I saw the faint glimmer of a grin on his lips, I was suddenly aware that I was no longer standing still.

It wasn't until I'd got his perfectly placed blue shirt and his dogs-tooth check suit jacket in both of my fists, I knew I'd now got hold of him. I was walking forward quickly with increasingly longer strides and his feet were stuttering around underneath him as he attempted to keep himself going backwards and upright against my sudden attack. With my face no more than a couple of inches from his face, I watched his expression change from grinning to shock and then from shock to terror. His hands came up to mine to try to tear them away from his clothing, but my grip was stronger, fuelled by my anger.

I kept moving forward, forcing the bastard to keep up with my momentum. His face changed colour, turning puce as his blood pressure rose in his panic.

I heard chairs and tables scrape across the floor in our wake and then bang onto the tiles as they were sent flying in all directions. Metal joined in the cacophony of noise as the already laid place settings were disturbed and sent clattering to the floor.

I heard Lauren shout out my name, trying to get me to let her fiancé go.

Her voice should have brought me to, it should have damped down the fire in my blood, but instead all I could picture was her putting his fucking ring on her finger where mine was meant to fucking be and the only coherent thoughts that travelled around my body were of absolute fury.

Finally, we came to a halt as his arse met an old walnut sideboard next to a decorative fireplace. I put more strength into my hold and pushed him backwards knowing how uncomfortable the position would make him as his spine curve the wrong way. I didn't stop pushing until the back of his head smacked onto the bare brick wall. A small sense of satisfaction crept through me as I watched him recoil in pain.

'RAFFERTY, ENOUGH. PLEASE... Please stop.' Finally, Lauren shouting my name crept through to me. Then I heard the emotion in the words she used as she pleaded with me to let him go.

Blinking a couple of times as the red mist began to clear, I looked down at the man trapped beneath my strength and anger. He was taking small breaths as his body reacted to his panic. His hands were flailing around slapping mine as he attempted to tear my hold off his clothing. His eyes were open wide in fear, his skin was a reddish purple and was now covered by a light sheen of sweat.

Then I turned to look at someone far more important. As my head twisted to look over my shoulder, I could see the woman I loved with tears rolling down her face. Her hand was over her heart as she tried to protect herself from me. It was her body language that felt like a knife to my back. I'd never in my life set out to hurt her, but every fucking time she seemed to get caught in my wake. Then my eyes fell to the path of devastation I created in her beloved Fairy Garden.

Enough.

The material I was holding began to groan in protest as its fibres strained against my skin and I began to slowly loosen my hold on the bastard's clothes. I stepped back and pulled him to stand upright. Sarcastically, I patted the front of his clothing down as I attempted to straighten him out.

Flustered, he looked down at my patting, condescending hand and then back up at me as the purple drained from his face and he tried to regain his equilibrium.

'You're a bloody maniac.'

I heard him speak, but made no response. Instead, I turned on my heels, pushed my hair out of my eyes and looked back at the woman I loved. She may have only been twenty feet away but the distance and pain in her eyes as she stood and stared back at me told me that she had moved far out of my reach.

'I don't understand, Lauren.'

I started to walk back towards her, picking up chairs and doing my best to right the tables that I'd forced out of the way in my anger.

As she watched me walking towards her, I saw her pull herself up taller and I knew whatever she was going to say wasn't going to be anything I wanted to hear.

The pain I'd been keeping in check, forced itself to the surface. I knew that right at that moment I would do anything to persuade her to stay with me. I tore my eyes away from hers and bent down to pick up some of the knives and forks my actions had spilt to the floor.

'Just leave them, Raff… please leave them and go.'

On autopilot, I sank to my knees, looked back up at her and opening my arms up wide I began to question her.

'What do I need to do, Loz?'

She shook her head as more tears cascaded down her face and she sobbed a wordless no.

'I'm on my knees here, tell me what I need to say. Tell me what I can do. I'm begging you.'

I didn't care that we had a fucking interloper in the room and I couldn't have given a shit that she was wearing his ring. She was mine, I just had to make her see that.

'It's over, Raff. We don't know each other anymore, in fact I'm not sure we ever did. We can't keep clinging to the past.'

'Like fuck it is. You know me like no one else does, not anyone, Loz. Something has happened here today. I don't know what the hell happened between me leaving here this morning and now, but mark my words, I will find out.'

Anger took over her beautiful features, her freckles began to disappear and her eyes ignited with fury.

'Fool me once, Rafferty, shame on you. Fool me twice, shame on me.'

Silence enveloped the tearoom as I stared back at her. I hadn't a fucking clue what she was talking about. Slowly, I stood back up to my feet and dumped the silverware I'd picked up onto the nearest table with a loud, deliberate crash.

I closed the small gap between us until she was merely inches from me. With my arms down straight by my side and my hands clenching into fists, I breathed her in and willed myself to calm down.

I lifted my hand slowly and lifting a long, thick wave of her chestnut hair, I put it behind her shoulder. The knife of pain twisted slowly in my heart as she turned her head. She shied away from my touch and exposed more of her neck towards me. I rocked back onto the heels of my boots as I attempted to turn away from her and to leave like she'd asked, to save myself. But, the glint of a fine silver chain caught my eye.

No, it can't be?

She wouldn't have kept it after all these years, would she?

I knew she didn't want my hands on her, but before I walked away I needed to know.

I lifted my hand up slowly to the side of her neck. Her head righted itself and from the corner of her eye she watched my slow movement. She appeared to be unable to move away, so she prepared herself for my touch. Her breathing stuttered and I deliberately slowed my finger down, so I could appreciate the connection between the two of us.

Her lips parted slightly as she unconsciously welcomed me home and I knew without even hooking my finger on the chain, it held exactly what I thought.

Finally, the nail I kept deliberately long to play the guitar, picked up the chain and lifted it away from her body. I ran my nail slowly towards the front of her body, pulling the chain up from out of her sweatshirt. At last the half heart flicked out of the top of the round neck. I took it between my thumb and forefinger and rubbed the tip of my finger over the one word that was written there.

Always.

A sob left her then, effectively breaking the spell that had surrounded us for a few too short minutes.

I dipped my head and with my mouth close to her ear, I whispered, 'And forever, Lauren.'

I forced myself to release the chain I was holding and watched it gently fall back down in place. I took her face in my hands and made her look up at me as I ran my thumbs over her cheekbones.

'No… we're not forever. Not anymore. It was a stupid dream, a childish, rose-tinted dream. We no longer know each other. You seem to have a habit of discarding people, when you no longer have a use for them. Well not me… never again me. I can't let you.' She tried to twist her face out of my hold, but I held her firmly, not wanting to hurt her, but needing to see her beautiful face as she spoke the words I didn't want to hear. 'We're over,' she finally whispered. Her face contorted slightly, almost as though just allowing the words to cross over her lips, gave her pain. Her eyes filled with tears, but biting on her lower lip she forced them to stay put. Effectively, telling me what I already knew, I wasn't worth her tears.

Her hands came up and flicking up the back of hair she released the clasp on the silver chain. I knew what she was doing but refused to release my hold on her face. I refused to empty my hands, then she couldn't give me the chain.

'Don't do it, Loz. You're mine, no one else's.' I shook my head at her. 'This isn't over. You can try to hide how you feel but I can see it in your eyes,' I whispered down to her and then placed a kiss to her forehead. 'Remember what I said when we were together. I gave you a choice. If you let me in, you were mine and I was never, ever letting you go. Whatever has happened here today, won't keep me away. The words you've spoken, won't keep me away. Giving me back the chain you've kept for years won't change anything between us. Those two words are engraved on our hearts and nothing can erase that.'

Lifting her right hand up, she gently peeled my left hand away from her face and with her eyes still full of the tears she refused to cry for us, she placed the still warm chain in my hand and wrapped my fingers over it.

The pain in my chest expanded and I gulped several times to clear the emotion trapped in my throat. My grip tightened on the precious chain in my hand, until my knuckles started to turn white. My teeth were clamped together so hard in my mouth I could now taste the unmistakable metallic tang of blood.

'I told you that you weren't welcome here, you need to leave.' The fucking bastard I had managed to ignore until now interrupted the moment and I knew right at that minute I could have killed him with my own bare hands.

I hadn't heard him scuttling up behind us, but hearing his voice once again ignited my blood.

So, I took a step away from her as I prepared myself to go. On my terms and not his, I released her. Letting her go flicked a switch inside me. Holding her in my hands had held me solid and in check, now without that connection of skin on skin between us, the rage and anger began to once again take hold.

Without thinking I twisted myself around quickly and placing him where I'd heard his voice last, I swung my left arm with its already closed fist towards his face.

'JUST. SHUT. THE. FUCK. UP.' I roared at the unwelcome bastard.

The feeling of satisfaction as I watched him fall to the floor onto his backside was powerful. The crack as one of the chairs from the tearoom broke underneath him wasn't.

I heard Lauren scream and another woman's voice from the doorway.

'What the hell is going on in here?' Her shout vibrated throughout the empty space.

Unconsciously rubbing at the knuckles of my still clenched fist, I made my feet move and walked towards the doorway. Lifting my head up, I found the confused looking face of Winter as she took in the sight of Lauren and the debris around her.

'I'll be right back, Lauren. I need to take care of something first,' she called over my shoulder, before she grabbed my forearm tightly and digging her talons through my jumper, she dragged me outside and slammed the door closed behind her.

The cold winter air hit my face as I stepped back outside and into the courtyard. I looked down to where Winter still had hold of my arm.

'You can let the fuck go.' My voice came out more threatening than I meant it to and I hurriedly sucked in a cold breath to calm the fuck down.

'Can I? Can I really?' She was younger than me, but her tone of voice sounded like she was speaking to a petulant child.

'YES, for fucks sake… yes.' I pulled my arm abruptly upwards and out of her vice like grip. Once I'd been set free, I made myself walk further away from the building that held the woman I loved, before I forced my way back in there and threw the wanker she'd got engaged to out on his arse. My hands began to twitch as they almost goaded me to do just that. Holding the chain she'd placed into my hands, I wound it tight around my index finger, still feeling the warmth from her skin radiating from it and groaned out loud. Then linking my hands together, I placed them up behind my neck and willed them to stay right there. Unconsciously, I started to walk around in a small tight circle as I did battle with my inner demons. Coming to an abrupt standstill, I spun back around to focus on the angry looking face of my sister. Her arms were crossed over the top of an expensive cashmere coat and yet another Louboutin shoe tapped up and down as she ran her disappointed gaze over me. The setting behind her could have been that of a perfect fucking Christmas card, snow topped Victorian buildings, twinkling lights from the tearooms and the rich, deep green colour of the surrounding tall evergreens. The only thing wrong was the look of fury on her face and the anger inside of me that was threatening to spill the fuck over.

'What's happened?' she questioned, turning a little to wave one open arm at the building I'd vacated.

'I'm *fucked* if I know,' I replied, spitting my words out into the cold air.

'That's not good enough.' I watched her turning in disbelief, looking at me and then through the condensation filled windows of the tearoom at Lauren.

'I. KNOW. THAT.' I shouted out into the still of the empty courtyard and knew my voice had travelled into the tearoom when in my peripheral view, I saw Lauren's hurt face turn to look out of the window and then just as quickly she turned back to him. I grimaced and looked away. I pushed my hands down deep into the back pockets of my jeans, then filled her in on what had happened last night and this morning, as quickly as I could. 'I know it's not fucking good enough, but it's all I've got.' I spoke again trying hard to keep a lid on my anger.

'She's accepted his ring?' she replied after listening to what I had to say. Her eyes opening wide and the disbelief in her voice gave me hope.

'Yeah.'

'I don't believe it.'

'Oh, you can fucking believe it. I watched her put his ring on her finger all by herself. As of twenty minutes ago, the only woman I've ever really loved got engaged to that fucking twat.' I pulled my hands from my pockets and linking them together I put them behind my neck.

'She put it on?' she replied with her face contorted in question.

For a few seconds, silence filled the space between us. I watched as Winter tried to take in what I'd said, and then as she looked in disbelief through the opaque glass of the arched windows of the tearoom. Thankfully, and fucking painfully all at the same time, I could no longer see Lauren through the steamed glass. Just finding her once in his arms would have been the death of me... or maybe the death of the arsehole in there with her. Releasing my hands from behind my neck, I began to fidget, until I was pacing around and around the courtyard. Trying to push the thoughts in my head away, I pushed up the sleeves on my jumper and began to sort out the many twists of leather and chains on my wrists. Winter stepped nearer to me and placed her small, perfectly manicured hand onto mine. She squeezed slowly, trying to offer me consolation. Then she lifted it quickly and tapped her fingers on mine as she began to speak again.

'Look, Raff. I need to go in to her. I'm trying to work this all out. I saw her with my own eyes last night when you both came to help us look for Amy. Honestly, I can't remember having ever seen her so happy. She was right where she was meant to be, at your side with you holding on to her. If everything happened just as you've told me it did, then something went wrong this morning, while you were back at The Manor.'

I stabbed the front of my old brown boots into the snow on the ground and flicked small pieces of loose snow up as I thought. 'How did you know I went back there?'

'That doesn't matter, not right now,' she forcibly pushed into the conversation, shaking her head.

'But what could have happened while I was gone? She was here looking after the kids.' As I uttered the words, understanding came crashing down. 'Flint,' I whispered, remembering words Lauren had spoken. 'She said I discard people when they're no longer useful.'

I watched Winter nod and then grab my arm in solidarity. 'I'll do what I can from this end. You need to talk to Flint, you know how mixed up and angry he is.'

'But, what the fuck could he have said that would have made her react like this?' I questioned her and felt my forehead pull into a deep frown.

'I don't know, that's what you need to find out. And I'm sorry, but I need you to also see Brody and find out what he's playing at with Amy. Read him the riot act if you need to. I've got one heartbroken friend in there,' she tilted her head towards the tearooms, 'and I don't need another.'

Lauren

'Bloody hell, look at this mess.' I turned at the sound of her voice to witness Winter re-enter The Fairy Garden. Her hands found her hips as her eyes perused the furniture all over the floor.

I couldn't offer her anything. So, I acknowledged her presence by just about managing to nod my head towards her.

'Okay, I've got a while. So, lets sort out this place, shall we?'

I watched her lose her camel coloured coat and reveal the immaculately put together outfit underneath it and had never been more grateful for her organising capabilities than I was at that moment.

I let go of a juddering exhale and dropping the cold wad of paper towels I'd been half-heartedly holding against Toby's right cheekbone, I sank down into the chair I knew was still behind ne.

Winter's here and I can let go.

Amy, Winter and I knew almost everything about each other and I knew I could rely on her to help me through this. The emotions colliding inside of me were too much to ignore any longer. I needed to let them out. I could feel the storm rising up and smashing against itself. The tears that had been building up inside me for too long began to chase each other down my cheeks and I could taste the salt on my lips as they ran over them to then drip off my chin. I made no attempt to wipe them away, I hadn't the strength.

An audibly loud sob left my mouth and I knew I'd effectively uncorked what was about to happen. No napkin tearing, or number crunching, was going to stop what was about to happen to me. The pain gathering inside of me was far too big to keep stored any longer.

My heart began to pound as the anxiety began to assemble itself inside me and I knew it was only a matter of minutes before it took over.

'Okay, Toby. I think I can take it from here. Lauren doesn't look too well and you need someone who can help you with your face… Is your mum at home?' I heard Winter's voice as she grabbed Toby by the elbow and tried to make him stand, to guide him towards the doors.

Sitting further back into the same chair I'd been sitting on, on and off all day, I watched as the tearoom began to fade into the background. The vibrant Christmas decorations lost their strength and seemed so washed out, it felt like I was watching a B movie. I could see Toby standing up and looking over at me as I drifted away. Then I watched Winter's mouth moving and then her pulling him by the elbow she had a firm grip on, as she directed him to leave the building.

My heart rate began to accelerate and the air I was drawing in was now only arriving in small gasps. My head began to spin and just when I didn't think it was possible, my heart rate increased again. Blood whooshed past my eardrums over, and over again and holding my hands out in front of me, I could see my new engagement ring and my Christmas red nails with hand painted snowflakes on them tremoring. I grabbed one hand with the other and dug my nails down deep into the soft flesh underneath them. The pain was sharp, but it wasn't nearly enough. It was nowhere near enough. Very quickly I recognised that the whole of my body was beginning to shake, I tried hard to relax into it, but I knew it was no use.

I was no longer in control and my anxiety was.

As Winter closed the door behind Toby and slid the bolt with a resounding clank, I watched him gratefully vacate the porch area and walk to his car. I knew he couldn't cope with my attacks and I was happy to no longer have him around to witness my breakdown.

A cry of pain that sounded like a wounded animal in the dead of night escaped my mouth. I thought fleetingly how very poignant that was. I was wounded, mortally wounded. My heart was broken and I felt like I'd been left behind floundering in the darkness. I slammed my hand over my heart to push against the heightened sense of pain trapped within me as it tried to burst free. I heard Winter's shoes click hurriedly across the tiles and suddenly she was stood beside me.

'You're okay, Lauren. I've got you... use this.'

Kneeling in front of me, Winter, with a flick of her wrist, opened one of the pink paper bags we used for takeaways and grabbing hold of my hands she held them and it in place over my mouth and nose. Her beautiful violet eyes found mine and never left. Together we looked deeply inside each other and I knew she didn't shy away from what she found.

'That's it... calm breaths. In through the nose, hold it and out through your mouth.'

The touch of her warm caring hands on mine and the strength and stability in her voice gently persuaded me down from the height of the strangulating anxiety that had wrapped its hold around me like a python. Slowly, following her voice as we held the paper bag together, my breathing deepened and my heartbeat began to slow as the python once again relaxed its coils and began to release me.

'In through the nose, out through the mouth. You've got this, Lauren and I've got you… in through the nose and out through the mouth.'

Gradually, I released the hands I had been desperately holding on to and relaxing our arms together we let the pink paper bag drop from the front of my face.

'Thank you,' I whispered up to her.

'There's no need to thank me,' she answered as she pulled a chair up behind her to sit back onto and then gently pulled me into her hold. For a while we rocked each other slightly side to side, while I cried the rest of my fears and emotions onto her shoulder.

'You must think I'm weak?'

She pulled apart from me so she could once again look into my eyes.

'Don't you dare think that. I know what you've been through and what you live with daily. Don't ever think that… Have you taken a good look around you?'

I gently shook my head at her. 'Well do so and take in all that you've achieved.' She gesticulated around us at The Fairy Garden and I managed a small half-hearted smile.

'Do you want to tell me about it?' she questioned.

I nodded, but not knowing quite where to start I took the easy way out and replied. 'I've got engaged to Toby.'

'That means nothing, engagements get broken all the time.'

'Not this one. I've made my bed and now I'll lie in it.'

A loud sigh left her. 'This isn't the nineteen fifties you know. That sort of martyrdom is no longer required.'

'He'll look after me.'

I watched her stand up in front of me and looked up at her to see a flash of irritation move over her fine bone structure.

'Lauren, how can you possibly think that? I'm sorry to sound like I'm rubbing your nose in it, but he can't even cope with your anxiety attacks. You don't need to marry someone to be looked after. I know you don't feel it now, but you're more than capable of looking after yourself and when you're not... well, we're here to help you.'

'I understand and I'm grateful for you and Amy, but I want more and at least he won't hurt me, Winter.'

She stepped back and flung her arms up into the air in frustration. Then her eyes were back on mine.

'As opposed to...?' When I didn't answer, but only shook my head she asked the question another way. 'Who will hurt you?' When I still said nothing, she carried on, having made her own conclusion. 'So, that's it?... You're giving up on the HEA you've always dreamt about, the one that you've told Amy and I was out there for all of us...' I rolled both of my lips over my teeth, and nodded. I watched her begin to shake her head at me in disbelief. 'If that's the truth, then you're right. Toby probably won't hurt you. But, that's not a basis for a good, loving marriage.' She studied me a little closer and then carried on. 'If you marry him, then you're going to do a damn fine job of hurting yourself. You won't need anyone else to do it for you.'

'Winter, you don't understand.'

She let out a slow exhale and shaking her head at me she spoke again. 'Then explain it to me? Tell me what happened in here this morning. Flint obviously said something to you, because it couldn't have been Brielle. You've pushed Raff away and I can't work out why.'

'I'm sorry.' I shook my head at her, knowing I couldn't betray Flint's confidence and remembering that Raff was her brother, and her sympathies would have to be split between us.

'What are you sorry for?' She reached out and took my hand in hers.

'Raff and I... you've been left piggy in the middle.'

'Forget all about that, you're my friend first. Tell me what went on here today. Tell me what I only saw the finale to. I haven't seen an anxiety attack like the one that had you in its grasp, in years and I know something huge triggered it.'

I watched her beautiful, animated figure in front of me and shook my head at her a little.

'Not this time, Winter... I can't. I need to move on with my life and not dwell on the what might have been.'

'As your friend, I want to shake you until you share it all with me.' She studied me closely and raised a questioning eyebrow at me as I sat silently under her perusal. 'But, I won't. I'm always here for you, day or night. All you need to do is pick up the phone. Do you understand me?'

I offered her a nod and a small smile at her words, although it was more a smile of relief that she was going to let it go. Normally, Winter was like a dog with a bone.

'But, I need to say this... You're using Toby as a shield, Lauren, and it's not right. Not for him, not for Rafferty and most definitely not for you.'

Having driven her point home, she leant over to hug me briefly and when she stood back up, I could see that her emotion for my situation had once again been held in check.

'Right, so I'll make you a cup of tea, then we'll set about clearing up this mess.' Her head turned around as she surveyed the damage her brother had left in his wake. 'It shouldn't take too long, the only thing broken is the chair that Toby's fat arse fell heavily onto.'

'Winter!' I berated her, feeling a smile twitch at the corners of my mouth.

Bending over she righted the nearest chair to her and pushed it under the table.

'Oh, sorry... I shouldn't have said that. Let me rephrase, the only thing broken is the chair that your fiancé smashed into with his fat arse.' She grinned at me and I smiled at her in return. 'Good you're back.'

'Thank you,' I replied, smiling at her.

Still sitting, I watched as she started walking towards the kitchen.

'Don't be too quick to thank me. After that cup of tea we're having and while we tidy up in here, we're going to discuss what sort of vibrator to buy you.'

'WHAT?' I shrieked at her disappearing figure.

'Men are trouble, Lauren. It's about time you and Amy realised that they're only around for the short haul, whereas a vibrator with the right batteries... well you can't go wrong,' she shouted from the kitchen. 'It does the business without all this emotional shit to deal with.'

I let her words sink in for a moment and had to admit, I was starting to come around to her way of thinking.

Chapter 29

Raff

It took everything I fucking had to drive away from her. I'd sat for a while in the empty courtyard, touching the single word on the half heart and rolling the silver chain around in my palm. Finally, Winter had arrived at the door holding the bastard who was now engaged to my fucking girl, by the elbow. I knew by the look on her face that she'd taken charge and she'd convinced him that he needed to leave. Leaning forward on my steering wheel I stared at him through my narrow windscreen, loving that even from this distance I could see the swelling and bruising on his right cheek that I'd put there.

He deserved it and so much fucking more. He'd read her right and taken the opportunity as it presented itself to him. I admired the bollocks of the bloke, but at the same time I would have happily cut them off the fucker.

I wasn't normally a violent bloke. Sure, I could stand up for myself and had been involved in a few fights here and there. But, the love and passion I had for Lauren added to the hate I had for him, brought out every aggressive and vicious response I had in me.

Even the feel of being behind the wheel of my brand new car couldn't mask the tsunami of emotion threatening to engulf me.

How in the space of a few hours could all my hopes and dreams come crashing down so monumentally around my ears?

'FUCK IT!' I slammed my open palm against the black dashboard.

Either my shout or the bang travelled over to Winter, who with a wave of her hand and a tut which I couldn't hear but could make out on her lips, told me it was time to leave. Reluctantly nodding at her, I made my sleek machine pull almost silently out behind Toby's ten-year-old, silver rust bucket.

I revved my engine several times as we travelled through the narrow archway and onto the single lane that would either lead us left to the country lane, or right up the long winding driveway that led to The Manor. The moment the gravel track widened enough, I overtook and went alongside him. I jammed my foot down quickly on the accelerator and one-handed, turned the wheel quickly right. I knew anything loose on the track would be sprayed all over his vehicle. As I flew away from the junction, I looked into my rear-view mirror and winding down my window, I gave him the finger.

For about ten seconds my childish behaviour gave me a sense of happiness, then as the electric window came back up into place, closing me into the small space, my true feelings flooded my system.

I stopped myself from travelling too fast up the driveway the moment I saw a few of The Manor's guests wandering around as they admired the white covered countryside of our new venture and home. Seeing children with their parents as they played in the snow brought me back to earth with a bump. I slowed the Bugatti down to watch them, until it was so slow I could almost hear the engine crying. The expensive car, the fact it was crawling by, started to get a few admiring and interested looks.

Not wanting to face more of an audience than I had to, I turned the car to follow the track that would lead me around to the back of the house, the kitchen and the delivery entrance. I was trying to not think at all, in a bid to keep the pain inside me to a level I could cope with. I switched off the car, pulled myself out of the door and still holding tight to Lauren's half of my heart, I made my way towards the back door. Without any thought as to what I was going to do next, I pressed the correct sequence of keys on the keypad and pulled open the heavy door.

As luck would have it I found Brody sorting out a hamper in the large kitchen area and I knew it had to be for Amy.

'Well, look what the fucking cat dragged in.' I watched him freeze as he became aware of my presence. 'If it isn't Daniel.' I carried on letting him become aware of my accusation in the sarcastic tone I used. We'd learnt he wasn't being truthful about who he was. Amy had told the girls she was seeing a bloke called Daniel, when she was actually seeing our lead singer, Brody Daniels. Winter and Lauren were scared that with her past, finding out she was being lied to would break her.

So, even with everything that was going on in my life, here I was trying to sort out his fuck up too.

With his back to me, I heard the knife he'd been hacking at the bread with click, as it was slowly put down onto the board in front of him. He turned himself slowly around to face me and the accusation I'd left hanging in the air. Any other day and I would have entered the building and thrown my arm around his neck and pulled the bloke towards me, told him to treat her right, stolen some of the food he was making and left with a laugh as he told me to fuck off.

But this wasn't any other fucking day.

Today, was the day I lost Lauren for the second time in my life and I was barely holding it together. I needed to make Brody see that if Amy meant something to him, and I was convinced that she did, looking at the picnic he was packing up for her, added to the fact that he'd virtually gone AWOL for the last couple of days. Well, I had to make him understand what he was doing, so he could take the only chance he might have to do right by her. He took me in for a few seconds, leant his arse down onto the polished metal preparation area behind him and sighed in acceptance, crossing his arms over his chest.

I pulled up a stool behind me and sat down on it, mirroring his defensive body language. For a few seconds, we stared at each other.

'Just slow the fuck up, I know where this is coming from.' Brody held up his open palms to me, shoved his hands into the front pockets of his jeans and then shrugging his shoulders at me he began to speak. 'I never lied to Amy, she heard Cade calling out "Daniels" and she just took it from there.'

I moved my head from side to side as I mulled over what he'd said and then pulled my mouth into a sneer.

'Yeah, I'm reasonable, I can see that. We all call you Daniels, instead of arsehole, from time to time when we talk to you, but what about now?'

'Oh, ha fucking ha, you're a fucking comedian. Whadaya mean, what the fuck about now?' His voice rose in volume in defence, he pulled his hands from his pockets and crossed his arms again.

'You're packing up a picnic, and it's for Amy, don't fucking tell me anything different.'

'It could *be* for anybody,' he snarled back, looking pissed that I knew what was going on.

'Winter guessed that the "Daniel" Amy was talking about, was you. She and Lauren had a conversation with Amy after you slept with her the first time. Then last night, she disappeared from the drawing room next to where we played. The room that you were seen escaping into after our set. We looked around for about an hour before Winter put two and two together and we all realised she must have gone back to your room with you.'

'Yeah, I was escaping. Hell, if it means that much to you all to know my business, you might as well know that we didn't do much fucking sleeping… either night.'

'Fuck, Brody! Don't play fucking games here. What the actual fuck do you want with her?'

He uncrossed his arms quickly, rubbed the hair on his head and started pointing his finger at me and my accusations.

'Believe me when I tell you I'm not playing around here. This has the possibility to be so different from anything else I've ever had.' I felt my eyebrows raise at him in question and yeah it had to be said, surprise. He crossed his arms yet again to stop his aggressive finger pointing in my fucking direction. 'She hasn't a clue who I am, and it's seriously the best fucking thing ever. I know I will have to tell her. Eventually.'

'Soon,' I pointedly interrupted him.

'Yeah, okay, fucking soon. I do know that. But just for a few days I want to be the guy she's just met, the one who makes her heart flutter and her breathing quicken, just because I'm me and not some rock God. I want her to *want* to be with me for what she finds in here.' He smashed his closed fist into his chest. 'I'm sick to the fucking back teeth with the false fucking shit that's been in our lives and that comes into our lives on a regular basis, because we're in a band. Tell me you understand that?'

'You know I do.' Watching him, I could feel his pain. I knew how sad he was to be having this conversation and in turn that helped me to slowly put a lid on my over spilling emotions.

'Then just give me a few days.' His voice was quiet and almost pleading in its tone.

'Look, I grew up around here, with people like Amy. They're not used to having people like us around.' He raised his eyebrows at my "people like us," not quite sure exactly what it was I was getting at. But, I could see that his brain had added two and two and come up with millions of reasons why someone like Amy wouldn't want him and his troubled past in her life. I carried on trying to appease him. 'I didn't have a lot to do with her when we were younger, as you know I didn't hang around here very long. But, she means the world to Winter and she's Lauren's cousin. So, you could say she's like part of the family, just don't hurt her. I do know that she has dealt with more shit in her life than a fucking pig farm.' I caught the look on his face. 'Yeah, I know you have too, but I'm serious. Do the fucking right thing by her, have your couple of days and then tell her who the fuck you are and let her make her own decision about it.'

For a few seconds, there was silence in the kitchen as the last sentence hung in the air between us. Then he nodded resolutely at me. I pushed myself off the stool and walked up to him, and we man hugged for a few seconds before we slapped each other on the back.

'So, how's it going?' he countered as I pulled away.

'How's what going?' I followed the words with a deep sigh, I knew exactly what he was asking.

He smirked at my pathetic attempt to divert where the conversation was now heading.

'Lauren,' he added.

'Oh… Lauren. Mmmm… Well, she's just got engaged and it's not to me.' I could feel my face contort with pain as I spoke the words.

'Fuck,' was all he could offer in answer.

'Yeah, see ya later. Have fun, but do right by her and be good to her, take it from me you may never get the opportunity again.' My voice was heavily laden with regret.

I walked towards the kitchen door, feeling his eyes boring deeply into my back as the door opened I stepped through it quickly and out the other side. I knew he meant well, but I hadn't got the answers to the many questions I knew he wanted to ask and I was grateful to leave the conversation behind.

Raff

It was a relief to make it to the start of our private wing. I'd come past several members of staff and a few guests on the way through the building. I'd managed to nod or offer them a half-hearted smile, when I was convinced a few of them had wanted to exchange a few words with me.

I wasn't in the mood for conversational small talk and I didn't want to inflict my ugly mood on anyone else. They didn't need it, and I didn't need the questions and the possible fall out that my anger was sure to bring.

I needed some down time.

I needed some time to think, to come up with a plan.

I always had a plan to help everyone else. Now, I needed one to help me.

I almost jogged the last few steps at the thought of being a few paces away from peace and solitude. But, the view that met my eyes as I swung around the final corner had me stopping dead in my tracks. The corridor that led to our rooms was full of people.

'Thank fuck, dude. You're here.' Cade uncrossed his arms and propelled himself off the wall behind him and started towards me.

Looking around his large figure I could see my mum and step-dad. Just seeing him in the place I was once again happy to call home, knocked me off fucking kilter. *What the actual fuck?* Then it dawned on me.

Of course, they'd stayed in the hotel last night, after the opening day.

'What's happening?' I asked Cade as he strode on towards me, but as soon as the words left my mouth the loud sound of a drum kit being worked up into a fucking frenzy hit my ears.

'Flint?' I questioned him as he stopped in front of me.

'Yeah... I've never seen him like this Raff. He came back before lunch, gave Brie her cookies, burst into tears and locked himself in his room.'

From the noise he was making, I could picture him behind his kit, using every part of his body to hit every single drum he had. The noise was loud, aggressive and repetitive. It wasn't a defined beat he was keeping to, not one that any musician would recognise as a song. But as his dad, I recognised exactly what he was playing. The crescendo of noise showed me his anger, pain and most of all his fear. It reminded me that my son, who was now only a few inches under six foot and who so wanted to be treated like an adult, was still a child and he was struggling.

'Why?' I had a feeling that I knew exactly why, but the stupid sodding question came out anyway.

Cade shrugged his shoulders at me. 'Luke and I have both tried to get him to open the door. He doesn't reply, just goes from playing his kit until he's probably near exhausted and then to sobbing.'

Lauren's parting words re-entered my head. *"You seem to have a habit of discarding people."* I shook my head, trying to dislodge the sentence as it ran around on repeat.

'Why didn't you call me?' The question I'd asked came out louder and angrier than I meant it to. I watched Cade's nostrils flare, his eyes narrow and one eyebrow lift in question at me.

Luke having heard my accusing question walked up behind Cade, twisting his phone between his fingertips and asked. 'Whoah, take a fucking step back, Raff, and let us ask you a question. Where's your phone?'

Instinctively, I slapped at the back pockets of my jeans with both hands and found them empty. 'I must have left it in the car.'

'Exactly, we *did* phone you,' Cade replied.

Taking a deep breath, I held both my empty palms up to them and shook my head. 'Sorry.' Suddenly a cacophony of noise hit my eardrums and I knew Flint had started up again. 'I need to get in there.'

'Maintenance are on their way up.'

'Thanks.' I looked at them both and moved forward, walking in between the two of them as they moved aside. I knew my mum and step-dad were further down the corridor and knowing what a shit day I'd already had, I refused to look at him and focussed my eyes on my mum.

'Oh, Rafferty. Flint won't talk to us either.' My concerned mum was stood to one side of his door. 'I'm sorry, we've tried.'

I placed my hand on her shoulder and squeezed it as I smiled my thanks to her.

'Trouble at the mill, Rafferty?' I heard his voice behind me, but I couldn't turn around. I knew if I did, that with all fucking certainty, he would be the second arsehole I put on his backside today. It wasn't always what he said, but the way he said it and in that tone of voice that was always reserved for me, or the people he deemed beneath him. He spoke to me in the same tone that he had always used with the staff at home, when they hadn't followed his orders and were in the wrong. Every nerve in my body was on edge and the hairs on my neck stood to attention.

Eight years had gone by after I left England for the U.S., before I finally listened to my mum and Winter. Unable to stand being caught between the two of us, Winter had begged me, for our mum's sake, to try to move past what had gone down between me and him. I'd promised her nothing, I couldn't forgive him. I hated the man and everything he stood for, but for the sake of the women in my family I agreed to at least stomach being in the same room as him. Being in the U.S. had made what I'd agreed to easier, I made sure I was only ever in the same room as him once a year or less if I could manage it, and that room was always full of other people.

He'd had his once this year, and that was fucking yesterday.

It was bad enough that he was taking so much satisfaction from the situation we were all witnessing, and was enjoying rubbing my goddamn nose in it. But, taking pleasure in the fact that my boy was locked in his room, with his heart breaking, was too fucking much. My body acted on instinct and even feeling my mum grab at both of my forearms didn't stop me. Every muscle in my body was tense and straining to let loose and I shook off her hold and turned around quickly to face him.

At first, he saw fit to smirk at my reaction, the reaction he had incited. That single action immediately transported me back in time to his mahogany panelled office with its smell of cherry and vanilla. I lifted my head, stood taller and stared at him a little harder, looking deliberately down my fucking nose at the bastard. For the first time, it dawned on me that I was seeing the older, weaker man he'd become. His arrogance melted away when he recognised what I saw. His eyes flicked down to where my hands had clenched tightly into fists and then looked back up to my face. As his throat moved, I watched him swallow a gulp and knew he wasn't worth my anger and without a fucking doubt he didn't warrant my time.

'Please, Rafferty,' my mum pleaded from behind me.

'You can leave.' I spoke quietly, but so vehemently that I saw my own spittle connect with his perfectly waxed moustache. Removing my eyes away from the pathetic excuse for a man stood in front of me, I turned back to Flint's door and stepped up close to it.

I knocked once with the hand that still held Lauren's necklace and then leant my forehead onto his door. 'I'm here Flint and I'm coming in.'

'Mr. Morello, Gary from maintenance is here can I send him in?' I heard the voice of Maria one of our brand new receptionists, as she arrived at the entrance to our private wing and spoke to Cade.

I rolled my forehead around on the door, as I listened to my boy sobbing again and with tears in my eyes I followed her voice and looked down the corridor.

'Yes, thanks,' I called over to her before Cade had a chance to answer and offered her a smile of gratitude. 'This door please,' I spoke to the guy who had appeared like magic behind her and pushed on the door handle, making it flick back into place, showing him why I needed his help.

I watched him work, effectively blocking everyone else out. Slowly, as they began to one by one disappear, my anger followed them.

I waited until everyone had vacated the corridor, before I pushed open Flint's bedroom door. After he'd heard me speaking to him through the door the drumming had started up again.

I opened the door up quickly and slammed it shut, and with one hand still behind me on the door lock I twisted it to send it home, effectively making sure that no one could disturb us. Whatever happened in here in the very near future was between Flint and I, it had been a long fucking time coming and I wasn't letting either of us leave until we'd cleared a pathway through the crap life had thrown at us.

Only after feeling the lock hit home did I have the guts to lift my head up and focus my eyes on him. The scene I found was like a punch to the gut. In that single moment, as I took in his posture, I felt more ineffective than I'd ever felt in my life. The realisation of what he must be going through tore into me.

My son, the boy I would move heaven and fucking earth for, was sitting behind his kit, driving his protesting body on and on to keep hitting the hell out of it. I knew watching him that his drum kit had become his life, his hopes and dreams and right here in this minute he couldn't see any way through the pain and confusion to the other side. His long dark hair was wet with sweat and was stuck fast in several places to his face. I couldn't see his eyes through the damp strands, but I knew if I could that I'd find them red and raw with the anguish that was seeping from his body. His dark grey sleeveless vest was marked with sweat and was stuck in places to his adolescent body.

The tears I'd been holding in since leaving Lauren, spilt down my face and spurred on my need to hold him in my arms.

I moved quickly away from the door and towards the small bay window to where his drum kit had been set up when I'd had the room decorated especially for him. When I was only two feet away from him, his head lifted as my feet found their way into his peripheral view.

'NO!' he screamed, aiming that one word at me as he tried to keep me away.

His drumming stopped abruptly. Lifting both of his knees up he landed his feet centrally into the bass drum. The whole of the carefully set up kit collapsed; drums, stands and cymbals were sent spewing in all directions. I stopped dead in my tracks, unsure of where to tread next as the debris landed into my legs and rolled over my feet.

The room that had been so alive with noise was suddenly still.

'Go away, leave me alone... I don't want you in here.' Flint spoke in between the sobs he was releasing and then almost inhaling again, as his body went into spasm in his distress.

'I'm sorry, Flint, but I can't do that. I can't do that because you're my son. I can't do it because I love you too much to.'

For the first time since entering the room I saw a flash of his stormy grey eyes behind his wall of dark hair. He raised his left hand quickly and threw the only things he had left in his arsenal. The drumsticks were well aimed and although I saw them coming I didn't lift a hand to defend myself.

I wanted to feel his anger. Hell, I was sure I deserved it.

The sticks hit me square in the face, causing me to wince in pain and then they clattered to the floor.

Now, he was fully exposed and vulnerable. And so was I.

I shifted the strewn equipment away from the path I needed to tread, pushing it to either side with my boots and carried on walking towards him.

'Don't you ever listen to me. I don't want YOU HERE!' The words he started to speak got louder as he tried to stop me advancing.

'Too late, Flint. I'm your dad and I'll always be here. Whether you want me to be or not.'

'I don't want any of this and I don't want you.'

He moved quickly off the stool he'd been sitting on up to now and retreated further into the bay window behind him. Sitting on his backside with his black, denim-clad knees bent and his arms wrapped tightly around them, he dipped his head. His face was completely obscured by the long lengths of dark hair as it fell forward. I knew he was crying as I watched his body shake and shudder as he tried to breathe through it. But, at least the manic frenzy seemed to have passed and I was fucking grateful.

I moved forward until there was enough space for me to turn around. Using my boots, I carefully shifted some more of the wreckage out of my way and sat down. I leant my back against the cold, outer wall behind me and taking a deep breath I put Lauren's silver chain away in my pocket, reached for him and pulled him into my arms.

I was worried he would fight and push me away, and although he didn't assist what I was trying to do, he willingly came into my hold.

Thank fuck.

I don't know how long we both sat there, time had no significance. I could see out of the window and watched the early afternoon sky beginning to darken. The snow gently fell outside and I tried to take the sense of calm it gave the world as it blanketed our surroundings. I had leant back against the wall with my legs initially open in a large V shape. Once I'd pulled Flint's side to my chest and wrapped one arm around his now shivering body, I bent my knees and joined my feet together, effectively sealing him in against me. I couldn't remember the last time he'd allowed me to even hug him, but this now, we both needed.

I stroked my hand over his head, trying to soothe him as he quietly cried in my arms and when I felt the time was right, I began to speak to him.

'You can tell me anything, Flinty.'

I felt his head shake against my chest.

'It doesn't matter how old you are, wherever in the world your feet take you. You will always be mine and your mom's baby, we'll always love you.'

I knew he was listening but again my words got no response.

'Your mom and I don't get everything right, I know that. But I can promise you we're trying our best.'

'You didn't love me enough to stay together.' And there it was, I knew I was beginning to unpeel the layers that would lead to whatever it was that had caused his meltdown.

'Us getting divorced has nothing to do with our love for you. You are, and always will be, the greatest thing your mom and I ever achieved together. We never wanted to hurt you by separating, but we knew without a doubt that us staying together would have become so toxic, we couldn't have avoided you being hurt in the fallout...' I took a deep breath and tried again. 'What I'm trying to say is, we don't love each other anymore, but we love you with everything we have.'

His head lifted slightly under my chin and I knew he was taking in what I was saying. Uncomfortable in the position I was in, I leant my neck against the windowsill, tilted my head backwards and closed my eyes. I was happy to hold my only child in my arms for as long as he needed and then some.

'I wasn't enough though, was I?'

'What?' I felt my brow crease up as I gently asked the question.

'You wanted more children.'

'I'd love to have more than just you, Flint. Because you're fucking amazing and you're the very best thing I've achieved in my life. But, if you're all I ever have, I want you to understand that you're more than enough.'

I tightened my hold on his body and felt his hand hold on to my forearm.

'Can I ask you something?' he questioned.

'Anything.'

'If Mom had managed to have any of the other babies, do you think you would still be together?'

Holy fuck. How the hell do I answer a question like that truthfully?

'You have to remember that Mom and I have been separated for a long time. A child…' I stopped and bent over to kiss the top of his head. '…isn't responsible for keeping a marriage together and it certainly isn't responsible for breaking a marriage up. That, son, is completely down to the adults involved.'

'But, I heard you, Dad.' My heart lifted at his reuse of a title he'd subjectively stripped from me a while back, but immediately sunk again at what he may have fucking heard. We'd had many loud screaming matches before we'd eventually gone our separate ways.

'You heard me say what?' I tentatively asked.

'I was outside Mom's hospital room after she lost the baby at the beginning of the year. You said to her that you weren't willing to be by her bedside again as she lost another baby… So, what you're telling me is a crock of shit.'

A loud sob wracked through his body as he emptied his heart of the pain he'd been carrying around for far too long. My hand left from stroking his head and now using both of my arms I wrapped them both around him tight. I wanted him to feel how loved he was, but equally I knew we both couldn't afford for him to push me away now. The relationship we were set to have for the rest of our lives as father and son, I knew now, hinged on my answer.

'I think your mom and I have both done wrong in keeping things from you and I can only apologise for both of us. We thought we were protecting you and I can see that by doing that we've caused more damage. I know we only divorced this year, but we've been separated for years. Although, to you that probably didn't seem much different with me always being on the road.' I sighed not knowing how to word what I needed to tell him next. 'Look, Flint, there's no easy way to say this, but the last two babies your mom lost, well... they weren't mine. We were still married and the paparazzi reported that they were.'

'What?' he replied as he tried to sit up to look at me.

I held him tighter, needing to hold on to him while I got the rest of the words out. 'She was already involved with Travis; those pregnancies were his. I needed him to take responsibility for her and them. That's why I walked away from her in the hospital.'

Silence filled my ears as he thought over what I'd said.

'Why didn't anyone tell me? I'm not a baby and you shouldn't treat me like I'm stupid either.'

'I know you're not and no one thinks you're stupid, but you're not an adult either. This in between bit is hard for you to steer through, and us. We didn't want to hurt you and we didn't see the point in telling you stuff you didn't need to know.'

'One or both of you should have told me.' His tone was accusing and I couldn't blame him.

Finally, he pulled himself out of my arms. I hesitantly released my hold over him and he turned around to face me. I used my now empty hands to push my hair off my face and back onto my head where it belonged. I watched him wipe his wet face with the back of both hands as he tried to show me how grown up he was.

'Flint, I'm sorry… I know how stupid this sounds, but we honestly thought we were saving you from the hurt. Truthfully, our marriage was over when you were about five or six. Neither of us wanted another relationship, your mom was happy being the lead guitarist of Default Distraction's wife and I just went with it. We thought once you got a bit older, some things might be easier for you to understand and hear.'

'You've got to be fucking with me, Dad.' I watched him turn his head to look at the devastation of the drums around us. 'The truth is always the best thing to hear, even if it hurts like hell in the beginning.'

I shook my head at him. 'Your mom and I could learn a lot from you.'

'Right, well here's something else you might want to learn… I don't want to be a drummer anymore.'

'Okay,' I replied, still wondering at the fact he taken in all that information I'd given him and was now onto something else.

'Is it though? I'm not sure Mom will see it the same way. Being in "the business" is in the blood.'

'Flint, I don't care what you want to be, all I care about is that you're happy. You leave Mom to me… anyway she's got Travis to mould now. So, she'll let you off the hook for a while, won't she?' I offered him a smile and my insides lit up when he smiled back.

'Yeah,' he replied and then his smile was gone and I watched his head drop. 'Was Lauren alright?' He shifted his body a little and his fingernail started to pick absentmindedly at the charcoal grey carpet in his room. 'When you saw her this morning?'

'Why?' The pain of what had happened between Lauren and I engulfed me and I inhaled a steadying breath. Clasping my hands together, I placed my elbows onto my knees and moved my back off the uncomfortable wall, leaning forward towards him. His head lifted slowly and his eyes once again found mine.

'I told her some things this morning, that were wrong. But, I didn't know that until now. I really like her and... I'm sorry, Dad.'

I shook my head at him, letting him know he wasn't to blame. 'I had a feeling you might have.'

'I know she's the girl you loved before Mom.' His words were coming out so fast he was almost tripping over them.

'How the hell did you know that?' I could hear the surprise in my own voice as I answered him.

'Just... well, just from things Mom said.'

'Let me get this straight, Mom told you about Lauren?'

'She never said her name, but she said you'd loved someone else before her and that she lived in England. I knew it was her, Lauren I mean... in the kitchen the other day when she looked at me like she was seeing a ghost. Then you walked in and she got up immediately and walked out... I really like her, she's kind and I sort of wanted to warn her about you... Mom said you were coming back for her.'

He said no more, but it all made perfect sense to me. I could almost imagine their conversation and the words that Lauren had left me with, once again went around my head.

You discard people that are no longer of use to you.

I guessed what he'd told her. I could hear in my head how he told her I'd left Ashley when she'd lost another baby, because that's what the poor kid believed at the time.

'Did you tell Lauren what I said to Mom at the hospital about me not staying around anymore?'

He nodded his reply, looking guilty.

'Don't worry, Flint. You didn't hurt her, I seem to manage to do that all by my fucking self.'

Managing to smile at him, I leant further towards him and ruffled his hair with my hand. 'I'm glad you like her, she means a lot to me.'

'Do you still love her?' As he asked the question, I was suddenly aware that I could feel her chain in the front pocket of my jeans.

'Yeah, I do.' I nodded at him.

'Then, Dad, I hope you manage to get her back.'

'I aim to.' Now I had absolute proof that she'd only got engaged to keep me at arms' length, nothing was going to keep me away. 'After New Year, we're going to go back to Vegas. We've got some awards thing to go to. After that, me, you and your mom need to sit down and talk. We need to get everything out in the open... then I'm back here. I don't know how I'm going to prove to her how much she means to me, but I'm going to spend the rest of my life trying.'

I knew my conversation had probably gone far too deep, so I ruffled his hair again with my hand and smiled.

'I can come back too, can't I.'

'Yeah. I'd love you to.'

'I can tell Lauren that I got it wrong and apologise.'

'I'm the one who needs to apologise, not you, Flint.'

The door being knocked made both of our heads turn in its direction.

'Uncle Riff, Flint... can I come in please?' Brie's voice hit our ears.

I looked at Flint and he nodded. So, jumping up, I made my way over the mess in the middle of the room and unlocked the door for her. She entered immediately and gave me a huge smile, before she turned all her attention to Flint who was still sitting on the floor.

'I saved you some cookies, Flinty. Dad has gone to get us some milk, so we can dunk them.' I watched as she sat down next to him and offered him the white box.

'Thanks, shorty. That means a lot.'

The door opened and Cade and Luke appeared. It was obvious they'd sent Brie in first to check the coast was clear. Once she was allowed in, they'd followed.

Within ten minutes the drum kit had been reassembled and we were all sat on the floor dunking the kids' cookies into milk.

In turn, I nodded at them both to show I appreciated them being here.

We were a family.

We weren't fucking conventional.

But somehow it worked for us.

Lauren

Christmas Day

'Well that's a bloody relief, I'm pleased she's okay,' Winter exclaimed as she entered my flat in front of me, walking out of her heels and hanging up her coat.

I watched as she walked towards the log burner. She left our presents on one of my small settees and made her way over to stoke the embers of the fire.

'Do you mean Nan or Amy?... Are you staying tonight?' I gesticulated to the settee, knowing Amy's stuff was still in my spare room.

'Both... it's been a hell of a week for us all, hasn't it? And yes, but I'll share with you if that's okay?'

'That's fine, of course you can.' At least her being there might erase the thought of the last person to share my bed. I walked further inside the threshold and pushed the door closed behind me by leaning on it. I couldn't use my hands as I was holding the Christmas present we had just found outside of my front door close to my chest.

'Are you going to open it?'

I don't know, am I? My eyes came up to find hers as I thought over my predicament and then fell straight back to the box in my hands.

I placed the beautifully wrapped, square box on the small, protruding shelf next to my front door. I shrugged out of my wool coat, pulled my bobble hat off my head and placed it next to the present that I still couldn't take my eyes off.

'In a minute.' I looked up to meet her gaze. 'Do you know anything about it?'

'Honestly, no. I haven't spoken to Raff since I told him we weren't coming to their fancy dinner today at The Manor. My big brother was pissed, not sure if that was because he would have to spend more time with my dad without a large crowd, or if it was because you weren't spending the day with him.'

'I suppose it might not be from him.' My eyes wandered back to the gift.

'Hey, girl, this is me you're talking to…you *know* it's from him… If you're not opening it now…Well, I can't watch you any longer. I can't stay if all you're going to do is stare at it and contemplate… So, can I shower first?'

I nodded at her. 'Yes, you know where the fresh towels are and there's clean PJs in the normal drawer. I'm going to throw some more logs on the fire and grab a drink. Do you want one?'

'Please,' she called out as she walked towards my bedroom door. Then her voice drifted off as she disappeared into my bathroom and I just managed to hear, 'Something on the side of stronger would be good.'

I listened to the sound of the water starting and Winter singing in her very own, unique off-tune way. Then I walked away from the box and busying myself, I pushed as many logs as I could fit onto the log burner and slammed the door shut quickly before they attempted to roll back out. Picking up a dark red fleece from the back of a settee, I wrapped it around my shoulders. The weight of the fleece settled me a little and I knew I'd grabbed at it more for comfort than for its warmth. Finally, lost in my own thoughts, I went over to pour us a couple of whiskeys. I drank my first one straight down, then I refilled my glass. Relishing the burn in the back of my throat and the fumes which entered my nostrils afterwards, fleetingly I closed my eyes. On the way back to the sitting area of my large open-plan living space, I carried the cut glasses with the fingers of one hand and picked up the box as nonchalantly as I could with the other.

Eventually, I placed all of them down on the thick cream carpet. I crossed my legs underneath me and sat down. Sipping at my whiskey and listening to Winter murder "Fairy tale of New York" in the shower, I sank back into the settee behind me in tiredness. There I stayed, motionless, staring at the beautifully wrapped but unmarked Christmas box.

'I know it's from you, Raff,' I whispered to the silent room.

Still wearing the deep red fleece wrapped around me, I leant forward, reached out to touch the box and let my fingers toy with the bow on top. I played with the green velvet ribbon, sliding the soft fabric between my fingers as I worked up the courage to open it, and I thought back over a week that had seen so much change in our lives.

The Fairy Garden had been full to capacity, from Tuesday through to our last opening day before Christmas, Friday. My small business was thriving, if only I could say the same for myself.

I had managed to be too busy to see Toby at all and that was an enormous relief, not only to me but I thought probably to him as well. His mum was now ill with the flu and although I didn't wish that one on her, it was a relief to know he would be caught up looking after her. I knew that although our sudden engagement was something we needed to have a conversation about, it wouldn't be happening anytime soon. Even without talking about it, I felt we both understood that it wasn't going to stand the test of time. He, never wanting to lose at anything especially to Raff, had seized an opportunity and run with it. I, on the other hand, had grabbed at the only way out I could see in that moment. So, for the time being his too tight engagement ring on my finger, remained the shield that Winter had insisted it really was.

Every day during this week, I'd seen Raff. He'd turned up in the tearoom at different times of the day and had always managed to secure a small table or sofa in the room, to sit and drink for a while. Thinking about it, I knew the girls who worked for me must have been secretly helping him to achieve that. But, I never questioned them about it. His presence in the tearoom checking up on me every day had helped me get through the week. I hoped he was biding his time, allowing me the space I needed to work everything out in my head. The fact he came every day reassured me that not only did he remember and understand how I ticked, but also, he was patient and determined enough to let me work through everything in the only way I knew how.

In the few glances I'd allowed myself of him, I'd taken in everything about him. Every time I'd allowed myself a fleeting look, I knew without a doubt even though his face didn't change in expression, his eyes were on me. He'd sat every day brooding and watching for me, as I'd busied myself. His dark hair was always messy and he used it like a curtain, looking through the longer strands as he surveyed the room. The man was a crowd pleaser, daily the people in the tearoom had caught on to who they were sharing their light breakfast or afternoon tea sitting next to. Luckily, they seemed to be disciplined enough to leave him alone, only on an occasion had people stopped by his table to shake his hand and remind him of a time gone by when he'd delivered their papers as a paperboy, or how they'd gone to school together. He'd smiled politely and even signed an autograph or two, then the conversation had very often fallen flat. He had then smiled his well-practised goodbye at them and they had vacated his space, this left him once again free to search me out.

Even casually dressed, he had given off an air of magnetism that was hard to disguise. I could see that even those who didn't know him, or quite who he was, were intrigued by him. He had worn old T-shirts under checked shirts, which shouted comfortable and relaxed. His choice of clothing didn't leave the women, including me, around him relaxed, because there was no way the old clothes could disguise how they stretched over his solid, muscular chest. With the sleeves of his shirt casually rolled up, all eyes fell to his large forearms, which were only covered by the strips of leather and the cuffs he always wore. And when he stood, the old, well-worn jeans he wore with them, accentuated his muscular backside.

His clothes were as comfortable as he seemed to be, as he relaxed back into whatever chair he was sitting on that day and stretched his long legs out in front of him. His body language screamed that he had nothing to prove to anyone. Then his eyes would find mine and for a few seconds he would let me see past the smoke screen that he was creating. Just long enough for me to see how uncomfortable he was. Then I would remind myself that he had everything to prove to me and force myself to look away

Every day this week I had tried to steer clear of him. Just once he'd touched my arm and asked me to sit down. I'd pulled it sharply away and ignored his request. Then he'd narrowed his eyes, twisted his head in question at me before rolling in his bottom lip and biting down on it. From then on, I'd tried to stay out in the kitchen or to find jobs that had to be done in the office, but often the tearoom had been so busy that I was required to help. All the time I'd been out front, I had felt his eyes follow me around as I worked. Most of the time I tried to stop my eyes from wandering over to him, but more often than not they'd drifted over of their own accord and I'd taken a small look at him, conserving every single piece of him to memory.

Like I needed more to torture myself with.

The day he had brought Flint and Brie with him, was worse. I had my false engagement ring to use as a shield and he used the children as a lance, as he tried to penetrate my defences. I'd managed to somehow outwardly ignore him and spent the few minutes I could spare talking to them and then getting the children to collect a small edible treat from the kitchen. Flint and Brie seemed happy to see me, but it was obvious that Flint wanted Raff to be included in the invite to the kitchen with them. I watched as they wordlessly looked at each other and wished I knew what was passing between them. Raff, after looking at me, had shaken his head at Flint and had stayed put, but when he and Brie had left the kitchen, Flint had caught my arm and whispered, 'Thank you for the cakes and I'm sorry.'

I hadn't a clue what he was sorry for.

If I hadn't understood it before, I knew now that I didn't understand the opposite sex at all, so I pushed it out of my head.

Raff still coming around and my reluctance to talk to him or face up to anything, had meant my anxiety had shown up in different ways. For the past few days I had been methodical with looking after my diabetes, using it as a form of number crunching to keep my bubbling emotions in check. It was crazy, I should have treated it this way years ago. That was positive, but the resulting negative had been that there was no way I was going to win a best boss award this week. I'd felt agitated and this had resulted in me being defiant and sometimes angrier than I should be. I'd apologised to everyone yesterday as I'd handed out their tips and a little extra as a Christmas bonus and put it down to the stress of the year.

They'd smiled back and said they understood, and I could only hope they did.

All the time I'd been avoiding him and my feelings, Amy had been avoiding Winter and me. Her shifts had been done at the tearoom and I would see her in passing, but never long enough to have a meaningful conversation with her. But, I knew we reacted in a very similar way to emotional upset. We were avoiders and we did our best to avoid any form of conflict until it smacked us in the face and we couldn't ignore it any longer.

Life had smacked us both in the face on Friday, when our family had been given the news that our beloved matriarch, our nan, was now deemed too ill with dementia to return home after her six-week respite care in the care home. The same respite care that I knew she had signed up for herself, to give Amy a break. It was our nan that I had turned to when I needed to follow Raff over to the U.S. When I realised that even at only sixteen I couldn't live without him. I knew once she'd listened to me that without a doubt she would help me book the flight I needed. I couldn't ask my mum or dad, because I knew that although my parents loved me, they would do anything they could to stop me leaving. Thankfully, our nan had always believed in love.

Not only had Amy had to cope with the news about Nan, but the shit had hit the fan yesterday evening, at the Christmas eve wedding of one of the boys we grew up with. Default Distraction had taken to the stage, having been asked last minute to perform when the snow had stopped the previously booked band from attending. All our hearts had been broken as we watched her comprehend that the man she had recently fallen in love with hadn't been telling her the truth about who he was.

Most women would be happy about the discovery that the man who'd fallen in love with them was the lead singer of a huge rock band, but not Amy.

And last, but by no means least, Winter had been given the job opportunity of a lifetime. Cade and the others had offered her the contract of overseeing the opening of their next three hotels, as she'd done such a fantastic job with The Manor. The next one was opening in Vegas and she'd be going out there soon with Cade, and the thought of that made me smile to myself.

In the space of one week, it seemed that the three of us who had been going along under the false pretences of *happy and content with our lives,* had been thrown under the path of several oncoming trains.

They were all shit hot rock stars, with bodies and looks to die for.

Now, the three of us had choices to make, we either stood up to watch our oncoming fate or we got the hell out of the way and fast. I could see what path the other two were already working towards, me, I wasn't too sure.

I was shit at making choices, as I'd proven only a few days ago.

Then I thought back to today. Winter and I had cancelled our plans to have Christmas dinner at The Manor with Raff and her family and I couldn't have been more relieved. We had managed to get Amy to open the door and to accept our apologies for not telling her sooner about Brody. We were also able to convince her of the truth that all we'd wanted was for her to have a chance of happiness. Then, having cancelled our dinner out, the three of us scraped around in the back of Nan's freezer and we'd eaten a Christmas dinner of waffles and fish fingers sitting in the middle of Nan's large bed.

It had been different, but I think different was what we all needed.

We'd spent the afternoon with Nan. I'd taken the too tight ring off my finger, saying that it was because I didn't want to confuse her, but that had been a lie. The truth was it had been a relief to remove it. Although Nan had dementia, she always seemed to be able to be the nan we needed when we needed her the most, and I didn't want to worry her. We'd then spent Christmas afternoon in her company trying hard to forget all about the changes that were happening in our lives and hers.

My fingers dropped the ribbon I'd been toying with as I thought over the last few days and I looked over to where I'd placed the presents I'd received today. My eyes flicked up to the same papercut Nan had given all three of us as a present today.

I spoke the words out loud. 'Be with someone who can understand three things in you. The sadness behind your smile. The love that enflames your anger and the reason behind your silence. Be with someone who accepts you for you.'

'Just undo the bloody thing.' Winter's voice penetrated my thoughts and I heard her sigh as she tried to persuade me. I'd been so lost thinking back over the last few days that I hadn't even noticed that the water had stopped running. My eyes shot up to find her standing in the doorway, twisting up her long blonde hair into a messy bun.

Resolutely, I nodded at her.

Pulling the green ribbon, I watched as it fell away. I took one end and wrapped the velvet around my hand as it came away from the box, then I lifted the lid. Red tissue paper filled the inside. Taking a deep breath, I unfolded the pretty paper, sheet by sheet.

The first thing that caught my eye was a glint of silver and my heart sunk that he'd tried to return my necklace. I picked up the silver shape, realising quickly that it had no chain. In between my thumb and forefinger, I could feel that the inside of the shape was thicker than the outside rim, as I rolled it around in my fingers I quickly recognised that the unusual shape I was holding was a plectrum.

Raff's plectrum?

'Is that his plectrum?' I heard Winter's question and I nodded at her in answer.

I remembered when I watched him sing and play for me in the ballroom back at The Manor, seeing a flash of silver in his fingers.

Placing it in my palm I turned it over to find a faded "forever" in the centre.

Tears pricked at the corners of my eyes as I realised what I was holding. I wrapped my hand around it tightly, feeling the metal warm in my hand and in turn that warmth then spread to the whole of my body.

He'd kept it. I was shaking my head in disbelief, tears pricked the corners of my eyes.

'His plectrum was made out of…' I started.

'I know, I can see it. I can remember you both wearing your chains,' she gently interrupted as she stepped near enough to read the word.

'After all these years. He could have had a solid gold one made with all the money he has. I can't believe it, even having been married to someone else, he kept it.' My heart was frantically banging in my chest in anticipation of what else I might find.

Rummaging a little further into the tissue paper I pulled out a strip of old photographs. The strip was folded into four, the edges of the paper were worn and the colours had faded. The film was peeling off and separating the layers of paper in places.

'It can't be,' I whispered.

Before I even turned them over I knew what I was going to find. They were four small pictures we'd had taken a long time ago. We were squashed into a photo booth, laughing and playing around as we kissed and held each other. The four photos had captured us so perfectly then, that as I ran my finger down the four of them I was taken back. I could hear our laughter, sense his arms around me and feel the touch of his lips on mine.

I lifted the hand holding the photos and ran my knuckles over my lips absentmindedly.

'How could something so right, go so badly wrong?' I hadn't even realised that I had spoken out loud, until Winter who had now arrived beside me answered.

'It's called life, and personally, the more I bloody think about it, the more I think there is more to this crazy box of frogs than we're all aware of... I think you need to start asking a few questions of certain people and I've told Raff the same.'

She retrieved her whiskey and plonked herself next to me on the floor, making sure her shoulder was touching mine in solidarity. Then she raised her arm and pulled me into her hold.

'It's too late,' I answered. 'Too much water under the bridge.' I laid my head on her shoulder.

'It's only too late when you both give up or give in.' She kissed my head in reassurance.

'Has Raff given up on me?' My voice sounded smaller than I wanted it to, but I was apprehensive of her answer.

'What do you think? Would he have kept those things if he had? I don't think he would have done if he'd moved on... Do you? And if he's had enough and moved on *now*, why would he have sent them to you?'

I opened my hands and looked at the small gifts that had brightened my day.

'Is there anything else in there?' Winter questioned.

I looked back inside, rummaging in between the sheets of red paper and finally found a small piece of card. The writing on the card read.

I've kept your smile and laughter captured in these photos safe in my wallet since the day they were taken. When what I wanted to do was to keep you safe with me. When I couldn't keep you with me, the hardest decision I ever made meant you were at least safe.

When the chain broke on our forever, I changed it into something that made sure you would always be with me. I've held this plectrum in my hand every day, when what I wanted was to hold you in my arms.

You need reminding that we're "Always and Forever." So, I'm lending them to you, but you can only borrow them. Like I'm borrowing the necklace you gave back to me.

You're my girl and you need to understand that you were never discarded. One day I'll prove it to you. I know you don't want to talk to me yet.

But one day I pray you will.

Until then, I keep and hold you safe in my heart.

We will *always* be *forever.*

'Oh, brother of mine,' I heard her whisper as she read over my shoulder.

I clutched the gifts he'd given me as gently as I could and held them to my heart as I fell into Winter's arms and sobbed at the ridiculously unfair situation I was in.

Can I trust him?

Those few words went around my head as my heart screamed to be heard. They went unanswered until my head finally forced my heart to shut up.

'Give it time, Lauren. All things come to pass in time,' Winter whispered to me as she held me close.

I mulled over her words, thinking they were the truest thing I had heard in a while.

Chapter 32

Lauren

Five weeks later

I was ensnared.

My life had fast become likened to an old-fashioned record, with its needle stuck. I was still whirring, still producing the noise I needed to, in order that people knew I was still operating, but the track of my life felt like it had run its course and I couldn't see how to start it again from the beginning.

The weeks between Christmas and the end of January were strange. I was in the clutches of the weird twilight zone that becomes the dull of winter after Christmas. It had left me not even knowing what day of the week it was. I went to work when it was dark and gloomy and when I came out of the tearooms late in the afternoon it was once again dark. The forecasted month of snow stopped just as the weathermen had predicted it would and the roads were at last completely passable. But, the deep covering of snow in the fields meant that the countryside around us was still picturesque and peaceful, which was more than I could say for my mind.

I had to be honest with myself, I was in limbo because my heart was broken again. The pain of losing him again was too much to bear. Every day felt like an eternity as I outwardly got on with my life, but inwardly I was beginning to mentally fall apart, as daily I argued, twisted and tried to sort through the various scenarios in my head.

Maybe I should talk to him?

Let him go, he doesn't deserve you.

Perhaps there was a valid reason for his actions?

You can live without him, you've proven it before.

My life felt like it was running on automatic. I was existing but not living and it didn't matter what excuse I came up with in my head to warrant the way I was acting, I knew it couldn't last much longer. I didn't feel brilliant, I was tired and grumpy and felt sure I was fighting off some sort of virus. But, instead of having a day or two off sick, I worked every day we opened, because in my head, I knew I had to make sure that when I went upstairs to my flat at night, I was completely exhausted.

Amy was away training for her new job, Winter was busy preparing for her new position and these things gave me the perfect excuse to lock myself away with only my head and heart for company.

It was painfully and slowly killing me.

But, the first week of February at last saw some change.

With our busy period being now well and truly over and knowing that the spring cleaning in The Fairy Garden was done, I decided to take the week off and although I was dreading it, I had a monthly doctor's appointment to make and I also knew I needed to rest.

I spent the first two days of my week off with Winter. I think the term she used was, we both required some much needed retail therapy. The term I would have used was, we both needed an escape. I was happy to be with her, but my heart wasn't in it. I had however, put on make-up for the first time in forever and had willingly trailed around behind her as she tried on everything that even remotely caught her eye. She either shopped like a mad woman or found herself several men to warm her bed, when she was trying to ignore something else in her life.

I was thankful that this time she was only shopping.

The second day she had booked us both in for a Spa day. We had every treatment known to man in the space of eight hours and I tried so very hard to relax, but it was useless. We had been friends for so long, we had got through Raff leaving us both before and then the heartbreak of me having to come home. But, this time it was different. There was a wedge between us. She was trying so hard to be my friend, but I knew without a doubt she was struggling being stuck in the middle of me and her brother. It appeared that even spending time with her wasn't enough to give me the peace I needed.

On the Wednesday, I woke up to find that a handwritten letter had been posted through my door. The letter was from Toby who I hadn't seen, much to my relief, since our farcical engagement just before Christmas. His mum was now at home after having been admitted to hospital suffering with complications that arose from the flu. Initially he'd stayed away from me because he was busy looking after her, but he wrote what I had been desperately hoping he might realise. Our time apart had given him the time to see that we weren't suited to be together and he asked to be released from our engagement and that I return his ring ASAP. He wished me well and hoped he hadn't broken my heart, then the letter had been ended with how Lucy his assistant had been a great help to him when his mum was ill and he was going to ask her to marry him just as soon as the ring was once again in his hands.

I'd gone through various emotions as I'd read his words, liberation was the first, quickly followed by the overwhelming relief that I wasn't going to have yet another conversation with him about why I didn't want to be with him. Then I'd spat out my cornflakes and laughed until tears ran down my face when he wrote about needing the ring back ASAP to get engaged again. My hysterical laughter soon turned into sobs and I felt guilty because I knew those sobs weren't for Toby and I, but once again for me losing Raff.

As soon as I could pull myself together, I pulled on some leggings, an oversized hoodie and some Hunters. I'd dropped his ring into an envelope and had driven as fast as I could. Without interacting with anyone in the village, I'd put the envelope through his letterbox that same morning. As the brass metal snapped its pseudo jaws shut around its prize, I turned and rushed back to my car, grateful that I could at last close that chapter of my life.

I knew I was supposed to be off and relaxing, but after the two days with Winter and today with only my own morose company to contend with, I'd had enough. Even watching my favourite films tucked up on the settee for the rest of the morning, with a pot of ice cream, didn't help.

I had to face it, I couldn't stand my own company anymore, so I relented and went down to the tearooms.

After wandering around the quiet tearoom for twenty minutes looking for something to occupy me, I quickly realised that Debbie and Kirsty, my full-time staff, had the place completely and annoyingly all in hand. I stood in the middle, warming myself by the log burner and absentmindedly turned around in a circle. I was looking at the various places in the tearooms that Raff had sat. I could see him sitting there watching me, waiting for me to come to my senses. I looked down at the table I was nearest to and stepping towards it, I tidied up the place settings that needed no tidying and sighed loudly. Then I lifted my head as I held on tightly to the back of the chair I was stood behind and managed to catch myself in the Baroque mirror over the fireplace. For the first time in weeks, I took in how I really looked, not just the pale, sad creature on the outside, but the broken shell of the woman on the inside, and I realised that enough was enough.

No more.

I couldn't put off what needed doing anymore.

'You're both doing a great job,' I called out to Debbie and Kirsty as I pulled my gaze away from my reflection in the mirror and started to move. I turned and watched as they looked at each other knowingly and then back to me. 'But, then you knew that without me telling you.' I smiled at them both and walked nearer to them.

'I'm not sure what you came down here for in the first place,' Kirsty retorted and offered me a small smile.

'I'd say she misses someone. I mean even I miss him being in here every day… but it must be worse once you've actually had those lips on yours,' Debbie answered her.

'I do miss him and yes it's much worse.' I heard the words I spoke and took a few seconds for them to wash over me.

So, what are you going to do about it?

With that thought in my head and Winter's words about us both needing to start asking questions to get to the truth, I turned suddenly and moving quickly towards the arched front doors I grabbed my coat down from a hook.

'Good luck,' they both called out as if they could read my mind, then the door closed with a bang behind me.

I walked a few steps, feeling the gravel crunch under my feet and then jumped into my red Mini Cooper. Switching on the engine I paused for a moment before I pulled away, enjoying the feeling that my body was finally beginning to settle as it understood that I was going to do something proactive at last. I pulled out of the courtyard and under the archway, followed the single lane track. I came to the T-junction that separated the main road from The Manor's driveway and I glanced in The Manor's direction for a second, before I swung the car left.

Stop it! He isn't even there.

I knew he wasn't, but I hadn't been able to help myself. All of Default Distraction had flown back to America a few days after New Year and for one reason or another they were still in the U.S. After Christmas, I'd taken the Google alert off Raff and the rest of the band, so I hadn't seen any pictures or read anything about them. But, I'd been told by Winter that they were attending some music awards gala, then had given several interviews to the tabloids and TV stations. They'd stayed longer than they first thought because they had family stuff to attend to and the Vegas hotel to sort out. Although I knew that was why I was no longer seeing him almost daily sitting in The Fairy Garden, not seeing him these past few weeks waiting patiently for me to listen to him was eating away at me.

I drove quickly around the narrow lanes, enjoying the rush of adrenalin that was running through me as I accepted what I needed to do to move forward. But, even as the adrenalin lit me up with hope, the tiny feathers of nervousness moved around my stomach as I contemplated that I might not get the answers I wanted to hear.

I finally reached the village of Falham where we had all been brought up and where Nan's shop had been before it had quickly sold two weeks ago to a property developer. I slowed the car in accordance with the speed limit for the village, and looked at her old place as I went past it.

Nothing had changed there yet. I knew it would soon and I took in the view of the old Victorian frontage, feeling a sense of comfort from looking at it and reliving some of the happy times we'd all spent in there.

I needed to see Nan and now I'd made the decision I couldn't get there quick enough.

I could only hope she was with me today and I was able to get her to answer a question for me. It was only one question, but where I went to next was dependant on her answer.

The avoider in me was slowly awakening. I was beginning to face up to what I'd known all along. If I wanted any sort of a future, with or without him, I had to start asking some questions. I needed to piece together the jigsaw and hopefully then that would give me the peace of mind that comes from knowing the truth.

I knew that discovering the answers might in their own way cause me pain, but nothing could be worse than what I'd lived through for the last seventeen years.

As I walked down the corridor that led to Nan's room in the home, I could hear her voice, she was singing to one of her old records. I was eager to see her and to talk to her, but I forced my feet to slow to a standstill. I wanted to appreciate the happiness in her voice as she sang to one of her favourite songs. Finally, I pushed open the door a little, as well as listening to her sing I knew she'd be dancing and I wanted to watch her.

As the door opened a few inches I peeked around the white, glossed wood to see her waltzing around by herself, to **I won't forget you – Jim Reeves.**

Nan looked up the moment the door moved and smiled a welcome to me to come in, not once did she miss a word she was singing or a step in her waltz. I moved over the threshold and pushed the door closed behind me. She opened her arms and gestured that I should walk into her hold and join her. I dropped my coat and did as she asked, remembering another time when as kids we'd taken it in turns standing on her feet as she waltzed us around the living room above the shop to this exact song.

Times had changed, I was a few inches taller than her now, but I followed her lead and embraced the times passed. She sung the words to me holding me close to her and I held myself in check thinking how poignant they were. She sung about forgetting many things, but she would never forget her only love. I refused to cry, I so wanted to with everything that was going on. But, I wanted her to sing the words and to feel happy, this song and this dance wasn't about me. It was about her and her memories, her happy memories with Grandad that were fading fast.

After letting the record play twice more, she released me, switched off her record player and collapsed back into her high backed, winged armchair. Taking her embroidered hankie from her cardigan pocket she dabbed at her face.

'You're a beautiful dancer, Lauren. Thanks for the twirl.' She looked up at me smiling.

'You're the dancer, Nan. I just followed your feet like the old days.' I smiled my answer over to her and watched her eyes twinkle as she remembered something.

'Oh, yes,' she whispered as she grinned back. 'I'm not a collector of things, you know, Lauren. But, I am a collector of wonderful memories and although I can no longer still see many of them up here.' Her arm came up as she pointed at her temple. 'I will always feel them in here.' The same hand came down and she held it over her heart. 'In here, I will feel my memories until the last breath leaves my body.'

I leant nearer to her to place my hand on hers over her heart and cleared my throat, trying to swallow down the emotion that was building up inside me and sitting down on the footstool next to her chair, I reached over to take her other soft hand in mine.

Gripping my hand a little tighter, she jerked my arm towards her.

'So, what's going on?

'Oh, you know.'

I felt the moment she snapped to attention and I knew she was with me. It always seemed weird that even as the dementia came and went, the moment we really needed her she knew. Somehow, she managed to get the disease to recede for a short while so she could help us.

She reached over to take my other hand in hers. Her thumb absentmindedly ran over the small mark Toby's ring, which had been too tight for me, had left on my ring finger.

'Well, this is new.'

'Mmmm,' was all I could reply.

'What was on there?'

'A ring, but it's gone now,' I answered her question

'It wasn't from Rafferty...' she stated.

'No, it's wasn't, but how did you know that?'

'He would have told me.'

I raised my eyebrows at her as I thought hard how to answer her. My heart sank as I appreciated that she might not be able to answer my question after all. I wasn't sure now whether her memories were intact and what year she even thought it was.

'Would he?' I replied. The trepidation inside me made my voice sound a little unsteady.

'Yes, he was only here the other day... I can't remember which day, because I've probably slept since then.' I could hear the subtle change in her voice as she panicked slightly at the fact she couldn't remember what she wanted to and then as she gave me the answer she always used as her get out clause.

'He was?' I questioned.

'Yes, he was telling me all about the old place he's doing up, can't remember its name. It's on the tip of my tongue.'

'Falham Manor.'

'Yes, that's it... He's doing up Falham Manor?' she suddenly questioned as she remembered the old place.

'He is, well him and the rest of his band... So, he told you about Falham Manor?' Hope swept through me as I tried to place her on the track I needed her to be on.

'Yes, that's what I just said, didn't I?' she quickly answered me, in her "I'm not stupid" voice.

'What else did he say?' I knew I was pushing my luck and her for that matter, but I needed to know. I hoped that asking her the question, wouldn't cause her too much stress as she tried to remember.

'Oh, this and that... He's having trouble with his son.'

'Flint? Is he? Did he say why?'

'Not that I remember. Now stop asking me questions, Lauren. Who's ring were you wearing and why aren't you wearing it now?'

'It was Toby's ring.'

I saw a look of puzzlement spread over her face. She had met him a couple of times. I'd known that she wouldn't remember him, because every time she met him her nose had wrinkled up in distaste and let's face it she couldn't remember things she used to love, so why would she bother with someone she didn't even like.

'Oh, him,' she replied. I knew by her reply that she couldn't put a face to the name but was pretending she could.

'I've broken it off.'

'Good.' It was refreshing that my nan always said exactly what she thought, but she snapped the word out so quickly, she took me aback. 'Because you still love Rafferty, don't you?'

'I've always loved him, Nan.'

'I know you have.' She held my hand a little tighter as she acknowledged what I was saying.

'When I went out to Vegas to be with him, you booked my flight for me, do you remember?' I hesitantly asked.

'I did, I got into so much trouble with your parents for that?' She laughed a little as she reminisced.

'Sorry, Nan.' I'd apologised before, but felt it was necessary to do so again.

She waved her hand at me, telling me to forget it.

'I'd do it all over again for you, Lauren.' She moved towards me and stroked my cheek with her fingers. 'I always felt that you two were meant to be.'

'I only just about had enough money to pay for that flight, didn't I?' I prompted.

'Yes, my love. All that hard-earned babysitting money, and I had to put a little to it as well to cover it.'

'I didn't realise…' My voice trailed off, before I asked her the final question. 'Do you remember if the flight had travel insurance with it?'

'No…'

My heart sank. I knew I was asking too much and that the answer I needed was too insignificant in her life for her to have filed away.

I smiled and shook my head gently at her. 'Don't worry, Nan. I don't need the answer.'

'Lauren, I did answer. I didn't have enough money to buy insurance too.'

For a few seconds, I just looked at her as the information she'd given me filtered through to my brain first and then to my heart. The fear and pain of the truth became overwhelming, before a wave of sickness washed over me and the world blurred in front of my eyes. I dipped my head quickly down to my knees and fought with everything I had to ward off the rising bile and the light-headedness that accompanied it.

Raff

I picked up my black leather holdall with both hands and with one swift shake I aggressively tipped the contents all over my bed and looked at the mess. With one hand, I swept the mess to the floor. I couldn't be fucking arsed to sort through it.

Jetlag was beginning to hit me and fast.

But, I knew it wasn't the fucking jetlag that had me feeling this way.

Moving away from my bed I walked towards my window, crossed my arms tightly over my chest and stared outside. Then lost in my thoughts, I pushed my hair away from my face and back on top of my head and clasped my hands together at the back of my neck as I looked up to the ceiling and tried to work out what had gone down between Lauren and me.

I'd arrived back at The Manor half an hour ago. As luck would have it, I'd caught sight of her and Winter through the large, arched glass doors that filled the entrance. With my heart beating faster from having not laid eyes on her for more fucking days than I cared to think about, I pulled my luggage quickly out of the boot and slammed it, not even bothering to lock my prized possession. I'd swung the bag over my shoulder and quickened my step to make sure I bumped into them. Despite the look that I'd got from Winter, I'd ignored her and had continued to walk up to them both.

We'd passed the time of day and I gleaned the information that they were here to see Amy. I'd told them in return that although Luke and I were back, Cade and Brody were still in Vegas, sorting out the hotel with Cade's family. I kind of hoped that Amy might want to know, then what I'd been looking forward to for fucking forever was over. We'd parted ways as they'd knocked on Amy's office door and had then disappeared behind it.

Like a fool, I'd stood in their wake as I tried hard to read between the lines.

Lauren had smiled an almost sad sort of embarrassed smile and said hello, but that was it. As we were in public and with Winter, I couldn't question her. I couldn't apologise for being away for longer than I'd first thought I would have to be. I couldn't explain that I'd had to spend the time with my son as Ashley and I worked hard to sort through all the shit between us for his sake. I didn't ask if she'd understood her Christmas presents and the words I'd written down especially for her, as I'd tried to explain everything that I'd long ago shut away in my heart.

She was my greatest love, my greatest regret and she would forever be the other half of me. But, still we'd stood to one side of the foyer making small talk. Talking about meaningless shit that in the grand fucking scheme of things meant absolutely fucking nothing.

I righted my head and staring back out of my window, as the world got on with their lives and mine came crashing down around me, I went over and over those all too short minutes and tried to read between the lines.

She looked tired and something else.

I could sense something. Something that she'd been telling me without using words.

In my head, I pictured her again.

She was wearing a thick winter coat in a green colour that made her amber eyes pop. The rust coloured pom-pom hat on her head showed off the different colours in her hair and when she'd hastily pulled it off her head as I'd called out to them both, my eyes had been transfixed into watching the thick waves of her hair fall back onto her shoulders. I'd been taken back to a few weeks ago, remembering brushing it off her bare shoulders and winding the thick lengths around my hand, as she'd sat on me while we fucked.

I closed my eyes as the memories in my head engulfed me.

Then as I went through the tiny clip again in my head, it clicked and my eyes flew open. I watched her hand pull the hat off her head once again and saw what I'd been waiting for.

The ring was fucking gone!

Finally, taking notice of the world outside my window, I saw her red Mini Cooper disappear around the last bend of the long driveway.

'What's going on, Lauren?' I questioned the empty room and spinning around quickly I walked hurriedly towards my bedroom door and grabbed my keys from the bedside table.

'Jetlag be fucking damned, I'm not resting until I work this shit out.'

By the time the door slammed behind me, I was already at the top of the first flight of stairs.

As I jumped down them two at a time, my brain was whirring, going through all the various scenarios in my head.

She was no longer engaged. It was fucking fantastic, but...
Why?

Where was she speeding to get to? She hated people who sped around the lanes here, I remembered her calling them dangerous and reckless.

I couldn't come up with an answer, but I knew in my heart she was leaving me a trail to follow, even if she didn't know it herself.

I ran to the car, jumped in and started her up all at the same time. I pulled out of the carpark like a fucking lunatic, spewing gravel in all directions, hoping that there was no one walking anywhere near to the driveway. I was driving far too fucking fast as I sped up the narrow exit. It was all going well and I knew I had to be making up time on her, when I had to come to a screeching halt at the turning to The Fairy Garden.

Well that's fucking ironic.

The back end of my car slipped and I just managed to control it. I pulled up with only a few feet to spare from the delivery truck. It appeared that he had got himself stuck trying to turn into the narrow archway entrance to the tearoom carpark.

'FUCK!' left my mouth with force into the empty car.

The driver looked at me, obviously hearing me swear and raising his hands, he showed me his ten fingers as he gesticulated how long he was going to be. Although, by the look on his face, I could see he thought I was a fucking arsehole and he would probably take longer just to fuck with me.

I nodded at him and lowered my head onto the top of my steering wheel.

'Now what?'

Lauren would be long gone.

After looking around the village, without being able to locate Lauren's car, I'd pulled up in front of the building that contained a woman who I knew I could open my heart to. My heart was pounding, frustration was running riot around my body and I needed a dose of reality.

I spent just over half an hour with the lady, who against everyone else's wishes and instructions, had always believed in us. The same lady who meant as much to me as my own grandmother did. I knew that she was suffering with dementia as Winter had kept me up to date over the years and since I'd been back I'd visited her a couple of times already.

But today was a bad day for her, her carer had told me as much as soon as I walked into the building. Although, taking in the look on my face, she said I could still visit, if Vera was happy for me to be there.

Vera offered me a smile after I poked my head around her door after knocking, and taking that as an invitation I put my problems to one side and went in and sat with her. She spoke to me like she was sitting in the kitchen at Lauren's mum and dad's house and I'd arrived to pick up Lauren for a date. I went along, happy to reminisce with her and I enjoyed watching as her face lit up as we discussed the beautiful young girl that was her granddaughter.

When she started to doze off, I took my cue to leave. I placed a kiss on the hand of hers that I'd been holding and put it back onto the arm of her chair.

But as always, Vera somehow managed to give me the information I wanted and needed to know.

Her carer stopped me as I put pen to paper to sign out of the building.

'Sorry, Rafferty. Vera gave me this yesterday and she was most insistent that you had to have it as soon as possible. I should have remembered earlier when you came in... but it's busy in here today. Anyway, I've remembered now, so here you go.' I looked down at her fingers which held on to a small square, florescent yellow post-it note that Vera had written on.

I took it, thanked her and walking back to my car I read the words she'd written especially for me.

Now, lost in my own thoughts I drove out of Falham village and towards where I was now convinced I would find Lauren. Knowing what I was about to face, my head went back to where it had all started.

"Operator, how can I help you?"

"I need help to make a call to England, please."

"Do you need to reverse the charges?"

"Yes..., yes please and can you tell them it's an emergency?"

"Of course, can I have the number, please."

Gripping hold of the receiver, I gave the number to the operator and leant my forehead against the cool metal of the aluminium of the false wall behind the phone. My heart was pounding. I could hear Cade walking around behind me and Cerise's soft crying, as she sat on Luke's lap and let go of her fears.

I forced my conscious thoughts back to the phone as I heard the operator speak again.

"Connecting you now."

"Thanks," I murmured into the phone and closing my eyes I willed all the strength I had, as I prepared myself to ask for help from

the man I had long ago sworn never to ask for anything from ever again.

"Well this is a surprise, Rafferty."

I ignored his condescending fucking tone and tried to rise above it. I'd long ago realised that I would do anything for Lauren and I drove myself forward when my hand twitched to be allowed to slam the receiver down on him.

"I need help, Rupert."

"Well, well, well."

I hated the fucking bastard with everything I had.

"I wouldn't ask for me. But, it's not for me, it's for Lauren. She's ill. We've brought her to the ER in Vegas. I will pay you back, it would only be a loan."

"You need money?"

"Yeah," I answered, sighing into the phone.

"Not a star yet then?"

"No. Look, I know what you think of me... I'm begging you to help us. I'll do anything to get what she needs... Please can you help us?"

I heard him tut into the phone and could imagine the look of pure joy on his face as he took in my desperation and pain. "What a mess you've created, boy. Just think, if you'd have followed what I wanted for you, you'd both still be here with your families around you. That poor girl and it's all down to you."

I rolled my bottom lip over my teeth and bit down as I forced myself to remember the bigger picture and how much Lauren needed help. So, I took a deep breath and ignored him, effectively letting him carry on. "I'm sorry to hear about your difficulties." In my head I rolled the words 'I bet' around when he paused mid-conversation. "But, unfortunately, you've called the wrong place I'm afraid, I don't have any money. So, I can't help you."

His words made the pain and fear already travelling around my gut expand to the point of being excruciating.

"You don't have any?" My voice got louder as I spoke the words back to him in disbelief. "I know you fucking hate me, but this is her life we're talking about and you're telling me that you don't fucking have any."

"Don't you raise your voice at me, my boy. Unless you want me to take out yet another loan on this dilapidated house and put your mum and sister's stability in possible jeopardy, I can't help you. Is that what you want me to do?"

"Two minutes left," the operator's voice interrupted us both and for a couple of seconds I removed the phone from my ear and looked up to find Cade staring at me. I watched as he shook his head and gesticulated he would make a call and get what I needed.

I shook my head at him and spoke back into the phone.

"No, I don't want you to risk them."

"I didn't..."

I'm sure he had more to say, but I pressed the button and ended the call. I didn't need to hear anything more come out of his mouth. After waiting a couple of minutes, I released the button I was pressing down. I'd been holding it down so forcibly that my finger was turning white with the pressure and lack of blood flow.

I was so fucking pissed off with him.

"Operator."

"Hi, I need assistance please to make a call to the UK."

I gave Lauren's mum and dad's number and the fact I needed them to accept the call because it was an emergency and then I waited. As the phone began to ring thousands of miles away, I turned around in the stark, white corridor with its few plastic covered chairs and bright lights. I closed my eyes, allowed my knees to bend and my back to slide down the wall. The phone wire was stretched to capacity as I sat down on my haunches and tried to hold it all together. Once they'd stabilised her, and I hoped with everything I had they would do, at that point we either needed a credit card that worked or some sort of insurance that would cover her hospital stay.

What we needed was a miracle.

"Rafferty." The accusation flooded through the phone without him saying another word.

"Mr. Harper. I'm sorry. Lauren has been taken into the emergency room at Summerlin Medical centre here in Vegas. She's very ill. She needs your help please. I need your help."

Raff

I pulled up a few cars behind Lauren's and reversed into the empty parking space, feeling a sense of relief at finding her. I could see she was still sitting in the driver's seat. I took a quick look at my wristwatch, working out she must have been here just under an hour, and I tried hard to get into her head as I wondered why she still hadn't gone inside.

We sat like that for about ten more minutes, then I saw what she was waiting for. Her dad arrived in the flat-bed truck he used for his landscaping business and it all clicked into place.

He pulled forward and reversed in one fast movement onto the drive of Lauren's family home. I watched as he lifted his hand to wave at her and then he disappeared from my view.

I stared, waiting for her to get out of her car.

My phone vibrating in the front pocket of my jeans broke me out of my trance and adjusting my position I manged to retrieve it, pulling it from my pocket.

Ignoring the notification, I opened my messages and started to type.

'**Are we going in?**' Then I pressed send.

I saw the moment she read my message as she turned her head to look for me. Grabbing my jacket from the seat next to me, I pushed open my door. I placed my hand up onto the roof of the car and pulled myself out of the low sports car. Thrusting both arms into the jacket, I back kicked my driver's door closed, not giving a fuck if I marked the new paintwork and jogged past the couple of cars in between us.

Her head turned slowly and then her eyes found mine as she looked through the half steamed up glass of her driver's door.

I could see that she'd been crying

Offering her a small smile of encouragement, I wrapped my fingers around the car's door handle, pulled it open and offered her my hand. Much to my relief, without any hesitation whatsoever, her gloved hand came up to find mine and I stepped back so she could get out. As soon as she was standing, I used the one hand I had to pull her into my body. It wasn't an action that I'd spent any time thinking about, but an action that was so natural to us.

She fell into my body with force and I wrapped both of my arms and my open jacket around her and held her close, trying to warm her up. Looking up into the grey, gloomy sky I sent up my thanks to whoever was looking down on us.

'Don't be kind to me, I pushed you away and I don't deserve your kindness and I just can't cry any more,' she whispered into my chest.

'I promise not to be kind, if you promise never to push me away again.'

I bent my head down, allowed my nostrils to fill up with the scent of her shampoo and then I gently and slowly pressed my lips to her head. When she didn't flinch, or recoil away from my touch, my heart literally expanded to twice its size with hope.

'You deserve everything, Lauren and I mean to make sure you get it. Here today, we're going to start with the truth.'

'How did you know where I was?' she questioned.

'One word… Vera.'

'You've been to see Nan?'

I nodded, with my chin resting on her head I knew she could feel the action.

'I spent some time with her and somehow she told me what she sensed I needed to know. I'm here because you're here, it's that simple. We're both here because we both deserve to know what happened all those years ago, don't we?' Steam left my mouth when I spoke, it was freezing outside, but with her wrapped up in my arms I knew I would stand here for eternity.

She nodded against my chest.

'We have some answers, but it doesn't fit together, does it?'

'No. But, as much as I want to know, I'm almost scared to. I came here yesterday after speaking to Nan and didn't go in. Because the missing pieces to my greatest ever heartache are there inside that house with my parents, who I love and who I know love me.'

'I know you're scared and so am I… But, we can't go on like this. It's like we're slowly killing each other. I arrived back in the country today, having had to stay away for far fucking longer than I wanted to and the first thing I saw was you. It fucking killed me to greet you like we were just friends and then, in a few minutes, our conversation was over. You went in to see Amy and I went up to my room. I can't live like that, seeing you, but not being able to touch or kiss you.' I moved my feet as I thought over what words I needed to find to carry on. 'I stood in my room trying to control the anger inside me at having to let you walk away and I knew there was something I was missing. In my head, I went over the few words we'd spoken, but the answer wasn't there. It was more about what you weren't saying.'

'After all these years, you still understand me.' I could feel her shaking her head a little against my chest.

'Lozzie, where are you? The kettles on, love,' her mum shouting travelled over to us.

'I can and there's a million other things I remember and cherish about you and as much as I'd like to list each and every fucking one, I think first we both need to go inside there.' I leant my head towards her mum and dad's house and I knew she understood what I meant, even though she couldn't see me. 'Because, I think we both deserve the truth, don't you?'

Her arms that had been caught between us both started to move and I relaxed my hold on her just a little. Once they'd been released she wound them both underneath my jacket and around my body.

I inhaled deeply as my T-shirt moved with her movement and the bare skin of her wrist touched my flesh.

Fuck! The connection I had with her even after all the years apart was unlike anything else I'd ever witnessed. It still had the strength and power to shock me. Even in the emotional circumstances that we were about to embroil ourselves in, my body jumped to life at the simple touch.

'Thank you for coming.' She squeezed her arms around me just a little tighter.

'Always and forever, Loz,' I whispered back.

Reluctantly, I released my hold on her, but I couldn't let go completely. Walking up the path to her parents' home side by side, I reached out with my fingers to hers, threaded them together and took hold.

Lauren

With my arm behind me and gripping hold of Raff's fingers tightly, I pushed down the handle and opened the inner door to Mum and Dad's house.

Even though Raff was here with me as we sought together for the truth of what had happened all those years ago, I felt tense and apprehensive at what the truth would bring in its wake.

I loved my family, we'd always been close.

I'd always felt their love for me and although over the years we'd had our ups and downs like most families, we were, or so I thought, close. I couldn't believe they would intentionally cause me so much pain.

Raff closed the door to the porch behind us quietly and my mum's head appeared around the kitchen door.

As she wiped her hands on her apron, her smile fleetingly disappeared as she took in who was accompanying me on my visit. She looked at us for a few seconds and took in that we were standing in her hall holding hands. Then after the initial shock she regained her composure and called out a greeting.

'Hello, you two. Would you like a cup of tea?' She didn't wait for us to answer, but carried on regardless. 'Yes, I think we'll all need a cup of tea. Lauren, take Raff into the living room, the fire's lit. Go and take a seat and make yourselves comfortable.'

'Hello, Lisa, it's nice to see you,' Raff finally answered from behind me.

Mum nodded at him and pursing her lips together she held her emotions in check.

Leading Raff by the hand I turned left and walked into the shabby, but homely living room of my childhood. I sat down on the faded, floral settee and pulled Raff into the space next to me, but neither of us sat back to relax. Instead, we perched on the edge while we waited for them both to come in. As we waited, he lifted my hand onto his lap and rubbed his thumb reassuringly over my fingers.

'Are you okay?' he whispered.

'No,' I truthfully replied.

'We have to do this, Lauren. But, we can...'

'We can what? Raff you know we need to confront this today... otherwise neither of us can move on.'

Our whispering was interrupted by the arrival of my parents at the doorway together. My dad looked stoic, but my mum's hands were shaking ever so slightly as she carried in our tea on a tray.

'Thank you,' I replied and I offered her a smile, trying to reassure her.

I waited a few minutes as my mum sat down and my dad stood beside her chair. I knew why he chose to stand there, having lived with them for years I knew his body language. He wasn't comfortable with the situation that we'd presented to him, so he couldn't sit and he wanted to offer my mum the comfort of him standing beside her.

As I looked over at them, I went through all the many ways I could ask them what I needed to know, but absolutely nothing sounded right. My mouth opened and closed a couple of times as I tried in vain to start the conversation we so desperately needed to have.

I didn't want to confront them, I didn't want to accuse them and I hated the thought of losing them once I'd found out the truth. I'd watched Amy for years missing the link of parents in her life. I loved my mum and dad and not one sentence that came into my head seemed to be the correct way to go about what we'd come here to do.

Raff stood up suddenly and without releasing my hand he leant towards my dad and offered him his hand to shake. For a few seconds my dad looked at it and then finally he relented and after what looked like a strong, firm shake Raff sat down beside me and spoke.

'I'm sorry, Mr. Davenport.'

'And tell me, just what are you bloody sorry for?'

My dad's anger came spilling out into that one question and I moved, getting myself ready to jump into the conversation, but Raff gripped my hand tighter and I knew it was to discourage me.

'I'm sorry I encouraged Lauren to leave home at sixteen. I know now as a parent how much that must have hurt you both. And I'm sorry she fell so ill under my care. I'm sorry for anything I've ever done that's hurt you both, or her.' He stopped speaking for a minute and gathered my hand back up onto his lap and then he covered both of our hands with his other one and held on tight. 'But, that's it… I'll never apologise for loving your daughter and for wanting her to be with me. Not seventeen years ago, nor now in the present. Because it would be a lie. And I may be a lot of fucking things, but I've never been a liar.'

I turned my head towards him after listening quietly while he spoke and without even thinking twice I ran my fingers through his hair and lifted the hair that had fallen in front of his eyes back up onto his head. Slowly, his head turned to look at me and he moved my hand from the side of his head to his lips. He placed a kiss onto it as he looked into my eyes.

The gesture was simple and honest and I felt it deep down inside with every beat of my heart. I knew I'd been wrong in pushing him away. There had to be another explanation for what Flint heard between his parents. Raff's words had made me remember, he had never been dishonest and I knew he wasn't now.

'Are you two back together?' My mum questioned as she watched the interaction between us.

'Not yet, but with your help today, I plan on fighting with everything I have, to get Lauren back into my life. We've loved each other for forever and I believe that it will never be too late for us. Because for a love like ours, there will always be a way back to who we once were.'

A loud sob left my mum's mouth and my dad sat down on the arm of the settee to pull her close to his side as he offered her the comfort she desperately needed. Then he looked back at Raff and spoke again.

'I appreciate your apology, Raff. And I sincerely hope you never have to experience what Lisa and I went through after Lozzie left us and then subsequently, what we went through as her helpless parents, when she fell so bloody ill.'

Raff answered by nodding back at my dad.

'Please tell us how you paid for my hospital care in Vegas?' Finally, I'd found my voice and I asked the question as gently as I could.

'I will, but before you judge us you have to understand that we needed to have the money upfront to pay for your care and to get you home. It's a decision that's haunted me since we took it, but one which I know your mum and I would make all over again to provide you with what you needed.'

'Oh, fuck… It was him, wasn't it?' Raff's body became tense next to me and I turned my head between my parents and him as I tried to understand what they all seemed to be grasping and what I was missing. Unable to sit still as we waited for my dad to answer, Raff stood up and tried again. 'Wasn't it?'

'Yes.'

'Fucking hell, the evil twisted bastard. And I bet there were provisos too?' Listening to Raff speak and the way his tone changed as he did so, I now knew exactly who he was talking about.

My dad exhaled loudly as he braced himself to answer the man who was standing at my side with anger falling off him waves, but the same man that held on to my hand firmly but gently as he refused to allow his anger travel through to me.

'You two were to never know he'd lent us the money. If you found out he would pull in the loan… But, looking at you both now, the worst thing he asked was that we did whatever it took to make sure you stayed apart. If you got back together and he felt we could have stopped it, again he would pull in the loan.'

My head was pounding, the full cup of tea that I was still holding in my hand was shaking a little and tea began to run slowly down the sides. My cup looked like I felt inside. I was about to explode with emotion and anger.

'How could you both?' My worst fears had come true.

'We're so sorry, Lozzie. We had no choice.'

I stood up, still holding the cup of tea in my hand. 'There's always a bloody choice!' I screamed out in my anguish. 'I understand that you needed the money for me and I'm sorry to have put you in that position, but it was seventeen years ago. Raff told me he called here a few times, he even told me that you'd told him I was getting engaged to Bryan of all people.'

My mum cried louder at my words and turning her head she pushed her face into the dirty work clothes my dad was still wearing. Dad held her close, rubbing up and down her back as he tried to reassure her.

'We hoped in time, Lauren, you would move on,' he answered.

'AND. HAVE. I?' My anger bubbled over as I screamed at them both and understanding that this was everything I had been dreading it would turn into, I sank heavily back into their old settee. 'I've never stopped loving him, never stopped wondering all the what if's and truth be told, I've never stopped hoping he would come back. You should have told me, maybe not in the beginning, but after Raff married you could have told me.'

'How much do you still owe?' Raff speaking made me stop.

At his words, I stopped the harsh words that were flying out of my mouth, because once out and into the world they would be so hard to retract even with an apology. I took another look around my parents' shabby home and guilt hit me like a ton of bricks for all the accusations I'd flung their way. Everything made sense. They both worked so hard, Dad with his gardening and Mum with her cleaning, but they had nothing to show for it. No holidays, flash cars or even new clothes.

'I'm sorry,' I whispered to them both. 'I shouldn't have said those things…'

'Loz.' Raff interrupted me and I turned towards him. Pulling me by the hand he hadn't let go of since he helped me out of the car, he stepped towards me and lifted my chin with his other hand. 'It's okay, we can make this right.'

Then he turned back to my dad. 'Get him on the phone and put it on speaker. Let's find out exactly how much it is that you still owe.'

My dad looked at me, released my mum and then stepped towards the phone on the side table. Pressing a few buttons the sound of a dial tone filled the now silent room.

'Colonel Davenport.' I heard his condescending voice, my dad's reply and question, and it was all too much. I watched as the cup of tea in my hand fell in slow motion to the floor, splashing its contents in a far-reaching circle and the expressions on my parents' faces change from worry and guilt to looks of concern.

Then the world went black around me.

Raff

I heard his voice answer that they still owed several thousand pounds and leant towards the speaker on the phone.

'You've been found out to be the fucking bastard I always knew you were and now I'm going to finish you.'

I felt Lauren pull on my hand and then her grip as it relaxed its hold on mine and I turned my attention from the phone to her as she began to fall and then her mum began to scream.

Lauren

'There she is.' I heard what I thought was our doctor's voice and confused, I opened my eyes to look and check.

And sure enough, it was him.

'Don't worry, Lauren. You're still at your mum and dad's. Lyn and I were passing when your dad phoned us and here we are.' He smiled down at me and I realised I was now laid out on the settee.

'Dr. Carpenter?'

'You fainted, Lauren. I hear from Rafferty and your mum and dad that you've had a bit of a shock.'

'Yes, I did,' I replied, as I remembered hearing the Colonel's voice on speaker phone and understanding what his role was in keeping us apart for so long.

That meant that Raff had never wanted to leave me.

I searched around the room for Raff, and I sighed out loud as I found him. He was standing at the bottom of the settee with his arms crossed over his chest, looking extremely solemn. I could sense he was tense and his grey eyes had darkened in anger. He smiled at me as my eyes found his and his posture relaxed slightly.

'How have you been of late?' Dr. Carpenter continued to question me while holding my wrist in his hand as he checked my pulse.

'I've been feeling a bit off for a few weeks, but there's been a lot going on. But, my blood sugar has been steady,' I offered him as I tried to convince him I was fine.

'Have you fainted before?' Dr. Carpenter's eyes came up from his watch to find mine as he asked the question.

'No, but I have felt woozy a few times recently.'

I heard Raff exhale as he took in what I'd just said. Concern once again spread over his face.

'Okay, I'd like to run a few tests on you, if that's alright?' Dr. Carpenter carried on.

'Of course. But honestly, I feel fine now. I could come in later in the week?' I watched as he nodded at me and smiled back at the same time.

'That's as maybe, but I've got you here now and I know what you're like at making appointments, I think I'll do them today. Let's get you sitting up and when you're ready I'll need a urine sample please. Until then, let's do a glucose test and see how that is.'

My blood sugar result was good and after about ten minutes of sitting up, Raff helped me to my mum and dad's downstairs loo and I did my sample.

I thought, as I sat on the cold toilet seat, about what had happened in the last couple of days and shook my head at the news we had discovered. Then I sighed at the way I had shouted at my parents when I discovered their part in our story. I stood up, sealed the lid on the pot, washed my hands and opened the door. Raff was waiting, leaning on the wall outside the door, so he could help me back to the lounge. On the way past my ashen-faced looking parents, I grabbed hold of their hands and squeezed.

'I'm sorry for shouting at you, I know you never meant to hurt either of us.'

My mum held my hand for a few seconds and happy with my words she let me carry on with Raff, back to the living room. I handed over my sample with a smile and sat back down on the settee.

'I'll be back in a minute, Lauren. What I need is in my car.' Dr. Carpenter left the room and suddenly Raff and I were alone for the first time.

'I can't believe all of this,' I offered as Raff sat down next to me.

He placed his arm around my shoulders and pulled me closer to him. His hand ran up the side of my face and he gently threaded his fingers into my hair. I leant my head instinctively onto his chest and over the steady beat of his heart. My arm came around him and moving his T-shirt up a little with my hand I then placed it on his bare skin and held him close. 'Are you okay?' I questioned Raff.

Raff exhaled and I felt his chest contract under my head and then expand as he prepared himself to speak.

'I'm so fucking pissed. I want to kill him with my bare hands. I'm struggling with my hatred for him. But, then I remember that I'm sitting here with you and holding you in my arms and it's giving me the hope that we can move forward from this fucked up mess to have the life we were intended for and I'm holding myself together because it's what you need me to do.'

'I can't be angry at them, Raff. They did what they had to do at the time.' I spoke to the chest I was resting on and gently toyed with his bare flesh at his waistline.

'I'm not pissed at your parents, Lauren. They were as much pawns in his game of vengeance as we were. It's just all those years we've lost and the knowledge that I should have come back years ago to force the issue.'

'But you're here now.'

'I am and I'm not leaving. The burning question is, do you want me to stay? Because I seem to remember a few weeks ago you agreeing to *anything* to keep me at arms' length.'

I swallowed, lifted my head and looked up at him.

'I was told something. It had me running scared... I'm sorry I pushed you away, but I couldn't risk you leaving me again. I knew I wouldn't survive it.'

His lips came down to mine and he pressed them down hard as he attempted to show me his love. Just the touch of his flesh on mine comforted me. It meant we were together, just as we always should have been. The kiss was chaste, but the feelings flowing between where our skin touched each other's as we savoured our connection, was anything but. Eventually, he slowly pulled away and his silver grey eyes once again found mine. The love I found there within them took my breath away.

'Do you want to tell me what you were told?' he whispered to me

'No, not really.' I couldn't hurt Flint, so I reluctantly refused.

'You'll make a great step-mum and an even better friend.'

My eyes opened wide and then narrowed at him. 'So, you know what Flint told me?'

'Yeah, I've known since the day he told you and I sat in your tearoom day after day hoping we could talk about it. But, knowing you, I could see you weren't ready to listen.' He pressed his lips to mine again and when he pulled away he was smiling. 'God, I've fucking missed you and it was even worse after getting you back for those all too short fucking hours.' He grinned at me, sucked in his bottom lip, looked longingly at my lips and then back to my eyes.

'I've missed you, too. But what took you so long to get back?' I smiled at him as I gently teased him.

'Flint... He's the reason I stayed in the U.S. for so many weeks. It was fucking hard staying away from you, but he needed me and as his dad, I had to spend that time with him. I had to be there to force Ashley into sorting out the shit storm she'd created between us.' He stopped talking and loudly exhaled. 'Honestly, I've never met someone so fucking greedy for "celebrity" status, although a lot of her continued involvement in my life was my fault, because I let her get away with it... But, it's hard to fight over something you don't give a fucking shit about.'

'I understand, but once you saw it affecting him, you knew it was time to work it out for his sake. I've missed you, but you're his dad and you did the right thing staying with him. Children must be our priority, look at my poor mum and dad and what they had to do, because I was their priority... Is he okay now?' I asked.

'Yes, he's good. Finally, Ash and I sat down with him and treated him like the nearly adult he is and told him the truth. He told you that I'd left her when she lost a baby, didn't he?'

I nodded at him. 'Yes... And now, it makes sense. Flint apologised to me last time I saw him.'

'Did he? He's a good kid and I love the bones of him...That baby and the one she lost before that weren't mine. I'd have never have left a woman because she lost my child or couldn't give me a child. Surely, you know me well enough to know that?'

I nodded at him. 'My heart knew, but my head was trying to protect me. I'm sorry.'

He closed my mouth by applying gentle pressure on my chin and placed another kiss on my lips. Once he broke away, he spoke again. His lips were so close to mine I could feel the warm air that left his mouth as he spoke. 'No more saying sorry, we've had enough to last us a lifetime.'

'Agreed.'

For a few minutes, we sat in the peace and quiet, looking at each other, not quite able to take in that we were in each other's arms at last. He broke our contemplation by placing a kiss on the end of my nose. 'So, how did you get rid of the fucking wanker?'

I laughed at his question and then replied. 'He let me down gently and is probably engaged to his PA by now, using the same ring.' The laughter that left Raff's mouth was sudden and loud. His head rolled back and I watched his prominent Adam's apple as it moved up and down through the long, dark stubble on his face. It was so cathartic watching and listening, that very soon I was laughing with him. Dr. Carpenter walking back into the room caught our interest and we pulled ourselves together enough to give him the attention he deserved.

'That's a great sound, I must say. Your mum and dad have just been catching Lyn and I up on what happened.' I heard him tut and saw him shaking his head in disgust at what he'd just been told. I'd forgotten how close our two families were. I grimaced at him in answer and watched as he pulled a straight-backed chair away from the wall and nearer to us both, so he could sit down.

'Okay, I've tested your urine. Would you prefer me to speak to you in private, Lauren?'

My heart sank, knowing his previous fears about the subtle increase of protein in my urine. We had discussed the possibility that this was the start of a decrease in the function of my kidneys. 'No, Raff deserves to know,' I sighed.

I felt Raff stiffen next to me and tighten the hold he had on my body.

'Well, it appears the reason you've been feeling woozy and light headed just recently is because you're pregnant.'

My ears began to buzz as the still room fell silent. I heard Raff audibly swallow and I could hear all the unspoken thoughts running around his head as he contemplated what we'd heard.

Dr. Carpenter looked between us both.

'I can see you're both surprised.' He nodded at us both and smiled. 'I want to offer you my congratulations, Lauren.' He stopped suddenly as if he was choosing his words carefully.

'Thank you.' Stunned, I forced the words out of my mouth.

'I know a child is something you've always longed for... But, as your doctor I must warn you that this won't necessarily be an easy pregnancy. In fact, as much as I'd love to leave you to your joy at the news, I need to make you aware of all the risks to you and possibly to your unborn child. Some obstetricians would even go as far as to say that it might be easier for you to terminate the pregnancy.'

There are some conversations that as you get older you imagine having, or at least I know I did. I always wondered how I would feel and react if I was ever told this or that. Never in my wildest imagination or dreams did I ever think I would be told I was pregnant on one hand, but that it might be so risky to me and my unborn child that some specialists would consider the best option might be to terminate. My heart was beating frantically in my chest as I answered him. 'Is that what you're recommending?'

'No, Lauren. It won't be easy, but I know it's far from impossible for a diabetic type one woman to carry a baby and for Mum and baby to survive the strain that a pregnancy will put on you. In fact, with the right monitoring and care, the percentage of survival for both mother and child gets higher every year. But, I must make you aware of the situation… I want you to know that I, as your Doctor, will support you in whatever decision you make.'

Instinctively, my hand left Raff's waist and came down over the top of my jeans as I sent my love through to our child. I was listening to everything Dr. Carpenter was saying as he spoke about the potential risks to my already under pressure kidneys. He spoke about the risk to our unborn child and how it might not even be possible to carry her to full-term.

But as he spoke, she spoke to me too. Listening to her voice as she replied to me, and me telling her in my head that I already loved her, I knew she had to have a chance.

As her mum, I would give her the opportunity to live, because I loved her too much already to let her go.

'I'll leave so you two can talk. I'll be in your mum's kitchen eating her cake if you need me… By the way, it's good to see you back home, Raff and thanks for stepping in at the last minute to play at Jack's wedding, it was much appreciated.'

Chapter 37

Raff

I felt bereft as Lauren removed her arm from around my waist. Then I watched as she gently ran her hand onto her still flat stomach and I understood why she'd removed her touch from me. Then and there, at that very minute, I knew that without a shadow of a doubt I would help the woman I had loved for forever, fulfil her dream of becoming a mum, because it's what she wanted.

My head was fit to explode with the revelations we'd already heard, but my anger and hatred towards the man who had caused us both so much fucking pain was now an afterthought as my concern for Lauren grew. He and his plans of fucking vengeance against us didn't warrant any more of my time. I had more important things to think about. I would make sure he got the money that was outstanding to him and I would repay Lauren's mum and dad, too. I owned the house he and my mum lived in. I wouldn't demand she kick him out, but I would make sure that my mum and sister knew exactly what Rupert was capable of. They would have to understand when I let them know with absolute certainty, that neither I, Lauren or Flint would ever be in the same room with him again. But, I wouldn't force either of them to choose between us. Life was too fucking short to cause the people I loved more pain.

Now, I was thinking on all the things Dr. Carpenter had told us and slowly trying to filter through the risks he had spelt out to us both.

I can't lose her again, was the one thought that ran around my head over and over. But, I refused to be a selfish prick by voicing it out loud.

'Hey.' Pulling myself together, I broke the silence in the room, leant forward and pressed a kiss to her cheek. Then with the tip of my finger I began to run it down her nose and then to count the freckles on this side of her face that seemed to be appearing as I smiled at her.

Slowly, Lauren turned her head to look at me and it was like seeing her for the first time ever, I was floored by her beauty. Gone was the pale, worried complexion from earlier. After hearing the Doc's news, she was once again vibrant, with colour in her cheeks and her eyes were bright with hope. I lifted a long piece of her hair away from her face, wanting to see all her stunning features without it obscuring my view and placed it behind her shoulder.

'How are you feeling?' I gently questioned.

'Shocked, but *so* happy, I could burst.' A broad smile swept over her face.

I felt tears prick my eyes and I sniffed them away as I laughed a little at her words and nodded back to her.

'How are you?' she asked with devilment dancing in her eyes.

'It's been an enlightening couple of fucking hours but I'm getting there.' I couldn't help but feel hope after taking in the expression on her face.

Looking at her and taking in the brewing excitement inside her, I knew what I wanted to do next.

'I need to talk to your dad, wait here.'

A.S. Roberts

Reluctantly, I released her and jumped up from the settee. I opened the door and walked through to the kitchen. Four heads turned to watch me walk in and I grinned back at their questioning expressions. Then I stopped walking and pushed my hands down into the back pockets of my jeans. I'd been on stage all over the world in front of thousands of people, but only ever once did I remember feeling this fucking nervous in my life. That was when I'd been grilled by Lauren's dad as a teenager in the lounge, before he'd agreed to let me take her out.

The four faces smiled back at me, waiting for me to start.

'Mr and Mrs Harper.' As I began I realised I was shifting my feet around with uneasiness.

Just get the fuck on with it.

'I'd like your permission to ask Lauren to marry me... please.' The please slipped out as an afterthought in my bid to be fucking polite and to do what I had come out here to do properly. My hands came out of my pockets and as I waited for him to reply I started to crack my knuckles.

'Absolutely, you can.' The words came out of his mouth as he nodded at me. I nodded back and stayed long enough to see Lisa fling herself into his arms. I could hear their excited voices as I walked back to the lounge. I knew Lauren would have heard me, my voice was deep and would have carried.

I walked back in to see her sitting where I'd left her, with one hand over her mouth and one over her baby. Her beautiful eyes were wide with shock and from the creases in the corners of her eyes I could see she was grinning.

'So, what do you think?' I questioned her, twisting my head instinctively to the side and raising an eyebrow at her.

I watched as she nodded back her answer and I strode forward until I was stood in front of her.

Suddenly, she was too far away for my liking. I reached out to her and pulled her up and into my arms. Then I turned us both and sat down fast. The old settee groaned in protest, as I lifted her up and pulled her down onto my lap. Once she was there, I wrapped my arms around her and held her close to me.

'Just by looking at you I can tell you're going to have the baby. But, I want you to know that whatever your decision is, I'll be here with you... right by your side. Because I want us to get married as soon as we can.'

'Yes, I am... This little girl, I can't explain it, but I already love her so much. And, Raff I never doubted that for a minute, and me too... I want to be married to you so very much,' she replied and for a second my heart stopped and then restarted as I stopped breathing, gathered myself and carried on.

'Little girl?' I smiled as I asked her the question.

'Uh, huh,' she nodded as she answered me, then lifted her head to look at me. The amber in her eyes sparkled and I was as captivated by her then, as I was when I first saw her.

I inhaled a long, laboured breath and forced myself to ask what needed asking.

'Did you take in all the risks that Dr. Carpenter mentioned?' I hated myself for raining on her fucking parade, but the question had to be asked.

'Yes, I have, really I have. But, I already love our baby, Raff. Deep down inside I've always known I was meant to be a mum. I was meant to give her life.' I could feel myself nodding at her words, even though what she was saying was scaring me to fucking death. 'And if the very worst should happen, she'll have the best daddy and big brother anyone could ask for.'

Once again, my breathing stalled as I forced my body to calm the fuck down. What I wanted to do was to jump up and to shout and scream at her until she agreed that the whole pregnancy was far too fucking risky, then I could lock her up, and keep her by my side forever. But, life wasn't like that. I knew we all had to live life however we saw fit and we had to be allowed to take the risks we wanted to, so we could live it to the full and just because she had diabetes, she was no different. Suddenly, my brain went over what she'd said and almost like she could hear the cogs whirring in my brain, she pushed herself away from my chest to look up at me.

'I know you need to keep her, I understand. But, listen to me when I say, I can't lose you again, Loz.'

'Believe me, I plan to be here to watch her get married... Did you take in what I said, Raff?' She smiled at me as she placed both of her hands on either side of my face.

I nodded at her in answer, already knowing it was a forgone conclusion and ran over her words again. Then it clicked. 'The baby is mine?' I questioned, feeling my eyebrows move together as I spoke.

'Yes, she can only be yours.'

'But, you said you were on the pill, so I just assumed... well... the twat.'

'I haven't been with anyone since the last time you and I were together. I'm only a couple of weeks late, so she has to be yours... kiss me like you understand what I'm saying to you.' I knew she was reversing the tables on me and saying some of the words I'd spoken to her too many years ago to count and I smiled at the memory.

I put one hand up her back and pulled her slowly towards me as all the time I stared at her lips with intent.

'I understand... I wanted to marry you anyway. I'd have loved her as my own, even if she was his. But, fuck!... You, Lauren, have made all my fucking dreams come true. You are my first love and you'll be my last.' I ran one finger down over her nose and then kissed the tip, before turning my attention on her full and inviting lips.

'I love you, Rafferty,' she whispered to me, before my lips found hers.

I pressed my mouth softly to hers and remembering exactly where we were I reined in what I wanted to do to her. 'And now you need to understand this.' I lifted my hips and pivoted slightly, pushing my hard-on into the underneath of her bum and thighs. I watched her comprehend what I was doing and she giggled. It was music to my ears. I knew we had a lot to get through and I knew the path was going to be fucking difficult. So, for now, we needed to remember all the good, fun times between us, so once again I reverted into the adolescent kid she'd fallen in love with, to pull us out of our overthinking adult heads. 'And now, Lauren, I think it's time we got out of here. I need to "waylay" you some more, to show you how fucking much you mean to me.'

Raff

Seven months later

Tentatively, I pushed my hand into the circular opening and inched my fingers over to where her tiny hand with her beautifully formed long fingers rested on the white sheet underneath her.

Gently, I took hold of it and watched her fingers instinctively close themselves around my index finger. My eyes swept over her features and I took in how she was everything I'd hoped she would be.

It was simple, she was beautiful, like her mum.

'Daddy's here, Gabriella. That's it, you hold on tight. I'm not leaving you, not ever.'

It wasn't the first time I'd said her name or spoken to her, but this time was different. This was the first time we had been together without her mum.

Lauren had chosen her name days after we'd found out she was pregnant and named her Gabriella after the angel she was convinced she would be and the fact she was our Christmas miracle.

Every night as I climbed into bed with Lauren, I placed my head over her in the womb and told her something funny to make us all laugh. When she was around twenty weeks old, she would move around anytime she heard my voice, or so Lauren would tell me. Once she had grown bigger and I could wrap my arms around her and my gorgeously pregnant wife, she'd aim a few toes or knuckles in my direction, making Lauren and I laugh. We agreed that she was most definitely a girl, because she always had to have the last word.

I watched now as her body shuddered a little as she breathed in the oxygen being pumped into the incubator.

My heart leapt in panic as I looked at her and my eyes leapt up to the doctor on the other side of the incubator.

'She's fine, Mr. Davenport. She's preterm at thirty-four weeks and a little smaller than a full-term baby, at 5lbs and 6ounces. But, I don't see her being in here longer than twenty-four hours. She just needs a little help with the oxygen today and then afterwards possibly with helping her to feed. Other than that, everything is perfect with her and she'll soon be on her way home with you.'

I couldn't answer the consultant paediatrician we'd employed, I just nodded at her words of reassurance.

At that point, the tears I'd been saving up for the last couple of days began to flow. I placed my head on the side of the plastic container and let them go. The last forty-eight hours had been the most emotional fucking ride of my life. The whole pregnancy had been much more plain sailing than I'd even dared to hope for. With Dr. Carpenter's help and guidance, we'd employed a fantastic obstetrician who had worked with an enormous number of diabetic women. Between them and me we'd kept a close eye on her. The tearooms had been run in her absence by her staff and they'd done a fantastic job keeping her in the loop, but not letting her lift a finger and, for the first time in fifteen years, Default Distraction hadn't produced an album, much to Lawson's fucking disgust. Brody, Cade and Luke had decided, without me being present, that due to the circumstances Lauren and I were in, my time was much better being spent with her and I loved the fuck out of them for coming to that conclusion. We had the material. Hell, since Brody had met Amy all he did was write. And one day when the time was right again, we'd record all the new stuff he'd written. Those had all been the high parts of the last seven months. But, forty-eight hours ago my world fell around my ears when having complained of a headache and with swelling in her feet and face, Lauren's blood pressure then went through the roof. She was diagnosed with possible hyper-tension and pre-eclampsia and taken into hospital to be induced. When the birth didn't happen quickly enough, she'd been rushed out of the labour room we'd been in and taken for an emergency C-section.

As her hand pulled away from mine as she was hastily removed, my heart had descended heavily. I wasn't allowed to go with her due to the situation and it all came flooding back. I'd felt like a useless fucking teenager again, scared for her and Gabriella and I had to admit, I was scared for my fucking self. For the first time since she'd got ill in Vegas all those years ago, I felt impotent – money was useless and there was nothing I could do to help them. I had sunk to the floor and prayed for all I was fucking worth that the people she was with knew how much the lives they had in their hands meant to me.

I knew I didn't deserve them. I knew I could have been better in my life. I swore to anyone that might be in that empty room with me that I would do so much more if only they saved them both.

The paediatrician touched my shoulder and brought me out of my painful thoughts and then she left the room. I wasn't alone with Gabriella, but the nurse kept her distance and watched the monitors from the other side of the room.

So, to lift the pain away, I began to tell her all about her mum and I and how much we both loved each other and her. I told her about how we'd fallen in love and how after far too long apart we'd finally found our way back to each other. I told her about our love for her and her big brother Flint and how the two of them made our lives complete.

I knew I swore several times as I spoke to her, but I didn't care.

My baby girl needed me to speak to her, to show her she wasn't alone in her plastic bubble and I needed to tell her everything. I told her things about her mum that she would never witness, things from almost two decades ago when Lauren had been young and how she made my heart smile when she even so much as looked in my direction and caught my eye.

My words kept on flowing as did the tears down my face and she kept on sleeping soundly, unaware of what had happened in this hospital a few hours ago. But I knew she was listening to me. Holding her hand, I could feel the beat of her heart rhythmically slowing as she relaxed into the sound of my voice.

Or maybe I was imagining it, but it made sense to me.

It appeared my voice was as soothing to her as sitting here opening all my heart up, was to me. Finally, my tears and fears began to run dry and as silence filled the room, I watched Gabby with her eyes still firmly closed as she turned her head a little towards me and tried to find my voice.

'We're going to be okay, little one,' I whispered to her. Then I wiped my face on my sleeve and pulling myself together I spoke a little louder to let her hear what she was looking for.

'The doctor says we'll soon be taking you home. I surprised your mum with that one too. Only a month ago, I took her out for a drive and half way to where we were going, I pulled over and blindfolded her. When we got to the village I got her out of the car and made her hold on to my belt on my jeans as I led her into what used to be your great-nan's shop. Through we went, until we came out of the other side and into what used to be the apple orchard that was your great-grandad's pride and joy. You see I'd bought the shop, flat and extensive land behind it and had started to build a home there for us all. She hadn't got a clue. The shop has been restored and will always be there for Vera and the family to visit when they need to. I don't think I've ever managed to get one past your mum like that before.'

I smiled as I put my head down onto the plastic again.

As I did so, a sound came from behind me and I watched my baby daughter open her blue eyes.

'Hello, my girl,' I whispered as our eyes found each other's.

'I thought that was my title?' Lauren's voice rushed over to me and my heart leapt at the sound. I broke eye contact with our daughter to watch as Flint wheeled my beautiful, but tired looking wife's wheelchair into the baby unit.

'Always.' I nodded to her and mouthed that I loved her as Flint pushed her over to my side. I grabbed her hand and lifted it up to my mouth to kiss it and together we watched as Flint looked at his baby sister for the first time.

'And forever,' she whispered back.

With both hands, I lifted her hair from her shoulders. I placed the necklace I'd first given her so many years ago back around her neck and watched the pendant find its place against her skin, just above her heart. She looked down to watch what I was doing and then back up to meet my eyes and gave me a small smile. Denying myself no longer, I lifted her chin up higher using my forefinger and thumb. Then I placed a loving kiss onto the lips of the woman who held my whole life in her hands.

'Always and forever, my girl.'

The End

Thank you for reading!

I would be so very grateful if you would please consider leaving a review.
If you would like to follow my work, my stalker links are as follows.

Facebook https://www.facebook.com/A-S-Roberts-author-1482173865424420/

Readers group/Andrea's Anomalies
https://m.facebook.com/groups/363569640805168

Goodreads
https://www.goodreads.com/author/show/14846724.A_S_Roberts

Bookbub https://www.bookbub.com/authors/a-s-roberts

Instagram @a_s_robertsauthor

Twitter @authora_s

FATED

When naive, British physiotherapist, Frankie Jones, is offered the job of a lifetime, she decides that letting go and moving on is exactly what the doctor ordered. But when she comes face to face

with a sexy and irresistible blast from her past, she realises that she just can't walk away.
Even if it means stirring up old memories and pain...
Assertive and controlling CEO, Alex Blackmore, is shackled to obligations... obligations he didn't necessarily want. But now that Frankie is back in his life, he knows exactly what he does want... and will have. As their relationship intensifies, Alex's worlds collide and their past resurfaces, threatening to destroy what they're both working hard toward... letting go and moving on.
Can Frankie and Alex fight their demons and embrace the future they're fated for?

FREE: LINK: http://getbook.at/Fated

Facebook page https://www.facebook.com/A-S-Roberts-author-1482173865424420/

Chart topping U.S. rock band, Default Distraction have everything money can buy...

Brody Daniels, lead singer of DD has a life that many people envy. Money, fast cars, extravagant houses and a constant stream of beautiful women.
But he's tired of the rock n roll lifestyle, and so damn sick of the pretence.

He wants something real, something tangible...

Amy Harper has had more than enough of "real". She has nothing to call her own. Unless you count a large overdraft and a struggling village shop.

She's so tired of pushing against the tide, just for once she wants to be swept away with it...

An accidental meeting is all it takes for Brody to claim the reality he wants.
A few stolen moments are all Amy has to give, before once again her reality consumes her.

Can he convince her to take a chance on him when experience tells her to walk away?

To Buy Link: Mybook.to/BrodyDD

Printed in Poland
by Amazon Fulfillment
Poland Sp. z o.o., Wrocław